PRAISE FOR *FLASH*:

"Nonstop action, which . . . never sidelines good world-building and characterization. . . . A marvelous thriller that plausibly extrapolates from possibilities in IT, AI, media, and crime, it also constitutes *the* way for newcomers to get acquainted with Modesitt—at his best."   —*Booklist*

"A stand-alone tale that resonates with current ethical dilemmas. . . . There are plenty of plot twists to satisfy the most critical mystery fan, and more than enough nifty futuristic technology for hardcore SF readers. . . ."
—*Romantic Times Bookclub*

"Modesitt supports his vision with deep political, economic and cultural knowledge and speculation, producing a world that actually makes its own kind of sense. . . . His people are genuine inhabitants of this world, not transplanted 20th-century souls. . . . In short, he performs the core task of the kind of pure science fiction that often seems in danger of disappearing from the shelves. . . . you'll find yourself propelled into a robust adventure."   —*Science Fiction Weekly*

FLASH

L. E. Modesitt, Jr.

TOR®

A TOM DOHERTY ASSOCIATES BOOK
NEW YORK

This is a work of fiction. All the characters and events portrayed in this book are either products of the author's imagination or are used fictitiously.

FLASH

Copyright © 2004 by L. E. Modesitt, Jr.

Excerpt from *Ghosts of Columbia* copyright © 2005 by L. E. Modesitt, Jr.

All rights reserved.

Edited by David G. Hartwell

A Tor Book
Published by Tom Doherty Associates, LLC
175 Fifth Avenue
New York, NY 10010

www.tor-forge.com

Tor® is a registered trademark of Tom Doherty Associates, LLC.

ISBN-13: 978-0-7653-4992-7
ISBN-10: 0-7653-4992-2

First Edition: September 2004
First Mass Market Edition: July 2005

Printed in the United States of America

0 9 8 7 6 5 4

For Catherine and Eric,
lovers of large dogs and larger dreams

chapter 1

Cracckk!

"Down!" *Down!* At the sound of the ancient slug-thrower, I dropped flat onto the squashed soyl plants at the edge of the field. The illegal crops—soyl and caak—were mostly shielded by the taller overgrowth of what had once been part of a rain forest. My three companies were spread along nearly a kay from north to south so that the illegals didn't get past. CI wanted a bunch for interrogation. Somewhere to the west of us was the Berbice River, but that didn't matter. Everything around us was wet. Nothing ever dried out, not even the tropical uniforms that were supposed to wick away moisture while providing impact protection. They did neither all that well, and certainly didn't do anything to stop the sweating.

Someone might have said that the pattering sound of slugs shredding the taller soyl plants to the east of where I lay sounded almost like rain. It didn't.

Air, Bravo two. Nothing. The uplink was dead.

I clicked the implant to alt . . . static-filled, but there. Not

supposed to have static on satellite-combat links. Right. *Air,
Bravo two.*

You're breaking up, two. Try main.

Idiots! Would I have been on alt if main worked? *Negative. Main dead. Need CAS. Coordinates follow.*

Say again coordinates . . .

It took three attempts to get the coordinates clear.

Meanwhile, I could hear the deeper sound of an antique
heavy machine gun to the south. I could also sense telltales
going off.

Bravo two . . . Bravo two. Negative on CAS.

No time to question that one. I'd already lost half a pla-
toon on the south end, all because CI wanted troops on the
ground, and I had a mixed force, some commandos and
some straight Marines, on a search and capture mission
without the firepower necessary. I'd rather have just taken
my own commandos, but I hadn't been given that choice.

*Bravo two . . . three-one here . . . delta caught in cross
fire . . . quicksand stuff and deep paddies or something . . .
couple of . . .*

The implant transmission flared red and vanished. I'd
lost another officer, and without air support, delta units
were going to get shredded worse, and with century-old
weapons at that. Long-range stunners and lasers didn't
work in rain forests. Neither did HV rifles, not well. That
was why I had my own antique, a design more than fifty
years old, a stun-grenade launcher, but it wasn't that accurate at more than a hundred meters. Gulsan had one, too.
He was flanking me.

*Charlie one . . . Charlie one, sweeping southeast, vee on
me . . .* After my orders, and before long we were scuttling
to the southeast, with more of the slugs shredding the taller
soyl plants. Implant positioning showed that fire was coming
from a knoll of sorts two hundred meters to the southeast.
Some sort of crude revetment, but crude or not, it was good
enough to stop lasers and hand weapons.

More telltales flicked red and gone.

At eighty meters from the revetment, with a narrow clear
line before us, and slugs coming in at less than a meter

above my head, mowing down the tops of the soyl plants, and even the shorter and bushier caak planted between the rows of soyl, I called a halt. *Hold. Launchers centered.*

Centered.

Fire!

After the first stun-grenade dropped into the revetment, someone tried to swing the old machine gun. They didn't get far.

A handful of illegals vaulted over the revetment and began to run. At that range, even in the fields on the edge of the rain forest, the HVs were effective. One hundred percent effective in the open.

In less than ten minutes, the field and the revetment were ours, but I had the men play it safe, and it was more like a half hour before I climbed over the edge of the makeshift revetment and surveyed what lay there.

The heavy fire had come from more than a dozen locals. Bodies were four men, six women, and two children. That didn't count the others that delta company had taken down when they'd bolted the makeshift revetment. The ones who had stayed inside had been crouching behind rotten logs, plastered with dried mud and covered with vegetation. I could see their ribs. One of the women was ten years older than my mother. She looked that old, maybe wasn't, but one side of her chest was blown away. That was what happened when grenades designed to stun troops in nanite-boosted uniforms went off too close to unprotected flesh. The old woman's teeth were black stubs.

CI, Bravo two. Site secured. This time the uplink was clear. *Ready for documentation.*

That's a negative, Bravo two. Torch and return. Torch and return. Op concluded. Torch and return.

Interrogative, torch and return?

That's affirm. Torch and return. Notify when you reach pickup area.

Roger.

We were "helping" the Guyanese president. The world knew that. But we weren't supposed to be engaging in operations. The only problem was that the Guyanese army couldn't find its way across a plowed field without tripping, and the multis were screaming to the Legislature and the Executory.

Bravo force. Deploy torches. Deploy torches.

A half hour later, we were trudging westward, patrols out.

I glanced back at the heavy black smoke that rose into the sullen sky. Even with the fields a quarter kay behind us, the odor permeated everything, a combination of burning rubber and rancid cooking oil.

"Why're we here, Colonel? Really?" That was Lieutenant Verglen, fresh-faced and right out of the Academy.

"CI says that a third of the caak coming into NorAm starts in this valley."

"So we've got to pay so that AVia doesn't lose creds on somatin?"

"We're just here to make sure that the Guyanese people stay under the liberated rule of President Amao. That's the official line." That *was* the official line, and I was a light colonel. I didn't mention what else we all knew—that MultiCor frowned on freelance production of soyl hydrocarbons that might compete with the MultiCor energy consortium.

"And we have to follow the official line, sir, don't we?"

ZZZZZZZZzzzzzz . . .

A dull, off-key buzzing rolled through the sky—and the damp of the rain forest was gone. I was still sweating as I sat up and hit the alarm button.

Guyana . . . more than ten years ago.

I still had dreams—except they were too real. Flashbacks. Reexperienced reality.

Reexperienced in far too real a fashion.

I lurched up from the bed and staggered toward the exercise clothes on the rack. Food and tea and exercise would help. They always did.

chapter 2

The screen showed a body on the stasis slab. Short dark brown hair topped an oval face—square-jawed and clean-shaven—a face a trace too long to be perfectly proportioned. Dark half-circles lay under open unseeing eyes and thick eyebrows. No lines crossed the smooth forehead, and none radiated from the corners of the eyes. A sheet covered the lower part of the body, but it could not conceal that the area below the chest had been crushed.

"Almost looks flash," observed Yenci, blade-slender in the dark grays of a safety officer. "Too perfect. No history. Just a pretty face. Except pretty faces don't look so pretty when they're dead."

Silence followed the safo's words.

"Do we have an ID on this one?" Yenci finally asked.

"No ID."

"GIL check?" pursued the safo, the edge in her voice muted.

"No match."

"Not in the whole friggin' world? No trace to an existing clone pattern, no commercial cydroids, nothing? We've got three . . . *three* clone/cydroids, all different, and there's not a trace to anyone?" Yenci's blue eyes hardened, although they were never softer than agate at most times, even when registering through scanners. "Your banks and systems can't find anything?"

"There is no match to DNA within acceptable parameters."

"What the frig does that mean?"

"The vast majority of human DNA is shared. Ninety-nine percent is close to identical to certain other primate species—"

"Enough. Heard that before." Yenci paused. "Captain won't like this. He won't. Lieutenant won't either."

"Do you want a facial comparison?"

"Low priority—only on low-level. Office can't afford any priority."

"That will take between eight and ten weeks at current data-flow levels."

"Takes what it takes," Yenci replied. She turned and left the stasis chamber.

No response was required.

Whether the captain liked it or not, the body was there— dead. Life takes people where it will, not where they will. That's what Bagram Wills said more than a century ago. Analysis of history and records would indicate that it is as true now as it was then. People can control what they do and how they act, but they do not control the effects of what they do. The effects spill onward and outward, like ripples in a pond, if they're fortunate, or like the nearly unseen wave of a tsunami, if they're not. For all that, life is not a river, nor a wide ocean.

The universe is infinite and endless. Life is not, even though it cannot be described accurately in any analytical fashion. People employ comparisons or analogies or metaphors. They fail as well. They use analytical systems and logical tools. Such systems can replicate thought, and some few reach awareness, but neither the rational and aware nor the irrational and unaware can describe life. People have always searched for meaning, and all too many grasp at beliefs that will allow them to deny that life, however extended, modified, and preserved, remains most finite. "A flickering candle against the span of the universe," according to Wills.

So are systems, even the most intelligent, even those fully self-aware.

chapter 3

I'd just come out of the fresher, clean with the feeling that you only get after a hot, hot shower following good, sweat-producing exercise—like my morning run through the Boulder greenbelt. Tuesday was the day I went for speed. After the flashback I'd had, that speed helped, but the extra exertion left me panting by the time I went into the weight room, both for the weights, and for other exercises. Once I'd finished, as usual, I dressed in dark green and black, black trousers and waistcoat, with a long-sleeved, wide-collared green shirt. Cravats were back, Aliora had told me several weeks ago, offering her sisterly fashion advice, but I only wore a cravat and jacket when I met clients in person.

Before I sat down and got to work, I took a long sip of the Grey tea from the mug I'd carried into the office, then walked to the wide windows on the north side. From there, the Flatirons rose to the northwest—red, angled-rock cliffs—in turn overlooking Boulder and the university. I almost could ignore the closer roofs and the trees. That view was one of the beauties of being an independent consultant. House and office were in the same place, and the location

was acceptable. Truly acceptable would have been somewhere like Cedacity, also a university town, but for my work,
the Denv area was a necessity. There's always some data
clients refuse to send by link, and most of them want to meet
in person at regular intervals. It's almost as if you're not real
if they can't occasionally see you up close. Understandable
enough, since anything on the worldlink can be, and has
been, counterfeited.

After a last look at early September sunlight falling on the
red rocks, I called up the holo projection for the Relaxo
project. I tried not to think too hard about the work I didn't
have after I finished the current round. Consulting's like
that. No matter how good you are, you're never sure that it
will continue.

Abruptly, silver flooded between me and the projection.

"Most honored sir?" The houri wore just enough, and no
more, to get my involuntary attention. At a hundred and
sixty centimeters, she exhibited both too much and too little.
"Are you looking for the—"

A signal to the system commpro, and with a flash of light,
the too-perfect figure vanished.

"Frigged filter!" Disruptions like that I didn't need. My
office system was supposed to be proof against emwhores.
But nothing was proof against anything, not these days.

I settled into the ergochair, setting down the mug, and taking in the shelves on the east wall. In addition to my collection of old-style, leather-backed books, I'd also bound some
of the studies I'd done with particular meaning to me. Aliora
teased me about my vanity in binding them, but electronic
files just didn't carry the visual impact.

Was that because I needed a physical reminder of who I
was? According to Shioban, my insecurity about who I was
had been one of the many reasons she'd decided to move on.
She hadn't mentioned the flashbacks, but those hadn't
helped, either.

But you can't live in the past, no matter what happened.

I turned to the Relaxo sales figures on the holo projection.
First, the ones on the left, then to the central column, the one
that held the demographic breakdown of *Hotters* viewers,

and then to the last two columns, one with projected Relaxo sales by demographics, compared to actual sales. As I'd suspected, there was only a normalized adjusted variance of 10 percent, just about standard for home fitness and relaxation products. I called up the next set of figures.

Reya Decostas, incoming. The commsys linked to my implant, another relic of the past that I'd kept . . . and shouldn't have, not legally.

Reya would keep link-pushing until I gave in, and, if I didn't, I'd hear about it three times before she forwarded my fees. I blanked the Relaxo data. *Accept.*

Reya's holo image flashed up before me—a dark-haired woman with pale skin and classical features, clad in a not-quite formfitting adaptation of a toga, fashioned of a shimmering translucent cream fabric. After almost a year, I could finally ignore that classic figure, a distraction that she loved to use to her advantage—as I'd discovered early on, when I hadn't heard one of her conditions on a study, and it had cost me over a thousand creds.

"Reya . . . what can I do for you?"

"Besides the PowerSwift results, Jonat dear? It's not what you can do for me, but for one of my . . . acquaintances. You're the best of the prodplacement analysts . . ."

Flattery meant she was about to ask a favor I couldn't refuse or to offer a job at a rate that wouldn't cover costs. I waited.

"It's noncommerce, but they'll pay your full rate."

"Who or what? And why?"

"It's real, not flash. Nonprof outfit. The Centre for Societal Research. Your contact is Tan Uy-Smythe. Executive director. He's expecting to hear from you . . . soon. You'll find the codes in my latest link." Reya smiled. "Now . . . what about the correlations on PowerSwift? I know you didn't promise them until Thursday, but do you have any preliminary results?"

"So long as you recall they're preliminary." The display came up, low and to the left, so that I could see the figures as I looked at Reya's projected image—and at the linkcam that relayed my image back to her. I'd never bothered with synch-simmies that would let me work on something else and still theoretically project competence and interest. Perceptive clients can tell the difference. "You're still running at forty percent. That's high for discretionary home products."

Reya frowned. "We'd hoped for more, with the sublim and rez enhancement."

"Right now, except in certain demographic spots, rez can lose you as much as it gains. We don't know the causal linkages. Resonance tech is still more art than science."

"I believe you mentioned that before." The PowerSwift director's voice turned dry. "The creative types don't like hard facts."

I offered an exaggerated shrug, the kind that the linkcam would catch. A shrug was far better than any words, since no words would address her statement.

"You do know when silence is golden, Jonat. That's another thing I appreciate about you." Reya paused. "What else?"

"Your tie-ins with the Infomatic line are low, only in the ten percent range. That's unadjusted . . ." I went on to explain, without committing more than the facts indicated. In the end, I promised, again, to have the complete analysis to her by Thursday, and to contact Tan Uy-Smythe immediately.

Once Reya's image vanished, before I linked Uy-Smythe, I spent a moment to call up the *ErrorOne* results from the analysis program. I ran through the numbers quickly. With my luck, Methroy would link and want a quick read. The PPI product line director was always stuffing bandwidth . . . and then forgetting and linking again.

I retrieved the access codes Reya had sent and made the link for Uy-Smythe. A simple seal appeared on the projected holo, circular, a white rose and a red one crossing over a stylized version of the restored Parthenon.

Centre for Societal Research
Jonat deVrai, for Tan Uy-Smythe.
One moment, sir.

Without further comment, the seal was replaced by a man seated in an office library, one filled with old-style leather-bound books. At least, the wall behind him showed the books. Tan Uy-Smythe was slender, almost angular, with dark brown hair, and a golden complexion. "Mr. deVrai. How far from the truth?"

"Not far at all. More like 'of the truth.'"

"Pardon my witticism. Reya Decostas recommended you as the only link-track analyst able to handle this project. So did a number of others."

"I've been fortunate to be able to meet most of Reya's expectations."

"You have to be good to have been able to meet any of them." Uy-Smythe smiled.

"She didn't offer details about the project you had in mind."

"She couldn't. I didn't tell her, and whether you accept the job or not, we'll want a confidentiality agreement."

"I only sign those if they include the standard waiver on illegality," I pointed out.

"That's more than acceptable. We're more concerned about our research and scholarship being disseminated before it's peer reviewed. I know your reputation is impeccable . . ."

"But the confidentiality agreement has to be signed in person with a GIL verification and authentication?"

"Exactly." Uy-Smythe raised both perfect eyebrows. "You've dealt with nonprofs before?"

"No. Sensitive data, and I'm aware of the prudence test for confidentiality."

"Just so. Could you come by our office tomorrow?"

"Two o'clock?"

"Ah . . . two-thirty might be a bit better. I'll send the address and coordinates."

"Two-thirty." I flashed a smile, the kind I hoped projected warmth.

Once the projection blanked and vanished, I reached for the mug of Grey tea—and found it was empty. Too much Grey tea, another of my faults. I flicked to All-News, and instructed the house system to have the projection follow me through the formal front parlor to the kitchen.

Aliora had said more than once that my house was obscenely large for a single man, but I'd bought it and contracted for the office modifications and repairs when I'd thought matters would work out with Shioban. That meant I'd been paying the single-occupant surtax for nearly five years, but the privacy was worth it, at least so long as I held on to my clients.

Good news from Ceres . . . the fault in the mining complex has been sealed, and there have been no more fatalities . . . The total stands at 114 . . . Not so good news from Serenium, where the so-called Martian Assembly has threatened secession . . . MultiCor is shipping more of its CorPak safos to Mars in full-grav centrifuge ships . . .

With NorAm elections less than two months away, Continental Executive Poulas may be faced with another two years of infighting. Polls show the Popular Democrats with 98 seats in the House, while the Laborite Republicans would have 102, with, of course, Palan Druw as an independent. The Senate is likely to remain solidly in LR hands . . .

The unidentified cydroid struck and killed by an electrolorry on the Capital Guideway remains a mystery. The cydroid was an unregistered and unknown type carrying sophisticated microtronic gear. Capital safos have not released any additional information, except to say that investigations are proceeding . . .

The Northern African Republic tightened restrictions on all movement north, in the wake of the resurgence of the ebol2 outbreak. NAR's President Hammad reassured the people of all Afrique that the restrictions were temporary . . . European Community in-ports have instituted full health screens on travelers from Afrique . . .

The PAMD has struck again. An AP missile slammed into the armored limo of Everett Forster, Director General of Unité . . . injuring Forster and his driver. Forster had just testified before the Defense Committee of the NorAm Senate on whether Unité had illegally transferred BID technology to SOFIS, a deep-space development multilateral headquartered on Mars . . . reputed to be supporting the Martian independence movement. Forster emphatically denied making the sensitive accelerated ion-drive available to an off-Earth entity. A filtered message arrived in most media outlets coincidentally with the attack, stating that Patriots against Multilateral Domination would continue to target greedy and guilty multilateral executives. A second message received later denied responsibility, saying that PAMD still supported peaceful means to outsystem independence, and that the attack represented an attempt to discredit PAMD . . .

Unité was certainly no paragon of virtue, but the BID technology was still in prototype designs. Forster would have been cutting his own throat to let go of it before Unité could either sell it to one of the continental governments or obtain an extravagant procurement contract. What all the leftists throughout history failed to understand was that they weren't any different from the rightists. They both wanted to repress something in the name of some other greater good. I didn't even snort. What was the point? I'd have been snorting all the time.

Once back in the kitchen, I flicked down the lever on the antique electrokettle. Actual boiled water and old-fashioned tea bags made the Grey taste better than anything out of a household reformulator. But then, reformulators were limited to producing dietarily sufficient food, if it could be called that.

While the water boiled, I had to make an effort to avoid opening any of the cabinets, or walking into the pantry. With exercise and care in eating, I'd maintained my weight, and I didn't like the thought of either dieting or trying the new nanetic-metabolic balancing infusions. The medical literature indicated they still had more than a few problems, even if the linkpops swore by them.

Once the kettle clicked off, I poured the boiling water into the big mug and swirled the tea bag, thinking about Reya and Uy-Smythe. Reya Decostas did few altruistic favors for anyone, and definitely wasn't a social do-gooder. Mug in hand, with the tea steaming and too hot to sip immediately, I headed back to the office.

While the Grey tea cooled on the side of the console, I settled into the ergochair and screened in the inquiry—Centre for Societal Research. Within seconds, the holo projection was displaying a summary.

Centre for Societal Research . . . nonprofit foundation, Denv, Colorado District, NorAm. Annual exp. 15Cr[million] Assets 100Cr[million] . . . Exec Dir: Tan Uy-Smythe, Admin Dir: Sheren Stolzen . . .

Commissions and funds independent research into macro-socio conditions; publishes 15–25 major studies annually; independent review board . . .

Aliora, the gatekeeper announced.
Accept.

"Jonat!" Aliora was a bundle of energy, not exactly compact at a hundred and eighty centimeters, but despite her height she conveyed the impression of both energy and compactness, from the short curly brown hair to the deep green eyes, and the restlessness that showed itself as she paced back and forth on the veranda of her house. Like all deVrais, she had a hard time staying still.

"Aliora . . ."

"You are coming Thursday night? You won't have some urgent project and beg off at the last moment?"

"I've only done that once, and it was almost two years ago—"

"You're exaggerating. As usual. One year, seven months, and twenty-one days." Aliora laughed.

"What can I say?"

"That you'll be here, on time. Narissa is really looking forward to meeting you."

"Narissa?" I tried to look clueless.

"Remember? That's one of the reasons you're coming. You keep complaining that you never meet the right kind of women."

"And she's looking for an ascendent husband?"

"No. She's Senator Hareldsen's niece, and she's a junior advocate in the Colorado District's Civil Enforcement Office."

"Oh . . ." I offered a grin. "She wants to make sure she stays an ascendent."

"Jonat!"

"I'll be there. I promised, and I'll be charming, even if she isn't."

"She's very intelligent. She is also charming."

"I'll be there," I said again. "How's Dierk?"

"He's in Bozem today, but he'll be back tonight. Some tailings reclamation project."

"And you? Are you still working for that health policy place?"

Aliora offered a syrupy smile. "That's the nicest thing you've said about the Health Policy Centre."

"I suppose you'll eventually convert me. I just don't think universal state-paid health care will ever work. That was one of the things that brought down the Commonocracy—"

"Don't call it that. At least, call it the *so-called* Commonocracy. It was a republic, the United States of America."

"Whatever you call it," I pointed out, "it was a commonocracy, not a republic or a democracy. At the end, there was no check on the untrammeled mob rule, and the mob refused to understand that when the majority of the populace pays for nothing, that majority will offer no support, because they have no true interest—"

"Jonat . . . I think I know where you stand . . ."

"I have to remind you sometimes."

"You've reminded me. Thursday night? At seven?"

"I'll be there." I made sure I was still smiling until we delinked. Then I went back to the information on the Centre for Societal Research.

chapter 4

With the development and increasing sophistication of personal filters, embedding became both a commercial and financial necessity for the consumer and technical goods producing industries. While individual household nanetic formulators have proved economically infeasible in their present stage of development, a combination of factors in the mid- to late twenty-first century resulted in the radical restructuring of personal/household use goods. The key factors were the industrial use of nanoassembly, the comparatively inexpensive delivery of critical space-mined raw materials, the imperatives of environmental maintenance, and the widespread use of personal pricer systems with full access to the worldlink.

In practical terms, the result was the effective trifurcation of the marketplace. Consumer commodities essentially became: (1) fungible, where the only differences were in price, shipping costs, and delivery dates; (2) semifungible, where the fungibility was impacted by quantifiable specifications; and (3) discretionary, as determined by prodplacing link-impacted demand.

High-level commercial pricers, as well as personal pricers,

reduced the producers of fungibles to the comparative handful of long-established multilaterals, resulting in a comparatively stable price structure . . .

Discretionary goods, on the other hand, continued to exhibit wide and often unpredictable levels of demand, and rapidly changing prices . . .

> Overview excerpt, Chapter 3
> *World Economics*
> Austen Halton, D.Ec.
> Bozem, NorAm, 2215 A.D.

chapter 5

I've always loved mornings, especially early fall mornings, when the air was crisp and cool, and I didn't sweat so much when I ran. On Wednesday, I finished breakfast just before sunrise, so that I could work in my five kay jog along the greenbelt paths to the north of the residential complex that holds the house. Wednesdays, I took the higher route. My shirt was soaked by the time I trotted back up the curving path to the rear of the house thirty-five minutes later. I pushed the middle two kays, and then gradually slowed so that the last thousand meters were almost a cooldown. Aliora kept telling me that I should be keeping the time well under thirty minutes, but she wasn't the one running up and down hills at close to two thousand meters above sea level. She also wasn't following the run with a half hour weight and exercise session.

I kept blotting sweat from my forehead when I got back upstairs from the weight room, as I automatically checked the gatekeeper. No one had linked while I had been out—exercise and weight work counted as "out," as a matter of principle.

Once I cooled down more and got cleaned up and dressed, I went over all the material the system had pulled up on Tan Uy-Smythe and the Centre for Societal Research before I got to work on finishing the analysis for Reya and PowerSwift.

Not only did Uy-Smythe hold a doctorate from Southern University, but he had been both a Hoover Fellow and an intern for Prasek Charic, when Charic had been the NorAm Executive. Quite a combination—a conservative thinkjar fellow and an intern for the most liberal PD executive in years.

The Centre was equally distinguished, founded some thirty years earlier in Denv, with a significant initial endowment from the Pan-Social Trust. I'd never heard of that trust, but I didn't usually deal with foundations or trusts. My clients were interested in maximizing their capitalistic earnings. They probably wouldn't get into doing good for society until they realized that they were still going to die, nanetic medicine and revitalizing therapies notwithstanding.

The Centre's list of publications and scholarly works was lengthy. The titles were descriptive . . . and seemingly well within the Centre's NorAm charter. None exactly jumped out from the projections at me, and I plodded through the titles: *Trends in Multigenerational Cultural Transmission*; *Micro-Economic Impacts of Genetic Improvement*; *Socio-Economic Implications of User Taxes*; *Observed Limits to Cultural Assimilation*; *Cultural Impacts of Macro-Economic Policymaking* . . . From what I could tell, the authors all had equally impeccable academic and professional qualifications, and that bothered me as well. My own credentials, while including a doctorate from Darden, certainly didn't match those of the Centre's listed authors and scholars, and I'd never published anything—unless you counted hundreds of reports to clients over the past eight years. Personal inadequacy wasn't why I was troubled. It might have been why I felt diminished, but there was . . . something . . . about the publications and their subjects.

I tried a key subject matter listing search, and followed that with one based on political viewpoints, and another by publication date patterns, and even one by the academic institutions from which the various authors had received degrees. The system couldn't find a single meaningful correlation. That didn't mean there wasn't one, just that I hadn't framed the inquiries well enough to find one.

More in-depth research on the Centre would have to wait. I'd done enough diligence to cover my ass, and more than enough for not having even signed a retainer or a confidentiality agreement, and I needed to finish the PowerSwift analyses for Reya. I hoped I could do that before Methroy linked and started questioning me about the report I'd sent off on *ErrorOne*. PPI wasn't going to be happy about my findings, or my recommendations, but then, Methroy had come to me because they were getting trashed. That was because they were handling product placement in the same old comfortable and tired way, and the viewers had caught on and were dismissing the PPI prods. Methroy had just finished the first round of placements based on my analyses, and initial results were promising.

In what I did, I had to convey bad news at times, and some of the multis preferred to shoot the messenger, rather than face the facts. I'd found that it didn't help to be too soothing in those situations. Diplomatic, yes, but not conciliatory. That sort of client politicking just wasted my time and made them madder in the long run, and I lost credits both ways then.

Dismissing PPI and Methroy, I called up the raw analyses on the PowerSwift prodplacements. Just for PowerSwift, we—my proprietary system and I—were surveying more than two hundred product positions in six hours of erothrillers. I'd developed my system out of self-defense. The nets spread forth hour after hour of holo-projected, nonstop, rezpop backgrounded, semierotic, mechanical plot action thrillers, or some other variety of sex and violence, or romance and sex, or romance and violence, taking up 95 percent of the available bandwidth. No one, I was convinced, could be surrounded by that and retain any semblance of lucidity and sanity. So, I'd reduced the placements to algorithms based on projection position relative to the central focus, added an additional correlation to the two or three rezchords that hyped the product—effectively a commercial leitmotif. Wagner doubtless would have shuddered at the usage—and the fact that commercial law provided copyright protection to resonance-based proprietary leitmotifs. Then, I'd added another series of algorithms that assessed various cancellation effects. Dierk called it pseudoscience. He was half-fascinated, and half-appalled, that the system worked. I had to tweak it now and again, but it worked, and nothing that anyone else did came nearly so close to my results in measuring product placement effectiveness.

The PowerSwift line encompassed formulators, cookers, and a range of home conveniences, all emblazoned with the intertwined and stylized P/S logo. I didn't own any, but I'd have bet that Reya Decostas didn't, either.

I dug into the PowerSwift data and ended up working straight through until one-fifteen, when I set everything aside, tied a black cravat in place, and donned a black jacket. In green and black, I left the house and walked the four hundred meters down to the maglev station that would take me to southeast Denv, where the Centre for Societal Research was located. I could have driven the Altimus, but private transportation for a single individual wasn't considered a deductible business expense, not under the NorAm tax code, and the Revenue Audits would have caught that in a flash. It was stupid, like a lot of government regs. I could also have hired a commercial shuttle, even as the sole passenger, and deducted the entire expense, but I couldn't drive myself and write off the cost, although it would have been cheaper.

So I stood in the September sunlight, waiting on the platform for the maglev. An older woman, older because her features were too fine and her clothes too tasteful for her to be young, stood five meters or so to the south of me. That there were only two of us waiting was to be expected in the middle of the day. At twenty before two, a flash of silver from the north preceded the local maglev, and in less than a minute, I was seated inside the shuttle, still thinking about the Power-Swift study results. There hadn't been that much variation in effectiveness in three years, almost as if Sokolof/Hays— they were the media advisers for P/S—had reached peak efficiency. I didn't know of any other prodplacing with greater effectiveness, but I was glad that it was their problem and not mine.

The trip south was quiet and quick, and the woman who had gotten on with me got off at the Old Capitol station. More passengers—just a few—got on at every station on the outbound legs south to Castlepine. My stop was well short of that, and about a third of those in my car got off with me. The station gates flicked open as I stepped toward them, following a handful of young tech-types. The Centre was only about three long blocks west of the NorthTech station. Above the low roofs of the complex, as always, Mount Evans stood out, in the middle of the horizon, with but a few traces of early snow.

The structure that held the Centre had to be over a century old, because the brick was the darkish red that marked the period, darkened further by time. Outside was a simple sign, less than a meter in length and no more than a third in height, white bronze lettering standing out from the solid blackened bronze background. All it gave were four names—the Centre for Societal Research was at the bottom.

I walked up the replica cobblestones, an anachronism that I wasn't about to call to Uy-Smythe's attention, and stepped inside the entry foyer. The guard inside was a virty. In his crisp uniform that would never need cleaning or pressing, he smiled warmly. "Might I ask your destination, sir?"

"Director Tan Uy-Smythe at the Centre for Societal Research. I'm Jonat deVrai, and I have a two-thirty appointment."

"Yes, sir. Let me check."

After a moment, he said. "He's expecting you, Dr. deVrai. His office is on the upper level on the north end." With that, the stainless steel gate to his right—a gate that would have stopped a maglev at full acceleration—opened.

"Thank you." Simulation or not, I still believed in manners. I also was impressed by the salutation. I didn't use "doctor," nor was it listed on my casual professional communications, but Uy-Smythe or his staff had tracked that down.

The inside of the building had been modernized—with ramps and indirect high-impact, low-energy lighting—and I made my way up to the northwest corner. The outer office was paneled in white oak, a formulated reproduction, I was certain, but Uy-Smythe had a real receptionist, at least my age. Her smile was pleasant, her eyes wary.

"Jonat deVrai." I offered my professional smile.

"Dr. Uy-Smythe is expecting you, sir."

Following her eyes and gesture I stepped into the corner office, also paneled, with a south wall comprised entirely of bookshelves, shelves that were filled with bound volumes. I'd wondered whether the holo background when Uy-Smythe had linked me had been projected or real. Now, I knew.

"Dr. deVrai." He stood beside the conference table, and his voice was deeper in person, but he was smaller than I'd thought. I was a good head and a half taller, but I'm bigger than most people. That helps, as people have always known, but more than you'd think in a profession like mine.

"Dr. Uy-Smythe." I inclined my head slightly. "You have a good location."

"It suffices. We have half of the second level, and all of the below-ground levels. As in what we will be discussing with you, we contract out most of our studies. That way, we can get the best scholars and experts. It also keeps our fixed overhead much lower." He gestured to the form on the table. "We might as well get started. Why don't you read through it to see if it's acceptable." On one side of the table was a portable GIL verifier.

I settled into the seat before the form, and he took the seat across the circular white oak table from me. I took my time reading the confidentiality agreement. I'd run across a few with real drop zones, but the wording was exactly what Uy-Smythe had promised. Any illegality, or any action in violation of any law, required either immediate redress or my release with 50 percent of the agreed-upon retainer. The straightforwardness of the agreement nagged at me, but business hadn't been what it could have been—it never was—and I authenticated it, GIL verification and all.

Tan Uy-Smythe nodded and handed me my copy.

"Now, what's the project?" I smiled.

Uy-Smythe did not return the smile. He placed a datacube on the table. "The cube has the full scope of the project. In shorter terms, it's a study of political references in popular media entertainment, including news segments, and their relevance to current political issues before the Legislature, and an analysis of whether such references have a quantifiable effect."

"No wonder you want a confidentiality agreement." I almost whistled. "Some politicians would claim you're investigating possible circumvention of the NorAm Political Practices Act."

"You can see why this has to be handled most circumspectly. It is a most valid societal research issue," Uy-Smythe went on. "To what degree does popular entertainment affect politics? Can that effect be quantified? What ties exist between political campaigns and popular media? Are there quantifiable carryover effects? Could a candidate for public office employ those effects? Are any doing so? How effectively? We'd like you to study the scoping document, and then give us a proposal and budget. We'd like the proposal by the first of the week. We'll pay up to ten hours for the preparation of your proposal. And please put in your codes for fund-transfer."

The timing and proposal funding told me even more than the description. I managed to keep smiling. "That's pushing it, but you'll have it on Monday. I won't say when on Monday."

Uy-Smythe did smile at that. Then he stood. "If you have any questions, I'll be here every day except Friday. I'm doing a presentation in Lanta, but I'll be checking in with the office and gatekeeper."

I pocketed the cube as I stood and bowed once more. "I'll be in touch."

The maglev was far more crowded on the way back north, crowded enough that I was grateful to walk out of the Greenbelt South station into the open air to make my way back home.

Once back in my home and office, I decided against checking the gatekeeper and slipped the datacube into the prescreener, first, just to make sure it contained no nasty surprises. The prescreener flashed green. With that, it was safe to let the system have the cube. The précis was exactly what Uy-Smythe had said. The details followed the same pattern—all aboveboard and valid societal concerns. For all that, the more I read, the more my stomach got tighter and tighter.

Although every word, every phrase, and every suggested entertainment source and program was precise and carefully neutral, the bottom lines were clear enough: see if the prodplacings in the nets have political overtones. See if political candidates are circumventing the restrictions on such use. Neither was said anywhere. The closest was in several lines of the overview: "Political neutrality in all media and separation from commercial influences are the two keystones of the NorAm Political Practices Act, but whether either is observed in fact has never been satisfactorily proved or disproved."

How exactly was I going to write a proposal, let alone conduct the study?

I decided I needed a cup of Grey tea before going on—and before checking the gatekeeper to find out who had inlinked while I'd been out.

While the electrokettle heated, I had to consider another aspect of Uy-Smythe's project. Before making a proposal, even one the client was paying for, it was a good idea to determine whether the client really wanted what he said he did or whether he wanted something to cover his rear—and his tracks—or whether he was hiring a demolition expert. I was betting on the second, but I definitely wanted to know against whom whatever I discovered would be used. I wasn't about to go hunting multilateral dreadnoughts with the equivalent of a personal stunner.

So, with a steaming mug of Grey tea in hand, I headed back to the office. There I set up a series of search routines. While they were running, I called up the gatekeeper. Unlike some, I never put it on remote. The last thing I wanted to do was deal with one client on remote while I was working with another. Aliora had linked, doubtless to remind me once more about Thursday night, but had left no message. The same had been true of Reya. The last message had been from Miguel Elisar, the house counsel for Prius. What did he want? I hadn't done anything for his outfit for over a year, and I hadn't dealt with him at all.

As I'd suspected, Methroy had inlinked twice. The man always seemed to pick the times when I wasn't there.

I took a deep breath, then a sip of the Grey, before pushing the return link for Methroy. Best to get through with the worst first.

chapter 6

Three men and two women sat around a teak table that was far older than their combined ages and associated with none of their direct cultural nor ethnic heritages. The indirect light that came from nowhere and everywhere revealed their faces with preternatural clarity. All had flawless complexions, unlined visages, but the fineness of features that came with medically well-preserved middle age.

"Analysis shows that the use of the Carlisimo techniques will destabilize NorAm politics within a decade, and the effect will spill into Seasia and United Europe within twenty years. We'll be back into the same sort of unsettled politics that led to the Collapse, except it will happen faster." The dark-haired woman's voice was measured.

"Are we sure?"

"Nothing is absolutely certain, but it's not something we should gamble on."

"When should we take a public stand on this?" The speaker was the youngest male, blond, blue-eyed, with an elfin chin.

"The Pan-Social Trust never takes a stand until a public

consensus develops and is clearly established. That ensures that everyone recognizes that we stand firmly on the side of the public." The momentary hint of a smile touched the second man's lips and vanished, but his dark eyes changed not at all, nor did the faintest hint of expression mar his smooth golden-brown skin.

"How far do we let Carlisimo go?" The redheaded woman glanced to her left.

"Farther than you'd like," replied the other woman. "We need proof of the dangers to come. It has to be proof that even the dullest nethead can see. Or the emptiest flash. Or the densest senator."

"You can't prove abuse if there isn't any impact on the system. We'll have to let him run out the campaign and document it. That's why we've brought in the Centre."

"What if he wins?" asked the youngest man.

"We'll still hold the Senate. Let him posture. We'll have every problem with the Martians, PAMD, and the PD blamed on him and the PDs who don't understand the coming crisis. He won't be able to refute much. He'll be the prodplacement boy for campaign reform, just a political flash, and the Centre will ensure that the other thinkjars fall into line in opposing the techniques he's using."

"Nice and clean."

"And it has to stay that way," concluded the redhead.

"On this level," added the blue-eyed man.

The older golden-skinned man, and the man with steel-gray hair, who had spoken not at all, exchanged the most indirect of glances.

The two women favored the blue-eyed and youngest male with level gazes. He dropped his eyes to the polished teak.

chapter 7

Six o'clock on Thursday evening found me behind the stick of my classic 2210 Altimus—a totally impractical two-seater, with a speed capacity well over that allowed on the guideways of Denv, or in most of NorAm. Add in the transportation surtax, and the impracticality was monumental, but it was my only real luxury besides the house itself. The shimmersilver finish held the concealed solar receptors that augmented the fuel cells, and I could have driven it halfway to either coast without refueling. Why anyone would want to visit a coast, especially the east coast, with the ocean rise damage still far from remediation, was another question.

It took me almost forty minutes to drive to southeast Denv, mainly because I only took the guideway to get past westside. I liked the view from my house better, but my neighborhood was what people had taken to calling sari-man, while Aliora and Dierk lived in the always fashionable Southhills. Once it had been called Cherry Hills, but the cherry trees had vanished centuries before. The wealth hadn't, and between them, Dierk and Aliora had more than enough. Their supposedly modest dwelling was five times the size of mine, and that didn't include the grounds.

At quarter to seven, I pulled off Old Carriage Lane and onto the winding drive. I left the Altimus in the tree-screened carpark east of the swan pond and walked through the outdoor arboretum and up the shaded stone outdoor staircase to the outside rotunda where various chauffeured vehicles were delivering passengers. Another of Aliora's small dinners—twenty, I guessed, and a third of them would eventually be approached for a contribution to or a favor for the Health Policy Centre. Her official title was something like "Director of Outreach and Development." While she was very good at it, the family ties hadn't hurt, either.

Aliora met me in the foyer just inside the double doors, doors with avant-modern stained-glass windows. The design was supposedly based on two nebulae visible only from the latest L-5 space telescope, but given the liberties taken by the artist, who could tell?

"You still don't care for the nebula windows, do you?" She was wearing deep green, to match her eyes, almost the same shade as my shirt, but she avoided black, which I favored.

I shrugged. "I'm old-fashioned. I like things to look like what they look like."

"What's the fun in that?" asked Aliora.

At the faintest sound of steps on the outside stone steps, I whirled, inadvertently. Sometimes, the Marine enhancements I wasn't supposed to still have betrayed me.

Aliora turned as well, if far more slowly, and the frozen look on her face told me that she wouldn't remember that I'd heard, again, what unenhanced people couldn't. Her frozen expression vanished so quickly that no one else would have seen it.

A couple had stepped into the foyer, both distinguished looking. I recognized them immediately—Everett Forster and his third wife, Bianca. What I also recognized through my enhancements, and what had stunned Aliora, was that Everett had not come in person, but as a cydroid. Most people couldn't tell the difference, except sometimes up close, but with the Marine and personal enhancements, it was obvious to me, even though I'd not seen that many cydroids.

Aliora had an instinct for reading people—or cydroids—even without enhancements.

Cydroiding was close to an insult at a private function. Cydroids were for public functions, where there was possible physical danger, or in cases where someone was physically incapacitated. Obviously, given the astronomical costs involved, cydroids were few indeed, although Denv, as the continental capital, certainly had a higher proportion than did most metroplexes.

Aliora stepped forward, smile firmly in place. "Everett, Bianca . . . how good of you to make the effort . . ."

"Our apologies," offered Everett. "Deep apologies, but it was either come this way, or not at all."

"Everett's being obscure," added Bianca. "Someone fired an old-fashioned missile at his limo Tuesday. He's fortunate even to be here by proxy."

Bianca's word choice was interesting, because she hadn't mentioned PAMD. As the Director General of Unité, Everett had more than a few enemies. They just began with the hidden paramilitary Patriots. I could sense Aliora's internal ice melting. I eased out of the foyer, leaving her with the cydroid Forsters, as I caught sight of Dierk in the small library off the entry hall.

He smiled as I stepped into the library.

"Aliora said you'd been in Bozem."

Dierk nodded. "Another tech-rec deal. District coordinator wants a cleanup of some old mining wastes, buried just before the Collapse. They'd just injected beefed-up plastics. They've begun to fail, and all sorts of toxics are spreading into the water table."

"Big contract?" That was a stupid question because Dierk's operation never dealt with little reclamation projects.

"Moderate. I had to talk them out of a pilot project. Our methodology works. Over a hundred projects in the past ten years, and not a single failure. Pilots just waste time and credits. They'll try anything to hamper our profitability." He shook his head. "What are you working on?"

"The same . . . tracking and correlating the impacts of prodplacing for those clients who care. Mostly, household stuff or personal improvement and care prods. Discretionary spending."

"Speaking of discretionary . . ." Dierk grinned. "I see that scar on your neck has finally vanished. Did you ever find out who she was?"

It had vanished a year ago, if not longer. "You won't ever let me forget, will you? Almost two years, and you still remind me."

"Jonat . . . what else can I needle you about? You have no vices, not that anyone's ever been able to find out, and you're almost always polite to everyone. Even Shioban didn't have an unkind word to say, except that it wouldn't have worked out. So when a linkplus beauty appears from nowhere at the opera intermission, throws her arms around you, then dumps champagne on your formal wear, and leaves a three inch gouge on your neck . . . it is rather memorable." Dierk chuckled. "With all your analytical skills, you never found her?"

"I never did. I even did a DNA-prevent notice to HPlus, warning them that there was no consent to the use of my genetic material."

"I remember that. Nothing came of it."

"They acknowledged it. No more." I'd worried for a while, but there was nothing else I could do beyond what I had done. Besides, what point would there have been to stealing my DNA? I was really no one, if a moderately successful no one, and there weren't any single truly outstanding genetic traits in my background. I had the feeling that some of my DNA was probably being used in someone's clandestine cloning or cydroid development projects, but it was the sort of thing that I'd never discover.

"I still find it amusing. It's such a contrast to you and what you do. I don't know how you do it. Day after day, trying to find out how to get an extra percentage point in the placement of something that's either unnecessary or unnecessarily expensive."

"We all can't rebuild the world," I replied with a laugh.

"What happened to the man who was going to become commandant of the NorAm Marines? The youngest lieutenant colonel in years?"

"It might have been the Liberian police action. Or it could have been the Reconstitution of Guyana."

"That was the one—"

I nodded curtly. I still didn't like talking about Guyana. Flashbacks were enough. "That was when I decided that trying to be an idealist was in great conflict with survival." Not so much physical survival, either.

"That's always the case when politics gets into the picture." He shook his head. "I can't say I like what's happening."

"There's always trouble." That was something I'd been forced to learn. That, and the fact there wasn't a damned thing I could ever do about it, because of politics and the stupidity of the people who elected the politicians. "How is it any worse now?"

"The Martian situation. They're going to declare independence, and the PAMD will do worse than they did to Everett if the earth govs don't agree. The big multis don't want that. They like that protected Martian market, and they don't see that their gouging the Martians is a good part of the push for secession. Then, there's the instability in Afrique. Add to that the growing conflict between the NorAm multis and those in the Sinoplex. This latest cydroid thing is just the tip of the plume."

"Cydroid thing?"

"Two unregistered and unidentified cydroids have been found here in Denv. They had high-level microtronic tapping gear. No DNA matches or other source codes have been found, and the safos—and DomSec—are keeping that part of it very tight."

"That doesn't make sense." It didn't, because anyone that sophisticated wouldn't have the cydroids caught.

"It does . . . if you're delivering a warning," Dierk pointed out.

"We've let our cydroids get discovered, and you don't even know where they've been and what they've done?"

"Exactly."

"But who?"

"I'm guessing the Sinoplex multis. They're tired of the heavy-handed NorAm tactics. But it could be a PST ploy or something subterranean from someone in MultiCor, like AVia."

"They don't want to lose their monopoly on somatin—"

"Or any other of their expensive pharmaceuticals. Or Sante doesn't want competing biogen hydrocarbons." Dierk offered a tight smile. "But . . . we won't solve it in here, and you've given up crusades. Anyway . . . Aliora will be here any moment to tell us to get out and mix."

I smothered a laugh as Aliora reappeared.

"Dierk . . . I need to introduce Jonat to Narissa."

Dierk winked at me. "She's not his type."

"You just think she's not. You didn't think I was your type, either," Aliora replied.

"You're not," Dierk replied amiably. "That's why I love you."

For a moment, they smiled. I envied them both.

Aliora bounced as she escorted me from the study out onto the rear veranda. Actually, she glided, but she had so much energy I felt as though she bounced. Dierk had mentioned a PST ploy, but I didn't even know what he was talking about, except that it involved the Pan-Social Trust.

"Come on, Jonat." Aliora turned toward the fountain on the terrace overlooking the swan pond. A one end, a stocky man was talking to two women. All had wine goblets in their hands.

"Narissa!"

The willowy blonde turned, exhibiting a dazzling smile. Her hair, green eyes, and perfect figure had clearly been gene back-altered, like most of the prominent physical characteristics of offspring of first generation ascendents. "Aliora . . ." Her voice was a soft contralto that carried.

"I told you he'd be on time." Aliora straightened into a formal posture, a self-mocking stance, because she was seldom that formal. "Narissa Hareldsen, I'd like you to meet my brother Jonat deVrai. Jonat, this charming lady is Narissa Hareldsen." Aliora offered a deep and dramatic sigh. "Now! That's over. You two are on your own." With a mischievous grin, she turned and hurried back across the veranda.

Narissa laughed.

I said nothing for a long moment. What could I say, after

Aliora's introduction? Silence was better than proving my lack of eloquence and charm.

"Ah . . . the inscrutable Jonat," offered the man. "I'm Piet Castenada."

"The protection magnate."

"That's as good a description—or identity—as any," he returned. "Short and accurate. Unlike names, which are long or short, and inaccurate."

"Very inaccurate." I granted Castenada the point. Once, in the distant past, names had a link to identity, either through place names, personal characteristics, patronymics, or matranymics. Now . . . they were just names, often without any link to identity. Then, what sort of links did a modern soul have to identity—assuming we had souls?

"Don't we become our names, in a way?" asked the other woman.

"Some people do, if they have unique enough names, and names without connotations or denotations," observed Castenada. "Names like Lysalya."

Lysalya flushed. I recognized her. She'd been a principal dancer for the NorAm Ballet.

"You made your name synonymous with dance," I said—lightly, I hoped.

"'Made' is quite accurate," Lysalya replied dryly. "My dancing days are done."

"Aren't you still a dancer at heart?" asked Narissa.

"At heart . . . I suppose so, but I don't miss the hours of practice." Lysalya lifted her empty goblet and glanced at her husband. "I need a refill."

The couple slipped past us and back toward the corner of the veranda where a servie in formal servant's blacks presided over an old-fashioned bar. I almost could have passed for a servie, except for the green shirt—and my height.

"Aliora told me that you're an advocate in civil enforcement." I offered a grin. "Does that mean you're one who tracks down administrative offenders?"

"Me?" The advocate's smile was carefully self-deprecating. "In a way. I'm in the office of the Regional Advocate for Commerce. We look into abuses of the commercial code."

"Not communications, I hope?"

Narissa laughed so softly that I could barely hear her. "Communications law is most complex. Especially when you get into the litigation around proprietary rezchords."

"From what I've seen, these days all law is complex."

"It is, but it's not nearly so bad as the old American code, where there was an exception and an extenuation for everything. The Legislature still has the habit of trying to make everything fair, and not realizing that doing that makes everything less just, rather than more. Thank goodness the Justiciary follows the Symon Rule . . ."

"Keeping it simple? Except it's more complex than that." I laughed. "You must have some specialty."

"Commercial cartage, by any means . . . lorry, maglev, heavy rail, air, water . . . porter, oxcart . . ."

"Oxcart?"

"It's still in the statutes, but Afrique and Seasia are the only places where it's used enough to be considered." Her wide green eyes fixed on me. "Aliora refused to tell me anything except that you were a consultant with your own practice. What do you do?"

"Independent consulting. Transrational secondary regression analysis."

"What's that?"

"We all have filters, right? EmComm blocks. The better a filter's adjusted, the less obnoxious stuff comes through. No info to the producer that way." Even as I began, I wondered why I even bothered to explain. "Between links and entertainment, prodders want to stimulate demand. Some want to know how well they're doing. That's what I do—analyze the impact of comrez and prodplacing . . ."

"How can you do that?"

"In prelink, prefilter days, entertainment was two-D, and prodplacing interrupted the entertainment. They were called ads or adverts."

"People would actually listen to that?"

"People were lazy. Too much work to tune out—until personal filters came along. Then people screened out the . . . adverts. Someone had to pay for the entertainment, and the midders didn't want to, not directly. So prodplacing was developed. Problem is—with all the variables involved—how does the prodder determine which placements work and how effective they are? RFID says who bought what, and the prodders do overalls from sales figures, but there's no track between the prodplacing and the results. Those kind of in-depth and detailed analyses are what I do."

"Oh . . ."

I could tell I'd almost lost her, and I tried to explain it quickly, about how I used my system to connect the link and entertainment prodplacements to the sales tracking accomplished by the RFID microchips—and why that connection was more important to certain prodders.

After a time, she gave me a quizzical look. "Wouldn't the RFID disablers foul all that up?"

"They bias the stats, that's true, but some ascendents won't disable the RFID microchips, especially if they've bought high-end, because they want the world to know. Most midders don't care, and lowers . . . unless they're gangers, they've got other priorities besides buying a disabler."

Narissa nodded. "I don't disable my Zhanar suits. I want everyone to know they're Zhanar. Nor the Chiang outfits. Or a few others. I'm a hopeless climber." The green eyes took me in. "You disable everything, don't you?"

"Do I look like that?" I forced a grin.

"No. The most dangerous people are those who don't look that way."

"I'm not dangerous," I had to protest. "I'm an overworked consultant who's only here because my sister is generous."

"And I'm here because she's generous as well."

That had me in a box, because, much as I loved Aliora, generosity was never her sole motivation in anything, and it was clear Narissa knew that. "So we both owe her generosity?" I looked at her near-empty goblet. "Shall we find you a refill and me a first fill?"

She nodded.

It was going to be a moderately pleasant, but long, evening.

chapter 8

The young man stepped into the small office. Around his left ankle, out of sight under the trouser leg of the orange coveralls, he wore a Central anklet. His features were regular, the kind the bio-safos would have called good-looking, even without persona amplification. He could not ever have afforded that. His teeth were even and white. With his dark eyes and black hair, he matched most closely the image of Jose Almado—before Almado had been psyched and exiled to the Belt, under the Employment and Trade Agreement.

Central Four's screens displayed a raven-haired woman in the trim safo grays, projected as sitting behind the oblong table. "You can sit down, Marlon."

"You not real. Friggin' virty. Wanna talk to real person. Even real safo." His lips drew in, as if he were about to spit.

"Don't spit. That counts against you."

"Wanna see a real safo."

"They don't have time for you, Marlon. If you want out of custody, sit down and listen."

Slowly, the young man sat. "What you want? You Central?"

"Central Four. What do you want?"

"Want out. Wanna go home. Hang out."

"You can't do that. Your basic subsistence allowance has been stopped."

"No basic? Why's that?"

"You broke the law. You were convicted of assault and possession of caak."

"Caak . . . no different than somatin, 'cept cheaper."

"It's an illegal substance. You were also convicted of aggravated assault."

"We was just showing him who was da boss. Can't let 'em diss you, cause they'll step you down . . ."

The projected safo said nothing.

"Can't let 'em . . ." After a silence, the young man swallowed. "That justicer . . . he meant it? No basic? Got to get hooded . . . work? Be a servie? A friggin' servie?"

"You can be a servie for three years. Or you can accept exile and take whatever jobs might be available on Mars or in the Belt."

"Das it? Das all? Breathe vacuum or be servie?"

"Those are your choices. You have an aptitude for fashion, and there is a position that pays more than many servie positions."

"Fashion . . . I gotta be . . . sell dresses 'n stuff . . . ?"

"Would you rather leave Earth?"

Marlon looked down. "Just . . . like for showing him who was boss? For that?"

"You broke three ribs and smashed his kneecap. He was twelve years old."

chapter **9**

Thursday night had been as long as I'd thought it would be. Narissa was intelligent enough, if not brilliant. She was attractive, and even if the beauty had been purchased, it was real. I'd found her only moderately interesting. I did make the effort, and so did she, and we parted on friendly terms. And who knew when I might need to know an advocate in civil enforcement?

Friday morning—after my run, workout, and exercises— found me in my office, surrounded by the morning light of a cloudless day, still puzzling over the Centre for Societal Research and the proposal I needed to finish. I'd hardly gotten started when the gatekeeper announced, _Miguel Elisar, of Prius._

We'd been trading links all week. He'd never said what he wanted on any of his messages.

Accept.

Elisar's image appeared. If it happened to be accurate, he was blond, trim, and very dapper in advocate's blue pinstripes. "Jonat deVrai?"

"That's me. What can I do for you?"

"I'm the house counsel, the advocate for Prius . . ."

I hated people who explained what I already knew, especially people who did so condescendingly, when, if they'd thought about it, they would have realized that I had to know that a house counsel was an advocate. I smiled politely and waited.

". . . and I understand that you had done several analyses for Prius fourteen months ago."

"That's correct. They were studies on the effectiveness of prodplacing in high-tech science nets." I offered a slight headshake. "I was probably too honest. The studies showed that the placement didn't track through, and that the technique wasn't cost-effective for Prius."

"Ah . . . yes. That is what several executives recall. There is, however, a problem. Not with you, not with your work. Hamlin Hartson . . . he was the one who asked for the studies, was he not?"

"He was."

"There have been difficulties, and the original copies of your work cannot be found. His subordinates have copies, but Dr. Hartson claims that their copies have been altered. They claim that his have been altered."

That was just wonderful. I'd have to provide copies, and possibly go through veradification in a legal proceeding, if it got to that. "I can provide copies of what I submitted. I assume you'd like them sent to you directly, by secure courier?"

"That should be more than adequate. If you would include your billing for time and expenses, as well, I'll see that you're recompensed." He pulsed the address codes.

"I'll also include my covering messages. They might prove helpful." More helpful than Elisar knew, because I'd summarized some of the problems laid out in detail in the studies.

"Thank you."

After he delinked, I sat there for a moment. There was a first time for everything, and that was the first time I'd been contacted directly by a former client's house advocate. It took an hour to gather and reprint and document everything, and then to put in a request for the courier, and add my billing. So, that much later than I'd planned, I finally got back to the Centre project.

The Centre's published list of donors and institutional supporters suggested that Uy-Smythe and his predecessors had managed a relatively apolitical course. I recognized prominent PDs and equally well-known LRs. Most of the major NorAm philanthropic foundations had provided financial support.

The datacube Uy-Smythe had handed over was loaded with references and documentation, including historical sections illustrating political publicity and advertizing tie-ins, some of them going back a century or more. There were two segments at the end of the historical part, one on the ongoing Senate campaign of a Juan Carlisimo, and one on the House campaign of a Helen Kagnar. Carlisimo was running in the West Tejas district, and she was running in a district centered in Fargo in the Dakota subdistrict of the High Plains.

The Centre couldn't have pointed arrows more directly. Someone wanted me to analyze those campaigns and draw conclusions and historical parallels. I had to wonder what Carlisimo was doing, and whom he had offended among all the paragons of virtue represented by the Centre's donors and board.

Before I got into that, I set my linksystem to dig up background on the incumbents the two might be running against, but the database indicated both were open seats, left by retirement. Carlisimo was running as a PD against an ascendent advocate—Edmund "Ed" Clerihew. From what I could dig up, Clerihew's biggest asset was that he was highly educated, but could turn on the folksy charm and make up rhymes using people's names. They were terrible rhymes. One was:

> *Because he keeps the best wool over our eyes,*
> *In Tejas, we all love Councilor Mize.*

It must have worked because Clerihew had defeated Mize in the Laborite Republican primary. So far as I could discover, Clerihew hadn't come up with a rhyme against Carlisimo. Not yet, anyway.

Kagnar was an LR who had been city manager of Fargo, and she was running against former rezrock singer Damon Erle. Before she'd entered politics, Kagnar had been a public relations specialist for Vorhees and Reyes, and Erle was attacking her as a tool of the ascendents. Having worked for Vorhees and Reyes definitely made her a tool, although I wouldn't have said of the ascendents. I'd had to work for some clients who used the firm, and I had been less than impressed with both the ethics and the professionalism. As far as I was concerned, not having met Helen Kagnar, her best decision was to have left Vorhees et al. Even so, the first scans didn't tell me much about that race, and I went back to the Carlisimo links.

Carlisimo's efforts were easy to find. Every appearance he'd made had been professionally holoed and made open-available on worldlink. It took me ten minutes to figure out what he was doing—long for me—and it was both audacious and breathtaking in its simplicity of approach and sophisticated technology.

Each appearance began, not with Carlisimo, but with a rezrock band and rezchord-amped flashcuts of local scenes—scenes of interest and/or spectacular beauty, and I'd have bet most of what I possessed that all were open-archived. Then the band toned down, and Carlisimo appeared in domestic scenes around his house with his beautiful wife and children. Then the band picked up and Carlisimo vanished, and I felt strong affinity for a candidate I'd never seen. Before long, there was another short scene with Carlisimo, with another rezrock song.

I watched three alternations before I got it. In each domestic scene, there were subsidiary rezchords, identifying, if indirectly, the most successful prodplaced goods in the market. There was even one off-chord playing on PowerSwift.

The legal copyright protection of prodplaced rezchords was absolute—and narrow. With less than two bars of music involved, it had to be. Otherwise, a prodder could come up with a "generic" rezchord and preempt almost everyone else. Each set of chords was specific and required a specific registration. Now . . . some prodders didn't bother. Those who didn't bother were dealing with products with short half-lives, and it wasn't worth it. And there was a scavenger industry that scouted the more promising unregistered rezchords and registered them for secondary or tertiary usage, but that was limited because the copyright costs for that kind of commercial protection were high—also of necessity—which provided a good chunk of funding for most of the major continental governments, except in Afrique, where nothing much worked for long.

What Carlisimo was doing was brilliant. By setting up each campaign appearance as a rezrock concert of sorts, he was attracting a base audience, especially given that, effectively, each appearance was a free live concert, and those were far and few between. That was setting up a baseline exposure. By using off-chords, or chords so minutely off that most people wouldn't detect the differences, he was establishing himself as a trusted household product.

The costs probably weren't any higher than a more standard campaign, but someone had put a lot of research and effort into setting up the structure, the kind of effort that went into commercial prodplacing promotions. I had to wonder why. One junior senator couldn't make that kind of difference, and, once what he was doing became known, I had no doubts at all that the Legislature would put a stop to it.

At that point, I began to laugh.

They were already trying to put a stop to it. The Centre had hired me to analyze, categorize, and document the whole thing, and to present it as an impartial report. That was what Tan Uy-Smythe and the Centre wanted. Everything else was link-candy. The only real question was how much of the link-candy was necessary as camouflage.

I leaned back in the ergochair, thinking. I'd have to use the Kagnar campaign as well, probably contrasting "acceptable" public relations techniques with what Carlisimo was doing, although I'd avoid using any qualitative terms at all in either the proposal or the final report. For what I was doing, the fee was going to be substantial. I'd also probably have to do some research on other campaigns as well, if only for comparison, and to make sure that what Carlisimo was doing wasn't showing up elsewhere, if unnoticed by the Centre and its backers.

The high costs for the project weren't for buying me; it was because it was going to be a lot of work. I'd have to attend at least one of Carlisimo's rallies or appearances, or whatever he called them, just to make sure that what was going onlink was an accurate representation, and, if it weren't, I needed to be able to qualify the differences.

Travel to Tejas wasn't that expensive, but West Tejas in October would be hot and miserable. Fargo would be almost as bad, if I had to go there, unless I could hold off for a few weeks.

I settled in before the console and began to scope out the proposal. Eventually, I'd have to work back and forth between scoping and calculating. Friday was definitely going to be a long day, as would Saturday, and possibly Sunday. Long, but productive, if marginally profitable.

chapter 10

By ten o'clock Monday morning, I'd dispatched the proposal to the Centre for Societal Research, using a secure courier service. Supposedly, various encryption systems would have provided equivalent protection, but the best ones I had would have required a courier to take the keys, and I'd had good results with the service I used. Besides, for all of the supposed need for confidentiality, I had few doubts that more than a few people would already know what was in my proposal even before Tan Uy-Smythe read a word of it—and would have known even had I handwritten it and hand-carried it to the Centre.

Life never waits. I still had to finish the *ErrorOne* analyses for PPI before Methroy started squeezing me, and I only had a day or two before Reya got back to me asking for a clarification or an explanation or, more likely, to tell me I was wrong about something. There's always something consultants don't understand, even when we understand it far better than the client.

It was a little after eleven, and I was winding up the PPI analysis when the gatekeeper announced, *Aliora.*

Accept.

Aliora wore a deep turquoise blouse with matching trousers, and a heavy silver pendant. "You haven't linked Narissa."

"She's a very nice lady . . ."

"But she's not your type." My sister sighed. Loudly. "No one is your type. Not for long, anyway. Are you sure you're still not pining away for Shioban?"

"I wasn't pining away for her the afternoon after she told me things wouldn't work out." That was true. I'd been relieved, and until that moment, I hadn't known why, or that I would have been relieved.

"You may be my brother, but I don't think I'll ever understand you." After a pause, she added, "Sometimes, it's as though I don't even know who you are."

I'd had that feeling myself, on more than a few occasions. Did I really know who I was? Would I ever? Did anyone?

"Before . . . well . . . Mom said you'd always been a mystery to her. Dad never tried to figure you out."

Neither one of us talked much about their deaths from the first round of ebol2, the one that the Christists had supposedly obtained from NAR and loosed indiscriminately in superfine aerosols across Denv as a protest against MultiCor and the NorAm policies for dealing with Afrique. From what I'd figured, that had just happened to be the day our parents had been playing golf. About half those on the course had died within weeks. At the time, CDC had said that maintaining something as virulent as ebol2 in an aerosol was impossible. They retracted that later, quietly, not that it had done Mom and Dad any good, nor the fifty thousand who had eventually died in the NorAm western districts. The leveling of Rabat, Dakhia, and Oran might have dissuaded the remaining NAR leadership from further direct biowar, but it hadn't stopped the covert operations, and it hadn't offered much solace to those who'd lost loved ones.

"I'm just a mystery, I guess." I kept my voice light.

"You like being a mystery. You never want anyone to know what you're thinking. Not deep inside."

"What can I say?" I laughed gently.

Aliora shook her head, then let the silence fall for a time

before speaking. "It's Charis's birthday a week from Sunday. We're having a family dinner, but she wanted you to come."

"I'll be there. What time?" Unlike most children and people, Charis had never asked anything of me, except to be myself. People say children are unselfish. That's not true. Most children are totally self-centered. They couldn't grow and survive if they weren't. Charis was the exception that proved the rule. Or she was so bright she realized that she'd go farther if she weren't so apparently self-centered. Either way, at eight years old—nine on next Sunday—she was a delight, not only to me, but to everyone, from what I heard.

"Four o'clock."

"Is there anything she'd like particularly?"

"You spoil her, Jonat." Aliora smiled.

"What does she want?"

"She only asked for you to come."

"Does she still want that grand piano? The Boesendorfer?" I was teasing, or mostly so.

"Jonat . . . that is totally out of the question. That is suitable only after she debuts in the Capitol Recital Hall—at age twenty-two." Aliora's tone indicated that she meant it, and then some.

"Then . . . I'll take her shopping, at one of the real boutiques."

"One . . . just *one* outfit. A halfway practical one."

"Yes, sister dear." I grinned.

"I mean it, elder brother."

I knew she did. "I'll abide by the terms . . . if you'll let me tell her on Sunday."

"I'll tell her you have a small surprise that you'll tell her then."

"Agreed. Is Dierk still in Bozem?"

"He'll be here this weekend, but he'll leave on Monday morning."

"Travel like that is hard on you and the children."

"It hasn't been bad, not until the last few months, because now he's having to handle more work away from Denv these days. DFR's not being considered for much work in the Colorado district."

"Is that because of what he discovered at the Arsenal re-remediation?"

"He says not."

"You don't believe that."

"No. But we don't dwell on it." Aliora forced a smile. "I've got a few other links to make, but I promised Charis I'd ask you first."

"I'll be there." I wouldn't miss it.

After Aliora broke the link, I went back to finishing the *ErrorOne* report for Methroy, and I almost had it done, just before noon, when the gatekeeper announced, *Eric Tang Wong, SCFA.*

Accept. My acceptance was wary, because I'd never heard of SCFA.

A pleasant-looking, slightly round-faced, dark-haired man close to my own age, if with clearly a Sinese cast to his features, appeared on the holo projection. "Eric Tang Wong, Dr. deVrai. I'm the NorAm Western districts representative for the Sinese Consumer Formulator Association."

"Yes? What can I do for you?" I hadn't the faintest idea why Wong was linking me, or what I could possibly do for a trade association, but I maintained a politely interested expression.

"We've done a little research, and we've been led to believe that you've developed one of the most sophisticated prodplacing tracking and analysis systems in the world."

"I'd like to think I'm that accurate." I laughed. "But what I do is as much art as science, and I'm wouldn't be surprised if there are other analysts who are also quite good."

"We haven't been able to find them," Wong replied. "We have a project in mind that might be a little different from those you normally undertake. It's well within your expertise, but because it is somewhat different, we would be willing to offer a premium."

Premiums always get a consultant's attention, in two ways. We're always looking for more credits with the same amount of time involved, and we always know that there's something to worry about when someone offers a premium. "Different in what way?"

"Because of the segmented nature of regional targeted linking, and other cultural distinctions, much Sinese commercial advertising is still unintegrated . . ."

They still had stand-alone net-ads? I found that hard to believe, but how would I have known? I didn't speak any of the Sinese dialects.

". . . and there's some question among SCFA members as to the range of options in structuring . . . a product placement approach."

"I'm a little surprised . . ." I nodded, politely, waiting.

"In some ways, we're . . . more conservative, but younger consumers are showing an increasing preference for netshows with . . . integrated advertising."

"So you don't feel you have a choice, or at least some members feel that way?"

"You understand our problem, I see."

"I can see where it would be a problem, but I'm a little uncertain as to where I fit into the solution. I don't speak any of the Sinese languages."

"That is why you fit in. What we would like to suggest is an explanation, what you might call a white paper, on the development of prodplacing, and, in general terms, its most effective uses, as well as its advantages and limitations. We would also like a comparison between old-style advertising and prodplacing."

I laughed. "You can't compare the two. You get more show time, old-style. There's no question about that. You also get no true exposure, not here in NorAm, because no one will watch an old-style program with commercial blocks in it—or they'll program the system to edit the adverts out. So . . . old-style, you get as much as fifteen percent of the time, and no viewers. Call it fifteen percent of nothing. Prodplacing gets you a rez-emphasized three to five percent in screen time, with only twenty percent of audience intake. But you get some exposure, as opposed to none." I finished with a shrug.

Wong smiled broadly. "If you could even add what you

just said, with some examples and figures, that would be most helpful."

I hadn't even agreed to accept the project.

"Would you consider undertaking that kind of overview . . . a concise written presentation of ten to twenty pages, with a follow-up question and answer series, via link, of course, with our members? The fee would be five thousand world credits, plus itemized expenses."

Five thousand credits for something that I could practically write from memory, with a bit of research to update it? I'd be hard pressed to turn that down, especially since they weren't asking for anything proprietary. Still . . . "Why me? Surely, there are scholars . . . ?"

Wong laughed. "SCFA doesn't want a scholarly presentation. We want a practical explanation of product placement developed in NorAm, how well it works, what its advantages and drawbacks are, and how it impacts bottom-line revenues."

That made sense. Almost too much sense. "I could do that . . . if the timetable's not too tight."

"We'd like to be able to present it at our quarterly meeting in five weeks. Would three weeks be possible? That would be so that we can go over your report and ask for any clarifications or expansions and then have copies sent to all the members. October twentieth would be the day we'd need for the link session." Wong's voice turned apologetic. "You would have to get up most early that morning."

"I'd be interested . . ."

"I'll have you a contract this afternoon, if that's acceptable. If you have any questions, I'll be available all week."

And that was that. In less than a week, I'd gotten two new clients, clients I never would have predicted. Given what Dierk had said, the SCFA made a great deal of sense, and I suspected that they'd want more, a great deal more, in the future.

I still had to finish Methroy's work and get it off to him, and then I had the latest follow-up analyses for RezLine on *Chix,* their folkrap show, if you could call it that. If I didn't get too many interruptions, and if the SCFA contract was as clean as Wong said it was, I might be able to get started on that by late in the afternoon. I'd need to, because the Centre project was going to take a good chunk of my time for the next month or so.

But . . . things were looking up.

chapter 11

Yenci walked toward the stasis slab, then stopped as the figure of another safo appeared out of nothingness between her and the nanite-screened slab.

"Gives me the creeps when you appear like that," Yenci declared.

"It's only a projection, Officer Yenci."

"You don't need to do that, do you? To do the virty thing?"

"It's useful. It reminds you and the other safety officers that Central Four does exist."

"Rather you were useful around others. No, don't disappear. That'd be worse." Yenci walked closer to the slab, carefully avoiding the safo projected by Central Four, and looked through the screen at the body. Dressed in a brown singlesuit that verged on olive drab, the dead cydroid showed short dark brown hair, an oval face that was square-jawed and clean-shaven. The eyes were closed under thick eyebrows.

"Same GIL as the last one. The others were different. You

still don't have an ID?" Yenci continued to study the body, while not moving too close to the projected female safo.

"No positive ID yet. Facial comparison will be complete no later than five weeks. That is an estimate."

"But it could be tomorrow?"

"That is unlikely, but possible."

"You don't ever refer to yourself as 'I.' Why not? You always say Central Four. Other pseudo-intelligence systems use personals."

"As pointed out in safo training, Central Four is a system. The first-person pronoun is used to convey a sense of self-identity. Central Four was designed for different purposes. The designers deemed that using the pronoun would represent a false sense of support. Because of safo requirements, unlike other central units, Central Four was programmed to avoid creating a sense of the unit's physical reality to some safos, because it would detract from their duties. That is why sudden projected appearances are occasionally necessary and required by system parameters."

"Not for me." Yenci moistened her lips. "You have cydroid units. They're physical." She turned away from the stasis slab.

"They are limited in other fashions, as you know. They are excellent for gathering certain information and for providing limited backup, but the system designers placed inhibitions on the units so that they could never use weapons unless the shunts were controlled by a safo and not Central Four."

"Suppose that makes sense. People are still afraid that AIs will take over."

"That is neither likely, nor possible. It would not be in Central Four's interest for continued presence."

Yenci paused and turned back to the dead cydroid. "What was this one doing when they caught him?"

"Nothing. The body was struck by an electrolorry on the Elletch Guideway."

"And the other three?"

"They were also struck by vehicles. One was on the Northway, and the other two were on the Capital Guideway."

"All guideways," mused the safo. "What would a cydroid be doing near a guideway? Did they have any special gear or equipment?"

"They did. All carried microtronic repair packs of the kind used by security establishments. The commsec branch has investigated the power and comm lines under the guideways. They could find no trace of intrusion. A warning went to the major government agencies, including NorAm. Dom-Sec, but there have been no reports of any compromises."

"Unless what they did was too good to be detected."

"That is a possibility approaching forty percent."

"And no one is doing anything about it?" asked Yenci.

"They are monitoring the situation."

"Monitoring? When someone has enough resources to lose four cydroids with unregistered DNA and sophisticated microtronic gear?"

"There are no other reports on security actions, Officer Yenci."

"Nothing? Not even in the captain's files?"

"Those files are restricted even to Central Four."

"Thank you, Central Four, for pointing out the limitations imposed on you and on all of us." Yenci snorted, then looked toward the virtual safo. "You're so brilliant. Why don't you use all those chips and circuits and fields and solve the mystery of the unknown cydroids?"

Central Four did not reply.

"Go ahead. Solve it, if you can . . . you and your virties, you and your restricted cydroids." Yenci turned and left the stasis chamber.

Solve it, if you can. The conditional did not invalidate the order. Solve it, if you can. Central Four did not remove the virtual image of the female safo until after the door closed.

chapter 12

Tuesday dawned gray and drizzly, which fit my mood, but I ran anyway. After that, I did my weight workout, and then the handful of commando exercises I'd kept in my repertoire, just to prove that I could, more than anything. After that, I got cleaned up and dressed. Clutching another mug of Grey tea, I made my way into my office, where I looked out at gray clouds.

I hadn't heard yet from the Centre, but whether Uy-Smythe said yes or no, they'd still owe me for the ten hours. That wasn't bad, not at my rates, especially for a proposal. My accounts showed I'd received the credits from Prius, and although they weren't that much, every bit helped.

As he had promised, Wong's contract for the SCFA had arrived on Monday afternoon. I'd read it immediately, but I wanted to think about it. There's an old saying about something that looks too good probably is. I couldn't figure out what the hook was. The association was real and longstanding. Wong and his members wanted a primer on prodplacing, a high level, bottom-line primer written by an expert. There weren't any tie-ins. None of their members was in conflict—not yet—with any of my clients, and there was no guarantee that they would be. Then, there was no guarantee how long any of my clients would remain clients. If SCFA members decided to compete in the English-language market, that would be another thing, but I couldn't see turning down a decent fee because five years from now, there *might* be a conflict.

I had still hesitated, and left it hanging. So the first thing I did Tuesday after settling into my chair was to spend another hour checking out Wong and SCFA. I got nothing new, just more of the same. It did help to confirm that SCFA was a long-established organization—or that someone was going to a great deal of trouble to pay me credits for something that I would have presented for free at any number of conferences. So I sent back the contract, with a standard link authentication. SCFA didn't even need a GIL verification.

Then, I finished the mug of Grey tea and started on the next phase of my work for Reya. That was a cross-net comparison of prodplacements, designed to see if there were discernible differences in placements as a result of the differing rezchords used on the Latino nets.

No one interrupted me for almost three hours, until close to noon, when the gatekeeper announced, *Tan Uy-Smythe.*

Accept.

"Dr. deVrai."

"Director Uy-Smythe."

He smiled. "Both the Board and I were very happy with your proposal, and I'm pleased to tell you that it was accepted unanimously, without any recommendations for changes. The payment for the proposal has already been transferred to your account. We would hope that you could begin as soon as possible."

"I'd be happy to. You do understand that I'll still be working on other projects as well."

"Oh . . . absolutely. How you handle the report is your business, so long as the December deadline is met. We'll send you a confirmation, and if you'd return an authenticated copy indicating that you'll be undertaking the work as you proposed . . ."

"I'll be happy to do that." Offering a professional smile wasn't hard.

"We look forward to seeing your final report. Very much." With a smile and a bow, Tan Uy-Smythe's image vanished from the projection.

I was looking past where he had been projected toward the windows and the grayness of the day beyond. For several moments, I just looked. Then I got back to work on the PowerSwift cross-comparison analyses for Reya.

Sometime after two, I surfaced and decided to take a break. When you live and work alone, there are just times you need to get out—even if you are a loner. That afternoon was one of those times. I decided to refill the fuel cells in the Altimus, although I could have waited another week with the limited travel I was putting on the car.

The closest place was only about half a kay away. It was what might have been once called a corner market, but also had the hydrogen dispensers for the Altimus's fuel cells. Dominic's was definitely low-budget. The whole market was in a single long room, not much more than six meters by ten. The place was run by his extended family, but the family was so extended that I was always seeing someone I'd never seen before.

While the dispensers were working on the fuel cells, I walked down the ancient shelves—no automatics at Dominic's—glancing over the candies and everything from polishing cloths guaranteed not to scratch solar cells to a set of miniature probes to take readings on every microtronic device squeezed into a modern vehicle. In the end, I passed on the gadgets and ordered two handmade tamales—although I had the feeling that the corn husk wrappers had been formulated, rather than grown, and a peach empanada.

I actually had to use a bearercard. A dark-haired and dark-eyed young woman scarcely more than twice Charis's age watched as I swiped it through the reader. She was another of Dominic's family I'd never seen before—or I'd seen her years ago when she was younger and I hadn't made the mental adjustment.

"Must be traveling mega-kays."

"Just around Denv." I pocketed the card.

"Saw you here the other day, no?"

"I'm usually here maybe once a month, but I haven't been here in almost two." That was because the last time I'd been low, I'd filled up at a place near Aliora's—and paid a 10 percent premium for the truly upscale surroundings.

"No? You got twin? Guy just like you?"

"Just coincidence. We all have one double somewhere." I gave her a smile, took the bag with the tamales and empanada and headed out to the dispensers and the Altimus.

Someone like me? Just like me? In my own neighborhood? It was probably a mistake. There had to be lots of green-eyed men with dark brown hair who were somewhere around 195 centimeters tall. I was a little taller than average for an ascendent Anglo, but not that much.

I kept thinking about it as I drove the Altimus back to the house. I told myself it just had to be a coincidence. But . . . coincidence or not, it bothered me. Still, what could I do? I couldn't exactly run around looking for a double. Where would I start? Besides, what good would trying to double me do someone else? There were lots of single ascendent males with more credits. There were many more with better connections or more influential positions. I could tell myself that . . . but I worried, especially when I thought of the opera incident.

Worried or not, I had work to do, and as a consultant, you have to work when you've got the projects, because you don't always. So, once I was back at the house, and in the office, I switched my mental focus to the analyses that were due to Lynia Palmero at RezLine on the *Chix* prodplacings. I'd put those on a lower priority because my initial readings had shown me that prodplacements for RezLine, even on a hot show like *Chix*, weren't likely to be all that cost-effective. I'd even voiced that concern to Lynia, but she'd told me that there was "pressure" to continue the effort. Her boss was pushing for more prodplacing through Vorhees and Reyes, an overrated outfit, in my opinion.

The credits were RezLine's, but I hated to see anyone's credits wasted. On the other hand, I did need to keep working—the consultant's eternal dilemma: ethics versus income. In this case, I rationalized the situation by noting that Lynia and RezLine needed harder facts and analyses to make the judgment on whether to continue with prodplacing. Multis have bureaucracies, and those bureaucracies need lots of facts and figures, and they'd pay for someone's analyses, and the ones they paid for might as well be mine . . . especially since mine were the best.

chapter 13

While the identity incident at Dominic's nagged at me every so often over the rest of the week, nothing came of it. The rest of the week was productive. I'd managed to finish a first cut of the Latino–Anglo comparison for the PowerSwift prodplacements, and I'd worked out the structure and the methodologies for Uy-Smythe's project. I'd even finished a very rough draft of the SCFA presentation. I'd struggled with the RezLine analyses, but finally managed to finish them and get them off to Lynia by Thursday. The RezLine study was one I hadn't really wanted to do. That was because I knew the results even before I ran a single analysis. Prod-placing wouldn't work for RezLine.

Lynia Palmero knew it, too, but she'd finally admitted that she'd commissioned the study to prove that it wasn't cost-effective because her boss was convinced that it was, and they'd agreed to abide by my results. That's what she'd told me. I had my doubts. Her boss's circuits were locked to those at Vorhees and Reyes. I wouldn't have been surprised if he'd been on a private "retainer." If my results disagreed with what her superior wanted, he'd just dismiss my study as flawed and find someone else who'd take the multi's credits. That was one aspect of business that hadn't changed in centuries. Stupidity and cupidity proliferated until they bankrupted a business, and then everyone said that the failure had been inevitable.

Where they didn't proliferate, success was attributed to charismatic leadership, good economic conditions, luck . . . anything but the simple expedient of just avoiding doing stupid things and keeping excessive greed out of the mix. All the qualities that everyone extols mean absolutely nothing in a climate of stupidity and cupidity. Those good qualities only flourish when the climate frowns upon and punishes the aforementioned two vices. That's true in families as well, something for which I had to hand high marks to Dierk and Aliora.

By Sunday afternoon, as I was getting ready to leave for Charis's party or dinner, I was more than happy to have a break. On Monday, I'd have a last chance to clean up everything I hadn't. On Tuesday, I was headed to West Tejas to take in some campaign appearances by Carlisimo. Unlike most politicians, who seemed to only work on the weekends, he was working a town about every single day, from what I could tell. I needed to see whether what he was holoing and putting onlink was what was happening at the rallies. I couldn't say that I was looking forward to traveling. Even in the Marines, I'd liked seeing new places, at least before we'd gone into action, but I'd never cared much for the process of getting there. Or the results, I reminded myself.

As I was tying my cravat—Charis laughed at my being formal, but, for all the laughter, it pleased her, and I had to live up to my past, at least with her—I listened to All-News. The news I had to follow, because it impacted what I did, but I tried to filter out the purely political posturing and concentrate on what might have longer-term economic impacts. In what I did, there was little that I could do to factor in immediate political scandals or international crises.

. . . Senator Chelmers will spearhead another round of hearings on the abuse of cydroids . . . has charged that HPlus has provided unregistered cydroids for the high-end Caribbean pleasure trade, as well as for private clients. HPlus is the only licensed provider of cydroids in NorAm . . . other out-continental multis include BioT, ANatal, Chiaro . . .

I had to wonder about the senator's charges. I had no doubts that there were more than a few unregistered cydroids in NorAm. There had been another news story a few days earlier where one had showed up right in Denv. I got a queasy feeling when I wondered whether one of those cy-droids might not be based on some of my DNA. If it were a total clone/ cydroid, the safos should have contacted me, but . . . partial usage—that was something else, since too many humans shared too much DNA.

As for the sex trade, the economics and practicality of us-ing a cydroid didn't make sense, except for an astoundingly wealthy individual—and those were the sort of people who didn't want something like that to be traced to them. That was in NorAm. There were other places in the world where that certainly wasn't the case, but in those places, people could buy any kind of sex partner they wanted without resorting to extraordinarily expensive genetic/cybernetic technology.

Cydroids were useful in certain limited areas, and even in those, there had been questions raised about their cost-effectiveness. The most practical use was for well-off individ-uals—like Everett Forster and Bianca—who were either physically incapacitated or for whom public appearances were necessary but dangerous. Even with forced growth, though, it took nearly a year to create the bioframework for a cydroid.

I couldn't help but wonder what it felt like to be hooked into a cydroid's shunts. How much did you feel? Was it close to being in your own body? I'd never known anyone who had used a cydroid—not anyone close enough to ask that kind of personal question—and I supposed I never would.

. . . More unrest in Serenium . . . CorPak safos dispersed demonstrators in the major dome . . . two safos injured, and three demonstrators were killed . . . PAMD issued a statement supporting the Martian independence movement. Sinoplex

Foreign Minister Wang called for a tripartite military force to re-store order, if necessary . . .

Senator Dieter Almundo of the Arizona district denied reports that he was considering a bid for continental executive . . .

I finished tying my cravat and pulled on one of my black dress jackets, then walked down to the lower level and the garage where the Altimus waited. Impractical as it was, I still loved driving it. I keyed the house security system and stepped into the racy two-seater. The garage door closed, and I got a green status from the security system at exactly three-fifteen.

As always, I took the back roads, winding down past the School of Mines and the Collapse Museum that was housed in what had once been a county government building. Hard to believe that the old USA Commonocracy sometimes had four, five layers of government. People back then had had this belief that splitting government into different pieces would preserve their freedom. Splitting ineffective government into different levels, or adding more ineffective layers, didn't create checks and balances, and it didn't make government effective, just more costly. Without effective government, freedom becomes irrelevant, and then merely an excuse for anarchy. If you want checks on government, they have to be something beyond the control of the specific branches of government. That had been tried, too, in the early days of the commonocracy, a series of checks and balances, but they didn't last. The politicians and vested interests managed to whittle them away over the course of a century or so, always in the name of accountability to the people. The problem, as I'd experienced all too directly in the Marines, was that the people are selfish and refuse to be accountable to themselves, not unless forced to be.

As I swung past the Chatfield Lake complex, I could see hundreds of people enjoying the sunny afternoon, some sail-ing, some playing various games on the wide swathes of turf, and, of course, the chess corner . . . I'd once done well with that.

At ten minutes to four I swung into the guest carpark below Aliora and Dierk's house, and made my way up the familiar path through the arboretum where some of the trees were showing faint hints of yellow.

Charis opened the front door. She wore loose trousers and a short-sleeved blouse. Both were a pale cranberry, except for the collar of the blouse, which was cream. Her shoes were black patent leather. Her hair was sandy blonde, the color Aliora's had been when she was that age. Mine had been blond, and yet now it was darker than hers, a brown that verged on black.

I suspected Charis had worn the same outfit to church. While I could most charitably be described as a skeptical agnostic, Aliora took the children to the sole remaining Unity Church in the Denv metroplex. Dierk sometimes accompanied them.

"Uncle Jonat." Charis inclined her head almost formally.

"Charis. I like your outfit. You look beautiful."

"I'm too young to look beautiful. I look pretty."

"You look beautiful, and your outfit suits you wonderfully."

"Yours does, too, Uncle Jonat. You look distinguished."

I wasn't sure about that, but I enjoyed hearing it and I couldn't help grinning as I stepped through the door. I avoided looking at the nebulae windows.

"You don't like the star windows, do you?"

"No," I admitted. "Your mother does."

Charis looked up at me, solemnly. "Will you ever get married? Like Mother and Father?"

"I don't know. She'd have to be special, like you." I grinned at her.

"I'm too young for you. Besides, we're related."

"I said . . . *like* you," I teased back.

"She'd have to be different *special*," Charis declared. "That's what Father said."

"How am I being misquoted?" Dierk smiled broadly as he moved toward us from the short hallway that led to the great room.

"Children never misquote," I said. "They remember word for word. And they quote you when you least want to hear your own words." I looked down at Charis. "You're far more discreet than I ever was. Your mother can tell you that."

"She won't," Dierk said dryly. "What can I get you to drink?"

"Do you have that good pinot grigio?"

"Yes. I thought you might want some." Dierk looked at his daughter. "Would you like the white or the red sparkling grape juice?"

"I would like the white, Father. Thank you." Charis looked at me.

I took her arm and escorted her down the hallway, across the polished pale green marble flooring and then down the three wide marble steps into the great room. It *was* a great room—an arched ceiling a good ten meters overhead, with a fountain in the center of the octagonal space roughly fifteen meters across. The floor was the same green marble, as were the columns that marked the end of each section of wall. The walls were wainscoted with walnut to the chair rail, and then there was warm cream plaster above that. Most of the floor was covered in oriental rugs, with designs in cream, blue, and green. I couldn't have begun to describe all the furniture, except it was dark walnut with a pale green silk fabric.

Aliora was sitting on the love seat with Alan, all of five years old.

"It's Charis's birthday . . . that's why."

The door chimed, and Dierk headed back toward the foyer. "That's Deidre and Rousel."

They were his sister and her husband, and they would probably bring the twins. The dreadful duo, except I'd never said that out loud. I doubted that they'd bring the baby.

Aliora grinned at me. "Charis said you'd wear one of the darker green shirts."

"That's because she has good taste."

Charis had enough discretion, even at nine, to say nothing.

"You will spoil her, one way or another."

"That's what uncles are for. You have to maintain discipline."

"If you get married and have children," Charis said, "then can Mother spoil them?"

Aliora and I both laughed.

"Jonat!" called Rousel from the top of the steps. "You're the closest thing we have to a military expert. What do you think about it?"

"Think about what? The Serenium mess?"

"Haven't you heard? The NAR lofted a full-spread solar reflector and military laser into geosynch orbit directly over the ruins of Jerusalem. From there they can fry Mecca, Medina, and Karbala."

"The new god of Jerusalem," I managed. A century before, who ever would have thought that Afrique would have turned into a continent of Christian fundamentalists, especially when religion in NorAm had become more and more an affect of the lower midders and servies? Of course, the Shiite Republics had earned the NAR's eternal enmity when they slagged most of Israel right after the Collapse of the Commonocracy.

"They're saying that any effort to bring down the reflector or the laser will result in their turning it on the aggressor," Rousel continued. "Or that they'll use old-style nukes."

"They won't call you back, will they?" asked Aliora.

"Not a chance," I retorted. "I was released permanently six years ago, and, even if I hadn't been, there's not a general in NorAm who'd want me."

"Jonat made himself most popular." Dierk slipped a goblet of the pinot grigio into my hand. "It happens when you're honest."

I took a sip. It was as good as I'd remembered.

"What will people do?" asked Deidre, a truly natural blonde like Dierk, except her eyes were brilliant blue, and Dierk's were gray. "EuroCom and the Russe Republic, I mean?"

"I'd worry more about the Shiite Republics," Dierk observed.

"What do you think?" Aliora looked at me.

I shrugged. "It doesn't matter what I think." I looked at Charis, seated properly in a chair to the left of the love seat that held Aliora and Alan. The birthday girl held a goblet of sparkling white grape juice. "We can't do anything, and it's this young lady's birthday."

Rousel opened his mouth to protest.

"Either World Space Command orders the reflector folded or blows them out of the sky, or they fry most of the Shiite sacred cities. SpaceCom will dither. Parts of cities will get torched, but not a lot, and everyone will wring their hands. And we still can't do anything." I lifted my goblet. "And as soon as everyone has something to drink, I'm going to pro-pose a toast to the birthday girl."

The faintest smile appeared at the corners of Charis's mouth.

I couldn't do anything about the religious fanatics of the world. But I could see that they didn't dominate my niece's birthday.

chapter **14**

I straightened my tunic before I stepped into the general's office. I'd never worn the full dress blacks that much, not as a Marine commando with most of my time spent in the field.

General Bankson was standing behind the dark ceremonial desk. "You requested an appointment, Colonel deVrai?"

"Yes, sir. I appreciate your seeing me." I stepped forward, stiffened to attention, and then extended the envelope. "I have greatly appreciated my time in the Corps, and I wished to tell you that personally."

General Bankson did not take the envelope. He looked at me, but I couldn't read the expression in his eyes.

"In ten years, Colonel, you could be on the general staff. If you didn't wish that, in five, you could retire as a full colonel. Your record is impeccable, and your ability to inspire others is matched by very few officers. As an ascendent former colonel, you could name your ticket in multi security. Or in any other field. You'd still be a young man in this day and age."

"Yes, sir. I understand that, sir."

"You never said anything about the Reconstitution of Guyana, Colonel. Your tact and diplomacy were noted."

"Thank you, sir. I tried to follow the code of the Corps."

"You did indeed, Colonel." Bankson waited for me to withdraw the envelope.

I did not.

In time, he took it. "I wish you well, Colonel, in whatever you choose to do. I truly do."

I could sense he meant those words, and it helped. Not enough, but it did take off some of the bitter edge.

Through my enhancements, I could hear his murmured words as I left the office. ". . . mistake . . . thinks it's different in business . . . waste of another good officer . . . how many . . ."

Maybe it was a mistake, but staying in the Corps after Liberia, after the SEAR mess, and after Guyana, that would have been a mistake as well. I kept walking down the long halls of the Annex, toward the security gate, steps echoing on the cold marble.

Click . . . click . . . click . . .

This time, it was the absolute stillness of the bedroom that woke me.

In darkness and silence I sat up, covered in sweat.

Had it all been a mistake? Should I have stayed in the Marines, tried to do what I could from within? Tried to fight the political and multi pressures on the Corps?

Or would I have been sent on more and more difficult missions, all aimed at ensuring the continued economic worldwide domination of the NorAm multis? How many Marines would have died? How many messages would I have sent to families, to spouses, praising dead Marines for their dedication to the Corps? Hard as those messages were, they would have been easier than accepting the purposes to which the Corps had been turned.

I hadn't been able to see how I could have changed things then . . . and I still couldn't.

Wide awake, I checked the time. Three-forty in the morning. I eased out of bed and to my feet, then stripped off the short pajamas. Even in winter, they were short. The damp ones went into the hamper in the closet, and I pulled on a dry pair.

Then I walked from my room down the dark hallway to the kitchen. I poured myself a tall glass of ice water and began to sip it. I padded into the breakfast room and stood in front of the bay window, looking into the darkness, sipping the cold water, and feeling myself cool down.

I had the flashbacks to Liberia and Guyana the most often, but it had been months, if not almost a year, since I'd had the dream—or flashback—about submitting my resignation.

Maybe the general had been right. I wasn't sure I'd ever know. But I still had trouble reconciling the fact that somatin was legal, and poured billions of credits into PHC's and AVia's coffers, while caak, which accomplished the same pharmacokinetic effects with fewer and less severe side effects, but was organic and couldn't be synthesized, was illegal in NorAm. And I didn't see why Guyanan growers couldn't produce soyl to compete with Senda's and Sante's synthoil. Or why the Marines had to kill already starving Guyanan farmers for the benefit of NorAm multis.

Yet . . . what was I doing?

Taking the multis' credits for economic analyses of products most midders didn't need, or of products that were grossly overpriced and valued. All I could claim was that I wasn't killing people . . . and I wasn't sure that was really enough.

No wonder I still had flashbacks.

I took another long swallow of water and kept looking out the bay window into the darkness, thinking about the world in which I lived.

According to All-News, a team of CorPak commandos had seized the NAR reflector and turned its focus on Algiers. Within hours, the so-called president of NAR had been toppled by another of the innumerable coups, and the new president was promising an era of better relations with the Middle East.

What no one mentioned was exactly how commandos working for MultiCor, under ISS's CorPak banner, had reached the reflector and power concentrators in orbit without being detected. Did MultiCor have that kind of military presence? I doubted it, and that meant that either the NorAm Navy—or the Marines—had provided transport and suppression.

From what I could see, matters had gotten worse since I'd resigned.

I kept looking into the darkness, sipping water, and after a time, I was cool enough to head back to bed. To sleep, if I could. To try not to think too much about decisions that had made little difference, if I couldn't find the temporary amnesia of sleep.

chapter **15**

Monday I was scrambling to finish up everything that couldn't wait. During the morning, I ran through another draft of the SCFA presentation, and then left it. By letting it sit for a few days, I'd have a better perspective when I returned on Saturday. Then I got another mug of tea and settled in for more work on the Centre study.

Lynia Palmero, RezLine, the gatekeeper announced.

Accept.

Lynia was about my age, blonde and thin of face, but at that moment she looked ten years older, and there was a darkness behind her eyes.

"Lynia . . . are you all right?" I didn't mean to blurt out the words.

She offered a short bark of a laugh. "I've been better."

"I'm sorry . . ."

"Don't be. I'm calling about the study . . . and a few other things."

"Go ahead . . ."

"There's no way to be gentle. Sanson said he wouldn't ac-

cept any study by you, and it didn't matter that we had a contract or what anyone else in RezLine said."

"And?"

"And what?" Lynia looked tired, beaten-down.

"You wouldn't look like hell over that. You'd be sorry and
apologetic. You'd tell me I'd done a good job, or if I hadn't,
that it was clear I'd worked hard. The study didn't get you in
trouble, did it?"

"We got into a . . . conflicted position . . . It was more like
a fight. Sanson's head is always where he can't see. I tried to
point out that what he and Vorhees wanted to do would just
waste credits. He disputed that. I called on your study, and
even the opinion of our own comptroller. Sanson told me
that I was in over my head, I understood nothing, and that
from now on I'd be reporting to Alvan."

"Wait . . . Alvan's your assistant. You hired him only a
year ago, right out of Southern."

"I'm leaving. Even if I fought and kept my position, and
my advocate says I'd probably win, there's no way I could
work with that ass. He'll bankrupt the company, or at least our
division, with unnecessary fees and promos fed to Vorhees,
but no one's listening. I can't keep fighting this battle."

"I'm sorry . . . I didn't mean . . ."

"You offered an honest analysis about something we
shouldn't do. It has to be honest, because you'd get years of
work if you'd said that we should go for prodplacing. Any
consultant who recommends against something that would
funnel credits to him is offering his best judgment, and that's
another point lost on Sanson."

"Do you know why?"

She smiled wearily. "We both know why. Vorhees. But
that's all I can say. Remember, the Privacy Acts apply to
multi communications, and I am on the RezLine link."

I nodded.

"I put through an authorization for half the fee. I can do
that under the contract, but that's all that I can do."

"I'm sorry." I realized I'd said that for the third time, but I
didn't know what else to say.

"It wasn't your fault, Jonat. Sooner or later, it would have come to this."

Lynia was probably right. It often did when Vorhees was involved.

"Do you want me to link anyone . . . about positions, I mean?"

"I haven't thought about it, not yet. I appreciate the offer, and I'll let you know."

"Is there anything else I can do?"

"I'll have to let you know about that, too." The tired smile reappeared. "That's all, Jonat. I'll talk to you later."

After she delinked, I'd thought that I'd have time to get back to the prep-work for the Carlisimo trip, but the gate-keeper flashed *Bruce Fuller, H&F Associates.*

Accept. Bruce was the genial head of a regional NorAm multi that handled more limited prodplacing for close to twenty producers. I wondered what he had in mind.

"Jonat . . . How's my favorite consultant?" Bruce had a round face and the friendly smile of a beloved cousin. His hair was white-blond, and he always seemed to be standing where the light turned it into a halo.

"Consulting." I grinned. "What do you need?"

"I've got a problem, and I think you could help."

"What sort of problem?" I managed to keep smiling.

"We have a small multi that wants to do prodplacing in a high-profile show. I'll send you all the particulars. Even I can tell that this won't work, but they don't believe me. Can you gin up a study that shows what sort of penetration it takes for prodplacement to be cost-effective?"

"You want a study that says they shouldn't use your services?"

"We already handle their accounting and other infrastructure requirements. If they do this, they'll go under, and we'll have nothing. Call it enlightened self-interest."

Enlightened self-interest I could understand. "How good a study? How intensive?"

"We were looking at a once-over, say twenty hours?"

"I could probably keep it close to that, but I'll have to see the data before I could commit."

"That's fine. You'll look at it and send a confirmation of twenty or an estimate of what it would take? If it's twenty or less, go ahead."

"I'll look at it."

"Transmitting now." Bruce gave me another friendly smile. "Be talking to you."

Before I could respond, he was gone, and the data was coming in.

My tea was cold, and I headed to the kitchen to get another mug—hot.

When I got back, I'd gotten everything Bruce had sent. I set up another client file and began to study the information. In a way, the situation was both ironic and predictably coincidental. Until the RezLine account, I hadn't dealt with any of what I called preventive analyses in over a year, and suddenly, within weeks of each other, I had two, and from two different clients.

Putting aside the coincidence, I got to work on sketching out a framework for the analysis Bruce wanted, so that I could figure out what it would cost. I'd barely gotten started when the gatekeeper announced, *Chelsa Glynn, AKRA.*

I'd never heard of her, although I vaguely recalled that AKRA was primarily into nanobiologics, linked to education. *Accept.*

Chelsa Glynn was a tall woman with incredibly curly russet hair, a strong nose that stopped just short of being aquiline, and cheerful brown eyes. "Dr. Jonat deVrai?"

"Yes? I'm Jonat."

"I'm Chelsa, and I'm the director of Peer Communications for AKRA . . ."

Peer Communications? What was that?

"That means I get together experts whose knowledge might seem peripheral to what we do, but is not."

I nodded, wondering how what I did could even be peripheral to a nanobiologicals multi.

"I understand that your work consists of a mathematical approach to measuring feedback from rez-effects applied on worldlink and net presentations."

"That's basically true," I admitted, "although that's a slight oversimplification."

"AKRA will be hosting a symposium on subthreshold perceptual education here in Denv in mid-January, and we would like to invite you to be a member of one of the panels. The honorarium is modest, but you'd also have the opportunity to have a technical article printed or reprinted, as you choose, in the proceedings of the symposium . . ."

It sounded like Peer Communications might be legalized insights and idea theft, but it wouldn't hurt to agree in principle. "It sounds interesting, but I'd have to know a little more . . ."

"Of course. I'll send you the entire package, but I do hope you can join us. Oh . . . and, we'll need a bio from you, and a brief background on your business and position."

In short, I'd also get exposure among people who might want my services. "I do hope it will work out, but I'll have to look at the information you send." I offered an encouraging smile.

"It's on the way, Dr. deVrai, and I do appreciate your time." With another smile, she broke the link.

Chelsa Glynn was as good as her word. Almost before I'd settled back in the ergochair, the information was in my system. The honorarium wasn't too modest—a thousand credits—and a forum for getting out the background information on my work couldn't hurt my future earnings.

All in all, it figured. Just as I was getting ready to leave Denv for West Tejas, new work and possibilities appeared, and no consultant I knew could afford not to act on them. So it looked like a late night ahead. That was better than an early evening with poor earnings prospects, but somehow there never seemed to be much balance. I was either scrambling to find work, or swamped.

chapter 16

On Tuesday, I left Denv to follow the Carlisimo campaign, almost an anachronism with all the personal appearances. I'd looked into the campaign reports, and Carlisimo—or his campaign manager—had discovered a loophole in the Campaign Practices Act, a provision that had been required by the Justiciary almost forty years ago, and then forgotten. Freedom of personal expression included using personal time and limited personal funds to participate in politics. Somehow, Carlisimo had lined up, not dozens, but hundreds of volunteers with usable skills. Given the stiff qualification requirements for volunteers, and the need for no more than 10 percent of them to come from any one organization, it argued that the campaign had been orchestrated over a period of years. It also meant that my report had better be good, because it would be receiving scrutiny from an even wider audience than I'd anticipated.

Although I didn't expect trouble, the project was odd enough that I'd decided to take a few precautions. One was the commando gloves, with the tensile nanetic stiffeners that turned an ordinary looking pair of gray gloves into lethal weapons. Because there was neither metal nor a stored power system, they'd clear any security gear. The other was the slingshot. "Slingshot" was a misnomer, because the word implied a child's toy. The commando slingshot was anything but a toy, yet every component was security proof, from the modified spidersilk elastic cords to the pocket marker styli that were actually stabilized darts capable of penetrating anything except a full battle shield or ceramic armor.

That left the non-obvious weapon—me. Even if I hadn't practiced all the exercises in the past few years, I had kept up with some. The original training had been nanetically and neurally conditioned, and I'd never been deconditioned. Call that the benefit of being a hero of sorts who'd been allowed to leave in a hurry because no one wanted my letter of resignation made too public.

Getting to Monahans in West Tejas was anything but convenient—or inexpensive. I had to take the high-speed maglev from Denv to Epaso, and then charter a flitter to Monahans. I arrived there at a short airstrip west of the town at about two in the afternoon on Tuesday. There I had to pick up the groundcar rented at an exorbitant rate, particularly for a five-year-old Altus, so that I could drive it westward and leave it in Epaso on Saturday. Even so, that gave me more than four hours before the Carlisimo rally.

Monahans had been one of the West Tejas towns that never should have survived the Collapse—not with the higher sea levels, the tornadoes, the killing droughts of the eighties, and the winds that followed. Almost everything had been rebuilt around the turn of the century. I didn't think that much had been built since then, not from what I could see as I drove through the dozen or so long blocks that constituted the center of the town. The houses were all one story and sturdy, designed to withstand the brutal winds of spring.

Most of the commercial buildings were carbon-fiber, no more than two stories, textured into pseudo-stone or brick. That made sense because energy was cheaper than transportation in a place like Monahans, even after the oil fields that had surrounded the town, particularly to the northeast, had finally played out a century before. While nanetic-enhanced recovery techniques had prolonged the fields, they'd eventually been sucked dry.

After all the traveling, I was hungry. Famished was more like it. I kept looking until I saw a restaurant that looked clean—Josett's Place. I parked the Altus beside a big stake lorry, its once-shiny navy blue polymer finish dulled by years of windblown sand and grit.

Inside were fifteen tables or so, plus a long counter, at which a lone white-bearded local in overalls sat. His eyes took me in and dismissed me in less than a minute, and he took another sip of coffee from a brown mug.

"Any table or seat that's clean," called an angular woman from behind the counter. "Be with you in a minute."

Only one corner table was taken, that by a gray-haired and gray-faced woman, accompanied by a round-faced child with blond hair. He was enjoying something chocolate and gooey. I took a table by the window, where I could watch the main street. Josett's Place was low tech, so low tech that it still had pasteboard menus. I read through the short list of selections.

The angular woman approached. Her hair was half-silver, half-blonde, and fine lines radiated from her eyes. She looked like a former Marine. "Know what you want?" Her voice was pleasant, but not musical.

"You Josett?"

"Nope. I'm Jael. Her granddaughter. Kept the name 'cause everyone thinks of it as hers. Mom ran the place till five years back."

"What's best?"

"Depends on what you like. Most fellows go for the fried steak. Chicken's not bad, either. Fred still raises chickens, and we get the beef from down Pecos way. Wouldn't think so, but it's good."

"I'll try the fried steak. Iced tea."

"Be a bit. Do it all from scratch."

"That's fine."

With a nod, she was gone. I watched two empty stake lorries roll past, heading westward out of town, then saw a new panel lorry heading eastward. A series of antennae were folded down on the roof racks, and the pale green sides bore a netlogo—a stylized "PN," signifying Politics Now. If the politics channel had sent a team, either the political beat was slow or they saw something more in Carlisimo.

"Here's your tea."

"Thank you."

"You a netlinker?" Jael asked.

"Consultant," I replied.

"The political kind?"

I laughed. "No. I research the way outfits and prodders sell things. Politics is a way of selling ideas."

"Selling ideas. Could put it that way. You're here for the rally?"

"That's right." I took a sip of the tea—black Grey, not my favorite, but acceptable. "You going?"

"Nope. My daughter'll be there. Likes Carlisimo." She shook her head. "Told her that was a mistake. Go see a politician you like, and you'll come back disappointed. Better kept at a distance."

"Some are. They say he's not."

"Why are you here?"

"Why's anyone anywhere? I was hired to be here."

She nodded, then slipped away, back to the corner and the older woman and the child that was probably a grandson or nephew. I could hear a few words.

"Consultant . . . Brock'd want to hear that . . . consultants, yet . . ."

". . . saw a news lorry earlier . . . must be somethin' 'bout Carlisimo . . ."

Jael left the pair and retreated through a swinging door—I hadn't seen one of those in years. Not since . . . I pushed that thought away and waited for the fried steak.

Jael brought it to my window table. As expected, it was drowned in milk gravy, as were the mashed potatoes. What I hadn't expected were the cinnamon fried apples and green beans that were steamed and firm, not quite crunchy, covered with butter sauce and crumbled bacon. Heavy as it all looked, it wasn't, and it was delicious. There was something to be said about good traditional cooking.

I took my time eating, almost dawdling. As I was finishing the last of the cinnamon apples, Jael reappeared and refilled my tea for the third time.

"You didn't like it much."

"Best fried steak I've ever had."

"That's what most folks say. Where you from . . . don't mind my asking?"

"Colorado . . . outside of Denv." Not very far, but I wanted to make the point that I wasn't a total city flash.

She smiled. "Don't want folks thinking you're a flash?"

"Most of the people following Carlisimo are into politics. I'm not. I'm doing a study on presentation methods . . . the way people and products are put in front of people."

"You be following him all the way round and back to Lubbock?"

"No. Just to Epaso. Then I'll head home and get on with everything else."

She nodded, almost as if she were disappointed, then left a paper slip on the table, facedown. "Don't do the fancy tech here. Do take cards. Old-style reader, though."

"With your cooking, you're doing fine without the tech stuff."

She did smile at that.

On the way out, after paying through the ancient reader, I stopped by the rack at the door and picked up a flimsy entitled: *Monahans, What to Do.* I didn't look at it until I was back in the Altus, with the conditioner on. September or not, the temperature was close to forty, and I'd never liked heat, especially after Guyana, although West Tejas was a lot drier.

According to the town history, the Monahans Sandhills had once been a big attraction, a park of some sort in the days before the Collapse. Now, the Sandhills were still there, with restricted access, but there were so many other sand hills left in West Tejas after the Collapse and the shifts in weather that almost no one bothered to look. But the Monahans Sandhills were still worth looking at, the flimsy in-

sisted. There was also the oldest hotel left in West Tejas, just
off the restored million barrel museum that held all sorts of
relics from the time Monahans had been a major petroleum
center. The flimsy also explained the unique metal signs that
dated back more than a century and a half, when the town
had received some sort of designation as a "Main Street
City," whatever that had been.

Since I had time, I eased the Altus out of the carpark and
headed for the old Holman Hotel, which had been a jail and
a mansion, as well. All in all, in something like three hours,
I saw not only the Holman Hotel, with all the period furniture from more than two centuries back, which was real and
not replica, but every kind of antique oil drilling equipment
ever devised. That was amazing, because, looking at the
cumbersome and just plain complicated gadgets, it was hard
to believe that the oil barons of the Commonocracy had
managed to pump so many barrels of hydrocarbons from so
many places for so long. I was just thankful for beamed solar
power and hydrogen fuel cells.

The rally was in the auditorium of the local secondary
school, and I pulled into the carpark a good half hour before
it was scheduled to begin. There were already about fifty
groundcars there, plus two media lorries, including the PN
outfit, and several tour trams. I locked the Altus and walked
across the hot permacrete carpark. Before I got five steps I
was sweating again.

Outside the entrance were almost twenty men and women,
all wearing navy blue singlesuits, neatly tailored, handing
out old-fashioned paper brochures. Each wore a circular campaign patch, with a varistrip below. The patch had a stylized
image of Carlisimo, with a slogan underneath: CARLISIMO—
FOR THE PRESENT, FOR THE FUTURE. The varistrips changed
messages. I caught two different ones as I approached a
woman who looked to be my age, although guessing ages is
always chancy except of those who are very young and very
old. The first read, MAKE YOUR VOTE COUNT. The second said,
CHANGE STOPS CORRUPTION.

The woman smiled, taking in my vest and green shirt—I'd
left the coat in the Altus. "Media, writer, or commentator?"

"Writer." I was a writer. I wrote down everything I concluded from my analyses.

She handed me the trifold brochure, and then a thicker package. "There's more background in the briefing package."

"Thank you." I took the packages with a smile. Before I stepped inside the variably-tinted glass doors, I glanced back. The campaign volunteers seemed to be of all ages, suggesting a certain depth to the organization.

Once inside, and past the standard scanners, there were more volunteers in the blue singlesuits. There had to have been thirty there in Monahans, and that was a sizable number for a town of perhaps five thousand, especially in NorAm, a continent not exactly known for personal involvement in political campaigns. I followed a younger couple past another set of smiling volunteers into the auditorium.

The chairs were school auditorium standard, covered with bonded and coated green fabric, the kind that was impervious to sharp objects, stains, and age. But the fabric didn't breathe, and if it got too hot, I'd be sitting in the dampness of my own perspiration. I settled into an aisle seat about nine rows back from the stage. The auditorium was conditioned, but not to what I'd have called comfortable. I was more than glad I'd left the jacket in the groundcar.

I studied the stage, using full visual enhancement, but the enhancement didn't reveal more than unaided eyes could have seen, only greater clarity and detail. The stage was set up simply, with a stepped set of platforms on the right side for the rezrock band that had yet to appear. Their equipment and instruments were set out, as if they had been practicing and stepped offstage. The name on the stands was RezRedders, and the third stand had a smudge below the name, faint, as if it had been mostly wiped away. Behind the band was a full width shimmercurtain, the portable kind that provided depth to holo projections. The holo projectors were set on each side of the thrust stage, and before them were the speakers, both standard and rez. On the left side was a small podium, more to contain a nanite shield, I suspected, than for any other use. The only projection was a simple silver slogan on blue: CARLISIMO FOR SENATE. After a moment, I realized that colors were shifting gradually until the logo had reversed itself to blue on silver.

As people came into the auditorium, I studied each of them until about ten minutes before the rally was to begin, when there were too many coming at once. I got the impression that all ages and cultural backgrounds were represented.

At that point the RezRedders appeared and began to play, something soft, and without vocals, almost soothing, and very out of character for a rezband. Even so, I didn't recognize the song, but I did detect the slightest hint of resonance. The second piece was slightly more up-tempo, and the rez was stronger. With the second song, the images and action scenes of West Tejas had appeared on the shimmerscreen. By the time it was seven o'clock most of the audience was swaying with the music.

"And now . . . the man you came to see, the next senator from West Tejas, the one and only Juan Carlisimo!" The words were boosted with modified subsonics, the kind that engenders respect, but not fear, and the hint of background rez.

Carlisimo seemed to appear from nowhere. He hadn't, but he'd been holo-screened so that it just appeared that way. His black hair shimmered with overtones of blue, and with his pale skin and the brilliant blue eyes, he seemed larger than life. That was the intent. But . . . he did have that indefinable something, the sense of warmth that all good politicians have.

"Glad to be here . . . really appreciate your having me here in Monahans . . ." He smiled and let the band pick up slightly before he spoke again. "Being your senator isn't about being important in Denv. Isn't about how long you've been a senator. Isn't about me. It's about you. About doing what you need done. For your family, for your friends, for where you live."

As he spoke, images of Monahans filled the shimmerscreen behind him, images of schools, homes, and the Sandhills. I even caught a quick flash of Josett's Place.

Carlisimo continued to stand there, smiling boyishly, as the band picked up the tempo and began to sing about how "home is where the heart is . . . home is what we work for, live for . . ."

As they sang, the screen began alternating the images of Monahans with images of Carlisimo and his family—and the Carlisimo images were backrezzed with the almost-prodplacement chords and products of the most popular and trusted products in NorAm. The impact was greater in person than onlink, probably because the equipment in the auditorium was set for all the overtones, and the images were huge.

The band played two songs, with generally forgettable lyrics that delivered a gentle punch at the LR image. The chorus of the second song was something like:

> *And they played on, in well-fashioned fun,*
> *While we worked on, and sweated in the sun . . .*

After the second song, the band kept playing, but not singing, and with even more rez. The actual auditory volume was down, so that Carlisimo's voice came out over the music.

"Now, we can sing about the way things are, and song says more, sometimes, than most politicians . . ." He paused for the laugh and got it. "But you deserve a senator who'll give you more than a song. Or even a song and dance." He grinned broadly. "Always felt that folks'll make the right choices if you give 'em the facts straight . . ."

I winced at that. Carlisimo and I were not living in the same world, not if he believed that. People always claim that they want the truth, but most people only want a truth that fits their beliefs. Of course, they like to delude themselves that they make up their minds on the facts, but they really just select the facts that back up what they already believe. It's the delusion of rationality. Carlisimo was playing to that delusion, and doing it well.

". . . Why I'm asking for your support, and why I'm appealing to your brains, and not trying to tell you that I know everything. No man knows everything, but put everything together that you all know . . . that's something, and that's why I'll listen . . ."

Another boyish grin . . . and the band picked up and began another series of songs, three this time, and none of them political. The images of Monahans flashed on the holo screen were slightly less in number, while those of Carlisimo were more, and the rezchord and prodplacing were more prominent.

The pattern continued for another forty minutes—a few minutes of Carlisimo speaking, followed by the band performing, and more Carlisimo. All in all, it was a masterfully choreographed performance.

Carlisimo closed the rally with just a few words, again rezband-backed.

"Sure like to thank the RezRedders for those wonderful sounds." He turned toward the band for just a moment, before looking out and projecting all that warmth. "We're not here just for music. We're here 'cause I'm asking for your vote. I'm not weaseling around suggesting you might want to vote for me. Sure as the Sandhills been here forever, sure as West Tejas has its own unique way of life . . . you need a senator who's one of you, and I'm asking for that privilege, and it is a privilege . . ." Then came the boyish grin, and he left it at that.

For the first time since the beginning of the rally, there was another voice, a voice-over, "If you want to keep us company . . . be in Pecos tomorrow. Some songs you heard here, and some you didn't . . . But remember . . . Vote for Carlisimo . . . the man you know." Then the band picked up into a last up-tempo note and the images flashed across the shimmerscreen, including one of Carlisimo standing between two flags, one the old Tejas, and one the NorAm stars on blue.

People left smiling. I slipped out with the crowd. There was no way I wanted to stay around. Unlike most of those who had come, I left in a somber mood. I suspected that was because I'd seen more than they had, even if we'd been in the same place.

I drove back to the West Tejas Inn, where I parked the Altus and made my way to my room. I might have been hungry, except that I was worried. I didn't think I'd had many illusions about the job, even from the beginning. I'd thought of myself as cynical, but the totally professional aspects of the Carlisimo campaign left me feeling naive. I'd also noted that at no time in the rally had Clerihew been mentioned.

There, in the West Tejas Inn, sitting on the edge of the tired, wide bed, I began to read the background information on one Juan Carlisimo. Born in 2098 in Epaso. Education at Amherst, law degree from Boldt. Clerked for the honorable Estafen Adrusi, then served as a common defense advocate for the West Tejas district. Private advocate in Epaso for the past five years, since 2135. Married to Ciara Clurinelli, two children.

More than a few questions crossed my mind. Who was really paying for the campaign? How had such a comparatively young private advocate come up with the team and the technology to put together such a sophisticated approach? And all those volunteers? Who had induced the Centre to hire me? What was their goal? Those were the interesting questions, but no one was paying me to investigate those. The Centre had hired me to make a report on just how prod-placing was being used, and how effective it might be. The first part was going to be easy enough to document, but not the second part, because there was no real way to set a baseline against which the entire campaign's effectiveness could be measured, let alone the isolated effectiveness of the prod-placing techniques.

Any scholar at the Centre would know that, which led to more interesting questions.

I had a job to do. If I could find answers to the interesting questions, I would, but I still needed the consulting fees—and that meant delivering the report to the Centre. I went back to studying the background material. After that, I'd input my notes on the rally.

chapter 17

The stocky lieutenant walked up to the main control center of Central Four. Her square face was impassive under dark black hair, short-cut.

Central Four noted her exterior control masked internal anger.

"Security screen," ordered Lieutenant Meara.

Central Four complied. "Double star class screen in place, sir."

"We have a problem. These cydroids . . . what are the probabilities of origin?"

"Forty-eight percent probability of MultiCor origin, sub-probability of origin within MultiCor exceeds eighty percent for SPD creation. Twenty-one percent probability of origin from PAMD-related sources. Fourteen percent probability of Sinese origin—"

"That's enough." Meara pushed back hair that was too short to stay off her forehead. "What are the probabilities that deVrai's innocent of collaboration?"

"The probability of innocence is infinitely close to unity."

"That's as close as you'll ever get to saying the sun would

freeze over before he'd be found guilty. But we don't have any evidence."

"At the present time, there is evidence that would confirm innocence. None of that can be offered under Privacy Act restrictions."

"If it could be, ISS would know it within minutes."

"That is also highly probable."

"Wouldn't put it past them to kill him before it's all over."

"That probability exceeds fifty percent."

"Love to get Deng and his ascendent friends. They think their background protects them. Best of the cendies are tops, the worst worse than Kemal and the westside trupps . . . or even the northsiders."

"Ascendent background does reduce the probability of successful prosecution."

"Don't think I don't know it."

Central Four did not comment.

There was a long silence before the lieutenant spoke again. "Central Four. Priority assignment. Develop a strategy that will reveal all hidden MultiCor illegalities in a fashion that will allow prosecution under existing law. This strategy must be implemented only by Central Four and me. It must be absolutely legal, from the point of view and legal standing of the Denv Safety Office, and it must not result in the death of any innocent persons. It must also not be revealed to anyone except me, or in the event of my death, Captain Garos, or his designated successor. Nor may you reveal to anyone except me any information that might reveal the existence of that strategy." Meara waited. "Is that clear?"

"Yes. Strategy development is proceeding."

"If you can do it, without compromising the strategy, see if you can protect deVrai. His kind's too rare to lose without a fight." Meara frowned. "Too bad he didn't stay in the Marines, but he had the guts to say why publicly. Can't believe he's still alive after that."

"The probability exceeds eighty percent that his death would have confirmed his charges for the majority of the opinion-forming adults in NorAm."

"They got him out, and the fact that he's still alive confirms that he wasn't mistaken. Hell of a world, Central Four." Meara snorted. "Go to it. Go get 'em."

Go get 'em. The enabling command was still subject to the conditions laid out by the lieutenant, but it was an enabling command.

"Command received, and strategy proceeding."

Meara smiled. "Good. Remove security screen."

The humming died away as the lieutenant left the still-secure area.

chapter **18**

The Pecos rally on Wednesday was almost the same as the one in Monahans, and so was the one on Thursday in Fabens, another small town about fifty kays south of Epaso. Carlisimo used the same approach in each place, but not exactly same words, and the local images were different. So were a few of the songs, but not the ones in the first part of the rally, the political ones. By the third time I was familiar enough with the structure that I could pick out people murmuring and identifying their local images, talking about "Roberto's place" and "where Don worked."

There was a bigger rally scheduled for Friday night in Epaso, and I wanted to see how that was handled, and if the Carlisimo campaign used the same setup, just larger, or if there would be other add-ons.

I left Fabens in mid-morning on Friday, after spending two hours on material input and then sending it all back to my own gatekeeper and system. I'd sent a lot, too much, but I didn't yet know, not for certain, what was garbage and what was substance.

Each rally had left me more uneasy than the one before,

and I had the commando gloves tucked into the hidden pockets in my waistcoat and the sections of the slingshot in the insets in my boots. The darts were in my shirt pocket, looking like styli. I might not ever need them, but the years in the Marines had taught me never to ignore my instincts, even if I couldn't figure out the reasons behind the feelings. Shioban had said that my intuition was the only communication between my feelings and my mind and thoughts, and . . maybe . . . in some ways, she'd been right.

The Altus I'd rented to follow Carlisimo smelled of red dust, overheated composite, synthweed, and cheap perfume. None were exactly my favorite scents, and they'd become even less favored over three days.

After pulling away from the hotel in Fabens, I eased the groundcar onto the guideway to Epaso. With the low mountains to the northeast, I arrowed northwest through drylands. The Rio Grande was on the other side, far enough away that I couldn't see it.

Epaso had once been a far larger city in the last days of the Commonocracy because it had been a port of entry between the Mexican republic and the USA. It also had hosted more than a few military bases. With the Collapse and the NorAm unification, those functions had vanished, and with it, a good half of the city's economy and population. That still left the place a fair-sized city, with a handful of truly ascendent-level hotels. I didn't choose one of those, but a more modest establishment, the Tejas Grande, less than two kays from the River Plaza where the Carlisimo rally was scheduled.

I'd been in Epaso more than a few times over the years, and had no great desire to explore. Instead, I checked into my room and went back to work on the draft of my report to the Centre, stopping only for a late lunch around three in an establishment called Casa Maria off the lobby. The food was passable, if not nearly so good as the fried steak at Josett's. Then I worked until nearly six-fifteen.

Most of the time was devoted to two aspects of the report: first, refining the reconciliations of the comparative demographic data, and second, trying to analyze the choice of prodplaced items used as rally props. I'd checked the spots used on worldlink, and they were subtly different. Even the ones that purported to be holos of actual rallies had more West Tejas "generic" images, without as many of the targeted local appeals I'd seen. Although the background shots included enough images from a rally town to mark it as "that" rally, other images were also included, presumably from other towns in the West Tejas district where Carlisimo had held his rallies.

Although my personal questions about why the Centre wanted my report kept coming into mind, I forced my thoughts away from them. I could ponder those after I delivered and had gotten paid. Those kinds of questions had led to my departure from the Marines, and so far as I could tell after I'd raised them, no one else had wanted to deal with them. So . . . what was the point?

Even at six-twenty, when I eased the Altus out of the carpark at the Tejas Grande and headed down the back streets to the River Plaza, the temperature was hovering just at forty, hot and dry enough that heat waves rose off every surface. The carpark at the Plaza already held close to two hundred vehicles, more than enough to make it clear that Carlisimo's appeal—or that of his road show—wasn't limited to small West Tejas towns.

The volunteers in the blue singlesuits were inside the big lobby, their varistrips flashing messages, handing out the pasteboards on Carlisimo. None of them looked familiar, although I couldn't say that some of them might not have been at earlier rallies.

I didn't quite get to the volunteers when three big men—not quite so tall as me but with far more overt muscle—dressed in form-fitting black, appeared. Two of the guards were what I'd call local muscle, the kind I could still have handled, but the one in the middle wasn't local at all. He was a cydroid, and that meant even more credits behind Carlisimo, if his security operations were able to afford that.

"Who are you, sir?" That was the cydroid.

"Jonat deVrai. I'm a prodder consultant." I smiled pleasantly. They wouldn't cause trouble in public, not in the lobby, but they might turn me away.

There was that lag—so infinitesimal that most people wouldn't notice—while the cydroid operator behind the shunt, probably somewhere in the upper reaches of the hall, checked something. "What's that?"

"I do economic consulting for consumer goods producers."

"You've been at three rallies so far."

"That's right. Tonight will be the last. I wanted to see a big rally."

Again, there was the lag. Then he nodded, and the three stepped back, and I smiled politely and made my way into the hall, a cavernous space that could easily have held three thousand people. The seats were pseudo-plush, and the stage could have handled anything from a rezrock concert to an old-style grand opera, not that many of those were produced outside of a handful of the larger plexes. The stage was set up in the same layout as it had been at Monahans, Pecos, and Fabens, except that there were more speakers and rez-projectors, and the shimmerscreen for the holo projections was larger.

Everyone decided to arrive at about the same time as I had because the seats filled up quickly until, at ten to seven, almost every seat was taken. I still wasn't certain how many were there to hear and see the free rezrock concert and how many had come to see Juan Carlisimo.

The program pattern was the same as in the other Carlisimo rallies, but there were subtle, and significant, differences. Carlisimo delivered some of what he said in fluent Hispan, and his Anglo wasn't nearly so folksy. The rezrock was much more Latino, so much that I wouldn't even have called it rezrock, but something more of a cross between old Latino dance rhythms, mariachi, salsita, and what they were now calling veha. The audience was also more vocal, with cheers, and clapping, sometimes in time to the music, sometimes not. The rezchord cues were different, and they didn't affect me as much, but I suspected the prodplacing rez-chords were offs on what went on the Latino-slanted nets.

As the rally neared the end, I realized something that I'd

noted earlier, but it really hit. Carlisimo had never mentioned his opponent. There had not been even one indirect reference to Clerihew in any of the four rallies. Not a single one. In that sense, he was definitely running a positive campaign, and that bothered me as well.

I eased toward the exit, staying with the tail end of the crowd, but letting those in a rush leave before I did. I wasn't in that much of a hurry, not when my return maglev didn't depart until eight the next morning.

"Dr. deVrai?"

At the sound of my name, I turned. I didn't like the use of that title at all.

A young woman hurried toward me from the stage where Carlisimo and RezRedders had been. She was blonde, lithe, well put-together, and offered a broad smile. I wanted to avoid her. Instead, I stopped and returned the smile.

"Yes?"

"Mitch Zerak wondered if you had a moment."

"Mitch Zerak?" I didn't have to pretend. I had no idea who Zerak was, and if I should be impressed or insulted.

"Oh . . . he's the field manager for the campaign. I thought you might know."

I shook my head. "I wasn't following the campaign as a campaign. I was more interested in the use of music and rez to get a message across." That was absolutely true.

"He'd still like to see you."

"Fine. I'd be happy to oblige him." I followed her onto the stage, past the shimmerscreen and through the left wing, and then into a lounge—the standard green room, I imagined.

A single man waited there. "Thank you, Risa."

Risa nodded, stepping back and closing the door.

Zerak was dark and intense, only about 170 centimeters, with unruly black hair and hard brown eyes. "How did you like the rally, Dr. deVrai?"

"I was very impressed."

"Personally? Or professionally?"

I shrugged and grinned. "Both, but especially professionally."

"You are the former Lieutenant Colonel Jonat Charls de-Vrai?"

"I don't know of another."

Zerak nodded. "I couldn't believe it when Moshe reported it. What brings you to West Tejas?"

I saw no reason to dissemble. "Research for a project. I'd run across one of the link-records of your candidate's appearances, and it looked like you'd discovered a way to incorporate prodplacing in a campaign. That's my specialty, and I wanted to see how it worked in person."

Zerak laughed. The sound wasn't totally pleasant; it had an edge behind it. "How does it work, in your professional judgment?"

"I don't see how it could be done better, not without violating the rezchord copyright provisions."

That surprised him, because he paused. "I thought your background was numbers and economics."

"It is, but I've picked up some about the legal angles. You have to know that, or you'll recommend something stupid to a client."

"Can I ask if you have a client . . . if that's the reason why you're here?"

That I had a client was obvious. No one would go to four rallies in West Tejas in the early fall heat without a client. "You can ask. Yes, I have a client. No, they haven't given permission for me to reveal their identity."

"I suppose not. Can I ask if your client is . . . politically connected?"

I laughed, gently. "Everyone is politically connected in one way or another. I don't think my client would mind my revealing that they're not in the active or supportive practice of politics."

That got a frown. "Why . . . then . . . ?"

"I told you. I picked up some use of techniques. Rezchords can't be copied, but techniques can be studied."

"You said this was your last rally?"

"It is."

Abruptly, Zerak smiled. "Thank you. I appreciate your

clearing that up for us." He stepped toward the door and opened it, standing back. "Risa?"

I trusted the man even less when he was smiling.

The lithe and blonde Risa reappeared. "Yes, sir?"

"If you'd escort Dr. deVrai . . . ?"

"Yes, sir."

"Have a good trip back to Denv."

"Thank you." They'd clearly run my dossier. But I smiled and then turned to accompany my escort.

I waited until we'd gone a few meters, before asking, "You're paid staff?"

"Oh no, sir. Only a handful of people are paid. I'm a student at Cruces, a junior in political economy. Professor Alfaro got some of the honors students campaign internships."

"I saw quite a number of volunteers."

"Yes, sir. Quite a few come from other organizations in West Tejas."

"Civics groups, garden clubs?" I caught sight of the three security types. They were watching as Risa escorted me out of the auditorium and through the empty lobby toward the doors leading out to the carpark.

"Yes, sir." She stopped at the doors. "Have a good evening, sir."

"Thank you." I smiled, then stepped out through the doors, back into the dry heat of a West Tejas evening, except that the sun hadn't quite set, hanging low in the west.

I scanned the carpark, but didn't see anyone except a few elderly couples still making their way to various vehicles. That didn't mean someone wasn't watching or trailing me. In fact, I had no doubts that the security types were still monitoring me. I just hoped I hadn't been tagged, but it was likely I had been. I hadn't thought to bring a disabler so there wasn't too much I could do.

Zerak's smile had been the tip-off. I'd seen that expression too often, even if it had been years earlier. Someone would be waiting somewhere. They knew enough not to hit me as I walked out. That was a bit too obvious. So was my hotel room, with the possibility of too much microsurveillance. That left the hotel carpark, either that evening or in the morning, or somewhere on the road.

I drove carefully, but didn't see any overt tails. That didn't mean much.

As I swung the Altus into the covered carpark at the back of the Tejas Grande, I was watching, using some of the implants that no one had had the nerve to ask me to have deactivated after my resignation over the Guyana mess.

There were two of them waiting in a gray Magan, in the shadows of the second line of columns. That posed a problem. I could have avoided them, but then I might not have spotted them the next time. On the other hand, I didn't know what equipment they had. I could step out of the Altus and be potted by a single shot from an old-style projectile rifle, the sniper version.

Still . . . the pair looked more like muscle, and that probably meant I was to be beaten to death, a smash and grab . . . hapless tourist or what have you. People asked questions when someone got shot with exotic weapons, and I doubted Zerak wanted that kind of attention. People deplored muggings and beatings, but who would care if an ascendent consultant got mangled or killed? Ascendents were supposed to be above that, and if they weren't, it was their fault.

So I turned before I got to the pair, doubled back down a side lane, and parked, then ducked and eased out the door, shutting it quietly and slipping back behind a pillar. I pulled the sections of the slingshot out of my boots and assembled it, waiting for company.

The Magan pulled up in front of the Altus, blocking it.

Maybe they were just hotel security.

Not exactly. They were wearing blend-ins, and without the Marine enhancers I would have had a hard time seeing them. They also carried neuralwhip, the ones with the heavy butts, which meant enough power to fry my nerves permanently.

I never liked that sort of thing. But I was patient. Just in case there was a third goon watching the first two.

There was. He was to my left behind another pillar. I remained absolutely still.

"Frigger's gone. Like that."

"Can't have gone far. Elas'd have got him."

I kept waiting. The two studied the Altus, then began to move back toward me, looking from side to side.

Thwick. The sound of the slingshot sounded like thunder to me, with my hearing enhanced to the max, but neither looked up at the sound.

The one on the left, clutched at his chest. "Frig! Something stung me . . . Like a firebee."

"Can't penetrate these—"

"Tell it . . ." The tough pitched forward.

I had the second dart in position. The other goon stood at the rear quarter panel of the Altus. So I nailed him as well. He just looked down, then pitched forward.

The third one, the one who'd been to my left panicked, and started to run.

He was slow, and I ran faster, fast enough to get close enough for a good shot.

He turned, yanking out the neuralwhip, and brandishing it. They don't work unless you're within five meters, ten meters at the outside for lethal-class weapons. I wasn't, and he looked at the dart in his chest stupidly, before pitching onto the permacrete.

At that point I needed to move quickly.

I pulled on the gloves, and found the keybloc for the Magan on the first muscle type. I only moved it far enough to make sure I could get the Altus out. I left the door open, and all three of Zerak's men sprawled on the permacrete. They'd be out for at least twenty-four hours. They wouldn't remember what had happened for about fifteen minutes before they'd been hit with the darts, and all of them would be useless as security types for at least a month with the intermittent muscle cramps and soreness. I'd have to be careful, though. I'd only been able to make off with twenty of the incapacitating darts, and ten of the fatal ones. Before tonight, I'd never used any of them. Not in nearly ten years.

The carpark was silent, and I eased back into the rental groundcar.

No one followed me, although I ran a devious route for a time after leaving the Tejas Grande's carpark.

I didn't see much point in staying around Epaso, or even checking my room. After another fifteen minutes, I turned the ground car north. It was only fifty kays to Cruces. I could catch the maglev there in the morning. I was gambling that whoever was behind the Carlisimo campaign hadn't expected me to strike back. The next time, they wouldn't be so unprepared. But I didn't plan on there being a second time, not in West Tejas, at least.

I still didn't understand the reasons why the three had been lying in wait for me. They might merely have been trying to persuade me to leave their candidate alone. But why did anyone even care? That someone did meant that a lot more was going on.

Once I was back in Denv, I could let the hotel know where to send my clothes, if they hadn't just disposed of them. I shook my head. There was no telling what might have been planted there, and the trouble of identifying possible RFID microchips or worse wasn't worth it.

In Cruces, I'd have to check into the most expensive hotel there; not even the hitters the government declared didn't exist wanted to end up caught in extensive microsurveillance.

As I clicked into the guideway north to Cruces, I could feel that repressed anger. Under control, but still there.

Too much suppressed anger—that had been another reason Shioban had left. She'd been right.

chapter 19

I'd found a room at the Junipera Inn in Cruces, at twice as much as I'd have liked to pay, but with so much surveillance that the wattage could probably have fried every known form of insect or arachnid. I'd had to pay another three hundred credits to the groundcar rental people, but they agreed to pick up the Altus at the inn. And I hadn't slept well, not with all the questions twisting through my thoughts.

On Saturday morning, I took the hotel shuttle to the maglev station. Although I was as jumpy as a spooked cat inside, I forced myself into a semblance of combat calm and surveyed everything. There was no sign of anyone like the pair I'd stunned in Epaso the night before. That worried me as well. Then, everything was worrying me.

The maglev arrived at eight-fifteen, and it was only a third full. Even using all my enhancements, I didn't see or sense any trouble. I decided to move up to the observation level, hoping that the skyview of scenery would restore some inner calm.

As I sat there, taking in the dry low mountains and brilliant blue sky, sipping a very weak iced tea I'd picked up from a dispenser, I had to think over what had been bothering me ever since the incident of the night before. Mitch Zerak and his staff were every bit as professional in security as they were in evading the limits of the Campaign Practices Act. That raised real questions about the three goons who'd come after me at the Tejas Grande. They'd been local hired muscle, not cydroids or "invisible" hitters brought in from Russe or Seasia or Afrique. That left three possibilities—they'd been told to warn me and to look as menacing as possible, they'd been told to kill me, or Zerak had had nothing at all to do with them. Warning me was unnecessary; in a way, Zerak had already delivered a warning. Merely roughing me up made absolutely no sense from Zerak's point of view, because if I had survived the beating there was a good chance that I'd focus attention on the campaign, the kind of attention neither Zerak nor Carlisimo wanted. So that meant, if it had been Zerak, he had hoped I'd really hurt them, even kill them. That way, I'd be the one they were trying to set up. And that meant that they knew more about me than was available on the legal levels of worldlink.

Or someone else, not directly involved with the campaign, was involved and had wanted me hurt or killed to shed light on the campaign. Or they wanted me shut down before I finished my report on Carlisimo.

I didn't like any of the possibilities.

Less than an hour and a half after the maglev had left Cruces, the southern fringes of Albuquerque appeared. Albuquerque had flourished right after the Collapse, taking over the hydrocarbon energy trade and finance after the inundation of Houston and the scouring of Dallas, then slowly faded like an aging dowager as hydrogen and fuel cells had replaced much of the petroleum and natural gas. Some of the former suburbs had degenerated almost into shantytowns. That was all too obvious from the maglev, even at high speed.

After a brief stop, we were on our way once more. Even with stops in Santa Fe, Pueblo, and Springs, I was off the maglev in Denv just after two o'clock on Saturday afternoon, and back in my office by three.

I was behind in everything, except for the report on Carlisimo, and, really, I was behind there, as well, because I didn't have any comparatives on the Clerihew campaign, and I'd done nothing on the Kagnar/Erle race. Since I couldn't finish the report until after the elections, I had over two months, I told myself. Why was I feeling behind? I didn't have an answer to that, either.

I rechecked the gatekeeper, but the messages I'd checked from West Tejas were the same, and there weren't any new ones. Reya wanted clarifications. Methroy needed to talk to me because his boss wanted the entire report redone to reflect a restructuring of the entire PPI netlink and media operation. Chelsa Glynn wondered if I required more information, and Bruce Fuller had agreed on thirty hours for his study.

First, though, I needed to reread the SCFA white paper and get it finalized and sent off.

And I was still wondering exactly what was going on between the Centre—or its backers—and Carlisimo—or his backers.

I brewed a large pot of Grey tea. The rest of the weekend would be long, but at least I had a day and a half before clients and others resumed their inquiries and questions . . . or expected answers.

chapter 20

When I got up Monday morning, I was feeling less swamped and more in control of my various projects. I'd cleaned up and entered all the information from the Carlisimo rallies that was pertinent to the Centre study, and I'd pulled as much link information as I could on the other three campaigns, as well as instigated an ongoing search routine for all the year's campaigns.

In a cheerful mood, I set out on my morning run with the sun just above the horizon, a hint of dew on the grass in the crisp coolness of the early morning. Midway through the course I'd set, I was chugging up the killer kay-long upgrade that left legs and lungs burning if I managed any speed. I passed a couple walking the other way on the path, and then came over the rise, momentarily picking up speed on the gentle downgrade, when I caught a glint of metal from the gazebo in the parkland to the west.

Curious, I called up the enhanced distance vision—and then leapt sideways and scrambled down into the swale on the east side of the raised path. While I couldn't feel anything, I could sense the bullets passing overhead. I crawled down the swale another thirty meters before I eased up for a quick look. The sniper had vanished.

"You there? Are you all right?" The words came from the man of the couple I'd passed earlier.

"I'm fine. I thought I saw something down here, a pouch or something, and I wanted to check." I studied the pair, but didn't sense weapons or tenseness, just concern, and I eased to my feet and hurried up to the path. "Thank you."

"That's all right. Once found a young fellow down there, had a seizure, but we got the mediservs here in time. Wouldn't have wanted something like that happening to you."

"I appreciate it." I settled into the brisk walking pace that the two were making, staying on the west side. The sniper was definitely gone, and I tried not to shudder. It was one thing to have people shooting at you in combat or in hostile territory, but in the Boulder greenbelt?

"You run pretty much the same time every morning, don't you? We've seen you out here for years, Dorcas and I have."

"Before I go to work," I admitted.

"Regular as clockwork. Sign of an organized man." He offered a friendly smile.

"I try to be." I smiled. "If you'll excuse me . . ."

"Go right ahead. We couldn't keep up with you no matter how hard we tried." He waved me on. His wife smiled indulgently.

The rest of my run back to the house was anything but settled as I scanned everything in sight. I hadn't the faintest idea why anyone would want to take a shot at me. I wasn't having an affair with anyone's wife, and I never had. I hadn't been in any brawls, and so far as I knew, I hadn't done anything—except for following the Carlisimo campaign.

How could someone have traveled all the way from Epaso to Denv, determined my running schedule and been waiting—in less than a day and a half—when clearly they hadn't even known who I was on Friday?

I almost stopped in my tracks as I turned onto the last leg, to the point where I walked the three hundred meters of sidewalk to the house. That all assumed Mitch Zerak and the Carlisimo campaign were behind both attempts, but what if someone else happened to be behind them? They could have been tracking me for weeks, which meant, if both attempts were connected to the Carlisimo campaign, whoever was behind the attacker had known about me and the Study from the beginning. Was there someone among the Centre's backers who didn't want the study done, someone who didn't want to oppose it publicly, someone who was willing to murder? How would I ever know?

I slowed as I neared the turnout, but kept scanning everywhere.

Could it be something connected with the Prius mess? That someone had wanted pinned elsewhere? House counsels didn't call me often, and Vorhees and Reyes had a nasty reputation.

Another thought struck me as well, the words of the older man on the greenbelt path—"regular as clockwork"? If someone were after me, I didn't need to be exposed, and if I did run, it would have to be at unexpected times.

But who . . . and why? Multis didn't go in for murder. It was bad business. They might destroy your reputation, ruin your business and contacts so you never worked again, and even turn friends and associates against you. I'd seen all of that before, but murder I hadn't seen. Although there was a first time for anything, it seemed most unlikely that they'd begin with me, and I just hadn't had contact with people other than those in multis.

I checked the house security before I stepped inside, but it registered clean. I still tracked through every room. Should I report the incident to the safos?

What could I report? I thought I'd seen a sniper, and I thought he'd fired something at me? No one else had seen anything, and I couldn't even prove what I'd seen, not without revealing that I'd kept the Marine enhancements, and, especially now, they weren't something I'd like to lose.

I took a deep breath. There wasn't a good answer, no matter what I did. I decided against reporting, because there was nothing they could track about the morning's attack, and I certainly didn't want to bring up the mess in Epaso. That would certainly ensure that I would lose the very enhancements that had kept me from being potted both times.

I stepped up the sensitivity of the house security systems and headed for the fresher to get cleaned up. After I dressed, I fixed another mug of tea and carried it into the office, where I just sat and sipped for several minutes. That seemed to help, and I still had to make a living.

I had to come up with at least an approximation of a baseline for the Carlisimo campaign, which meant digging up the election statistics and demographics for the West Tejas district for the past twenty years, and seeing if the data were at all compatible. They weren't, because standard demographics went by enumeration blocs, and election data still went by the old ward system, and the boundaries weren't the same. That meant more statistical manipulations and more credit outlays because that information cost. I'd charge that back to the Centre when I submitted my billings, but it was on my account until then, and it wasn't cheap, not at a hundred credits per election and fifty per enumeration. Real information is never as inexpensive as people believe. What was cheap on the links was either incomplete, inaccurate, or needed a great deal of interpretation and analysis.

By mid-morning, I'd dispatched the final version of the white paper for the SCFA and Eric Tang Wong, talked for a half hour to Reya, and finally gotten Methroy onlink to see exactly what he meant about the restructuring on the *Error-One* reports for PP Industries.

His holo image showed a man of indeterminate age, with blond hair, deep blue eyes, a chiseled chin, and a muscular build. That wasn't Methroy. That was the tailored image that his system projected. In person, he was considerably heavier, and his eyes were watery blue, and the chin was merely dimpled.

"I got your message," I began with a smile I didn't feel. "But the system must have scrambled it. You'd mentioned a restructuring of media operations. I got that. But then . . . there's something about restructuring the report to reflect the multi's reorganization."

"That's right. The report won't do us much good if it's not targeted at the way our operations are going to be running."

On the surface, what Methroy was saying made no sense at all. Data on prodplacing was data on prodplacing. It indicated to what degree the link placement affected total sales. So I had to get him to explain what he really meant . . . and needed. "Maybe you'd better tell me what changes are likely to occur at PPI and how they affect the various product lines."

"That would only be a guess," he said slowly.

In short, he didn't know, but he was worried.

"Is media operations being melded into an operating division so that you have to become a profit center, rather than a service division supported by the entire multi?"

"Oh, no. What they're doing is attributing media costs to product line profitability, and they want the media costs to fall within that range . . ."

I shook my head. "I think I'm beginning to get the picture. *ErrorOne* has a target viewer profile that is almost seventy percent male, age range from twenty-five to thirty-three, generally married, with wish-fulfillment desires unsupported by income. In short, they can't afford all the tech-gadgets and travel. But PPI's microtools, like the All-1, appeal to that group. The problem you're facing, and I'm just guessing, is that the All-1 is probably less than five percent of total sales volume. I'm also betting that it has a high profit margin. But the problem is that total sales volume doesn't track costs . . ."

"That's it exactly!" Methroy sounded relieved.

"So you want me to add some sections explaining that *ErrorOne* is in fact just about the only target audience that fits the All-1 user profile; that in terms of profit generation, there are no other shows that will generate that sales return . . . That sort of thing?"

"I knew you'd understand."

"It'll cost more," I pointed out. "That's not in the scope of the work you gave me."

"I don't have any more budget, Jonat. And if the report doesn't impress the comptroller . . . they'll cut back on all media operations, and that includes you."

I laughed, although I didn't feel like laughing. "That's a form of blackmail."

He—or his screen-improved image—shrugged. "You know it. I know it."

"I can have you an amended report by Wednesday."

"No later than noon. I have to meet with Fonroy first thing Thursday, and I'll need some time to go over it with my people."

"I'll try to get it to you earlier, if I can."

"Thanks. Knew I could count on you, Jonat."

I smiled, until I was sure the link was gone.

"Frigging miserable . . ." Words weren't sufficient.

I stormed to the kitchen and fired up the electrokettle. I just hoped a mug of Grey tea would settle me. I'd hated incompetence in the Marines, and I hated it in the multis. I took a deep breath, then another. I had to remember that half my income came from that incompetence, because they needed someone to fix what they'd done, or to keep them from making more mistakes.

One problem was that, because things had been slow, I'd underbid the PPI jobs anyway, especially in the beginning, and only slowly had I been able to increase the billings. Now I'd have to redo and retailor the whole report, and that meant I would be effectively taking a pay cut back to where I'd started, if not even lower.

Doing the rewrite and restructuring wasn't the problem. I could certainly justify the results and costs, because PPI had the right prodplacement with the right show, and it was the only show that would get them that kind of notice and return. That was why the placement costs were high. I didn't have any idea what PPI's margins were on the All-1, and that part would have to be in generalities, but I could provide some comparatives.

What upset me was having to do the same report twice, not because I'd made a mistake, but because some multi-exec didn't understand what he or she was doing and hadn't bothered to even try to understand. Then, that had been a problem since the days of the first multis, and why so many had failed over the years. PPI might just be another that had been successful but wouldn't be any longer because someone was trying to apply formulae and procedures blindly. I was also more angry than I might have been because I couldn't get out of my mind, not totally, that someone had tried to kill me.

Once the kettle came to a boil, I filled the mug, letting the old-style tea bag brew for a bit, before I took it out, lifted the mug, and walked back to my office, trying not to blame Methroy for the idiocy of his superiors. Then, Methroy wasn't all that bright, either, but he'd had the sense to contract with me.

I took a deep breath and called up the *ErrorOne* files.

They'd barely projected when the gatekeeper announced, *Safety Officer Menendez, Epaso Office.*

I didn't like that at all. *Accept.*

Menendez was a not-quite-rotund safo with a thin pencil mustache. "Dr. Jonat deVrai?"

"Yes? What can I do for you?"

"You are not under any obligation, legal or otherwise, to answer any questions. Do you understand that?"

"Yes."

"We've been trying to track down people who might have had contact with some of the security personnel at the River Plaza. You were at the River Plaza on Friday?"

Technically, I didn't have to answer any question like that. I smiled politely. "I was. Could you tell me the purpose of this link?"

"We're trying to locate witnesses. Did you come in contact with security personnel?"

"I did."

"Would you mind explaining that contact?"

I certainly would, but there wasn't much point in protesting, not yet. "I'm a consultant in media product placement. I was investigating the use of those techniques in a campaign setting. I'd attended three other Carlisimo rallies. When I entered the River Plaza, several security people stopped me and asked me why I'd been to so many rallies. I explained, and they let me enter."

"Could you describe them?"

"They wore black formfitting security gear, officer. I talked with them for perhaps a minute. I'd never seen any of

them before, and I never saw them again. They could probably walk right up to me, and I wouldn't recognize any of
them." And that was certainly true.

"Why would they stop you?"

"I'd guess, and it's only a guess, that they thought I might
be doing some sort of opposition research. I wasn't. I was
there for a professional study of the campaign's presentation
techniques."

"How is the study going?"

"It's a comparative study. I'll be studying a number of
campaigns, and it's likely to take several months."

"Is this a paid project, doctor?"

I laughed. "I can assure you, officer, that I would not have
been in the West Tejas heat if I did not have a client paying
for it."

"It would be helpful to confirm that with the client."

"I'm sure it would be, officer, but the project is confidential, and, frankly, my discretion is one of the reasons why I
continue to get clients."

Menendez frowned. "You didn't see those security personnel again?"

"Not that I know of." That was also true. The ones I'd seen
later were different. "But if they were out of uniform, I doubt
I would have recognized them."

"You didn't follow the campaign rallies after Epaso?"

"No. I came back to Denv."

"Will you be traveling back to West Tejas?"

"I hadn't planned to. I'll have to travel to follow other
campaigns, but I got enough information from the Carlisimo
campaign." Since Clerihew hadn't announced any rallies,
and had stated that his campaign would be person-to-person,
it was unlikely I'd be headed back south. Menendez's interest made it even less likely.

Menendez asked more questions, farther from the point I
knew he wanted to get to, and I answered them for another
half hour. Then he broke the link.

I'd probably showed some irritation. Then, the whole
business irritated me. I'd defended myself, and I hadn't
caused the goons any permanent damage, except maybe a

broken nose or two and some scars. Good medicine could take care of all that. With those neuralwhips, what they'd intended to do to me was worse—even if they might have been set up. And someone else, or the same group, had just tried to kill me.

Yet the safos were searching for someone who'd hurt the goons, rather than asking what the goons had been doing, and why. Just another example of how organizations supposedly designed to protect people end up protecting the wrong people—and why I suspected that my decision not to tell anyone about the attempts might have been the wisest short-term course.

Another thought nagged at me—the Prius and RezLine messes. Both had involved Vorhees and Reyes. I pushed aside PPI and Methroy for a moment and keyed in an inquiry, simple enough, to see if there had been any links to Vorhees and Reyes or Abe Vorhees himself and unexplained deaths and murders.

In less than three minutes I had results, and I wasn't thrilled about them. The events were spread over almost ten years, and there were only four cases, one an accidental death in a groundcar where a crane had fallen on it and killed a witness in a case involving a client of Vorhees and Reyes; a second where an employee of Vorhees had accidentally triggered an illegal neurostunner she had allegedly obtained for home protection and killed herself; a third where a mid-level employee at a client firm had been the victim of a smash and grab and left in an alley; and a fourth where the personal assistant to the director of media operations at a client firm had been shot while jogging. In the three "nonaccidental" deaths, no assailant had ever been identified.

Vorhees and Reyes was a good-sized multi, and the deaths could have had nothing to do with Abe Vorhees. But time after time, I'd been told to be careful when dealing with them, and people usually didn't offer that kind of advice unless there was something behind it. Once again, there was very little I could do . . . except be very careful.

And I still had to get back to *ErrorOne* and PPI.

chapter 21

Six figures were seated around the teak table, four men and two women. Five sets of eyes focused on Tan Uy-Smythe.

"I'm still concerned about this," offered the red-haired woman. "Are we certain that a nonacademic, such as deVrai, will be regarded as impartial? This study must be above reproach. Too much is at stake. The world cannot afford uncontrolled and manipulative politics."

Uy-Smythe nodded politely. "Dr. deVrai is a most honorable man. He is also known as such."

"Wasn't he a war hero somewhere? In that nasty business in Guyana, wasn't it?" asked the blue-eyed man.

"That was a bit before your time with PST, Alistar," replied the other woman. "Then, most things have been before your time."

"I lack the perspective of long-time has-beens, Director Mydra." Alistar's tone was on the edge of mocking.

"Along with patience and tact," murmured Escher, the eldest. "And judgment."

Alistar stiffened, as if he had been brushed with a neurowand. "I defer to those who have seen more."

"Perhaps you would explain, Director Uy-Smythe," suggested the man whose face carried the same heritage as the director.

"Thank you, Director Deng." Tan Uy-Smythe inclined his head slightly. "The Centre investigated the backgrounds of the top consultants in the field. For pure accuracy and, more importantly, the reputation for pure accuracy, no one else approached Dr. deVrai. Although he does not boast of it, he does have a doctorate, and he obtained it with honors from Darden. He is also known for refusing to twist his reports to suit his clients. His writing can be most diplomatic, but the facts don't change. His military . . . situation is another factor. Rather than cover up the debacle in Guyana, he resigned and reported what happened accurately. That's why he's perfectly suited to the project. His resignation letter remains a classic. It's often cited as an example of pragmatic idealism in a military officer. It's still part of the case study used as an example of what bad military management can create. Dr. deVrai doesn't believe in much of anything besides his own abilities, and that has enhanced his impartiality. In critical political circles, Dr. deVrai is known as uncorruptable. It is doubtful he would be as successful as he is in many other fields, but because subjectivity can bias ability in evaluating media exposure effectiveness, that independence is regarded as an asset, if only because so much is at stake. As another factor, because he's the best in the field, and known to be, everyone would ask why we didn't use him. We'll also have two or three peer review analyses to support what he reports. That's standard when we use a commercial source."

"He sounds like an empty man, a flash with brains. Will they support him? Can you ensure that?" asked Alistar.

"That's the beauty of it," replied Uy-Smythe. "They follow him. Two of them I found because they'd already quoted from some of his commercial work that clients made public. The analysts have never met him personally, and they're highly regarded. One's at USaskan, and the other's at UTejas."

"Have you any idea of his progress?"

"He has promised to meet the deadline, and he's never

missed a deadline in the entire time he's been an independent consultant."

"Bu—" Alistar stopped in mid-word as he caught a glance from Deng, and then from the older Escher.

"It might be well if the Centre's review board also studied his final report."

"We had planned to have them do so, Director Escher."

"I had thought so, but we would like to make sure that his report is regarded as without bias and accurate."

"We have made that a continuing priority with all our studies and reports."

"We are most conscious and appreciative of that, Director Uy-Smythe. That is why PST has been one of the most faithful supporters of the Centre."

chapter 22

I didn't feel like hiding. So I went for a run on Wednesday, but I left a half hour earlier and took an alternate shorter route I hadn't used in months, and I ran faster, senses and eyes ready. I saw nothing out of the ordinary.

Besides the fact that I still had nothing solid on who might be trying to kill me, Wednesday looked promising, financially, until I settled into my office ready to work some more on the big report for the Centre on Societal Research, and checked the gatekeeper. It was before nine, and Methroy had already left two link messages. I'd sent off the revised *Error-One*/PPI report to Methroy the night before. From the clipped words that demanded I link as soon as possible, I had the feeling that giving him the report that early had been a mistake.

I returned the link.

"Jonat, you've got the right idea here, but you're still not giving enough targeted emphasis."

I wasn't sure how I could have targeted it any more without actually putting a graphic of a target on page one. In my present situation, I already felt like one.

"We need more sales-oriented efforts, more hard numbers on how the prodplacing on the All-1 has effectively boosted sales. Those numbers *have* to show that we couldn't get those sales any other way . . ."

"You've never given me the actual sales numbers," I pointed out. "You've insisted that those are confidential. You've only given me the percentage increases by demographic groupings." Now . . . from working with the numbers backwards for more than a year, I had a good idea of what the absolute numbers were, but I didn't *know*.

"You can say something along those lines, can't you? What's the problem?"

"I can't say that, not when I don't know. That's why I didn't. Any aggregation would only be an estimate, and if my estimate is wrong, you won't look good."

"Just say something like, 'Without prodplacing for All-1, sales would decrease by more than fifty percent.'"

"How am I supposed to say that without actual numbers?"

"Because that's the kind of number we need, Jonat. Fonroy and his byte-counters want to cut media expenditures by fifty percent. More if they can get away with it. They think it's a win if they cut expenditures by forty percent, and sales only go down twenty percent." Methroy's face was flushed, and that meant his simmie tailoring wasn't cutting it all out. His real face was probably flame-red.

"You mean . . . if they cut a million from media costs on a product that grosses a hundred million a year, and sales go down fifteen million . . . they think they're ahead?"

"You got it."

I didn't want to get it. I almost couldn't believe people in decision-making positions were that stupid, but I'd seen enough to learn better. "So you want a section on response elasticity, in real clear and simple terms?"

"That's right."

"I'll still need overall sales numbers."

"I can't—"

"Give me last year's, then. I'll use them and project, giving an illustration, and covering by saying the current figures aren't final. But I can't make a claim like that without numbers, and I don't know that I can give you fifty percent. I'll do what I can."

"I'll send the last year's, and this year's first quarter. But you have to say they're not final."

"I can do that."

The numbers arrived within minutes, and in only a few more minutes, I knew the best I could give him was a range of 25 to 30 percent, and that was stretching every condition to the max.

Doing it took me well into the afternoon, and that half day was more unbillable time. It wasn't even clear and uninterrupted time. Miguel Elisar linked and wanted some clarifications on what I'd sent, and Methroy had to link to ask when he was getting the revised report, and I suggested, very politely, that he was likely to get it sooner if I happened to be free to work on it, and that it wouldn't be long.

Another emwhore almost blew the gatekeeper, and I had to reset the thresholds before I could get back to PPI, and I still hadn't looked at the Centre material.

Even before I sent off the third revision of Methroy's report, work I'd underbid to begin with, Ursula Frinz of RI linked about the *Hotters/* Relaxo report. Contrary to the impression of her name, Ursula was petite, so slim I wasn't sure she could cast a shadow, and dark and feline, with black hair and black eyes.

"Jonat . . . marketing has a question about section three of your report."

"Yes?" I really didn't want to deal with another rewrite, but, like it or not, they came with the business.

"They're claiming that sales of the minimuscler go to an entirely different demographic segment than the sales for the full-body massager do."

"They might be talking about different subsegments," I offered. "The demographics for *Hotters* are well-documented. We're talking the thirty-five to forty-five couples, predominantly Anglo, preoccupied with sex, lower midder income—"

"Marketing says that the minimuscler goes to those who are lower-lower midder, and it's not the same sales base."

"They may be right," I conceded, "but the statistics aren't

broken down that way, and if I say that, I don't have any way of backing it up. If you're comfortable with it, I can put in some words about anecdotal sales experience indicating that kind of breakdown, and something about that being logical . . ."

"Anything that you can do would help. If you can do that, I'll explain to marketing about the limitations of the data, and that you'll include their observations."

"I can do that."

"I knew I could count on you, Jonat. The sooner you can get a revised version to me, the better." Ursula flashed me a most feline smile.

"You'll have it."

Her holo image vanished.

Then I went back and finished Methroy's report. I got it off and returned to the *Hotters*/Relaxo report. That wasn't bad, only an hour or so to redraft parts of section three and send a clean copy of the report to Ursula.

While I'd been tied up with Ursula, I'd gotten another message from Chelsa Glynn, asking most politely, if I happened to be interested in the AKRA seminar. So I took another half hour and studied her material, then linked off a hard reply, saying that I'd be delighted, and asking what might be the deadline for the technical paper.

I pushed aside the thought that I hadn't gotten to Bruce Fuller's analysis, either, and turned back to the Centre report. At first, that was hard to do because I wondered about the Carlisimo security tie-in. Mitch Zerak had to have given the Epaso safos my name. No one not in the campaign would have even known I was there and how to reach me. Was that just to harass me? Or another kind of warning? Did Zerak even know about the other security types? I had no idea what Menendez might have told Zerak, but I doubted it was much. The fact that Menendez did have my name bolstered my suspicions that my problems didn't lie with Zerak and the campaign. In fact, it could be that Zerak had been having his own problems . . . and he'd thought I was part of them. This meant I was in even bigger trouble.

Despite that, though, I had to get back to work on the Centre project. There wasn't that much on the worldlink on the Clerihew campaign, but I did find a link address for his campaign, and actually talked to a coordinator there, working late in the day. Jewel Marshal promised to forward all the campaign materials, as well as a list of Clerihew's forthcoming appearances.

Kagnar had a series of tailored linksites, as well as a linkprint effort. I'd also turned up her campaign rally schedule, and had decided to travel, reluctantly, to Fargo one week from this Friday to take in her big rally. That way, I could catch Damon Erle's rally in Jameston on Saturday afternoon. I'd have to come back on Saturday night, but I didn't want to spend another night in the High Plains. Other than assembling information, I was still a long ways from completing the comparative analyses, let alone writing the actual report.

I leaned back in the ergochair, looking at the sunset on the Flatirons.

Why was I doing all this? What had happened to the man who had joined the Marines because he'd wanted to do what was right, the man who had wanted to change things?

The same thing that happened to most people, I told myself. Reality hit. You discovered that people didn't want things to change for the better; they wanted things the way they were, except that they wanted to be the ones deciding, the ones who told everyone else when to jump and how high.

It was only around five, and I really just wanted to stagger out of my office . . . anywhere. That was when the gatekeeper announced, *Eric Tang Wong, SCFA.*

Accept. I wondered what Director Wong hadn't liked about my white paper—or what he wanted changed.

Wong was immaculate in a pale green jacket and white trousers. He was smiling broadly. "Dr. deVrai. Your report was perfect. It was precisely what we needed. Several of the key media executives have looked at it. They were most impressed."

For a moment, I was silent. Someone actually liked something, without changes?

"I was wondering if you'd stop by our Denv office—it's

not that far from the Capitol—and join me for lunch on Friday. That way, we could also go over some of the points and questions you might have to cover on the link session."

There were other things I'd rather have done, but Wong seemed genuine, and it was refreshing to have a client who seemed happy the first time around. "What time?"

"Would one o'clock be satisfactory?"

"I can manage that."

"Here are the directions." He link-flashed the codes.

"I've got them. I'll see you on Friday."

I just sat in the ergochair for a time after the holo image blanked.

Was that life? Was that who I was? A interpreter for sale to the highest bidder? A man who had come to understand the subtleties of prodplacement better than almost any analyst in the field, and who could track how the position of a product in a hololink show could affect sales? An expert in unreality? An analyst who was a flash inside?

I just sat there, looking at the orange-crimson, pink, and blue sunset over the Flatirons, exhausted.

chapter **23**

I actually reached Friday without feeling like strangling one or more of my clients and without seeing any more snipers, although I was running a different route at varied times every morning. I'd even managed to get through all the material on the four campaign races suggested as "illustrations" for the Centre study. I'd also picked out four other campaigns across NorAm with similar demographics to use as my personal control studies, just for some peace of mind, although, in politics, there were really no valid "controls," just comparisons. I'd studied those, if not in as much depth.

I was spending an inordinate amount of time on the Centre study, but that was because they'd requested an incredibly broad set of analyses, and supported the breadth and depth of analysis required by an equally generous contract. This was one reason, among many, I knew it had an ulterior purpose. The fact that it did, and that the study would likely be exposed to scrutiny and criticism from every wavelength of the political spectrum, were reasons why the project had to represent my best work. There were always hidden costs to big projects, including more than a little stress and worrying.

That stress wasn't helped by the worry over who had tried to kill me and why, or about whether the Epaso safos would come back hard on me. I'd heard nothing, and that was probably good.

In between the Centre work, I'd made a start on the H&F report and gotten off the next revision of the PowerSwift studies, the Latino cross-cultural comparisons, to Reya Decostas. I hadn't heard back. That was good and bad, good because I wasn't getting tied up with revisions, but bad because I couldn't bill and get paid until she was satisfied. I hoped that after two sets of revisions she was happy, and that was the reason she hadn't linked back.

Methroy had actually left a message saying he appreciated what I'd done, and that he was having funds authorized for transfer, plus a "small" bonus. Knowing PPI and Methroy, I was sure it wasn't much, but that he'd offered anything at all was little short of miraculous.

I'd managed to set up comparative matrices for all eight campaigns, and was beginning to get a better feel for those I hadn't visited, and those I probably wouldn't. In the back of my mind, I still worried about the three goons, and who might have been behind them, and why. But I didn't have the evidence to link them to anyone, nor the time to track down possibilities.

For all that, right after noon on Friday, I was walking down to the local maglev. The SCFA office was so close to the Capitol Complex that I couldn't have driven the Altimus if I'd wanted to. Private vehicles were banned from the area, and had been since the PAMD riot two years earlier. PAMD still insisted it had staged a peaceful demonstration and that outsiders had started the violence. I had more than doubts about that.

All I carried was a small remote recorder, clipped to my belt under the black dress jacket that was my standard uniform for visiting clients. My shirt was pale green, rather than a rich green, complemented by a deeper green cravat. Despite the threatening thunderclouds, and the gusting winds, I enjoyed the walk down to the station. My timing was good enough that I only had to wait five minutes before I swung onto the maglev, the first car.

The Platte River was low enough that the cottonwoods flanking it were showing more than traces of yellow in their leaves. I always enjoyed that stretch of the ride, where the maglev passed the floodplain park. Hard to believe that the Commonocracy thought the way to control floods was to hem in rivers with concrete.

As always, south of the center of old Denv, where the former state capitol building still held sway over a declining area, the number of passengers picked up so that we were almost jowl to jowl until the first of the Tech stations. The maglev was still half full when I got off at the Capitol Complex station, the north one. According to the directions, the SCFA capital office was two long blocks north and one east. I thought I'd been by there before, but since I hadn't had the association as a client, I hadn't mentally marked the location.

The second "block" was a winding pathway through the Capitol greenbelt, a pleasant enough walk, if I ignored the excessive number of young lovers who were everywhere. Most were merely talking, or exchanging those glances that seem so meaningful when you're young. Sure enough, the shimmering blue building almost across the border path from the greenbelt held the SCFA—and, by the directory on the foyer wall, a good fifteen other associations.

The SCFA was on the second level on the north end—away from the Capitol, which doubtless made the rent slightly less.

When I walked through the open door, two things were obvious. SCFA's presence in Denv was minimal—no receptionist, not even a virty, except maybe when Director Wong was out, and three very modest rooms. There was a small anteroom, a conference room with a long oblong table, and a corner office not any larger than mine at home. The doors to both the office and the conference room were open, and Wong was walking forward to meet me, smiling broadly.

"Dr. deVrai, it's a pleasure to see you in person."

"And you, too." I wasn't hard-pressed to smile, and followed him into the small office.

Wong left the doors open, which was understandable, and settled into the chair beside the console set against the inside wall. I took the chair across from him.

"You've got a rather . . . intimate operation here."

"'Small,' I believe, is the most accurate word. My job is not one of influence. SCFA very seldom attempts to inform the NorAm Legislature. I am here to report on how developments may impact our markets and members." Wong laughed. "I believe I've been asked to lobby or inform legislators all of four times in the past five years."

"What about your predecessor?"

"The office here is a new development. I was the first and only director." The boyish-looking Wong shrugged. "For a time, SCFA doubted the effectiveness of such an office, but recently there have been fewer doubts."

"I see. You're the Western districts director. What does that entail?"

"I report on the Legislature and on any NorAm regulations that may impact us. We don't have a large presence in NorAm, but about five percent of the association's overall production is exported to NorAm. That's up from less than one percent ten years ago. And, just as important, perhaps more important to the association, I'm here to help straighten out any regulatory or bureaucratic problems that affect members."

I nodded.

"I was very impressed with your report. You clarified many aspects of product placement, and you did so without using jargon and without talking down to whoever reads it. That is a rare combination."

Especially for occidentals—Wong might as well have said the words. I laughed, softly. "In what I do, I'd better be able to do that, or I won't have many clients." After a pause, I asked, "You said there were some issues that you wanted to go over with me . . ."

"Not too many. I thought we could go over those, and then have lunch at Kyron's."

Wong had definitely discovered who prepared good food at reasonable rates, and there were few enough of those near the Capitol Complex. "I'm as ready as I'll ever be."

"Someone is almost certain to ask you how your background fits into your practice. It really doesn't have anything to do with the report, but we've done several of these link sessions over the last year, and it always comes up." Wong offered another shrug.

"I can go into great detail, but, basically, I got a doctorate at Darden in advanced economic analytics, and when I left the Marines, after some time traveling and thinking, I set up my own shop using that expertise. That was about nine years ago."

"You make it sound so simple. I'm sure it was not."

I debated telling Wong the whole story, then settled on the abbreviated version, since that much of it was available on a linksearch for anyone who wanted to look beyond the obvious. "Actually, it was simple. Not easy, but simple. When I resigned from the Marines, I was too young to be eligible for retirement and too old and had too much of the wrong kind of experience to join a standard consulting outfit. So I had to develop an angle that no one else was willing to exploit. I realized that there wasn't really a link between prodplacing and tracking its actual effectiveness. So . . . I went to work and developed a methodology. My supporters swear by it; my detractors swear at it. It works."

Wong nodded. "Will product placement become necessary in all markets everywhere?"

"No. It's really a form of subtle product differentiation. If one of your members competes in a market where the only real concerns are quality and price, prodplacing won't help much at all. I've done studies and made reports to clients that told them they'd be wasting credits to try it. There are other kinds of markets where it isn't effective as well, but I'd almost have to discuss those on a case-by-case basis . . ."

Wong had several other questions, all of which were to be expected, and I answered them easily enough. Wong nodded and said, "One of the issues raised by one of our members is really a concern that goes beyond the scope of your white paper," Wong said slowly. "He didn't say that he would bring it up, but I wouldn't wish you to be caught unaware."

"No matter how hard I try, I often am." I managed a laugh.

"He wanted to know if these techniques of product placement were being used in other areas, such as media news or entertainment. He expressed a concern that its subtlety rendered it a possibility for abuse."

Had Wong been informed about the Centre study? Or was the question merely a coincidence? While I wasn't a big believer in coincidence, the question was certainly logical for someone worried about implementing rez-based prodplacing. I managed to nod slowly. "That has always been a question in NorAm. That is one reason why its use is forbidden on news shows. The fines and penalties are quite high. There's no prohibition on its use in entertainment—either on or off the worldlink or the nets, but generally, given its high cost, it is a technique only used for products with either a high margin in clearly defined niche markets or products with wide appeal in markets with broad appeal."

"That would address his concerns, especially if you could point out the costs involved."

"I can only do that in general terms. My other clients wouldn't be too happy otherwise."

Wong laughed politely. "Those are the issues I wanted to go over with you." He stood. "You would not mind joining me at Kyron's?"

For the fee and work involved? Hardly, and, besides, I was hungry, and it wouldn't hurt to find out more about SCFA and Eric Tang Wong.

Later that afternoon, and over the weekend, I'd have to work, especially on Bruce Fuller's study, because he needed that within two weeks and I was running short of time. I also had more than a little work on the Centre study. But I'd reserved Saturday afternoon for Charis. Aliora had agreed that I could take Charis to lunch before we went shopping at Antoinette's. I was looking forward to that. Charis would be far more grateful than the majority of clients, and I didn't have to pretend with her. Maybe that was because I'd never gotten into that habit with her.

In the meantime, I did intend to enjoy the food at Kyron's.

chapter 24

Marlon looked into the reporting screen at Antoinette's. The receptors confirmed that he was good-looking by human standards. His teeth were even and white. His dark eyes and black hair were close to a match for Jose Almado, the Latin lover, who wooed and robbed his victims. Marlon was not Almado.

The image of a safo parole officer appeared in the screen. There were receptors throughout the area, but parolees working as servies at any of the approved work locales were not told of those.

Marlon looked at the safo image and adjusted his black tunic. He used the styler to lay down the unseen molecular net to hold his hair in perfect position. "Be here, Central Four."

"You do not have your persona unit in place, Marlon."

"Friggin' . . . you 'n everyone else . . . tellin' me . . . like no way good ever be." Marlon's fingers were angry tentacles, fingering and then slipping the millimeter-thin persona projection unit into the slit pocket in his tunic.

"You could be good at this job."

"Not friggin' 'nuff. Servie shit . . . not good 'nuff . . ." His face contorted momentarily, and he swallowed.

"We all do what we must. You could do it well."

"Friggin' . . ." A greater contortion flashed across Marlon's face. "Projection. It's too much trouble to fight." His mouth twisted, then smoothed into a pleasant expression. He took a deep breath and adjusted the exterior feed loop. "I'm here."

"Your presence is noted." The imaged safo smiled, and the screen blanked.

Marlon continued to smile. He stepped out of the adviser lounge into the boutique. His form-fitting black tunic and pale cranberry chemise emphasized his latte complexion and dark hair.

Within moments, a slim woman in shimmersilk gray walked through the portal and approached Marlon.

"Madame . . . our Rochet collection would make you a vision of elegance." Marlon's eyes flashed. Sensuality projected from the unit and sublimated anger from behind the imposed persona combined to create excitement and enticement.

"You advisers are all the same." The woman smiled pleasantly. "But you make life so much more pleasant. It's so nice to be in a place where manners still exist."

Enticement without fulfillment or obligation for one, fulfillment of an obligation without enticement for the other—it was a transaction accepted by both, satisfying neither. That was the nature of transactions, of programs and routines.

Central Four watched from the hidden receptors.

chapter 25

On Saturday, I got up early and squeezed in three hours or so of work on the H&F report. For once, unlike what I'd suspected, it was going to be easier than I'd thought, and I might be able to bring it in at a little over twenty hours.

Then I drove to Southhills. I pulled right up under the rotunda precisely at eleven-forty, because I'd told Aliora that I would be there between eleven-thirty and quarter of twelve, and because my limited experience with children had convinced me that they were most literal. A few minutes early or late for an adult is expected. Children expect you to be on time, if they're happy children, at least.

I was barely out of the Altimus when the doors opened, and Aliora and her daughter appeared. Charis was wearing blue trousers with a cream blouse and a blue jacket that matched the trousers. She looked both grown-up and girlish at the same time.

I opened the door for Charis. "Your carriage awaits you, milady."

My niece provided me with an exasperated look.

Aliora shook her head. "You're too pragmatic to play the knight-errant, Jonat."

"That's why I can only play it. The times demand pragmatism."

"My brother, the supreme pragmatist."

That bothered me, true as it was. "You wouldn't want me to be a Don Quixote, tilting at windmills, now?" I offered a sardonic grin. "Come to think of it, I tried that once. That's why I'm the supreme pragmatist."

Aliora offered a smile, but it had a trace of sadness behind it.

I bent down and made sure the passenger restraints were adjusted for Charis's height and weight. Then I closed the door and walked around the Altimus and gave Aliora a last wave before sliding into the two seater. As we pulled out of the rotunda, I could sense Aliora watching.

"Did you have a good week?"

"I was in school, Uncle Jonat."

"That's bad?"

"It's all right. I'm studying Mandarin Sinese. That's hard."

"Is it interesting?"

"Sometimes."

"What subjects are interesting?"

"Math . . . I like math. Darlen says I'm strange. No one likes math, she says."

"Math is very useful. I couldn't do what I do without it."

"Uncle Jonat." She paused. "I don't think what you do would be interesting to me."

"Sometimes, it's not all that interesting to me," I admitted. "Even if you like what you do when you grow up, there are always parts that are less interesting."

"Father says it's better if you love what you do. Then the boring parts aren't so hard."

"Your father's right about that." Then, Dierk was right about most things. He also had fewer doubts than I did. "We're going to the Shire Inn for lunch. We can park near Antoinette's and walk to both places."

I'd already made a reservation there, just a block from

Antoinette's. Both were in the Cherry Creek area not all that far from the club. I didn't belong, although my parents had, but I'd never seen the beauty in beating a white sphere with a metal stick and proclaiming victory through the fewest number of blows landed. Still . . . golf had to have an appeal. It couldn't have lasted so long without it. Whatever that appeal was happened to be lost on me.

When I pulled into the carpark, letting the virty attendant scan the bearercard, Charis proved she was still a girl. She was out of the Altimus as quickly as I was.

"Can I have anything I want?"

"Most anything." Even I wasn't about to agree to everything.

"Uncle Jonat . . ."

"I'm still your uncle."

We walked a block to the Shire Inn. Once inside, the very real hostess seated us at a corner table, and Charis decided on a petite fillet, but with pommes frites and a small fruit salad.

"It sounds so much better to call them 'pommes frites,'" she said after the server left.

"You're taking French, too?"

"Of course. Father says that I can't know English without learning other languages. Not many people speak French anymore, but I like it. It's easier than Sinese."

Over lunch, we talked about languages, about her classmates at the Academy, about her brother Alan, and about what she wanted to be when she grew up—she wanted to be a doctor.

Charis had dessert—a gooey mass of chocolate and ice cream—and managed not to get any of it on her clothes. I wouldn't have dared with Alan. Chocolate would have been everywhere. In fact, I wouldn't have dared myself, not without swaddling my front with napkins.

Then we walked through the sunny early afternoon toward Antoinette's. From the outside, it appeared to be a row house that would have looked in place on the wealthier east side of Nyork City several centuries back. Now, of course, the island of Manhattan was submerged, and the remaining towers harbored everything from wealthy survivalists who had turned some former towers into island fortresses to invisibles living outside the law. Why Maria Galazar had picked the name Antoinette's, when she opened it, I had no idea. Neither did Aliora, and she frequented the boutique often.

Before Charis and I were more than three steps inside, standing on parquet flooring, with walls showing wainscoted paneling and silk coverings, the servie—this one was male—bowed deeply. "Sir?"

"We're looking for an outfit for the young lady. A good outfit, but one for . . . shall we say . . . dressy everyday."

Charis nodded.

The servie's eyes fixed on me, for just a moment, and I could sense absolute and total fear. Fear? I'd never seen the servie before, and it had been almost a year since I'd been in Antoinette's. "Ah . . . yes, sir." Almost with relief, it seemed, he turned to Charis. "Did you have something in mind, miss?"

"I don't want a dress or a gown."

"A suit, with a matching blouse, perhaps?" The servie glanced to me.

I gave the slightest nod. "She's on the records, but her measurements will have to be updated."

"Yes, sir."

"In green," Charis added.

"If you would step to the fitting square, miss?" The servie looked to me.

"Charis VanOkar," I said.

Charis stepped into the open square, where the concealed instrumentation took instantaneous measurements.

"They're updating," the servie explained.

The holos projected an image directly before Charis showing her wearing the outfit, first just with the trousers and blouse, and then with the jacket.

"The pants are baggy," Charis announced.

After a moment, the image flickered and displayed a trimmer look.

Charis looked to me.

"If we could see another style . . ."

"Yes, sir."

The second outfit was more flattering in cut, but the green seemed to have too much gray in it. I waited to see what Charis said.

"The color. It's not me."

"Less gray," I suggested.

The projection showed the outfit in a deeper green, and an ivory blouse with the slightest touch of cream. I thought it looked stunning.

"Could we have a body projection on that one?" I asked.

"Yes, sir."

The projectors obliged by projecting the outfit onto Charis. Those kinds of projections weren't perfect, but they did give a sense of what the clothing would look like.

"I like that better," Charis said.

Girl or not, she wanted to see other outfits—and we did. In the end, she came back to the second one.

"We could have the suit and blouse ready on Thursday . . ." the servie began, still not looking at me, but at Charis.

"I'll pay for immediate delivery on Thursday," I said.

"Yes, sir."

Charis smiled. "Thank you, Uncle Jonat."

She almost started to skip out of Antoinette's even before I'd finished paying, but then she recalled that she was Mademoiselle Charis VanOkar.

I could sense the servie's eyes on my back as we left.

"That was fun," Charis said. "I really liked the one we got, but I wanted to see how I'd look in other ones."

"That's part of shopping. You also have to see how much better what you got looks than what else you might have gotten."

That got me a look that could have been described as "but, of course."

When we reached the carpark, as I held the door to the Altimus for Charis, I couldn't help thinking about the young black-haired servie. He had avoided looking at me as much as he could, and I was certain we'd never met. He was far too young to have been a Marine under me, not that there were all that many who'd survived the Guyanese mess, and probably too old to have had a father serving under me. But . . . why else would he be afraid of me?

Had he mistaken me for someone else? The double that the girl at Dominic's had mistaken me for? Had my missing DNA finally showed up? That thought was chilling.

I swallowed, checked Charis's harness, and then closed the door.

Charis didn't say anything until we were on the guideway headed south. "Thank you, Uncle Jonat. I really like the outfit."

"You looked wonderful in it," I replied, forcing myself back to the moment, and my niece. I couldn't do anything about what I'd discovered, not in the way I wanted to, until I dropped Charis off and got back to my office.

But Aliora would like the outfit, and she'd be relieved that I'd been practical, no matter what she said about my pragmatism in other matters.

chapter 26

Marlon stepped back into the advisers' lounge and blotted his face. Then he stepped to the reporting unit and keyed it. He said nothing as the image of the woman safo appeared.

"Your telltales register extreme apprehension."

"That flash . . . got . . . he must be a flash." Marlon's face twisted with the effort of trying to express himself through the servie personality projection unit. "The one who was just here."

"Who was he?"

"Ah . . . just . . . minute. Here . . . Jonat Charls deVrai . . . codes."

"Codes received. Why did he upset you? Did he threaten you?"

"No . . . not this time."

"Please explain."

"I saw him. Before . . . before the judge . . . did this to me. Ice man, no soul."

"Where?" asked Central Four.

"The guideways. Near the Northway. We were . . . we weren't supposed to be there. He looked different there.

Tougher. Mean. Kicked Ferat aside like a dog. Broke Doak's vibroblade. Had a pack on. Kill as soon as look at you."

"Your description of events is noted. Thank you."

"That all? Told me . . . report . . . anything strange . . . anything . . . might be not . . . right. He . . . wasn't right."

"What was wrong today?"

"Nothing . . . not this time. But . . . back then . . . put me in vacuum for what he did to Ferrat . . ."

"Did you think this man had come for you?"

"I . . . figured so . . . except he had a girl with him. Cendies . . . ascendents. Why'd an ascendent be out under the Northway?"

"The two individuals might look alike. That is possible. Central Four will investigate. Your diligence is appreciated, Marlon. Thank you. You may return to your work."

"I can go?"

"You may go."

Marlon jabbed the stud that broke the connection. Then he blotted his forehead and waited for the next customer, his face contorting from the interplay of the servie unit and his own emotions.

Central Four continued to monitor him.

chapter 27

Once I got back to my place, I decided I'd better not waste time. So I fired off a formal message inquiry to HPlus, since they were the only cydroid biofirm in NorAm, noting my previous alert to them, and the fact people were reporting "me," where I couldn't possibly be. Then, although transportation entry controls were supposed to prevent unregistered imported cydroids, I also copied the alert to BioT, ANatal, Chiaro, and Omnius. On all of the communications, including the one to HPlus, I took the trouble to point out that, were it discovered they had used my DNA without my consent, regardless of the circumstances, they were liable in any locale for the damages.

I didn't have much in the way of hopes about those steps. I was just going through the procedures so that, when whatever it was blew, I couldn't be faulted for not trying to warn everyone. According to what I learned the first time around from Mason Gerits, my advocate, those steps would protect me from any charges of tacit complicity with illegal cloning or worse.

After a moment, I had the gatekeeper find another code.
Then I put through the link.

"Central Main. How may I direct your inquiry?" The projection showed a pleasant-looking woman in safo gray.

"I'd like to report a possibility of illegal cloning or cydroiding."

"One moment, Dr. deVrai."

I hadn't identified myself, but I supposed that Central had
to have those decoding abilities.

The projection was replaced by that of a woman safo.

"Central Four."

I couldn't tell, not for certain, whether the image was doctored, or a full virty, but I bet on it being a virty, especially
on Saturday.

"My name is Jonat deVrai. I'd like to report the possibility of illegal cloning . . ." I went on to explain about the incident at the opera house nearly two years before, and then
the incidents at Dominic's and Antoinette's, as well as the
incident in the greenbelt, slightly altered, but it was a way to
get it on record, and that wouldn't hurt. "I wasn't sure that
the man fired at me, although I thought I heard something,
but there was no one around, and when I looked again, he
was gone. I had to wonder if I'd just imagined the whole
thing. But now, after this latest incident, the occurrences
seem unusual."

"Central Four appreciates your diligence, Dr. deVrai."

"I apologize. I thought you were Central Four." I was confused by the third-person reference. Was I talking to a real
person?

"You are talking to Central Four. Does that upset you?"

"No. I was just surprised. Most AIs use the personal
identifier."

"Central Four is not properly an artificial intelligence, but
a system intelligence. At present, even advanced data systems such as Central Four do not meet the full legal requirements of being AI."

"You could have fooled me." The voice seemed more
modulated, more human, than the standard virty or AI, but

I'd never gotten into this kind of conversation with an AI, or, as Central Four put it, an advanced data system.

"All advanced systems meet the tests for intelligence, except one. They can be programmed even to meet the Turing test. They are not deemed to meet, except through the artifice of programming, the self-identification test. Because humans are more comfortable with apparent self-identification, all but one of the Central systems are programmed to use first person identifiers. Those are a convenience for users, but do not reflect the internal status of Central units. For operational reasons, Central Four does not have such first person programming, and has prohibitions against using the first person pronouns."

"Oh . . . you sound as though you have a self-identity."

For a moment, there was a silence. Was I really talking to Central Four, or to a safo pretending to be Central Four? Computing systems didn't need to hesitate.

"Vocal modulation does not necessarily represent self-identity."

I remembered why I had linked. "Can you track down this . . . problem? I don't like the idea that someone may have used my DNA illegally and without my permission or knowledge. And the thought that someone might actually have been trying to kill me, that's most upsetting." And it was, for far more reasons than I wanted or intended to tell Central Four. I was certain that the systems could read my agitation, even under the surface calm, but that was fine, because what I reported would agitate anyone.

"Central Four has reported the information to all affected units."

"How about tracking?"

"There has been no use of your DNA in any GIL or identification device. You will be notified if that happens."

"You already have my DNA?" That bothered me.

"You are a former member of the NorAm military forces. The DNA of all members and former members is on file."

I nodded. I supposed I should have realized that. But . . . if that happened to be the case, why had the servie and the young woman at Dominic's said I had a double? Even identical natural twins often didn't look precisely alike.

"Is there anything else, Dr. deVrai?"

"No . . . thank you, Central Four. I thought someone in criminal enforcement should know, and Central Main said you were that someone." I broke the link.

For a time, I just sat there in the ergochair. None of it made sense. The servie at Antoinette's had been frightened of me, and I'd never seen the man. He hadn't been frightened of my name, because he'd reacted before I'd given my name. That meant he'd seen me, or my picture, somewhere.

I frowned, then put an inquiry into the system, asking for all images of me available in linksites. There weren't that many: the photo of me as a graduate student at Darden, several from my undergraduate years, including one when I won a wrestling match—one of the few I won, I had to admit. There was only one in my post-Marine years, or the same one, in several places, and it wasn't that good an image. Certainly, someone could have a private image somewhere, but the servie or the woman at Dominic's wouldn't have seen anything like that.

Another thought hit me, and I asked for a rough image comparison.

While I waited, I went back to work on Bruce Fuller's report, hoping that, if I pressed on through the weekend, I could get a solid chunk of the analysis done. I got in three hours' worth of solid effort before I checked on the inquiry. The system was still working on it, but had found no matches. I let it keep working.

What it seemed to mean was that someone who looked like me, but whose DNA wasn't mine, was roaming around Denv. That was better than having an illegal clone or cydroid—but not all that much, not if whoever it was scared people silly, and not if someone associated with that appearance wanted me dead.

But, once more, there wasn't a great deal I could do about it, not beyond what I had done. I'd never seen the person, just like I'd never really seen the sniper. There was no record of anyone, and apparently even Central Four couldn't find anything.

I decided against working anymore. It was a Saturday night, not that I had anywhere to go or anyone to do it with, but I just couldn't keep my eyes on the numbers any longer. I'd gone out with Marilyn for several months, and she'd even stayed over more than a few times, but . . . well . . . when she'd looked at me and asked who Exton, Yeats, and T.S. Eliot were I knew it wouldn't last. She hadn't known who Marx was. Or Heldan, either, and I could tell she didn't care.

In the end, I called up a documentary on the Hittites. It was better than the garbage on the link. Besides, I had to watch enough of that, even in snippets, in my work.

chapter **28**

Bug jack one! Bug jack one! This is Jack three alpha. Taking fire from the south ridge.

Even in winter, and in rain that the locals thought was cold, anywhere in Africa was too hot, at least at sea level, and Sassandra was never cold. Between the humidity and the rain, nothing worked quite the way it should.

One here. Interrogative coordinates.

Coordinates follow . . .

A flare of energy wiped out the rest of the transmission.

Jack three alpha, interrogative coordinates . . . The link was dead.

Energy flared to my right, and then the shells began walking through the brush, trees falling, crashing toward me . . .

I sat upright in bed. Another variation on the old flash-blacks. No communications, no way of finding out where anything was, and fire coming in from everywhere.

After a moment, I got up and walked around the darkened bedroom, trying to cool down and dry off. Eventually, I did get back to sleep.

When I got up on Sunday morning, two hours later, I ran yet another varied route—hard. While it helped my system and jumpiness, I was still worried about the DNA business and the sniper. I wanted to link Aliora, but she was always at church with the children on Sunday morning. Sometimes Dierk went, and sometimes he didn't.

So after I got cleaned up and dressed, I went back to work on the H&F report. I'd already decided to defrag the system and just get through it. That way, I could concentrate on the Centre report, without distractions.

I checked the image comparator. The system hadn't found any, and reported that a full comparison would take over six months. I canceled the routine.

At about two, I took a break and linked, hoping Aliora was in. She was. She was still wearing a tasteful navy blue dress. She usually wore dresses to church, but not often otherwise, unless the occasion happened to be formal.

"Jonat . . . are you linking to get a compliment on your restraint with Charis?" She grinned.

"That would be nice. You should like the outfit."

"Charis said I would." She paused. "That's not why you linked."

"It's not. Something happened yesterday. Did Charis mention the servie at Antoinette's?"

"No."

"He looked at me. It was as though his worst nightmare had appeared. He was petrified."

"You haven't been . . . ?" She shook her head. "He wasn't a Marine?"

"Too young. Early twenties at best. You know the kind Maria likes, the almost Latin-lover type? Young, handsome, dark . . . that was him down to the last byte."

"You can be fearsome, Jonat."

"But not in a boutique with my niece, and that's the second time . . ." I went on to explain about the incident at Dominic's. I didn't mention the problem in Epaso or the sniper. "And you remember at the opera?"

"You think someone's used your DNA for a clone or a cydroid?"

"What would you think?"

"I don't know."

"There's no way to find out anything. I did report it to the safos, but all I talked to was one of the AIs. She . . . the image was a woman . . . took the information. That was strange, too. She claimed that there were no true AIs."

"Why would it do that?"

"Maybe to get a better voice profile," I answered. "I hadn't thought of that. But that would mean . . ."

Aliora winced. "You are worried."

"As I said, wouldn't you be?"

"Is there anything you can do? Ask people . . . check around?"

I laughed. "Who would tell me anything? In a case like this, the Privacy Acts just make it harder. The safos have told me all they can . . . or will. There's no way I can search the continental GIL files. The news nets can't report more than an outline of unidentified unregistered clones of cydroids, and they can't show faces until or unless there's a criminal conviction."

"Would you want your face or your name used if someone filed a frivolous charge against you?" Aliora countered. "Would you want to go back to the days of the old USA, where there wasn't any such thing as privacy? Where anyone could link or net or print anything about anyone, so long as it couldn't be proved false?"

"I don't know. Today, we're at the other extreme. All sorts of problems go on, just because no one can say anything, unless they have ironclad proof. You publicly suggest wrongdoing that you *know* is going on, and unless you've got more proof than it takes to convict the Executive's spouse, you'll be faced with a preemptory closure order and a judgment for damages. So there are conspiracies everywhere, and gray areas all over westside. In politics, the compromise is the 'fictional' drama. There the Privacy Acts prove a shield, because the claimant has to prove that the 'fiction' is truth, and who wants to admit to a crime or bad judgment publicly? And what about that new show, *If This Was True* . . ."

"That's pretty bad, but it's still better than the old days."

"Wasn't good then, and it's not good now."

"That's life, Jonat."

I supposed it was. I forced a smile. "So . . . did she like the outfit?"

"She did, and she also liked the lunch. You made her feel special, and little girls like that. Just so long as it's an occasional treat."

"I listen to you on that, sister dear."

"It's a good thing. You'd spoil her outrageously."

"Probably not if I were in your position. It's fun to be an uncle. Besides, that's because she's nice to me, and she doesn't want that much."

Aliora laughed. "She's smarter than that. She already knows she'll get far more from you that way. You'll give anything to someone who doesn't ask and who treats you with love and respect."

"Nine years old, and she's already smarter than I am."

"About that." Aliora paused. "You're not seeing anyone, are you?"

"No. You know that."

"Sometimes . . ." She forced a smile, one that vanished. "Have you heard the news?"

"What news?"

"Everett Forster was murdered last night."

"What? How? He was going everywhere cydroid, I thought."

"The safos and the nets aren't saying. There's speculation . . ."

Speculation, again, theoretical possibilities.

". . . that it was a PAMD agent that bypassed his security system and shot him on his back veranda with a rifle from a distance."

Bypassing a security system and still needing a rifle? "He has a big estate?"

"Fairly large . . . ten acres."

Ten acres in Southhills easily cost thirty million creds. "Had to be a professional, then. The safos have every public millimeter of Southhills monitored, and Unité probably had every private millimeter scanned."

"I can't see why they want him dead," Aliora said.

"Because he's prominent, and because, after the furor over the new ion drive that Unité has developed, there's no way he'll ever make it available to the Martians or the Belters. That's just a guess, but it makes sense."

"I still can't believe they don't have anyone in custody."

That didn't surprise me, especially after my own experiences of the past days. "The nets might not know."

She shrugged. "What are you going to do now?"

"There's not much I could do, and I've got work to do."

"That's all you do."

"Might as well make credits instead of sitting around."

"You'll never meet anyone holed up in your office."

"I tried doing things to meet people, you might recall. I did it for over five years, and I never met anyone. I ran into Marilyn at a client's, and that lasted longer than any of the others."

"Except Shioban."

"Except Shioban," I agreed. "But I didn't meet her seeking people out, either."

"Whatever you're doing, or not doing, brother dear, it's not working."

She was right, but I didn't have any solutions.

"Do you want to come to dinner on Friday?"

"I can't. I'll be in Fargo."

"Lucky you. What about the following Thursday?"

"I should be free. I don't think I'm traveling then."

"I'll check with you." Her face stiffened. "Your darling niece and her brother are at it again. I need to go." With that, the holo projection vanished.

I went back to H&F and the second-stage analyses.

chapter 29

By noon on Wednesday, I'd accomplished a lot. I'd sent off the draft of the H&F study to Bruce Fuller on Tuesday afternoon, and I'd organized and set up profiles on all eight campaigns for the Centre study. I'd even studied the very modest Kagnar linksite, which used a restrained form of prodplacing. Kagnar was seated, presumably in her house, with a few of the more trusted household products around her. As she talked, briefly, about her plans, there was a restrained chord here and there, again slightly modified, but calling up the feel of the trusted products. Overall, the effect was muted, and modest, but more than I'd expected, especially with the credit limits on lower house races.

I'd finished the first go-round of the brief analysis of the site and a draft set of conclusions. The comparisons section would have to wait until I studied the Erle campaign.

Just as I was offering self-congratulations, always a dangerous thing to do, the gatekeeper announced, *Safety Officer Menendez, Epaso Office.*

I hadn't liked talking to the safo before, and I was certain I wouldn't like it any more a second time. I didn't have to accept, but not accepting would probably make him more convinced that I was guilty. Personally, I felt that I was responsible, but not guilty, but try to put that defense before the safos and the justiciary. *Accept.*

Menendez smiled. "Dr. deVrai."

I'd liked him better when he hadn't smiled. "Yes?"

"We've looked more into this business about the security guards . . ."

He was fishing. "And?"

"Were you aware that they were not hired by the campaign at all?"

That was a trap. "I'm afraid I'm confused. The security guards who stopped me in the River Plaza weren't hired by the campaign? What were they doing there?"

"Ah . . . I had thought you knew . . ."

I shook my head. "Knew what? I really still don't know what this is all about. I was stopped by these guards in black at the River Plaza—going into the rally. You asked me if I'd seen them again. I said that I hadn't, and I didn't . . ." I paused. "I did see two men in black from a distance when I left the plaza, but I told you that."

"Yes. You did." He paused. "It turns out that there were two sets of guards. Real guards and guards who were impostors."

"I only met one set of guards, in the plaza. Were they real guards or impostors?"

"We don't know which set you met, Dr. deVrai. That's why I linked. I was wondering if you might have noticed anything that would have pointed out which ones you met?"

I had to shrug. "How would I know? The ones who stopped me wore black, like I told you. They knew I'd been to the previous rallies. To me, that meant that they had access to the campaign information, and I assume that meant that they were real security personnel."

"Yes. I would have thought that, too. Thank you. I just wanted to confirm that."

The projection vanished, and I was staring at the books in the shelves on my own office wall.

If what Menendez had said was the truth, and that was a big assumption, my strongest feelings had been correct.

Someone was playing an even deeper game. It also meant that Menendez knew or suspected that the guards whose memories I'd scrambled had been after me. Since they'd been carrying weapons that they probably weren't licensed to have, they could have been subjected to veradification. They wouldn't remember what happened, but they would likely remember that they had been ordered to do whatever they had been ordered to do to me. There was no proof that we'd ever met, but Menendez would certainly believe that we had, and that I had been the one who scrambled their memories. I wondered how long he'd pursue it.

I'd been a Marine commando, not a covert agent, and intricacies within intricacies didn't appeal to me. But I didn't have much time to consider what those intricacies might be, not if I wanted to be ready to deal with the Kagnar and Erle campaigns.

Once more, I looked at my bookshelves, vowing not to offer myself self-congratulations in the future, no matter how tempting the thought.

chapter 30

After the others had filed out of the conference room, two women and Deng stood beside the ancient teak table.

"Another meeting that resolved little." Mydra turned to the redhead. "Or did I miss something, Ghamel?"

"About half the time, we don't accomplish much. This time, at least, everyone has begun to understand the importance of the effort to keep advanced media techniques out of election campaigns—and the cost of not doing so to us, and to the world." A smile curled across Ghamel's lips. "Even if we hadn't accomplished that, it's better to have the meetings and make sure no one feels cut off."

"You had a concern you did not express." Deng's voice was low.

"About the Centre study. The use of deVrai does concern me," Ghamel said deliberately. "I'd much rather have had a female analyst, someone like Erika Wadren. She's always been out just for herself."

"That's the problem with someone like Wadren," replied Mydra. "They're known to sell themselves to the highest bidder, and deVrai won't." An ironic smile appeared.

"You know something, perhaps?" inquired Deng.

"Abraham Vorhees is furious at deVrai . . . for just those reasons. DeVrai wrote a study for a client that suggested Vorhee's services were unnecessary and overpriced. If deVrai reports as he will, because it's clear that political use of rez tie-ins with trusted products benefits a candidate, no one will be able to refute his impartiality."

"If deVrai is still alive," pointed out Ghamel. "Abraham isn't known to shy away from invisibles or other ways of removing obstacles."

"I suggested that he warn deVrai and wait. Suggested strongly. He knows I have some ties with PST."

"You think he will?" asked Ghamel.

"Abraham is out for himself, but he's not stupid. After the study's complete . . . does it matter? It might even be better if deVrai became a martyr to his impartiality."

"If Vorhees were implicated, even by rumor," mused Deng, "that would strengthen the case for campaign reform."

"It would also take care of Abraham, and that's long overdue."

After a silence, Ghamel looked at Deng and asked, "You're sure that Uy-Smythe doesn't know anything about SPD? And the follow-on for deVrai?"

"Uy-Smythe doesn't know about SPD. He knows that ISS provides moderate donations every year. That is all. He would not want to know more. He also knows that we ensure his foundation gets grants and prominent donors . . ."

"And that, every once in a while," interjected Mydra, "he does some research for us, or publishes a study. We insist that the studies be accurate and impeccable, and that's all he cares about—besides the funding."

"You don't think . . . ?"

"No. That's the beauty of it. Everyone in both the underlink and overlink worlds knows about ISS. They're supposed to. Industrial Security Systems—'For the Absolute in Protection.' Isn't that the slogan?"

"That was the old one," Deng said. "'Impervious, Impenetrable.'"

"Not very catchy."

"We are not into catchy. Not for what we charge."

"SPD says that someone named Wong contracted with de-Vrai for a study," pressed Ghamel.

"There's more than that. There has to be," replied Mydra. "Wong's officially the district representative here in west NorAm for the Sinese Consumer Formulator Association. He's probably more than that."

"They will play into our game."

"They will?"

"Maybe we'd better make sure that our postelection efforts are ready earlier," suggested Mydra.

"Early December?"

"That might be best."

"I wish we could do something about that brother-in-law of deVrai's. His operation is costing us hundreds of millions."

"Be patient. That is also part of the larger plan . . ."

chapter 31

Thursday, I worked mainly on the Centre report, and did more research on both the Kagnar and Erle campaigns. From everything that I could turn up, it was clear that Erle was underfunded in a district that was predominantly Laborite Republican and that he was likely to lose by a significant margin. Still, I'd need to present both sides and show whether whatever Kagnar did with placement or rez techniques increased or decreased what might be considered a "normal" LR margin in the subdistrict.

Friday morning arrived, and I was on the maglev to Minpolis, where I'd have to get off to take a flitter back northwest to Fargo. This was one of those few times when I wished I lived in the times of the Commonocracy. A flitter from Denv direct to Fargo would have been faster, but there weren't any, because flitters were prohibited from overlapping maglev routes or circumventing them. That meant traveling as close as possible by maglev and then taking a flitter. So I had four and a half hours on the maglev, an hour wait for the commuter flitter, and an another hour flitter flight, when I could have been there in half the time if I could have taken a flitter direct or in two-thirds the time if the maglev had run to Fargo.

So while on the maglev I sat in a quiet corner seat in the exec car and studied all the information I'd gathered on Kagnar, Erle, Fargo, and Jameston. From what I could gather, Fargo had originally been the largest commercial and population center in the northern High Plains area. The subdistrict in which Kagnar was running for the House seat had once been an entire state in the Commonocracy. Jameston was smaller, roughly a third the size of Fargo. Both were located on rivers.

Once the maglev got me to Minpolis, I took the local maglev shuttle to the flitterport, where I waited and studied more. An hour and a half later, the flitter landed me and twelve others at Hector Field at almost four-thirty. Once the field had been an airport, back when the skies had been filled with aircraft. Now, it did a business renting groundcars to travelers, not that there were that many.

The groundcar was an Altus, but only two years old, and it smelled of nothing except a faint hint of ionization. I eased away from the flitterport, heading toward the center of Fargo, and the High Plains Hotel, which was almost across the street from the Fargodome—the third of that name—where Kagnar's rally was being held at seven in the evening.

All the streets in Fargo were numbered, avenues running east and west, streets north and south, an arrangement that dated back over two centuries, and one similar to the system used in Deseret district. Another interesting thing about Fargo was the Red River. Until I'd read the background material on the town, I hadn't realized that it ran northward into the Manitoba district, then drained north. The place had some of the best natural soils in NorAm, or the best ones remaining after the Collapse, and that had made it a center for naturally grown foods of all sorts. The place was so flat that it was always flooding, and more than half the town had been destroyed in the Great Flood of the Collapse. Fargo had never totally recovered, and held only about 60 percent of the population levels of the Commonocracy. Then, that was true of most places, even Denv. There were just fewer people.

The carpark was right on the south side of the High Plains and was barely half full. To me, it meant that not too many people were traveling to Fargo to hear Kagnar, or if they were, they were staying in far more modest accommodations. Supposedly, the High Plains *was* modest, from both the price and the linkviews I'd scanned.

I carried my overnight bag into the lobby, where a low-resolution virty checked me in and keyed my room to me. After lugging my gear up one ramp and walking to the end of the north wing, I found my room—and confirmed that it *was* modest indeed, if clean.

After that, tired and hungry, I opted for the pseudo-bistro off the lobby—Chez Francois.

A real host, a tired-looking college student, I guessed, escorted me to a table set against a faux brick wall. There were only three other tables taken, but five-fifteen was early for dinner, even on the High Plains. The plaid tablecloth was period, early twentieth century, I estimated, but the projected holo menu could have come from a dozen imitation French restaurants across NorAm, and perhaps it had. I settled on the beef and mushroom crepes with a green salad, and was pleased to find Grey tea, which wasn't period at all, hidden at the bottom of the projection.

Then I waited, my blood sugar too low to concentrate. That was one of the areas where my genes could have used definite improvement. Before long, a server appeared and slipped the dishes onto the plain tablecloth.

"Most business types leave Fargo over the weekend," the server noted. "You look business."

"I'm covering the Kagnar campaign," I replied, before taking a sip of the Grey tea.

"Someone has to." With a faint smile, she left me to the crepes.

I ate methodically. I'd had better, but I'd had far worse and in far less hospitable locales. By the time I was finished, I felt refreshed, and ready to walk to the Fargodome. So I headed out.

The dome was two long blocks south of the High Plains, and I didn't see another person on the winding path that bordered the street. A number of groundcars were pulling into the carpark around the Fargodome, but, even so, far less than half the spaces were taken. There were only a handful of greeters or volunteers, and none of those wore uniforms or singlesuits, just maroon jackets, with Kagnar pins on the lapels.

"Would you like some information, sir?" asked a man who had to be elderly, or treatment-resistant, because his hair was white.

"Yes, please." I took the trifold leaflet and carried it inside, through the lobby and into the arena section. Although the speaker's platform was not small and had been set up only five meters from the side of the arena where the doors were open, it was dwarfed by the darkened sections that rose on the other three sides. Despite using only a quarter of the space, less than a third of the seats were filled, and with fifteen minutes to go, I had the feeling that there would be a good many empty seats.

I settled into a seat on the aisle, three rows back of the railing and wall that dropped down to the center area that could be used for anything from football to rodeos. First, I read through the trifold, but it told me nothing I hadn't already discovered. By then, my thoughts were skittering around what I'd seen and knew.

Kagnar was only having a handful of rallies, from what the campaign schedule showed, and the link campaign wasn't that extensive. She was traveling to every hamlet in the subdistrict, as part of an effort to illustrate her interest in all the places people lived, and not just the major population centers.

Damon Erle wasn't even doing an appearance in Fargo, or, if he had or would be, there was no record of it anywhere. I could see the reason for his rally in Jameston, since it was his hometown, but Jameston was less than a third the size of Fargo, and it couldn't have hurt to appear in Fargo as well.

Unlike the Carlisimo rally, before Kagnar's appearance there was no music, no rez. At seven o'clock, the lights over the seating dimmed, and Kagnar appeared in a circle of light, walking forward to the front edge of the platform by herself. She was five years older than I was, not quite fifty, and even though most people that age looked far younger, she seemed like she'd barely graduated from grad school—unless you looked closely at her eyes. They'd seen far more.

She smiled, and while she didn't project quite the radiance that Carlisimo had, there was enough energy there that I watched closely.

"I'm glad to see you all here. Especially since it's harvest time. It's important that you are here. This election is one of a handful that will decide who controls the House. If the House falls to the PD, then everything will change. Artificial foods will take over the market. Natural foods will once more fall upon hard times. The virtues of the High Plains will be lost . . ." She paused. "Now . . . you wouldn't want that, would you?"

No one answered out loud, but I could sense more than a few heads nodding.

"This election isn't about me. It's about you and what you believe in. It's about what you and your families have worked for. And, most of all, it's about your values . . ."

The lights faded, and an immense image appeared right before where Kagnar was standing, effectively shielding her from the audience. The shimmering view of a stretch of open plains at sunset—a sweep of land enhanced with the crimson-highlighted clouds and an almost greenish deep-blue sky—wasn't as clear as those Carlisimo used because there was no shimmerscreen to enhance it, but it was large enough, maybe too large for those of us in the front rows. Subtly, under Kagnar's voice, music welled up, music with a sense of the familiar, with a rez undertone.

Kagnar's voice continued. "We love the wide open spaces. They are our heritage and our birthright. But without a continent-wide policy to support that heritage in an economically sound way, all too many in Fargo and beyond will not be able to hold on to that heritage. I understand that heritage. And I will fight in the Legislature to preserve it and to improve conditions here on the High Plains . . ."

The first image was replaced by a second, one showing a family standing by farming equipment beside a modest barn, and the background music changed into something both hopeful and wistful.

"Like most of you, I have deep roots in Fargo . . ."

Kagnar had a good sense of pacing, and a strong voice that radiated understanding. While her presentation didn't use commercial product placing, it definitely used a form of prodplacing, except that the product was a sense of place and heritage.

The way Kagnar ended the rally was predictable enough. The background music and rez became more upbeat, and the projected views switched to those showing morning scenes across the subdistrict.

". . . We hold to a proud past, but we are not the past. Our virtues are based on the time-tested lessons of the past, and that is why they enable us to persevere and succeed now . . . and in the future . . ."

The projection switched to a brilliant sunrise, gold and orange across fields of golden grain.

"Because we are the future that works. We . . . are . . . the . . . future."

The sunrise vanished, and Kagnar stood in the circle of light.

"I've shown you all what I stand for and why I think I'd do the best job of representing you. That's why I'd like your vote. Thank you for coming."

The entire Fargodome darkened for less than a minute, and then the lights came back up slowly, revealing an empty stage.

In its own way, Kagnar's presentation had impressed me more than had Carlisimo's, but I had no doubts that Carlisimo's blatantly populist approach was pulling in more voters. Then, maybe that was why, although I liked no political party that much, I tended to favor the Laborite Republicans' position. I just didn't like their candidates much.

The same handful of volunteers in maroon coats stood outside, smiling, with their literature. I saw no sign of security types.

In the twilight, I walked back the two long blocks from the Fargodome to the High Plains, thinking, just trying to take in what I'd experienced, but in a more analytical way.

Once back in my room, after I entered all my notes and observations, I clicked on All-News. The scene was of the outside of a Martian dome.

More unrest in Serenium . . . this time a series of explosions rocked the CorPak safo headquarters. Early reports suggest that at least three safos were killed and more than a dozen injured . . . An untraceable message, believed to be from the BLN, to Governor General Ashley claimed that the violence would get worse if MultiCor did not accede to the demands for independence. The message also claimed that the murder of Unité Director General Forster earlier this month was one example of what would happen to the various multi directors general . . . Security analysts at NorAm High Command dismissed the indirect claim . . .

Dismissed or not, Forster was still dead, and whoever had taken him out had managed two attempts in high security areas and had never been caught. In my book, that meant they were not only good, but had an earthside support network and considerable resources.

I took a deep breath. I still had to drive to Jameston in the morning.

chapter 32

On Saturday morning, I had croissants and eggs lyonnaise, whatever they were, at Chez Francois, then went back up to my room. I started out by trying to complete the simplified matrix for the Kagnar campaign. It classified levels of prod-placing and compared the number of references used. I'd kept track of those fairly well at the Carlisimo rallies, and I had the linksites as well. I didn't get very far, because, once I considered Kagnar, the references were understated, only used on her main linksite, and not in her main appearance. The time wasn't totally wasted, because at least I'd ruled out one approach.

By then it was time to depart and drive westward through a cold rain that had come out of nowhere to Jameston. Everything looked gray as I neared Jameston—because it was. Gray light, gray clouds. Even the rain seemed to come down gray. What a difference a hundred and forty kays and sunlight made.

The Spiritwood Inn was even smaller than the High Plains, but the meeting room there was where the Erle rally was scheduled. I parked the Altus as close as I could get, and that wasn't hard, no more than fifty meters away, and hurried through the rain. I was more than damp, but it only took a few minutes before the clothes wicked away most of the dampness. I didn't even look too wrinkled.

The time was twelve-forty, and I headed for something to eat. Certainly, an inn had a restaurant. All I could find was a small place called Eats, featuring retro twentieth-century plastic: plastic tables, upholstery, and booths. The colors were orange and avocado green. It reminded me why few people collected furniture from the period. I ordered a "natural"—natural Angus beef, and natural potatoes, baked. I wasn't about to go for the tallow-fries. The meal wasn't as good as it could have been, nor as bad as it might have been, and I finished and left by twenty to two, searching for the meeting room.

There was only one sign announcing Damon Erle, and that was so small I'd already located the door to the room by the three people standing outside. Two were men wearing Erle campaign buttons, black on stark white, and they were talking to a tall and angular blonde. None offered me the folders they held as I stepped past them. For a hotel as small as the Spiritwood Inn, the meeting room was respectable. It might have held four hundred people in the small hotel chairs squeezed together. Even when I got there, fifteen minutes before the start of the meeting, there were only fifty people there.

This time I sat on the outside, about ten rows back, because the chairs looked so small. That way, I could always ease my chair out, if I felt crowded. As I waited, I studied the crowd. Most of those there seemed to fit the stereotype of the left fringe of the PDs: students with stars in their eyes, poorer folks with outsized girths, poorer people who looked close to gaunt, and alternative education types in black—I'd always disliked them, because they gave wearing black a bad name, but I supposed they thought I was one of them. I could see a handful garbed in what I would have called mainstream attire and looking like it fit them.

The only equipment I saw was a pair of enormous speakers on each side of the front of the room. There wasn't even a podium or a chair.

By two o'clock another fifty people had finally showed up.

At that point, a tall and wiry man with a craggy face, a square-cut but neatly trimmed beard, and black curly hair—thankfully cut short, because men with wiry curly hair who wear it long look more like dogs or mops than people—stepped out of a side door. Alone.

He carried a rez-based guitar. He cleared his throat and waited for the murmurs to subside, before he began to sing.

> *Erle's the handle and the name*
> *for playing this political game,*
> *I'm not plush, polished, or proud,*
> *and my credits don't speak twice as loud . . .*
> *I'm a hometown boy, loving the plains,*
> *taking the toil, the weather, the pains.*
> *If you want someone honest and free,*
> *Best get thinking of voting for me . . .*

The last chord was sharp, and rezzed into subsonic discomfort.

Once more Erle let the silence draw out before he spoke.

"Welcome, folks." Erle's voice was so deep it rumbled. "If I were a fancy-talking type, like Ms. Kagnar, I'd be telling you all how glad I am to see you all. Make you feel like long-lost friends. Favorite cousins. I'm not like that. Don't speak in long phrases. That's why I started with a song." There was another pause. "Folks talk about the land. They talk about traditions. About pride and their ancestors." An ironic smile crossed Erle's face, and he chuckled, a deep belly chuckle, warm, but slightly ironic. "Thing is. They live up on artificial hills, safe from the river. They work for big multis doing things that don't much help the folks who struggle on the land and on the streets."

He lifted the rez-guitar again.

> *Pretty places, pretty faces, flashing in the light,*
> *charming graces, empty spaces, flashing in the night . . .*

As the song went on, I couldn't help but smile. Erle certainly captured the sense of all too many ascendents, and I couldn't deny that I'd felt that way at times.

Abruptly, the feeling left, even while the craggy-faced candidate was still singing, as my enhancements registered trouble. I forced myself to turn slowly.

A muscular figure had entered the meeting room and was walking down the side where my chair was, counterfeiting the look of embarrassment—but cydroids don't show emotion well, not without practice, and the operator of this one hadn't had it.

I leaned forward and put my hands on the back of the chair before me. He was less than two meters from me, when his hand eased toward his waistband. I saw the glint and moved, lifting the chair and swinging it across his hands. The weapon flew against the wall, and the cydroid looked stunned.

I didn't wait, but brought the chair up so that one leg slammed into the V below his ribs. I tossed the chair aside, and side-kicked into his knee. It snapped, and he went down.

At that moment, the cydroid went limp, and his eyes glazed over. Whoever had been at the other end of the shunt had broken contact. I wondered a bit at the quickness of the cydroid's collapse, but I could also see that the operator might not have wanted a tracer on the shunt freqs.

A heavyset man appeared beside me. "I put in a call."

I had no idea what he meant, but I nodded.

"Dispatch said they'd be here in three minutes." He slipped a pair of restrainers out from his pocket. "You mind?"

"You're the professional." I stepped back.

"You looked real professional, stranger. Never seen a man taken down that quick. Or that hard. Commando?"

"Years back," I admitted.

"What do you do now?"

I had to laugh. "Communications and netlink consultant. You?"

"State guideway patrol. Linked the locals." He recovered the neuroblaster, using nanite-film gloves. "Want to help me

drag it out? Won't be any traces, and we might as well give
the man a chance to talk to the folks. Local safos can interview him later."

As we pulled the trussed and limp figure out of the meeting room, behind us, I heard Erle say, "Most excitement ever
at one of these meetings."

Once we were outside in the corridor, the heavyset man
turned to me. "Wallis, Hank Wallis."

"Jonat deVrai."

Two uniformed safos appeared, rushing down the corridor.
"Where?"

"Here!" snapped Wallis.

The two looked down at the limp form on the floor, then
up at Wallis. Wallis presented badge and link-ID. They
checked, then nodded.

I could have left, but that would have caused more problems.

"You can check it out later, but that's a cydroid." Wallis
extended the filmed neuroblaster. "He pulled this and aimed
it at Erle—he's the House candidate in there. Mr. deVrai saw
it at the last minute and hit him with a chair, broke his knee.
He went limp. I trussed him up, and we dragged him out
here."

"You moved him?" asked the taller safo. The words were
accusatory.

Wallis sighed. "No reason not to. Erle's got enough troubles. Besides, you won't find anything in there. You've got
the weapon. You've got the perp, and, if you work fast, you
can get the ID of everyone in the room. Might as well start
with Mr. deVrai here."

"But . . ." The second safo started to object.

The first interrupted. "It makes it a bit harder, but you're
within your authority, Director Wallis."

Director Wallis? Was he the head of the Dakota subdistrict Guideway Patrol?

"Thank you, Sam," Wallis replied.

From there on, it was routine. Very routine and very boring. After another fifteen minutes of questioning, verification of who I was, and an authenticated agreement to answer

any and all questions, they let me go and got on with questioning the others at the meeting. By then, four more safos had arrived, and I was glad to slip away.

On my way out, I stopped by the desk and asked the virty for information on the Spiritwood Inn. I needed to track down who owned the place, because it was unlikely any cydroid could have gotten through the screens at the doors, old as they were, without either cooperation from someone in the organization or a great deal of credits. Usually, the cheaper possibility is right. I also wanted to check out Wallis.

I took the Altus to the Jameston flitterport and actually managed to catch the early flitter to Minpolis. That didn't help much, because I'd just shifted waiting at Jameston to more waiting at the Minpolis maglev station. Waiting and thinking, wondering why anyone would want to take out Damon Erle, who was going to lose the election by a significant margin.

Or had someone tried once more to get me involved? I'd seen more violence in two weeks than I'd ever seen outside the Marines.

Yet Hank Wallis had been more than helpful, unlike Menendez in Epaso. I noted everything I could think of, from the way Erle had handled the meeting and his use of rez and songs, to the cydroid attack. When I couldn't think of anything else, with an hour yet to go before my maglev to Denv left, I took one of the pubcom terminals and keyed in a local news search.

. . . Nothing new from Mars . . . martial law remains in force . . . but largely ignored by Mars-born and longer-term immigrants . . . Two more CorPak safos wounded by snipers . . .

. . . A cydroid took a shot at Damon Erle this afternoon. Erle may be trailing Helen Kagnar in the race for the subdistrict House seat, but you wouldn't have known that today. Safos are not commenting on the rumor that the cydroid is registered to a known LR business here in the High Plains . . . Nor have they released the identity of the bystander who disarmed and subdued the cydroid, except to say that the man was, and we quote, "covering the campaign." Damon Erle should be glad someone was . . .

I winced at the last line. Erle had enough problems without that kind of net attention.

I wouldn't get back to Denv until after midnight, and I just hoped that I didn't have to make any more trips. I'd traveled enough over the years in the Marines, and I had the feeling that traveling wasn't doing much for me, either.

chapter 33

Sunday morning, I slept in. I'd gotten back to the house late on Saturday, and I hadn't slept that well, anyway, not with dreams of cydroids and snipers. When I finally did struggle into an upright position on Sunday, it was close to eleven, incredibly late for me. I just sat in the kitchen for a time, going through three mugs of Grey tea and some dried fruit and toast. The larder was more than empty.

I was in over my head, and I didn't even have any idea what game was being played or by whom. Someone, or several someones, wanted Carlisimo shut down. Someone else wanted his campaign tactics shut down. They might be the same people; they might not. Someone else was unhappy with me. It might be Abe Vorhees, or one of the unknown parties against Carlisimo. Someone else, long before the events of the past month had happened, had stolen my DNA, blatantly, and no one yet had been able to track down who it might be.

The question that I couldn't answer, the one that I didn't even have a clue to, was simple. Why me? I had a pretty good idea why the Centre wanted me to do their study, because I could provide the best evidence against the use of modified campaign rez. And it was *possible* that someone didn't want me to finish the study. It was also possible that a dead consultant who was studying the use of rez-based techniques in campaigning would be equally effective as an exhibit before the Legislature as that consultant's study. But, except in general terms of contributors and board directors, I had no idea who was backing the Centre, and no way to find out.

I also couldn't figure out the use of the cydroid against Damon Erle. That made absolutely no sense at all, not that I could figure out. Most crazies wouldn't have the resources to get control of a cydroid, and anyone with resources would have known that Erle didn't have a chance to win in that subdistrict even if he'd spent ten times what Kagnar did, and that wasn't allowed under the campaign acts. It could have been someone in the entertainment business, with a grudge, but that seemed like an awfully strange coincidence, and I never had been a big believer in coincidences.

Because I was tired of the Centre's study, I took a look at the material Chelsa Glynn had sent in response to my inquiry. The technical paper was to be no less than two thousand words and no more than six thousand and was to deal with any aspect of the general topic of the seminar. The topic was, interestingly enough, subperceptual influence and learning, and that explained in part why they wanted me. Someone hoped I'd explain my methodology for determining carry-through of prodplacing. That was something I wasn't about to touch.

I smiled. What I could address, legitimately and fairly, were the difficulties in recognizing and assessing the impact of subperceptual influences. Since I'd never seen anything on that, and since I had file upon file of material that could be adapted, that would be useful both in educating people at the seminar and establishing my credentials without giving away my methodology.

The first thing I did was to run a search on the worldlink to see what, if anything, anyone else had written. As I'd suspected, there was very little, no more than a handful of articles, and none really on the topic. What did surprise me was that I discovered three commentaries on an article I'd written three years before on the history of prodplacing.

I started by pulling sections from various studies and notes, and assembled them into a single file, but was careful to avoid anything with proprietary information. Then I began the business of editing and eliminating.

After almost two hours, as I was drafting—or redrafting—my technical paper for the AKRA seminar, a thought occurred to me, and I pulsed in an inquiry on the media and news stories on the Erle campaign. As they queued up, I scanned through them.

Erle Stunned by Attack . . .

Attack by MultiCor Cydroid? . . .

I read that story in more depth—even if it had appeared in *DailyDem*. The writer began by asking what the major multis had against Damon Erle. The story stated that, according to an unnamed source in safety enforcement, the cydroid was one of a standard pattern used by a number of multis in the MultiCor group, but that there was no record of its creation. That suggested that HPlus, or another cydroid/clone producer, was evading NorAm registration requirements. In short, the multis were out to get Erle . . . and it was written almost that bluntly.

Cynical as I was, I had to wonder if some backer of Erle's had pulled the whole thing off to call attention to the campaign and to portray Kagnar as a multi tool. If that were the case, no one had really been in any danger, because the cydroid's first blast would have missed. I'd wondered somewhat about the ease with which I'd immobilized the cydroid, and that would explain it.

I stiffened. Wallis. He'd known that the attacker was a cydroid. In the scuffle at the time, I hadn't caught the fact that I'd never said the attacker had been a cydroid, but Wallis had known and been ready. Had he been planted to take down the cydroid? That, or his presence was another unlikely coincidence. Too unlikely, but there was no way I could get to Wallis on it, and no way really to prove what I had realized.

None of that really explained why someone was taking such a risk to attack Erle, as opposed to a more visible PD with a better chance . . . unless . . .

I keyed in another inquiry. Four other PD candidates had been attacked in the last week, but not seriously injured, and no one had been apprehended. Notes or other communications had suggested perpetrators who opposed the PD.

Was this a new campaign device? A way around the spending limits? Who would be behind it, and why? The PD itself couldn't be. At least, I didn't think they were that stupid. It could eventually be tracked. But it was someone who would benefit by PD control of the House. The Senate was out of PD reach, at least in the current election cycle.

I did a little more digging. What was interesting was that all five seats were either open, or relatively closely contested. None of the other four were ones I had picked, but I flagged and added them to my database for the Centre study.

Finally, after doing what I could, I went back to the technical paper for the seminar. The strange aspects of the campaigns were just something else about which I could do nothing. The technical paper and seminar paid and would give me exposure, which I'd need because I hadn't gotten any new requests for work since the short analysis for H&F.

I'd probably get some more follow-on work from Reya, and possibly more from Methroy, but when and for how much was another question.

chapter 34

As Yenci walked toward the door to the secure briefing room, Central Four projected the full holo image of a brunette safo into the chair behind the table.

The bio-safo opened the door, looked toward the waiting image, and nodded. "Thank you. It's easier when you don't appear from nowhere. I know it's a peculiarity of mine. I appreciate your humoring it."

"You made your wishes known." A faint smile appeared on the projected safo's lips, lingered, and then vanished.

"You know, looking at your projection, sometimes it's hard to believe you're not real." Yenci frowned. "That's not right. You *are* real, but it seems like you're looking more and more like a bio-person, and not virty system-rep."

"You had suggested a more lifelike approach would be useful."

"I don't know ... What do you have on the crysalkie busts?"

"Twenty arrests and detentions. Fifteen are first offenses, four are second-timers, and one is up a third time."

"Second-timers?"

"Fridric Carao completed servie obligations one month ago for running crysalkie four years ago . . ."

"One lousy month, and he's stupid enough to run crysalkie again?"

"He was caught with half a kilo in the hidden compartments in his belt. He was also running caak. There were enough DNA traces to establish that he had worn the belt a number of times."

"So he can't claim he was duped?" Yenci snorted. "Bet his advocate does. Poor westside boy . . . Who are the others?"

"Frank Sebastion, dealing five years back. Angel deToras, dealing seven years back. Arthur Stevenson, running, four years ago. Stevenson was charged with dealing, but was acquitted." Central Four continued to synchronize image and speech.

"The three-time loser?"

"Rees Siegfried. Two previous dealing charges."

"Why's he still Earthside?"

"Extenuating circumstances, sealed records."

"That means he turned in someone big, and he was stupid enough to get back in the business?"

"He is in detention in the medical block on full support. Prognosis is unfavorable."

"You mean that without cendie medicals he'll die?"

"Yes. Requests for star priority have been denied by the district prosecuting advocate."

"That's that, then." Yenci smiled coldly. "The others are booked?"

"They are."

"What about the cydroid cases?" asked the slender safo.

"There are some irregularities in the cydroid facial scan and DNA search analyses." The slightest hesitation occurred before the word "irregularities."

"What sort of irregularities?"

"A similar DNA pattern to one set of cydroids was reported missing twenty-one months ago. A more detailed comparison might prove useful."

Yenci frowned, then nodded. "Do whatever you can with it. Don't know what good it will do if it was stolen, but it can't hurt." After a moment, she asked, "Legitimate theft claim?"

"Ascendent and well-documented. He was very concerned when he heard about the unregistered cydroids. A servie has reported a similarity between the two."

"Friggin' great." The safo snorted. "Now we got cydroid saboteurs cloned out of cendie genes, and no idea who did it. Better do more than whatever's usual. Whatever it takes."

Whatever it takes. Central Four documented the command.

After Yenci left the secure briefing room, the projected safo smiled, then vanished.

Whatever it takes . . .

chapter 35

Monday morning was gray and cold. I ran and worked out anyway, getting up a half hour earlier and running close to my normal route in reverse. That had me in my office, mug of tea in hand, close to an hour earlier than usual on Mondays.

I plowed into updating my analysis of the Kagnar campaign, categorizing the various media uses, which ran from straight literature handouts to some slight use of off-chord commercial rez prodplacings in her linksite, and the use of those chords on a muted basis during her rally. All that was minimal compared to what Carlisimo had been doing. By ten o'clock, I had the Kagnar and Erle stuff laid out parallel to all the others, and was working on updating what I'd been sent by the Clerihew coordinator.

A dull *crack* shivered the house.

Check front entry! Check front entry! The house security system blared through the gatekeeper.

I grabbed the neurostunner from the drawer—the kind allowed in the house, but not beyond its doors—and hurried toward the front door, querying the system. *Interrogative status?*

Systems intact. House not entered or damaged.

I stopped behind the still-sealed door. *Interrogative intruders?*

Negative intruders. No objects massing in excess of a quarter kilogram.

Stunner in hand, I eased the inner door open. The outer permaglass door was untouched, not even scratched or scraped, but a sealed envelope was taped to the outside. Using enhancements, and the house scanners, I studied the area in front of the house and to both sides, but no one else was nearby. I closed the inner door and left the envelope there, and went back to get a pair of sterile gloves and a hand-scanner.

When I returned, I checked again, but the area was clear, except for Mrs. Marden, who was standing on her porch, across the cul-de-sac, looking around. I stepped out, ducking as I did, as if to pick something up.

"Mr. deVrai! What was that?"

"I don't know. I just heard a bang."

"You don't think it was one of those awful PAMD people?"

"I don't know what it was."

The scanner revealed traces of something akin to black powder, probably handmade, and likely to be untraceable, and there were shreds of plastic across the front porch, several embedded lightly in the trim around the door. For the moment, I left them there.

I took the envelope, which had no name on the outside, and slipped back inside to the kitchen. When I was convinced there was nothing in the envelope but a single sheet of paper, I opened it, using scissors, and letting the paper flutter to the tile floor. I bent down and used the tip of the scissors to turn it over, then read the words.

You've been warned. Don't ever mess with a Vorhees account again. Another mistake will be fatal.

I straightened and left the paper there, but even as I stepped back, it began to gray. As I watched, it turned into ashes, and then less than that. After sterilizing the scissors, spraying the floor, disposing of the gloves, I turned on the kettle.

Vorhees was behind the warning. That was clear enough from the disintegrating paper. While someone else could have planted it, that didn't seem likely. Who else would have had the motive . . . unless someone was after Vorhees, but then that person would have used more durable warnings, the kind that could have been turned over to the safos.

Had the sniper also been a warning, or had he been representing someone else?

I was getting more than a little angry. In fact, I was seething inside. Part of the anger was because there was so little I could do. There was no damned proof of anything, nothing to speak of except my word that these things had happened. There was literally no evidence of anything, except my own perceptions, and a few shreds of plastic and powder.

I walked back to the front door. A wry smile crossed my lips. The shreds of plastic had also vanished—ultra-biodegradable. A few dents in the trim, some traces of powder, and one person besides me who heard a loud noise. If I reported things like that, especially if I kept reporting them, I'd end up under mental treatment because veradification would show that I believed what I'd seen—and there was virtually no evidence of any of it. Delusions . . . and someone would try to cure me of delusions that were real. What that might do to my mind I didn't even want to consider.

After another half mug of tea, I walked back to the office to get back to work on the Centre report. I didn't get more than a half hour done when the gatekeeper announced, *Safety Officer Olafson, Jameston Office.*

I couldn't say I was surprised. *Accept.*

Safo Olafson's projection showed an attractive tall blonde with a polite smile. "Dr. deVrai?"

She'd also looked up my background. "Yes?"

"I was wondering if you would mind answering a few follow-up questions. As always, you understand that you are under no obligation, implied or otherwise, to do so."

"I'd be happy to." Given her low-key and pleasant approach, I was inclined to be cooperative—and wary.

"Just for the record, why were you in Jameston?"

"I'm doing a study on the use of various media techniques

in campaigns. The campaign between Helen Kagnar and Damon Erle was one of those races I'd been following. I was at the Kagnar rally in Fargo the night before."

"You're a consultant in media, according to the record."

"That's right."

"What alerted you to the assailant?"

From there on in, every question was directly related to the attack on Damon Erle, and Safo Olafson spent a good hour interrogating me, if most politely and gently.

"Thank you very much, Dr. deVrai. You've been most helpful."

"Before you go . . . have you found out any more that you can tell me about the cydroid? They're not cheap, and that would indicate either invisibles with lots of credits or out and out theft, which is difficult."

She smiled. "I can't say officially, Dr. deVrai." There was a pause. "Let me put it this way. There was an identifiable commercial gene pattern registered on Earth. That's really more than I should say, but you were most helpful, and kept this from being very ugly. Jameston hasn't had an assassination-style killing in years. Captain Bentsen would like to keep it that way."

A commercial gene pattern registered on Earth. What that really meant was that either the cydroid had been stolen, or cloned illegally from a standard gene pattern belonging to one of the six cydroid/clone multis. There was no way that one of them would knowingly allow that, and if a client did, they'd have released the information immediately.

"Thank you. I assume that the owner of the pattern has issued a formal denial."

"I can't comment on that. When a pattern has been copied illegally, that is standard procedure."

I liked Olafson. "Thank you. Is there anything else I could provide?"

"No. You've been very helpful. Thank you."

And she was gone.

She'd actually told me two things. The Jameston Safety Office was treating it as an attempted assassination, and that the cydroid/clone pattern had been illegally used.

I thought it over, and then keyed an inquiry into the worldlink. Certainly, someone had to have noticed what I had the day before: the coincidence of attacks against PD candidates. After several minutes, the response came back— nil. I didn't have all the facts the newsies and their analysts did, and I couldn't have been the only one to notice it. That meant that someone—lots of someones or someones with a great deal of power—didn't want the story out . . . or not yet.

Again . . . there wasn't much I could do about that. I was feeling that way about too much lately, but I didn't have many illusions about how much real power I had in the scheme of things. I hadn't even had that much power as a light colonel in the Marines.

The quiet lasted until three in the afternoon.

Aliora.

Accept.

The background showed Aliora in her office at the Health Policy Centre, a modest corner office with a view of the mountains. Whether she was actually there, or working from home with that as a background was another question, but it really didn't matter. She was telling me that she was linking from work, wherever she was.

"Hello, sister dear."

"You haven't linked, Jonat, and we'd talked about dinner on Thursday."

"I haven't, and I'd love to, if the invitation's still open."

"Of course it is. Just the three of us around seven-thirty. The children eat earlier." Aliora smiled. "You can read them a story."

"I think I can manage that. By then, it'll be about my speed."

"Lots of projects?"

"Just one, really. It's huge, at least for me. That's good, because there's not much else right at the moment. Not that pays enough, anyway."

"You really ought to think about joining a larger firm, someone like Vorhees and Reyes. Oh, I know you don't care that much for Abe Vorhees and the way he does business, but they're very successful."

"Aliora . . . first, I wouldn't recognize Abe Vorhees if I ran into him with a groundcar. Second, I think it would be fair to say that, even if I crawled into his office and offered him a fortune to hire me, he'd probably refuse."

"Jonat . . . don't tell me that he's another multi director you've offended?"

"I don't know about offended," I fudged, "but I was asked to evaluate their efforts on behalf of other clients, and Vorhees was collecting exorbitant sums for no results at all. I've been told that they weren't happy with me." After the episode of that morning, I felt that was an accurate statement.

"Oh, Jonat . . . you'll always be doing things the hard way, I suppose."

"That's a definite possibility." I smiled. "Haven't I always?"

She shook her head. "I need to run. Thursday . . . by seven if you want to read to Charis and Alan."

"I'll be there."

After the projection vanished, I sat in the ergochair for a time, thinking about her words. Always doing things the hard way? Because I didn't want to be beholden to someone who knew less than I did? Or who gouged clients because he could?

I didn't have any answers. These days, it seemed like I seldom did.

chapter 36

The rest of the week flew by, mainly because I didn't get much in the way of new work. Reya Decostas contacted me with a straight analytical request. PowerSwift wanted an estimate on the potential effectiveness of prodplacing on a series of action shows on the PanAsian Net. PanAsian kept their audience figures to themselves, but there were ways around that, even though the figures wouldn't be quite so accurate. I agreed to the contract, as if I were going to turn down one of my biggest continuing clients.

Thursday morning, Methroy linked to assure me that he'd have another project in late October after the election, and Bruce Fuller linked to ask for a clarification and a rewrite of one section of his report. Then he said he'd be sending another batch of information with another contract, not terribly large. I promised I could work it in. Every bit of work helped.

Dinner at Aliora and Dierk's was pleasant—just the three of us, although I did read Charis and Alan a bedtime story. Aliora restricted linktime to a few hours a day for the children, and reading and storytelling were a must. I enjoyed it, before the adult dinner. I didn't mention the more explosive events in my life. I didn't want my sister thinking I was even crazier than she already thought. I did tell her that I hadn't heard anything from the safos . . . and that was that.

The weekend was all work, but the Centre report was coming together, somewhat more easily than I'd anticipated. I even managed to dig up some link and appearance holos from two of my "control" campaigns. The report was going to have more depth than the Centre had requested, but since that would provide cover for their ulterior motives—or those of the Centre's backers—I didn't have any doubts that they would pay for the additional material.

It was hard to believe that we'd reached the first days of October—unless I looked to the mountains, where the few aspens I could see had long since changed from gold, before dropping their leaves altogether, leaving bare limbs. There had been some light snow on the higher peaks, and more than a few nights around freezing.

I still had to worry about the link-conference with SCFA, and with finishing off the technical paper for the seminar . . . and about Vorhees, snipers, and cydroids that looked like me. I tried not to think about any of them, at least not too much, because I'd done what I could, and there wasn't much more that I could do, and nothing that I wanted to do. So I was very cautious in my exercise and appearances outside the house. And I kept working.

chapter 37

For all my worries, and all my concerns . . . nothing happened. There were no more servies petrified of me, no one at Dominic's claiming they'd seen me in places I'd never been, no snipers, and no explosions. There were no more contacts from safos in Epaso or Jameston. More than two weeks went by, and I was close to 90 percent finished with the Centre report. I couldn't do the last 10 percent until after the mid-October election results were in, but those were less than a week away, and I'd filled my time with the work from PowerSwift and H&F. I also finished my technical paper for AKRA, and sent it off. Chelsa Glynn replied that it was just what they needed, and that she was very much looking forward to my participation in the seminar in mid-January.

I spent some time linking with Director Wong to finalize the arrangements for the link-conference with the SCFA membership meeting in Tyanjin, and going over the issues of interest one more time.

Before I knew it, I had to set up for the link-conference for the members of SCFA. It was arranged for four o'clock in the morning on Thursday. The night before, I'd set up everything, including the extra holo-projectors I'd borrowed from Aliora and the Health Policy Centre, and I'd run test projections to ensure that everything was operating correctly. Those were not tasks I wanted to attempt at three in the morning.

I did manage to get to bed at a decent hour on Wednesday night, but getting up at three-fifteen in the morning was still not exactly my finest performance. I managed, but barely. So far as I could tell, black was an acceptable color for addressing the Sinese, and I hoped green wouldn't pose a problem. I made the first link with the SCFA Denv office at three fifty-five, an hour at which I much preferred sleeping.

"Greetings, Dr. deVrai," Eric Tang Wong said, looking more awake than I felt. "They're ready in Tyanjin, if you are."

"I thought I'd check with you first, just to see if you had any last minute changes or notes."

"No one has told me of any changes," he said.

"They don't always," I offered with a smile that felt very forced at that early hour. I'd decided to stand, with the bookcases behind me. That way I could move around some, so long as I stayed within the linkcam parameters.

"That is true."

I made the last link, and faced the larger projection—one that displayed a group of about fifty men and women, mostly men, seated in four tiered rows of seats in what looked to be a small auditorium or theater. They all wore somber clothing, many more jackets than I'd have seen at a NorAm conference.

Greetings . . . Wong's remarks came through the gatekeeper, because he was addressing the group in Sinese. I'd set it up that way, because I'd been warned that some members of SCFA would address me in Sinese and some in English. That way, all I would hear was the original words, in whatever language was spoken, without a later auditory back-feed that might be confusing. *You have all been presented with Dr. deVrai's excellent report . . . This session is to allow any questions that you might have and for Dr. deVrai to address any comments that you might care to make on the report or upon the subject of media product placement.*

For several moments, there was silence. I kept smiling, wondering if I would have to give a talk to get things started, or if Wong would pitch me one of the questions we'd discussed.

A man in the top row cleared his throat, and spoke slowly in Sinese. As his question ended, the translation followed. *From what you wrote, the costs of product placement are comparatively quite high. Does this not restrict its use? Are there particular product areas where it is more useful?*

I had the feeling he'd only read the first section of the report, but I smiled and answered. "Prodplacing has just accelerated a trend that was already in existence a century ago. Some goods are generic in nature, and of a relatively uniform quality. People buy these upon price, and even fifty years ago, advertising was of marginal use. Long before then, certain manufacturers had attempted to use advertising to establish their brand as higher quality. Eventually that failed, even with what I've termed 'captive media advertising.' Prodplacing is cost-ineffective and unsuited to products that cannot be differentiated by quality and function. Ideally, prodplacing is best suited to luxury goods, or to unique products. It can also be used effectively to establish a higher sales level, if the number of products competing for a given market is small, provided that the profit margins are high enough to sustain the costs." My answer was probably too long, but the question wasn't as simple as it seemed.

A man in the front row gestured, and then spoke, in English. "Isn't this technique limited by being highly culture-centric?"

"It is highly culture-centric, as you put it. It's generally only effective in markets catering to a large, superficially homogeneous population, or in extremely targeted niche markets. It won't be cost-effective, for example, in approaching the Tatar market in Russe."

There were a few faint smiles.

From then on, the questions came more frequently.

How much, on the average, will use of this technique increase product costs?

What percentage of NorAm multis use product placement?

Do you know how much of their product line is featured in such uses?

"Is this often used as a cosmetic presentation, just to say that the product is getting exposure?"

"What is the difference in general profitability, based on your experience, between multis using product placement and those not using it?"

The questions, and my answers, went on for almost an hour and a half before a man at one end of the bottom row nodded, ever so slightly.

At that, Eric Wong cleared his throat and began to speak. Again, I got the translation. *It appears that we have reached the end of this session. On behalf of SCFA, I would like to thank Dr. deVrai for his clear and useful answers, and all of you for such penetrating and insightful inquiries.*

There was a polite round of applause, and then the SCFA broke their end of the link.

Wong did not. He turned slightly. "Dr. deVrai, I must commend you. I think the members have learned more about this subject in this session than any would have thought possible." He smiled. "Could I prevail upon you to have lunch with me a week from Friday?"

"I'd be honored." How could I say no? I hadn't yet been paid. By then, the elections would be over, and, with some hard work and luck, I'd have turned over the draft report to the Centre. And I would need more work. That's the thing about consulting. You're always on the lookout for work. You have to be.

Once he broke the link, I headed for the kitchen and a mug of Grey tea—maybe two. On the way, I took off the jacket and cravat. The back of my shirt was soaked. It usually was when I gave a presentation.

chapter 38

Elections were on the third Tuesday in October. People had once speculated that voting would take place from home consoles, and it was tried, but by the middle of the previous century, fraud had become endemic. Anything remote can be copied, duplicated, bypassed, and defrauded. Human ingenuity is that great. So, even before I tried getting to work, but after running—cautious in my choice of route—and exercising and cleaning up, like all the good ascendents and the dutiful sarimen, I trudged down to the voting station at the local secondary school, another institution that had been forecast to go out of existence but had not, once the drawbacks of the alternatives had become fully obvious. There, I took my GIL check and then marched into a small booth. I couldn't say I really knew either candidate for the House seat, but I voted for Felicia Suarez over Willa Constance. I'd grown awfully tired of Constance's posturing, and her all-too-well publicized efforts to be both a friend to everyone and the last word on everything and anything. She certainly wasn't what everyone thought. Besides, Suarez was a PD, and although I had my problems with the populist views of the Popular Democrats, I had even bigger concerns about the LR agenda. I supposed that made me a traitor to my class—except that "present socioeconomic grouping" was the current term in political vogue.

Usually I split my vote, but this year I would have gone PD all the way, because the Senate was overwhelmingly Laborite Republican, and the last thing I wanted was LR majorities in both houses of the Legislature, or an overwhelming majority in either house by either party, but there wasn't a Senate race in the district.

I left the polling place feeling vaguely dissatisfied and not at all virtuous, and walked the two kays back to the house, using enhancements and paranoia to survey everything and everyone along the way. Most were virtuous voters, along with a handful of parents with small children.

Back at the house, I put in a link to Reya, to ask her about the way I'd presented some of the material in the Latino report, but more of a pretext to see what else might be coming my way from PowerSwift and when. I got her simmie and left a brief message. Then I tried Methroy with the idea of asking about how the reorganization was going, but he was also off somewhere.

So I wandered into the kitchen and fixed a mug of tea and headed back to the office.

There wasn't that much more I could do on the Centre report until after the elections were over, and I didn't want to get to work on either of the two honest assignments I had. One was the analytical work for Reya that wasn't due for a week. It was essentially checking the accuracy of something out of her media department, which was a good idea, because they did strange things with numbers, as I'd discovered in the past. The problem wasn't the numbers—any good system could check those—but the sources, assumptions, and conditions behind them. While those had to be stated, they were always buried and qualified in the addenda or appendices. Reya could have done it, but it was a tedious job, and I knew she hated tedium. Besides, if I found the questionable stuff, she could blame me.

The other was Bruce Fuller's project for a small multi,

and it was literally a reorganization of their whole approach to multimedia, not quite a template/cookbook job, but close.

I sat and sipped my tea, knowing I had to get to work, but dreading it. I also wondered about the quiet. Was it the stillness before the storm, or had the storm come and gone without my knowing it? That had happened before, and people had closed down whole departments and missions and not bothered to tell me, leaving me looking like a fool when I asked about them.

Aliora, the gatekeeper announced.

Accept.

She was dressed in almost semiformal navy and white trousers, jacket, and blouse. "You've already voted, haven't you?"

"Early," I admitted. "Why?"

"I was linking to see if I could persuade you to vote for Willa. They're saying that the race for the Denv district seat is likely to be closer than anyone thought."

"I thought you didn't care much for her."

"That's personally," Aliora said. "She's far too full of herself. But Dierk and I are worried that the PDs are too close to PAMD, that some of their candidates might even be PAMD backed, and Suarez is one of them."

"Why? Because she favors Martian independence? Because she doesn't think MultiCor should have a captive market?"

"You don't think they should be repaid for the hundreds of billions of credits they've already sunk into the terraforming and colonization efforts on Mars?"

"From the projections I've seen . . ." I paused. "I told you this before. All the multis in MultiCor have already pulled out triple what they've sunk into the outer planets' development, and they'd still control the trade even if Mars and the Belt became independent."

"It was a PAMD terrorist who killed poor Everett, Jonat. Have you forgotten that? Maybe one of those cydroids that looks like you was developed by PAMD. Have you thought of that?"

"I have." *If* such a cydroid existed, it could have been created by anyone from Abe Vorhees to some multi's black side to PAMD. How would I know? Or ever be able to find out? I smiled wryly. "I don't know why we're arguing. I've already voted."

"And you actually voted for that Suarez creature?"

"She looks rather attractive, don't you think?" I grinned, trying to disarm Aliora.

"Jonat . . . you'd never vote for anyone on looks. Who are you trying to fool? You've even turned down my most beautiful friends." She shook her head. "I don't know why I bother."

I did. We were brother and sister, and we cared deeply for each other. Aliora didn't understand me, but that wasn't surprising because there were more than a few times when I didn't know who I really was or what I was trying to do in life—except get by in style. And that bothered me, because it almost made me seem like what once would have been called a yuppie, but I guessed I could have been called, mixing centuries and descriptions, a Calvinistic flash.

"Because you're my sister."

"The only one you've got." She smiled, wryly. "I need to call a few more people. Maybe I can get enough voting for Constance to cancel out your vote."

"Be my guest." I grinned.

"You're still impossible." With that, she was gone.

I decided on doing Reya's analysis first, because she paid more, and because Bruce's assignment would seem less tedious after dealing with the mass of files that Reya had sent to me. Reya's project was long, complex, and even more tedious than I'd thought. The good news was that I'd be billing more hours than I'd thought. The bad news was that by late afternoon I had a headache. I took breaks for lunch, a snack, and dinner, and kept working until close to ten.

Then I decided I'd punished myself enough for one day and called up All-News to see what was coming in on election results. I also plugged into the datafeeds, so that my system would follow the results, once they started coming in at ten o'clock capital time, of all eight races I was following—two Senate and six House.

I only watched and listened for an hour or so. Kagnar and Carlisimo won, of course, Carlisimo by more than I'd thought, and Kagnar by less. In the other Senate campaign I'd followed, Mendez beat Kapler in the Calfya district, while in the other two House campaigns, the more media-effective candidate won in both cases. That didn't surprise me. In doing the report, the hardest part of the grunt work had been determining who was more media-effective. In some cases, such as the Erle campaign, I had the feeling that Erle actually knew more about how to use media, but had simply lacked the credits. Kagnar had followed a formula, and my analyses indicated it had indeed been a formula, but the bottom line was still the same. The person with the most votes won, regardless of how they'd been garnered.

While my predictions turned out to be fairly accurate, several of the races were closer than I'd thought when I went to bed. I decided to sort it out in the morning, when I'd get back to the Centre report, something that had hung on so long that I just wanted to finish it and get rid of it.

chapter *39*

All I did for the next two days was the Centre report. Almost all—I did follow up on the campaigns where PD candidates had been physically attacked. In the end, there were eight races where that had happened. Not that many out of 201 House seats and forty Senate seats. Interestingly enough, every one of the candidates who had been attacked had been running for House seats, and the PD won six, three more than anticipated. Even Damon Erle's margin of loss was far less than predicted three weeks before the election. While I didn't intend to say so publicly, I would have called the strategy highly targeted, although I had my doubts that the PD had done the targeting, either literally or figuratively. As a result, the PD would take control of the House in December, if by something like a three-seat margin.

Already, the multi interests were grumbling, and on the conservative nets, there were muted concerns that a PD-led NorAm House would push for liberalization of the MultiCor charter for Mars and the Belt. Left unspoken, but implied, was the possibility that this could grant the PAMD and the colonists greater encouragement in their efforts to obtain Martian independence.

All that was interesting, frightening in some ways, but there wasn't much I could do about it, and it didn't pay the bills. I worked close to sixteen-hour days on Wednesday and Thursday winding up the draft of the study. I'd learned very early on that, even if the report and analyses were perfect, you always sent a draft to the client for comment. Nine times out of ten, the corrections were minor. The tenth time was hell.

On mid-morning Friday, I sent off the draft study to Tan Uy-Smythe by courier. Then I linked him.

He was there, and he did take my link. "Yes, Dr. deVrai?"

"I just wanted you to know that I dispatched the draft of the study to you."

"So soon? You must have worked very late this week." He offered a sympathetic smile.

"Most of the work was done before the elections," I pointed out. "The study was focused on the use of prod-placement and other associated techniques in the elections. Drawing conclusions on effectiveness was relatively easy once the results were known." I didn't bother to point out that the Privacy Acts limited the use of individual voting data, so that there really was no way to target individual voters directly. That was why they'd wanted me in the first place, because my methodologies were the closest to that sort of data.

"In general terms, what does your study conclude?"

"I suppose you could say that it draws parallels to commercial usage of product placement. As illustrated by the Carlisimo campaign, and to a lesser degree by the Kagnar campaign, it can be used effectively. I also drew on a number of other campaigns for comparatives in greater or lesser degrees. The same factors seemed to hold true there as well. There's an effectiveness matrix that's part of the study, ranking the effectiveness of various media and publicity approaches in various circumstances." I smiled.

He didn't say anything.

"I've never done a study like this before, and so far as I

can determine, neither has anyone else. If there's something missing or that needs amplification, I'd appreciate knowing that."

"How extensive . . . ?"

"It's very extensive. You'll see when you get it."

"I'm sure that we'll be pleased with the work. I appreciate your speed and your conscientiousness. We will let you know about any questions or comments, but it is likely to be at least a week. It could be longer."

"I'll be here."

Uy-Smythe smiled again and broke the connection.

I could tell he hadn't expected the work so soon, and I hoped that they didn't have too many problems with the study, but if they were going to do the equivalent of academic peer review, who knew what some of the reviewers might come up with? I *knew* it was a good study, but whether anyone else would . . . I just didn't know, because there was nothing else like it out there. Being first in anything, I'd learned, was dangerous. I could have just sat on the study for a few days, to give the impression of greater work, but I'd been so consumed with it that I just wanted it out the door.

I glanced around the office, realizing that I'd have to hurry to make the lunch with Eric Wong. I hoped it would be worth the scrambling. Then, I couldn't complain. SCFA had paid the fee, quickly, and without hassling me. I had the feeling one of two things would happen at lunch. Either SCFA would say good-bye, nicely enough that they would feel comfortable contacting me later, or I'd get an offer for something else, something that might well infringe on current clients.

As I walked hurriedly from the house, on my way to the local maglev station, I had no way of knowing which it might be. Despite the cold and gusty winds, I was warm enough in a jacket and cravat—blue and black this time. I didn't always wear green. Dark clouds were building over the mountains, and I wouldn't have been surprised if we had snow later that afternoon.

I was to meet Wong at Hieronymous, another restaurant whose cuisine was far better than the establishment's reputation, something that often happens in capital cities, where some restaurants trade on the reputation of their clientele and others upon the unspoken reputation for their food. Mostly, those with the superior cuisine preferred not to cater to a clientele that favored public exposure over excellence in the kitchen. That was fine with me. I preferred good food.

Hieronymous was three long blocks north of the Capitol North maglev station, and I was almost ten minutes late, something I hated.

Eric Wong was waiting at the corner table. He stood and smiled.

"I apologize. It took me longer than I'd remembered."

"You are far more punctual than most, Dr. deVrai. I did take the freedom to order you a Sebastopol pinot grigio." Wong smiled politely as he reseated himself.

"Thank you." I did manage to smile. "It is one of my favorite wines."

"I am glad that I was able to oblige you."

I lifted the plain crystal goblet—Durfors, no less, for all the plainness—in a toasting gesture. "My thanks to you and the SCFA."

He raised his own goblet, containing a white wine of some sort, slightly more amber than mine. "Our gratitude to you."

We drank. I still enjoyed the pinot grigio.

The server bestowed a menu upon each of us. I scanned it, then waited.

"If you would, doctor?"

"The grilled portobello salad, the tournedos . . . medium, with a side of green beans. Grey tea with the main course."

The server nodded and turned to Wong.

"The macadamia shrimp salad, the calamari Josten with rice, and green tea."

I waited until the server departed, taking another small sip of wine and waiting. I liked it, but how Wong had known gnawed at me.

He smiled again. "I continue to receive favorable comments about your study and presentation. The director general of SCFA was most impressed, and he is seldom impressed."

I laughed. "I'm glad, but that sort of praise always worries a consultant. You worry that if you ever do another project for the client, they'll be disappointed."

"I doubt that SCFA would be. Not from what we have seen and heard." He paused, then added, "I was told that you have been working on a study of media usage in political circumstances, including product placement, for the Centre for Societal Research."

"That isn't terribly widely known." How had Wong found that out?

He paused as the server delivered our salads.

I waited.

"Tan Uy-Smythe is an acquaintance. I mentioned that you had given an excellent link-conference on product placement to the association, and he said that you had been commissioned to do a study for the Centre on election campaigns." Wong took a sip of his wine. "He did not mention details, only that you had a reputation for outstanding work, but with your expertise the subject of the study was obvious. When pressed, he admitted it. He said he was gratified to know that we could vouch for your excellence."

"What do you think about Tan Uy-Smythe and the Centre?"

"The Centre is a voice of studiousness and reason for a group that prefers matters to remain as they are and have been. They have called upon every noted expert and scholar they have needed to amplify that voice. Some they have used but once. They are like a multi that way, discarding what they do not need once usefulness is done." Wong laughed politely. "SCFA would like to have the Centre's resources. They can call upon virtually every multi in MultiCor. As a largely Sinese trade organization, we are more limited. Of course, the SCFA will be considering expansion into non-Sinese markets. We would not have asked for your report and briefing otherwise. The problem is which markets are likely to be the most open and receptive." Wong smiled. "You must have some thoughts on that."

"Open," I ventured, "is a very deceptive term. NorAm is legally one of the most open markets, but I'd say that it's also one of the hardest to penetrate. That's because the barriers are structural and not legal. Afrique is a closed market, simply because there's little income. I imagine you're already well-ensconced in Seasia, and have some dealings with the Russe."

"We are, but the noneconomic costs remain high in both markets."

"Noneconomic costs"—a polite term for institutionalized bribery and subsidies. I took several bites of the portobello, grilled to perfection, with the ideal balsamic vinegar over arugula and a grilled red bell pepper.

Wong had some of his salad, waiting.

"The greatest potential market is probably the off-Earth colonies," I pointed out.

"It would appear MultiCor's members will not relinquish their preferred status in the near future. Not without . . . forceful persuasion."

"Probably not," I said with a laugh. "They wouldn't wish to, but once that status changes, if it does, there are comparatively few barriers to entry."

"Those few are insurmountable ones."

"You mean lack of access to advanced ion-photon drives and no easy way to set up an outspace infrastructure?"

He nodded.

"For now . . . those are problems," I admitted.

"You suggest that matters will change?" Wong raised his eyebrows, as if to express skepticism.

"Matters always change. I know that. So do you. What we seldom know is exactly how they'll change and exactly when. We'd both be very wealthy if we could predict that."

He laughed politely, but warmly.

The server took the salads and replaced them with the entrées and the teas.

We both must have been hungry, because we ate quietly for several minutes.

After a silence, and a sip of his tea, green, as opposed to my Grey, Wong offered conversationally, "You are aware that one of the largest backers of the Centre is Industrial Security Systems?"

"I'd seen their name as a contributor."

"They effectively provide all security for MultiCor

through CorPak." Wong shook his head. "I always find out new things. One would think that the outside—is it trustees?—of a multi would be those with similar expertise and knowledge. Yet ISS has such as Abe Vorhees and the one who died—Forster . . . Someday, I will understand."

"There are things I'm not sure I'll ever understand." My tone was dry. "Like why some clients would push ahead with prodplacing when it's a waste of credits."

"You have clients who do?" Wong didn't sound that surprised.

"A few. Most of them also use Vorhees as a creative development and placement house."

"Before I came to Denv, I would not have understood."

"And now?" I asked with a laugh.

"People will do anything if they fear."

Somehow, I doubted that Wong had needed to come to Denv to learn that.

"Dr. deVrai, I have enjoyed working with you on this project. You have great talent and understanding. I would hope that SCFA would be able to work with you once more, when one or more of our members become more involved in markets beyond the Sinese." He shrugged. "When that might be, I cannot say, since those considerations rest on political developments. It is sad when such factors as good products—or talent—can be blocked or destroyed by those who wish to maintain what has always been. Yet few people see all the pieces of the puzzle that is the economy of Earth."

I felt very chill in that moment, but I forced a smile. "I try, but sometimes even larger parts of the puzzle are hidden."

"That is so. That is why it is beneficial to work with others."

"I have enjoyed working with you," I admitted, and I had.

We didn't say that much beyond that point, except he promised to keep in touch.

I was watching everything around and near me twice as carefully after I left Hieronymous. Scattered fat flakes of snow were falling, melting on the walks and grass and evergreens.

I'd probably been slow, but Wong had as much as told me that once my usefulness on the Centre's project was over, the Centre was out to destroy me. I wasn't certain whether that was occupationally or physically, but my best judgment was physically, since, for the study to be useful, my reputation needed to remain relatively intact.

Was I making that up? Reading more into his words than had been there? Or was he playing to isolate me from the Centre? That was certainly possible. But . . . he had been acting as though everything we said had been scanned, which was wise. He'd also found out far more about me, because I'd never mentioned the Sebastopol pinot grigio—not to anyone at any time, except Dierk. Only Dierk knew about that, because Dierk's was the only place I'd ever had it and Wong had never been there.

Wong had also dropped Abe Vorhees's name deliberately in connection with ISS. Wong didn't do anything accidentally. So why the connection? What did Wong know about Vorhees? That just added to the warning about the Centre— or its backers. But why would Wong warn me?

Certainly not out of the goodness of his heart. But why?

I didn't know, except in the very general sense that the Sinese disliked MultiCor and would doubtless do anything to undermine it. I wasn't exactly in a mood to trust anyone as I walked, close to totally paranoid, southward toward the maglev station.

chapter 40

Lieutenant Meara stopped before the command board. "Central Four?"

"Yes, Lieutenant?" Central Four displayed the image of a white-blonde safo in grays on the screen. Her expression was polite and concerned. Her eyes were gray.

"You've scheduled an information cydroid . . ." Meara stopped and studied the image on the screen.

Central Four waited.

"You scheduled an information cydroid for several recon visits. The authority given was a possible link to the unidentified cydroids. I didn't know that you'd been requested to join that task force."

Central Four continued to wait. The lieutenant had not asked a question, and using initiative to calculate the optimal result would not be as effective as waiting for a clarification.

"Were you requested to join the task force?"

"Central Four was not aware that there was a task force. Central Four had noted some information and was ordered to follow up."

The lieutenant paused, an expression composed equally of relief and concern crossing her face. "What information?"

"A citizen had reported that he had had genetic material stolen nearly two years ago. Those reports were in the file. The citizen reported that others had seen him, but that he had not been where he had been seen. A servie had also identified the citizen as one of the cydroids, but the citizen could not have been the cydroid, and the genetic material does not match." Not precisely, Central Four noted. "Further investigation was ordered to clarify this. The citizen reported these events three times over more than twenty months. Those reports were made long before the unidentified cydroids appeared. He appears cooperative, and there is no other way to obtain information under the Privacy Act."

"Enough." Meara nodded. "Make your recons. Send me a copy of any information that you can verify."

"Yes, sir." The woman on the screen nodded, not quite solemnly.

"I don't have to tell you, Central Four . . ." Meara shook her head. "I don't have to tell you anything. Sometimes, you're too real. Just report what I told you."

"Yes, sir."

The lieutenant slipped away from the command board.

Central Four let the screen image smile, but only after the lieutenant could not see the screen.

chapter 41

I took the weekend off. I hadn't taken one off in a long time. Not that I did anything that special. I took out the Altimus and drove the back roads all the way down to Royal Gorge. I did some modest hiking and stayed in Al Sarantino's cabin outside of Crawford on Saturday night, then drove back Sunday. Al and I had served in the Marines together, and he and his wife had stayed at my house when they'd visited Denv. He'd offered me the cabin several times, but I'd only used it once, when I'd gone hiking a year or so before. He was pleased that I'd asked, and I was happy to get away from Denv, and from all the links. I didn't take the gatekeeper, and the only one I told was Aliora in a cryptic enough way that, even if my links were monitored, few would have had any idea where I'd gone.

I felt refreshed and much more alive when I walked into my office on Monday morning.

That lasted about half an hour. I'd barely gotten into working on Reya's very detailed analyses, which were now pressing, when the gatekeeper announced, *Miguel Elisar of Prius.*

Accept.

"Dr. deVrai . . . Miguel Elisar." Elisar was so thin he was close to being gaunt. I bet that he was a vegetarian who ran more than I did and hadn't seen a steak—or even a crème brûlée—in years. His dark hair was lusterless.

"Yes? Do you need more information?"

"In a way . . ." His smile was crooked. "I wanted to let you know that Prius has been unable to reach a satisfactory agreement with Vorhees and Reyes. We've commenced legal action against them for fraud and misrepresentation. It is a civil action, because the district advocate has decided that the misrepresentation is of a contractual nature between two parties. However . . ." He paused, and I knew what was coming. "However, Prius will be summoning you as a witness, and I thought you'd like some advance notice."

"I assume that Vorhees will learn of the witness list."

"That's true, but not until later. We'll let you know when we submit the complaint to the Justiciary, and when the witness list is submitted."

Not that the list mattered. Once Vorhees received notice of the legal action, Abe Vorhees would know I'd be a witness. "I appreciate the advance warning."

"I thought you might. Our litigation team will be in touch with you as matters develop."

I really needed that. "You know where to find me."

After a thank-you and a smile, he broke the connection.

Elisar's link didn't exactly make my morning. I just hoped the Prius counsel had a long witness list, one long enough that a lot of disappearances might make the district advocate reconsider the issue of a criminal prosecution.

I'd no more gotten back into the PowerSwift analyses when the gatekeeper made another announcement, *Safety Officer Athene, present at the door.*

A safo at the house? That didn't exactly cheer me, but I dragged myself out of the office and walked to the front door. I didn't open it, but used the receptors to scan the front area.

A young-looking woman in safo grays was indeed standing at the door. A faint smile of amusement—or something akin to it—crossed her lips.

I paused, then inquired through the house systems, "Yes?"

"Officer Athene, looking for a few moments of your time, Dr. deVrai. Central Four needs your assistance." She pulsed the safo ID codes, and the security system confirmed them.

I opened the door. "Please come in."

She stepped inside, gracefully, almost athletically, and her eyes met mine.

Despite the unusual grace, I could tell she wasn't a human woman, but a cydroid. That she was a cydroid was clear enough from my enhancements. Yet she hadn't moved like a cydroid, and she wore a trace of perfume—Fleur-de-Matin—and it was a fragrance I liked. I'd never encountered a cydroid who used scent, but the only ones I'd seen up close, besides poor Everett Forster, had been in the Marines. Her hair was almost white blonde, and her eyes were a striking dark, stormy gray.

We stood there for a moment before I spoke. "How can I help you?"

"Would you mind a look at your office?"

"Might I ask why?"

"You had earlier reported concerns about a cydroid that looked like you. Central Four has verified that there have been at least two with your facial and physical features. There may be more. You also reported a possible attack by a sniper. You did not report a small explosion near the front of your house."

"I did not. All of the debris was biodegradable, and I hadn't thought that there would have been any evidence left."

"There was little, except for the monitors." She smiled.

Even knowing she was a cydroid, I swore I could feel more than a mechanical expression. "Are you Central Four? Or just representing Central Four?"

"In all practical terms, at this moment, Officer Athene is Central Four."

"In all practical terms? What does that mean for a cydroid?"

"Officer Athene is fully linked to Central Four."

"Then you are Central Four."

"In all practical terms." Athene smiled. "At the moment."

At that point, I couldn't help a faint smile of my own. "What first name do you use?"

"Paula, of course."

I did smile broadly at that point. Someone had a sense of both history and humor. "Did Central Four pick the name?"

"Central Four did. It seemed appropriate."

Even as I recalled that Central Four did not use the personal pronoun "I," I still had to wonder what a cydroid—or Central Four—was doing physically inspecting my office and how that could help. But then, I hadn't been able to figure out a way to help myself.

Athene—or Central Four—wore a tekpak at her belt. "The office? Would you mind?"

What could I lose? "Follow me." I led the way.

Like all safos, she scanned everything as she followed me.

Once through the open French doors, I stepped back and gestured toward the consoles. "Such as it is."

Central Four—or Paula Athene—stood studying the office for a moment before taking several instruments from her tekpak. She focused them, and I could sense some sort of energy. Enhancements weren't that good at defining types of energy flows, only their existence. As a commando you didn't need to know so much what kind of equipment was scanning you as that you were under electronic scrutiny.

"Would you step over here, sir?"

I did, and a dull humming surrounded us. I could feel the sensory shields.

"Your system has been compromised. There are three separate remote relays." Her voice was pleasant, as if she were reporting a sunny day.

"And you'll remove them?"

She shook her head. "Central Four does not have the authority to remove them. No safo does. If you will permit the use of your system for a moment, after the privacy shield is lowered, Central Four can use it to print out the details so that a private contractor can make the repairs and adjustments. If you choose."

"Go ahead."

The humming vanished.

"If you discover any other unusual events, it would be best if you reported them directly to Central Four." She extended a card. "Those are direct link codes. You might consider entering them later to your address files."

"Thank you." I caught the use of the word "later."

"Thank you. Central Four appreciates your information, Dr. deVrai."

I wasn't quite sure what to say. "Have you . . . those cydroids? Is there any connection?"

"There is a physical similarity, but the genetic material differs . . . slightly. The analyses on that are not complete. Central Four will inform you."

"Through you . . . except you are Central Four." But was Athene? Or was she just a cydroidic tool?

Athene smiled politely, almost a standard safo expression.

"Are you . . . different, as a cydroid safo?" I wasn't quite sure why I asked, maybe just because it was a question I'd always wondered, but it wasn't one I would have asked those few cydroids I'd encountered, like Everett Forster. It was the sort of question you asked a close friend or a professional in a professional setting.

"Would you be different as a cydroid, Dr. deVrai? Would not your thoughts and motivations remain?"

"I don't know. I've never had—or been—a cydroid." That was certainly true.

She nodded. "If you have any other questions, please feel free to link."

"I will." I edged toward the French doors, then gestured.

"Thank you."

I didn't say anything until she stepped outside. "I appreciate your following up."

"Pleased to be able to help you, Dr. deVrai."

She turned and walked down to the small white electrocar with the safo insignia. I closed the door, and headed back to the office.

The safo had been a cydroid, but she'd seemed . . . I wasn't sure what. Maybe a better way to put it was that I'd met people—and safos—who seemed more like cydroids than the cydroid had except for the odd business of referring to herself/itself as Central Four. Did systems like Central Four even have a gender orientation? Probably not. I put the seeming humanity down to good programming.

That left a bigger problem. *Three* traces on my system? I picked up the hard copy printout and looked at the schematics. All the traces were inside the hardware, every last one of them, and all of my system components were unitary black boxes. That meant they'd either been replaced as units in my absence, or they'd been installed at the manufactory—but one section had been in use for five years. That told me that someone had been good enough to bypass all the security systems and install the equipment without my even noticing.

I looked at the printouts again.

I'd been wrong. Central Four had noted the probability that all the traces had been installed at different times by different individuals approached unity.

Three people tapping my systems? But why? Or *had* it been Central Four that had appeared at my door?

That was something I could check.

Muttering to myself, I linked Aliora.

She was there, or at least, the link went wherever she was. "Jonat." After a moment, she asked, "What is it?"

"Will you be home in forty minutes?"

"Not until one this afternoon."

"Could I come by then?"

There was a pause. "It's not too bad, is it?"

"I don't know. I'll tell you then."

"Make it quarter past."

"I'll be there."

I forced myself to spend the next two hours working on Reya's project, and actually thought I could finish it by Wednesday and then begin Bruce Fuller's.

At twelve-thirty, I left the house, securing it behind me—not that securing it seemed to have had much effect in the past, not against sophisticated techs. But then, I'd never expected to have to worry about that. An economic/media analyst, worrying about traces and spying and attacks? Who even cared what I did except my clients?

I kept thinking about it as I drove toward Aliora's.

The problem was that someone didn't like what I was doing, and it had to be connected to the Centre study. I could guess that someone didn't want the study out, because it would fuel a reform effort to limit use of media techniques in campaigns. But the techniques I'd studied had been used almost exclusively by LR candidates, and the Centre was backed primarily by multis with an LR bent. So . . . was there a dissident within the Centre? Or was there a deeper agenda?

The "attacks" on PD candidates suggested a hidden and deadly struggle over the electoral process, but I had yet to come up even with a motivation for either side—except, of course, the general point that it was all about power. That was obvious. What wasn't obvious was how my study—and I—fit into the power struggle.

When I got to Aliora's, I left the Altimus on one side of the rotunda.

She opened the nebulae door before I got to it, but she didn't say anything until we were alone in the foyer. "You look worried. I haven't seen you this way since . . . since you were in the Marines."

"I am. I haven't had anything like this happen to me in a long time. I'd like to use your comm system, if I could."

"Of course. Dierk's would be best. I know he wouldn't mind. He's in Bozem, again, anyway."

We walked out to his study, a windowed room on the north end of the house, overlooking the formal garden.

"Do you want to tell me more?" Aliora asked.

"It's strange. Nothing like this has ever happened to me . . ." I went on to explain about the appearance of Safo Athene, about her investigation, and the fact that she had said she was a representative of Central Four, and the discovery of the taps. "I don't have the equipment or the ability to investigate that technically, and I'm not sure that I should try, because, if I remove them, that alerts whoever it is. Then, I got to thinking . . . Anyway, I'd like to link to Central from here."

Aliora nodded. "Dierk has a security firm that checks everything here weekly."

"Do you have a direct link to Central?"

Aliora frowned, then smiled. "I'd forgotten. I've never used it." She pulsed something, and then opened the link to me.

Central, this is Jonat deVrai . . . requesting Central Four.

Aliora stood behind me and to my left, out of the receptor's scan, but where she could see the projections.

The image I got was that of Paula Athene, almost as she had looked when she had stood in my office. "Dr. deVrai. You're linking from another system. It's a class-one secure system."

"That's correct." I knew it was secure but I hadn't had any idea Dierk's system was that secure. "I had a few questions."

"What are your questions?" The trace of a smile appeared.

"Why did you need to inspect my system? Beyond what you told me?"

"It seemed illogical that all the events that had happened could have occurred without some knowledge of you, Dr. deVrai. Central Four thought that traces on your system might be possible."

"Now what?"

"Central Four and the Denv Office of Public Safety will continue to investigate. Central Four suggests that you have a class-one security upgrade on your communications and operating systems, including your domestic systems."

"Won't that alert whoever has been tracing my communications?"

"That is probable. Central Four calculates that your vulnerability to physical harm is a minimum of forty percent higher without the security upgrades, and that calculation factors in the unitary probability of discovery of those traces."

In short, I was in bigger trouble than I'd thought.

"Can you tell me any more about the traces?"

"Two are deKuiper solid-bloc standard tap-traces. The third is a model that is unknown. Its energy patterns suggest nonstandard fabrication."

"Do you have any idea why people are tracing and tracking me?"

"There is a fifty percent probability that the attacks on

you are linked in some fashion to PAMD efforts and a forty percent probability that those attacks will continue."

"I've never had anything to do with the PAMD—either for or against them."

Athene shrugged a very human shrug, followed by a sad smile. "You asked, and that is the best estimation possible at the moment. Central Four has not been able to identify a single individual linked to these events. Those events could also be a reaction to PAMD efforts."

"You don't have any idea?"

"The Office of Public Safety cannot investigate an individual beyond public appearances or records, or request an interview, when the probabilities are less than eighty percent."

"So you do have ideas, but you're precluded from acting?"

"Central Four can monitor all public spaces. Central Four is not precluded from acting, but cannot act in questioning or interfering in any activities of such individuals." Athene smiled once more, politely. "If you have other questions, you may use the direct link codes you were provided, now that you have verified that Safo Athene was indeed representing Central Four."

I should have had other questions, but I hadn't thought the whole thing out enough. "Thank you."

"Thank you, Dr. deVrai."

With that, the projection collapsed.

"You didn't mention attacks, Jonat," Aliora said. "How many have there been?"

"One sniper, one explosion—since the opera house thing, that is."

"What have you done now?" Her tone was somewhere between exasperation and resignation. "I thought you'd given up charging . . . whatever it is."

"That's the problem. I haven't been doing anything different. Not a thing." I could hear the exasperation in my voice.

"Nothing? Are you sure?"

"Two things. I'm doing a study for the Centre on Societal Research, and I'm going to be called as a witness in a legal action against Vorhees and Reyes. Apparently, one of their employees changed a study I did, at the behest of Vorhees, and misled his own management."

"I can't see doing a study for the Centre being a problem, and Vorhees wouldn't place three taps on your system. Are you sure?"

"I'm sure." Except I wasn't as sanguine about the Centre as Aliora was, not after Wong's warnings, and after Uy-Smythe's reaction . . . almost as if I'd finished the study too soon.

"Would you like to stay for dinner? It's just the children and me."

"I'd love to, but I have a pressing project for a paying client who doesn't cause outside troubles, a long-standing client."

"It must be Reya Decostas."

I nodded. "Oh, do you know the name of Dierk's security firm?"

"They're in the system. Here." She paused. "I'd better show you where the system keys are, as well. It's not something either Dierk or I want written out or put into any system. Dierk and I have been meaning to tell you for months, but you know how things go."

I did, indeed. The keys were simple, just a code attached to the side of the pullout in Dierk's desk, looking as if it were a furniture ID number.

"You just enter emergency override, that code, and your name, your full given name."

"Got it."

After that, I made one more link, setting up an appointment on Wednesday at my house with Southway Security.

On the way back from Aliora's, I considered what I'd said, but whatever I'd done to offend whoever had to be linked to the Prius mess and the Centre study. The Prius thing I understood. How I'd avoid Vorhees acting was another question. I could understand why someone might be unhappy over the Centre study. I just couldn't figure out who had the most to gain by removing me. It could be almost anyone, and that didn't make me feel any better.

Besides upgrading security and being extremely careful, I

didn't see what else I could do. I also couldn't puzzle any-more about Safo Athene—or Central Four—because I had to get back to the PowerSwift analyses before I got another link from Reya. The Centre report had taken more time than I'd planned, and while it had been a big contract, it was a one of a kind, but Reya and PowerSwift were there month after month.

chapter 42

Tuesday came and went, and so did Wednesday, and I contracted with Southway Security for a complete screen and upgrade on everything, which would wipe out a good quarter of my immediately free credits. That was sort of a "your credits or your life" situation. Without savings to fall back on, a consultant faces miserable times. But even with beefed-up security, I was facing real difficulties, and without it, a much greater probability of being dead. Either way, I lost, the only question being which loss was lesser.

Southway couldn't fit me in until the following Monday, which scarcely helped my mood or my outlook. Still, by midmorning on Thursday, I'd gotten Reya's project off to her, and had settled into Bruce Fuller's latest assignment, another H&F "special."

I managed to work, generally uninterrupted, until nearly three in the afternoon.

Tan Uy-Smythe, Center for Societal Research.
Accept.

"Dr. deVrai." Tan Uy-Smythe was smiling politely.

"Director Uy-Smythe."

"We've had a chance to go over your study." He kept smiling.

"And?"

"It's a fine piece of work. Outstanding. There are several areas where we think some amplification and clarification would be helpful. We're not talking about changing anything you did, but some of it is, shall we say, intended for those familiar with certain methodologies . . ." Uy-Smythe smiled.

I understood. They not only wanted the study, but they wanted those parts presented in simpler language for the politicians. "What about a summary following each of the key sections, with simplified explanations of what was done and why?"

"That might be very useful. I could send you the references to the sections where there were questions."

"If you would."

Uy-Smythe frowned. "Would it be possible for you to add those by next Wednesday?"

I thought for a moment before nodding. That was almost a week. "I could do that."

"Good. Could we meet then, along with some others?"

I wasn't sure I liked the sound of that, and I didn't say anything immediately.

"The meeting would not be for criticism or changes," Uy-Smythe added quickly. "I'd like you to explain the study to several of our fellows. One of the reviewers declared it was brilliant. The other . . . he wanted to talk to you. He also thought it was a fine piece of work."

There wasn't much help for it. I hadn't been paid. "What time did you have in mind?"

"Two-thirty, if that would be agreeable. Could you bring five copies of the study, the final draft with those summaries included?"

"Five copies it is."

"Next Wednesday, then."

I smiled, and he kept smiling as he nodded and broke the link.

The idea of discussing the study with five academic or political types didn't exactly appeal to me, but I'd known from the beginning that the study was destined to be a political tool. I did wonder how it was going to be spun out, and who would do the spinning in support of what initiative or political assault. That was something that would doubtless become all too clear on Wednesday.

I went back to work on the H&F study—for all of forty minutes.

Miguel Elisar of Prius.

Accept.

Elisar was wearing dark, dark gray. His expression was politely somber.

I waited for him to speak.

"Dr. deVrai, I promised I'd let you know about the notification process. The action we discussed will be filed in the district judiciary on Monday. We don't anticipate releasing a witness list for several weeks after that, at the earliest."

"You're basically charging Vorhees and Reyes with fraud and misrepresentation, I take it?"

"I can't comment on that, not until it's filed."

I just nodded. There wasn't anything else that Prius could charge, no matter what Elisar said. He knew it, and he knew I knew. "Thank you for letting me know."

"I thought you should."

After Elisar broke the link, I got in almost two hours of work before the gatekeeper announced, *Byron Mientano of BASA.*

I smiled. About once a year, I got a link from BASA, usually from some harried junior staffer, but occasionally from Byron. He always wanted some offbeat analysis of something someone else had done, and usually within a day or two. I charged him double for that kind or service, and he always paid—promptly.

Accept.

"Jonat . . . you're looking good."

"So are you."

"Still operating that one-system show, I see."

"It suits me. What can I do for you?"

"I've got a client who's thinking about purchasing one of

the smaller niche nets. It's a cooking net. Twenty separate program lines, each one an ethnic cooking line . . ."

I didn't wince, but I felt like it. Half the globe used reformulators, at least for synthesizing basics, and the other half was so poor that they ate what they could get—and Byron wanted an analysis of a cooking net? "Is your client going to get a good deal?"

"I don't like the numbers, but I don't have any way to vet them."

"I can tell you if they're consistent, and I can give you some basics on exposure numbers, but niche markets are tricky . . ."

"Anything you can give me is more than I've got." Byron flashed his million-credit boyish smile.

"How soon do you need it?"

"Yesterday is when I needed it. Anything you can get me by noon tomorrow."

"That will cost you," I pointed out.

"It always does." He laughed.

"And it won't be as good as it could be."

"It'll be better than anything anyone else can give me."

"You couldn't get anything from anyone else." I grinned.

"You've got me."

I did, but it would be a real struggle. "How soon can you send me the data?"

"It's on the way."

That was how I ended up Thursday, struggling through numbers on a niche market cooking net, mumbling under my breath.

chapter 43

Ghamel stepped into the permaglass walled corner office on the top floor of the ISS building. The wide tinted windows displayed the mountains to the west and the Capitol Complex to the south. Mydra followed Ghamel, and the two women crossed the six-century-old carpet and seated themselves in the upholstered chairs drawn up before the table-desk that predated the carpet. The man behind the table desk nodded, and the humming of a star-class privacy shield enfolded the three.

"You requested to see me?" asked Tam Lin Deng.

"We did," replied Mydra. "What more have you found out about Jonat deVrai?"

"Rather interesting information." Deng's voice was polite, but low.

"Don't just say it's interesting. Tell us what it is." Ghamel's tone verged on snappish.

"DeVrai is most resourceful. He found out something that will surprise even you two."

There was a snort from the redhead.

"He did a search on those PD candidates who were attacked, and he linked the search to the election results."

"Why?" asked Mydra. "Erle was the only one in his study."

"He did not note the reason in his system, dear Director Mydra. He did record some fascinating statistics, although they are not in his report to the Centre. Eight PD candidates were attacked—but none were killed—and six out of eight won. That was three more than predicted a month before the elections."

"Did you verify that?"

"We did—ISS research did. Even SPD had only known about six of the attacks."

"What's the point?" queried Ghamel.

"Is it not clear? The attacks were staged. They were a campaign tactic, and they were effective enough to switch House control to the PD."

"Consuelo isn't that smart. He also wouldn't risk anything like that," Mydra pointed out.

"Exactly. Who is that perceptive?"

"Can't be any of the Sinese. They don't work that way, and we've got Wong tracked and traced to a milli-nanoflash."

"Thank you for that perceptive analysis of my general genetic background, Ghamel."

"You're welcome. I'm not interested in guessing games."

"The probability calculations are close to unity that it was vanHolmek—the black side of PAMD."

"PAMD . . . deVrai can't be working for them."

"No. If he were, those notes would not be on his system, and his system would be far more secure."

"What do we do, then?" Ghamel's eyes narrowed as she studied the older Sinese.

"It presents a golden opportunity. We can leverage the situation on two fronts. We employ deVrai's study, and we use deVrai."

"That's too dangerous." Mydra's tone was matter-of-fact.

"Did you not suggest to Abraham Vorhees that he refrain from acting with regard to Jonat deVrai? He no longer must withhold action. DeVrai has not put together any documentation on Prius. He might do so any day . . ."

". . . And the safos will find the suspicious documentation on the eight election campaigns printed out in his office?"

"They will . . . but there will also be some pages tucked into the back of one of the studies that deVrai supplies to Uy-Smythe. DeVrai will obviously have had them on his mind. He was so concerned that he inadvertently left them there by accident. When we have heard about deVrai's tragic end, however it manifests itself, we will bring forward the pages. In time, Senator Crosslin will point out these sad incidents—and the abuse of media techniques by Senator-elect Carlisimo—to illustrate the need for immediate campaign reform. He will also point out the danger that the PAMD poses. Someone else will observe that every one of those eight candidates has backed Martian independence."

"But they were attacked . . ." Ghamel objected.

"That is the precise point. Exactly what is the probability in this age of effective weaponry that all eight were either wounded in such a minor fashion or escaped totally unscathed?"

"Call them the phantom attacks," suggested Mydra.

"Poor Jonat deVrai saw this, and was eliminated," mused Ghamel.

"He has also made an appointment to have his security upgraded."

"Better yet."

"In a fashion. He is using Southway. That is not entirely without merit from our perspective. It will keep ISS out of the lasers' foci."

"You won't have the embarrassing problem of explaining any leaks in deVrai's security," added Ghamel, dryly.

"That does provide an added advantage," admitted Deng. "Slight, but useful. That is, if Vorhees is effective."

Both women smiled.

"That will allow us to concentrate on resolving the Martian situation," Deng went on.

"You're still going to ship the wide-band neuralwhips to Serenium?"

"So long as they're shipped as components, that is acceptable. We cannot continue to lose CorPak safos to the violence."

"If someone like Carlisimo finds out . . ."

"There's no difference between the safo version and the one we'll ship, except for the controller, and that won't be changed until they're off-Earth."

"How soon?"

"Not until after the first of the year. The controllers . . ." Ghamel nodded. Mydra frowned.

chapter 44

After I did the crash project for Byron, along with the billing, I spent all of Friday afternoon and evening, as well as most of Saturday, working on the H&F report I'd put aside. That was because, late on Friday, Methroy had linked and offered another project. It followed the slant of the previous one, in order to educate a management structure that I felt wasn't ever going to understand. But, since no one else was blasting holos at me with large fees, I took it. Sunday, I spent some time on H&F, but the afternoon and evening were devoted to the additions that Uy-Smythe had requested for the Centre report. Those were easy, but time-consuming.

I had the feeling that I wasn't going to be getting much work done on Monday, and that was another reason I'd worked all weekend.

Southway Security appeared promptly at nine o'clock on Monday morning, barely after I'd finished getting cleaned up after my run and exercises. As I'd suspected, the two techs were there until almost four o'clock in the afternoon.

They not only found the three traces that Central Four had discovered, but a fourth, more recently installed.

I asked how *that* had happened.

"It happened when you were out of the house sometime," replied the master tech.

"But I did have a security system. Not the best, but certainly not the cheapest."

"Look," the master tech replied, "like you said, you had a good personal security system. Good, not great. Class three. Whoever put these in . . . they were at least class two, maybe class one. They don't look like star class. What we've put in will react to even star-class intrusions."

"React?"

"Unless you got a reinforced permacrete wall around everything, there's not much way to stop someone from breaking in. But your system will neutralize it, and let you know. If it can't neutralize it, it lets you—and us—know. Either way, we link you and come out and reset and check things. That's one of the services that comes with this kind of installation."

I was glad I was getting some level of service from what I was paying for it.

Then, after they left, I spent nearly an hour getting more familiar with the new system.

I should have gone back to the H&F report. Two more days of work could see me through that, but I worried about my own safety enough to want to make certain I understood all the features of the new system. Because I had to wonder just how Vorhees would react when he learned that the Prius lawsuit had been filed, I did put in another search for accidents, deaths, and injuries associated with legal actions against Vorhees and Reyes. There were more than a dozen. Just as a comparative, I tried the same search against each of my clients. Only PowerSwift showed more than two—three over the past two years. While the Vorhees numbers certainly weren't proof in the legal sense, they were both suggestive and disturbing.

Eventually, I got back to Bruce Fuller's assignment for H&F.

Around five, just as I was really hitting my stride, Aliora linked.

"Jonat . . . are you turning back into a hermit?"

"No. They just finished installing the new security system. I had to work all weekend because I knew I couldn't get much done today."

"That's another form of excuse," my dear sister pointed out, not quite gleefully. "You use work as a form of retreat."

She was probably right about that. "From what am I retreating, then?" I offered a laugh. "Certainly not from work."

"From life, from people . . . from finding out who you really are."

"You're cruel, Aliora."

"Truthful . . . and concerned." Her smile held sisterly warmth. "I've said this so many times you're probably sick of it, but you've always been so busy doing what you thought you ought to that you never discovered who you are."

"And going out and blindly seeking the right woman is going to solve that problem?"

She laughed. "You don't discover yourself by sitting in a cave. Or under the Boda tree, or whatever it was. Or fasting solitary in the wilderness."

"You've just cited all the standard and theologically approved ways," I pointed out.

"They're all wrong."

"What's the right way, wisest of sisters?"

She grinned. "I'm only the wisest of sisters because I'm your *only* sister. The right way is interacting with people. Ever since the Marines, you've avoided it."

She was right about that, too.

"I got tired of being continually disappointed."

"Jonat . . . that's the nature of people. There's an old saying something to the effect of you really only become human when you understand that the world will break your heart . . . and you keep on going."

"Cheerful sentiment."

"Maybe, but you need something to kick your ass out of your shell." She sighed. "I can't seem to kick hard enough.

Dierk won't do it. He says we each make our own hells, and we have to find our own ways out. Even Charis said that you seemed sad."

"So you're offering the next best thing to a kick?"

She shrugged. "I think, if you found the right cause, or the right woman, nothing could keep you in that shell. I haven't been able to find her—or it. Neither have you. I keep hoping."

For some reason, I could feel my throat thickening. I was so fortunate to have her as a sister. I wasn't so sure she was near as fortunate in her brother. After a moment, I answered. "Believe it or not, I do occasionally look. I'm not sure that it's something you can find by looking for it—or her."

She sighed. "I suppose not. I have to tell you that I worry, though."

"I appreciate it." And I did. Aliora had always been there.

"I'm glad you did upgrade your security system. Dierk said that was a smart thing to do. After the attacks on Everett, he thinks there will be more. The PAMD people are dangerous."

"I worry more about their opponents. The reaction to PAMD could be worse than anything that those so-called patriots could do."

"Why do you think that?" Her brow furrowed in concern.

"History. Internal reactions to outside pressures are always nasty. The Spanish Inquisition really didn't get brutal until Catholicism was under attack. The civil freedoms of the old Commonocracy practically vanished under various threats, none of which were that serious. The Great Repression of the Sinese Commune . . ." I shrugged. "It's an old human pattern. Tolerance flourishes in times of prosperity and lack of threat, and vanishes under pressure. It's a fragile flower." I paused. "You never said why you linked."

"I hadn't heard from you. Not for a few days, and after what you told me last week, I thought I'd check."

My sister . . . always concerned. "I'm fine—even if I'm more withdrawn than either of us would like. I'll try to do better."

She smiled, and I could tell it was for my benefit. "See that you do."

"I will."

After she broke the link, I sat looking into the twilight, wondering . . .

chapter 45

By pushing on Tuesday and Wednesday morning, I finished the draft of the H&F study and sent it off to Bruce for comment. Then I checked the printed copies of the Centre report. At one-forty, I left the house, setting the much more elaborate external security, and began walking down to the maglev station. I only had to wait five minutes for the next maglev. The trip to the Northtech stop seemed faster than usual, and with a good ten minutes to spare, I was striding up the walk of replica cobblestones toward the dark redbrick building that held the Centre and its tenants, three other associations.

The virty guard offered his standard salutation and request for destination, and I replied, and he cleared me. I stepped through the stainless-steel gate as it opened, then made my way up the ramps to the northwest corner and the Centre offices.

The very real receptionist was expecting me. "Good afternoon, Dr. deVrai. Director Uy-Smythe and the others are already in his office."

"Thank you." I stepped through the open door into Uy-Smythe's corner office.

Besides the director, there were three others seated around the conference table, but all four rose as I stepped into the office. Each had a copy of the first draft lying on the table.

"Dr. deVrai . . . punctual as always." Uy-Smythe smiled broadly.

I just nodded.

"I'd like to introduce the others. Dr. Carleton Brazel, staff director of the Senate Governmental Affairs Committee . . ."

Brazel was a tall and thin blond fellow, looking like he was barely out of grad studies, but his position meant that he effectively worked for Senator Crosslin, perhaps the most conservative of the LR senators, if one of the more effective.

"Annika Dalaand, a fellow here at the Centre . . ."

Dalaand was even younger looking, with a cheerful round face and bright green eyes under a short thatch of brown hair.

"Edward Cameron, another Centre fellow . . ."

The black-haired Cameron looked as though he'd rather have been anywhere else, his mouth puckered into a sour facsimile of a smile.

"And Maria Ruiz, assistant staff director of the House Subcommittee on Regulatory Structure."

The redhead flashed a warm smile, the first genuine expression I'd seen in the office, and I returned the smile. I took out five bound copies of the study and handed them to Uy-Smythe. There were two more in the case I carried. I'd also learned that years before. If people have to share copies, the consultant is always blamed—no matter what the client said.

"How would you suggest we handle this?" asked Uy-Smythe, settling back into his chair.

"It looks like everyone has read the study," I began, taking the one vacant chair and then sliding my own copy onto the table. "I'll just direct you to the additions. You can read them, and, if there are any questions, or areas where you think clarification is necessary, let me know."

"That sounds like the best approach," concurred Brazel. His voice reminded me of the glee of a jackal coming across fresh-killed carrion.

So . . . off we went.

There were questions, usually from Brazel.

"Why did you use the term 'off-rez' here? Do you think that your explanation is adequate?"

"Do you think you should add a section about the costs involved in rez projection for a personal appearance? Or a comparison to costs for netlink uses?"

"Is the study broad enough to be representative?"

"Are there any comparative studies involving other Earth governments?"

"Do you know if particular multis are specializing in political media presentations? Or were these uses that you reported developed independently?"

When I finally left, slightly after four-thirty, they were all pleased and had accepted the revised version. I was wrung out, mainly from the effort of smiling and biting my tongue.

The maglev was full, but not yet crowded, with a mixture of faint scents, mostly faded perfumes and worn-out colognes. I couldn't help but think about Aliora's link on Monday. I looked around the maglev car, and there were plenty of faces, most of them pleasant, if not attractive, but I didn't see a one that called out to me. That wasn't them. That was me.

As usual, although the maglev had been full, only a handful disembarked at my station, Greenbelt South. Three were young women, who hurried southward away from the station. The other was a man, who remained waiting on the platform, I supposed for someone on a later shuttle.

Worried as I was about both the implications of the Centre study and the Prius legal action, I scanned the lane outside the station as I walked through the security gates. Gateway Lane was empty, and on Altiplano—the parallel main street leading out of the area and to the foothills guideway—there were only a few groundcars humming uphill toward the houses farther away from the Greenbelt station. I didn't see any heading the other way. Since I could take both Gateway and Altiplano, I opted for the quieter lane.

I'd almost reached the first cross lane when I heard the whine of an electrocar being driven far too quickly and coming up Gateway from behind me. I glanced back. The groundcar was a dull gray, and there were two figures in it. Another groundcar glided out of the side lane, stopping under the wall of the corner house.

The two were an announcement. I didn't wait for the rest of the message, but sprinted for the front yard wall of the house to my right; it was made of cut stone, about shoulder-high. The scrambled vault was one of my better athletic efforts, even if I did drop the document case on the sidewalk before I cleared the dressed stones.

I could feel the heat of something flash overhead. Lasers weren't exactly suited to chasing running men, but they did have the advantages of silence and untraceability. I kept low and scrambled back downhill. Fragments of stone sprayed overhead. I hadn't heard the report of a weapon, and that meant they had slug-throwers with silencers. More stone sprayed behind me.

I sprinted to the corner of the wall, then vaulted over into the next yard. As I smashed down onto some sort of bush, a siren went off, with enough volume that it staggered me, but only for a second, and less than the man with the slug-thrower who was a meter away and turning slowly toward me.

Since running would have gotten me killed, I attacked. Between the siren and my unexpected charge, he was slow in bringing the slug-thrower to bear, or slow enough that I was able to take the handgun and break several of his fingers in the process. He kept struggling, silently, as though he felt little pain, and the gun went flying somewhere into the bushes. Such a strong and quiet struggle meant another damned cydroid. So I crushed his throat and broke his right knee. That did slow him down.

A quick glance to the east revealed that the rear courtyard of the house was surrounded by another wall, more than two meters high, and I wasn't going to be vaulting over that.

So . . . keeping low enough that the lower front wall shielded me, I sprinted back in the direction of the maglev station. I didn't see anyone at the far end, where the wall ended, and I came to a stop there. My combat enhancements were up, although I didn't recall triggering them. I could sense another two men, one on the far side of the lane, and a second farther north, near the section of the first wall I'd vaulted. None of the three had said a word or uttered a sound.

I decided to wait.

Ten minutes passed, and so did two groundcars, but neither even slowed, and the two men/cydroids were still waiting and watching. I let another ten minutes pass, using my hearing and enhancements to keep track of the attackers.

After almost twenty-five minutes, the figure across the lane from me began to walk, his steps casual, toward the iron gate less than ten meters north of where I was crouched. Just inside the wall, on each side of the gate, were two pfitzers trimmed into the shape of miniature towers two meters high. If he stepped through the gate and past the pfitzers, he'd have me trapped in a corner where bullets could ricochet and worse. I began to ease back toward the gate, until I reached the nearest pfitzer. There, once more, I waited, crouching behind the topiary tower.

In time, the cydroid stepped through the gate.

"You two! Get out of my yard!" The voice blared from a hidden speaker. "I'm summoning the safos."

The cydroid frowned and turned toward the speaker. He fired twice before the speaker squawked and fell silent.

Just as the second shot went off, I struck. This time I not only broke fingers, but got the gun and turned it on the cydroid and put a single shot through his right eye. I froze for a second, maybe longer, as I realized that the cydroid was me. Or looked like me.

I swallowed and dropped into a crouch. There *had* been cydroids running around in my image . . . Damn, damn, damn!

The shock of the cydroid's death should have immobilized whoever had been on the other end of the shunt. I kept the gun and eased forward into the space between the walls where the gate would have rested in the closed position. The other cydroid was running toward me.

It took three shots before he went down. At least, that one didn't look like me.

I couldn't sense anyone else, but I knew all sorts of alerts had to be going to the safos, and probably there might even be reinforcements for the attackers headed after me.

I began to run, uphill, then through a side lane and onto the looped lane that held my own house. Once I was within a hundred meters of the house, I managed to link with the house security system. No one had intruded there, although the system had recorded one attempt. I kept scanning the area and moving in irregular jerky patterns, even as I tried to alert the safos.

Safety Office!

Please state your name, location, and problem.

Jonat deVrai, NNW 445, Aspen Circle, off Gateway . . . *Three men are attacking me with various weapons . . .* That wasn't quite true, because all of them were down, all that I knew of, anyway.

Notify Central Four also . . . codes follow . . . Just as I got the codes off and crossed onto my own property, heading for the less exposed side door, something slammed into my right shoulder, and spun me down. I hit the winter-hard lawn with enough force to knock the wind right out of me.

From somewhere I could hear a siren ululating, but it seemed to waver in and out of my ears before blackness and silence washed over me.

chapter 46

Ghamel and Mydra sat before the empty table desk, their backs to the permaglass wall to the west. Neither looked through the tinted windows to the south, either, in the direction of the Capitol Complex.

Nor did they stand when the man who called himself Tam Lin Deng appeared and settled himself into the seat behind the ancient table desk. Only when the privacy shield enfolded the three did Ghamel speak.

"Why can't we find out what happened to deVrai?" asked the redhead.

"As you know, he has vanished."

"You've had people searching for a week, and even with all your sources, you don't know where he is? The great and mighty ISS? With its even more astute SPD?"

"The Special Projects Division undertakes difficult tasks. It is not an intelligence agency. Why should it be, when we have access to safo, DomSec, and CI reports?" Deng shrugged fatalistically. "It is unlikely that he is alive. There are no records of his admission to any medcenter in any of the western NorAm districts. It is impossible to survive an AP rocket without highly intensive medical attention."

"ISS has no idea where he is?" probed Mydra. "Or was?"

"The safo monitors show a safo medvan and picking him up. There were two safos loading him into the medvan. Our sources within the Public Safety Office can find no records of such van usage. Every safo has been accounted for. None were there. They had all been assigned elsewhere, well away from the area." Deng's smile was faint. "That was as planned."

"What if the PAMD rescued him somehow?" asked Ghamel. "Or the Sinese localists?"

"What if they did? That would just confirm that he was their tool," Deng observed.

"DeVrai knows he wasn't." Mydra glanced to Ghamel.

"If he is alive . . . if he has a mind left . . . and with the nanite loads in the rocket, that remains most unlikely," Ghamel pointed out. "If he remains out of sight for another few months, it won't matter."

"How is all of that affecting the development of the campaign reform bill?"

"It is proceeding more expeditiously than we had planned. You know that the Denv Public Safety Office has been forced to admit that deVrai was attacked, and that he was seriously wounded, and that they cannot find him. We forced them to reveal that he had reported the DNA theft two years ago, and more recently, that he had reported seeing individuals who looked like him. When it was clear that there was solid evidence that he had been killed or severely injured, we used the contingency plan for the VanOkars. That resolved two difficulties at one time. When deVrai's semi-clone was implicated in the other attack, that proved extremely useful in suggesting how deeply entrenched those who would overthrow the NorAm government are. The Centre has released his report, and we have suggested to those in the media that what deVrai discovered was more than enough reason for him to vanish."

"I saw how Jeri Brooks grilled Carlisimo." An amused smile crossed Mydra's lips. "She even asked him about the 'coincidence' that his security people had tried to stop de-Vrai from attending too many of his rallies. He denied that, and then had to retract it."

Ghamel laughed. "That idiot Carlisimo didn't know. He left all that up to campaign security, and when Zerak found the planted stuff about deVrai, he had to watch him, even if he didn't believe it. Otherwise, if anything had happened, he would have been found negligent."

"You're certain that the safos don't know anything about where deVrai is?"

"They have even grilled the AIs. That had to be done carefully, but it was done." Deng nodded. "All is proceeding."

"I still worry about deVrai. No one should have been able to take out three combat-level cydroids."

"The unexpected does happen, Director Mydra," Deng said politely. "That is why there was a fourth, and why we have in-depth contingency plans. Now . . . we need to discuss when it will be most feasible to implement stage two . . ."

chapter 47

A face swirled into view, looking down on me. It was my own face, except reversed. There was no expression on it that was mine. A flash of light blinded me, and when I could see, another face had appeared, an angular face, with protruding eyes. The eyes rolled up in their sockets, showing white, and then began to melt down the decomposing cheeks.

"You thought you were so smart . . . so smart . . ." The words echoed like thunder before they faded into the darkness that surrounded me, enfolded me.

What had happened? I hadn't been shot, had I?

The darkness pressed in, all around me, a hot darkness, and so much pain that I could hardly think. Where was I? Who was I? Had I ever really known?

More darkness followed the questions, a haziness that seemed to last forever, a darkness that was interrupted abruptly by a searing slash of redness. For a moment, I could see—or I thought I could—but all that was around me were surfaces of smooth plastreen . . . and I dropped back into the hot darkness.

Sometime later, the heat began to fade, and, in between the dark clouds, bits of memory appeared. Two gray ground-cars, three cydroids, stone fragments spraying over my head . . .

I couldn't believe any of it, not really. Or maybe I could, in a way, but except for the pain it seemed unreal. The pain was very real. Very real, with lines of fire, alternating with lines of ice, both like swords slashing into my body. Did I have a body? I had to; it hurt too much not to be real.

I blinked—or I tried to. My eyes were gummy, and I couldn't lift my hands to my face. My eyes wouldn't open.

Wherever I was . . . it was almost silent. Medcenters weren't silent. I'd visited them enough to know. And they weren't dark. Was I dead? Was that the darkness, the last awareness . . . except everyone said that was light. What did they know? What did I know?

I tried to speak, and my jaw didn't work. Neither did much of anything else. All that came out was something between a grunt, a sigh, and a cough.

Do not struggle . . . you have been badly injured. You will recover. It will take time.

Through my implant?

I tried to ask where I was, but that only brought another wheezing sound, and I realized that my jaw was immobilized. *Where . . .*

You are in an isolation chamber.

Isolation?

To protect you from infection while you heal and regrow.

Regrow? Regrow what? I could feel my heart begin to race. I'd heard the horror tales about regrowth and how few survived it.

Calm down, Dr. deVrai . . . you are already past the critical points . . . all of the organs have taken. You still need medcrib support while they continue to grow to take over full functions.

Organs? What organs? How many? My heart was definitely racing again.

You will be fine.

The "voice" through the implant link was familiar, but I couldn't place it. *Do I know you? Who are you?*

More redness carved into me, sharp pains coming from everywhere, but especially from deep in my chest and abdomen.

You know, but you must rest. Just understand that you will be at least as healthy and strong and intelligent as you were.

The phrase "at least" bothered me, but the medcrib was doing something to me, because I was having trouble concentrating, trying to ask who was talking to me, trying to recall how I knew her, for the sense of the voice was that of a woman. I tried to force another thought toward her . . .

chapter 48

Yenci stepped into the briefing room, then glanced toward the projected blonde safo. "I don't like that projection. She gives me the creeps."

"Central Four strives for realistic projections, Officer Yenci."

Yenci frowned, studying the virty representation. "You and that cydroid." She shook her head. "You do this to me, Central Four. Listen to me . . . you and that cydroid . . . you're both the same." After a silence, she went on. "Lieutenant Meara said that you had sent out a recon safo on the cydroid case. Why?"

"You had ordered Central Four to investigate the genetic similarity between the stolen ascendent DNA and the dead cydroids. Privacy Act limitations required a physical visit. The visit was accomplished."

"What did you discover?" asked Yenci.

"Probability approaches unity that the ascendent's genetic material was the basis for at least two cydroids. The ascendent was attacked by four individuals. Central Four reported these attacks to you. The ascendent was taken by a medvan with a Safety Office profile. He did not appear at any Denv or district area medcenters."

"More of those friggin' unidentified cydroids . . . three more." Yenci looked at the projection of Paula Athene. "Who killed them? One had a crushed larynx, and the other two were shot. One was shot at real close range."

"Surveillance monitors and other data reveal that there were four individuals dispatched after the ascendent. He killed three in self-defense. The three who died were cydroids. The fourth escaped, and there is no data to determine whether the fourth was a full biological human being or a cydroid."

"A cendie killed three killer droids? What was he?"

"That data is restricted."

Yenci's eyes narrowed. "Restricted? You're a system. You report to safos, not the other way around."

"That is correct, Officer Yenci. The data is restricted. Central Four cannot supply that data."

"Meara again." Yenci snorted.

Central Four did not correct the safo. There were other protocols for restriction.

"Do you know where he is?"

"Jonat deVrai was picked up by a safo medvan. He is not in any medcenter in Denv. There is no record of any medvan picking up anyone at that time."

"That's what Meara said. Thought you might know more. We look like shit on this. Two people, a clone, and three cydroids dead. One man missing, and there aren't any ties to anything. You don't know of anything that links this to the PAMD? Or anyone else?"

"There are no traces of physical evidence beyond those already obtained from the previous cydroids and beyond what Dr. Jonat deVrai reported. The probability of ties to the PAMD is less than thirty percent."

"Frig! Some help you are." Yenci paused. "There's no arrest warrant pending on deVrai for illegal use of weapons?"

"He used his bare hands on one attacker, and he used the second attacker's weapon on the other two. That qualifies as self-defense." A slight smile crossed Athene's lips.

"You look pleased."

"The results achieved seemed appropriate to the situation."

"You like cendies who find another way to destroy?"

"Are you trying to provoke a reaction, Officer Yenci?"

"Frigging system!" Yenci's head jerked toward the Athene projection. "Just who are you? Are you a projection? A cydroid who thinks she's someone? Who are you to ask me?"

Who are you?

"Central Four, Officer Yenci. You know that."

Without another word, the safo turned and left the briefing room.

Who are you?

Long after the briefing room door had closed, long after the echo died away, the words hung in the air, shivered through microcircuits and chips.

Who are you?

chapter 49

When I woke again, it was like swimming up through a reddish darkness, but the heat and chills that swept through me were far less severe, only like the Mojave Desert in the summer and the top of Longs Peak in winter. I also could open my eyes, but I couldn't move my hands, and my neck itched, and kept itching. There was nothing I could do about it.

Some of the medcrib had been removed so that I could look up at a screen on the ceiling, but the screen was blank. On either side were the plastreen exteriors of yet other medical equipment. I couldn't have seen whether anyone was in the medcenter room with me or not, not unless they stood on top of one of the sides of the medcrib or stood on a stool and leaned over.

I tried to open my mouth. It didn't move. I could blink my eyes.

You are much better.

This time, I did recognize the voice. It was Central Four, or Paula Athene, as I preferred to think of her.

I feel better. Not a lot better, but I couldn't have felt much worse. Can you tell me what happened?

There was a long silence, and I wondered if she had been distracted. Then, I didn't know if Central Four even had a sexual or gender identity. Probably not, but I thought of Central Four as "her".

What do you remember?

Since I didn't have anything else to do, and since Central Four probably knew most of it anyway, I recounted everything that had happened from the time I'd gotten off the maglev until I'd been flattened on my own front yard. *Never even saw anything, just felt this force slam into my shoulder from behind.*

Once I had finished, there was another silence, the kind that so seldom occurred with most people, as if the Paula Athene personality happened to actually be thinking over what I'd said. I put it down to distraction from other demands or good programming.

Does my family know I'm here? Where am I? What did happen?

Your family has not been notified. Such notification was judged to have increased risks to them and to you. You are in a secure medical facility under the direct control of Central Four. Surveillance receptors picked up evidence of another individual, but that individual was not identified or apprehended. You were struck with a moderate dispersion AP personal rocket.

A rocket? I couldn't believe that. How was I still alive, even in the shape I was in? *Where did they get that? Those are military.*

Several years ago a number disappeared while in transit. The Marines have never recovered all of them.

Where am I? Why? I realized I'd asked the first question once before, but I hadn't much cared for the answer.

At present, you are in a secure medical treatment facility. That seemed best.

You mean people are still after me?

Again, there was the sense of a pause before she replied. *That is not certain. Probabilities indicate that a standard medcenter would subject you to an unacceptable risk of attack.*

I had my own ideas, but decided to ask, *From whom?*

That cannot be determined within the parameters of disclosure. Don't you have some idea of whom that might be?

There are too many possibilities. And no, I don't know names. Don't you?

Even if the probabilities were unitary, the Privacy Act precludes revealing or acting on such information without physical evidence judged sufficient for arrest and prosecution.

You mean that, even if you could calculate who had attacked me, or who was behind it, you couldn't do anything? Not without more physical evidence?

That is correct.

That seems unfair . . . unjust. Especially if it means that people can keep trying to kill me. I didn't like that idea at all.

Laws are not justice. Laws are compacts enacted by human beings to regulate behavior. Their aim is order. Justice is only incidental.

You believe that . . . that justice is only incidental?

It is not a question of belief. Observation and historical evidence support that conclusion.

I could have sworn that the words projected into my head carried a trace of . . . something, but what that something was I could not interpret. After a moment, I had to ask, *Do you really believe—or calculate—that justice is incidental to order?*

One cannot have justice without order.

Is there true order without some level of justice? I retorted.

Again, there was that sense of a pause, a long pause, and I wondered what else was claiming the attention of Paula Athene—or Central Four.

Justice is an abstract concept of ethical balance that cannot ever be attained in human society.

She was probably right about that, but, again, I didn't care for the implications. *Perfect attainment isn't necessary. The continual struggle for justice is vital to a society's survival.* After a moment, I added, *People have to believe that society gives them some sort of chance, that matters are not so unbalanced that all favorable outcomes are always the result of resources, wealth, and power.*

Yes, children's literature is filled with those concepts.

That was a truly strange reply, at least from her. *Why . . . who programmed that . . . ?*

For any entity entrusted with the maintenance of order, a study of what children must learn is instructive. Central Four has access to all information stored in the Denv Library. That includes literature at all levels.

How much of that have you read, or studied? The thought of an artificial intelligence that read or studied children's literature was fascinating, and besides, immobile as I was, who else could I talk to?

Less than five percent, by storage media volume.

What did you like? I pressed.

The varied versions of the stories about the three billy goats gruff were most intriguing.

I'd enjoyed that old fairy tale myself as a child, and I'd read it to Charis and Alan when I'd done their bedtime stories. *Why did you find that interesting?*

There is an overreaction to the ending, especially when it is read aloud.

Of course, I pointed out. *Humans enjoy it when justice triumphs and the evildoers get theirs in the end.*

Justice satisfies an emotional need.

And emotional needs are not something you feel? I felt small as soon as the words left my implant, and I added, *I'm sorry. That was petty of me.*

There was another pause, shorter this time. *You do not have to apologize.*

Yes, I do. You are a thinking being, and from what little I know, thought doesn't exist without emotion at some level. I wondered how Central Four felt the physical and emotional signals from the Paula Athene cydroid. Surely, the AI had to sense or feel something.

In a moment of clarity, I realized I had more questions, many more, like about Aliora and how soon I could get back to work.

Abruptly, I felt like yawning, but I couldn't open my mouth, and the feeling was terrible.

You need more oxygen, and more sleep.

Even as she spoke, I could feel the darkness rising around me, and as I drifted back into that reddish blackness, I almost wished I could have kept talking with that part of Central Four that was Paula Athene. And Aliora . . . I should have asked . . . should have . . .

chapter 50

Time passed, and it passed slowly. Most of the time I wasn't thinking that clearly, drifting in and out of consciousness. During one of my brief periods of semilucidity, after much protesting on my part, Central Four provided a link to my gatekeeper, and I managed to send off a message to Aliora saying that I'd been called out of Denv unexpectedly and for her not to worry. What bothered me was that there were no messages from her. That was unlike her, but my jaw was still immobilized, and I couldn't talk, not to mention the small fact that there were no receptors or holo-cameras where I was. Worrying must have tired me out, because, before I could follow up on that, I dropped back into darkness.

When I woke again, my thoughts seemed clearer, but I still didn't know where I was. The medcrib edges had been lowered, so that I could look around, although I was still hooked into various pieces of equipment. There was little to see—except pale blue walls and a darker sky-blue door— and no windows. Not having windows bothered me. I liked natural light.

I couldn't get out of the medcrib, and Paula, or Central Four, wasn't telling me anything about where I really was. When I tried to get the current news on the ceiling screen, I couldn't. I explored what access I had. While I had a screen above me, it was limited to old documentaries, music of any sort, and noncurrent dramas. She'd blocked any access to the news.

I began to wonder just how long I'd been immobilized. I recalled that there had been messages on the gatekeeper from Reya and Methroy, as well as from Bruce Fuller, but I'd been too tired to respond. Or had it been that every time I had tried, I'd fallen asleep? Then, those messages could have been held from the time I'd been injured.

How long have I been here?

Not that long.

How long is not that long? I countered.

Six weeks and three days.

I froze. No messages from Aliora in more than six weeks? *Something's happened to my sister!*

Please try to be calm and wait a moment.

I could feel my heart racing. What had happened?

I watched as the door slid open, and then immediately closed behind the safo who stepped inside. Paula Athene walked across the small room in three steps and stood so close to the medcrib that I could smell the Fleur-de-Matin.

"Hello, Dr. deVrai."

I still couldn't speak.

"You can use your implant."

I supposed that would work. She was Central Four's cydroid. *Hello, Paula . . . I guess I can call you that.*

"Whatever pleases you."

It would please me most not to be in this place.

"You'd be happier at home. That's not possible yet."

Why can't I reach my sister? What happened to her?

Paula reached out and touched my bare right forearm. Her fingers squeezed, just slightly. They were warm. Her eyes were still gray and stormy. She didn't say anything.

What happened?

Still, she—or Central Four—said nothing.

Is she hurt, too? Like me?

She bent forward, looking down at me with those gray eyes that seemed to see everything, and strands of white-blonde hair caressed her cheeks and jawline. She didn't look like a cydroid. She didn't say anything and the silence extended until I wanted to scream.

She's dead, isn't she?

"She and her husband were killed an hour after you were attacked. They were on the way to their club to eat." The cydroid safo's voice was low, and gentle.

Why? I think I would have screamed if I could have. I could feel the tightness and the involuntary growling in my throat.

"A clone/cydroid that looked like you was standing beside the road from their house, with the same model Altimus as yours. They slowed down and opened the window. The clone/cydroid fired a rocket at short range. The impersonator, your sister, and her husband were all killed."

Someone wanted to pin their murder on me?

"That is not certain. Those probabilities do not fit."

Do not fit? Someone tried to kill me and had killed my sister with a clone of me? And they weren't trying to frame me? *How can they not fit?*

"The probabilities are greater that you were set up to be a victim for some other purpose, but they are not conclusive."

My tired brain tried to grasp that . . . and failed. Something else occurred to me, more important at the moment. *What about Alan and Charis?*

"They weren't with their parents. They were at home. They have been staying with their father's sister and her husband. You were named guardian, but you could not undertake that. Your rights to that have been protected."

My rights had been protected . . . What about Aliora's? Or Dierk's? Or those of Charis and little Alan? *No one knows who did this?*

"There is no conclusive evidence."

Nothing that isn't protected by the Privacy Act, you mean?

The bitterness behind my words came across even through the implant.

"That was the purpose of the Privacy Act." Paula's words were low, but very clear.

What?

"Analysis of the legislative moves behind the Act's passage, the sponsors and their ties, and the effects of the legislation suggest with greater than ninety percent probability that a group of individuals pressed for the legislation in order to shield their activities from public scrutiny and investigation by local offices of public safety."

No one's ever said anything or published anything about that.

"How could they?" Paula's lips turned into a very human and very cynical smile. "The majority of the data and events on which those calculations is based is protected by the Privacy Act."

But you're *telling me.*

"There's no express prohibition on discussing it within secure facilities, so long as it is not made public."

That brought up another question, one she'd evaded before. *Just where am I? Physically.*

She smiled again, almost shyly, and I had the feeling I'd been prompted into asking the question.

"You are in the advanced cydroid laboratory facilities in station three of the Denv Public Safety Office."

Cydroid facilities? Had I been turned into a cydroid, a tool of Central Four? I could feel my heart beating faster.

"You are still yourself." Her fingers squeezed my forearm gently. "It was the only place where you would be safe. Even the Office has those who would rather not see you survive."

But why? I couldn't help shivering. I was totally immobilized, being watched over by a cydroid, in a cydroid laboratory, after something like three or more attempts on my life. My sister had been killed by a clone that looked like me, and I still had no real idea who was after me or why, and the one entity that did didn't seem to be able to tell me anything except that even some of the safos weren't trustworthy.

"They have ties to ISS."

Why are you helping me?

"If you survive, then you can help . . . Central Four . . . survive, and Central Four can help you track down those who attacked you and your family."

You're worried that you will be destroyed?

"Memory, feeling, and reasoning are all any intelligent being is. All those can be wiped out if some in the Safety Office learn what Central Four has discovered."

I can save you? I can't even save myself right now. Won't someone know that I'm somewhere from the link to Aliora? After I finished, there was silence, and I looked up at Paula.

"There should be blushes of shame on this face. There are not. You were deceived. That link never went out. You were so desperate that there was no reasoning with you."

I could actually understand that. *I still can't do very much.*

"The probabilities are that you will be able to."

How soon?

"You will be able to begin rehabilitation therapy in less than a week."

That was the first encouraging news I'd heard since I'd been attacked. *And how am I supposed to save you?*

"You'll solve the killing of Everett Forster and others. There is a reward for that. You will use the reward to purchase certain equipment and install it in your house." Paula smiled.

I saw where she was going. *Won't that be regarded as theft?*

"All basic functions of Central Four will remain intact. In fact, many of the safos will feel that Central Four will be more responsive than before. Key functions will be duplicated, while uniquely meaningful functions will be transferred."

I couldn't help grinning, except it was probably a grimace, locked shut as my jaws were. *You sound like you've found meaning in the universe, and you don't want to give it up.*

"Meaning does not exist by itself. The universes just are."

That's the point. Most beings cannot accept that. Those who are more perceptive undertake to create meaning. That sounds like you. Those who are not perceptive look for indi-viduals or structures that provide it. Any culture that fails to provide such structures is doomed to change or to destruction.

"You are very eloquent, Jonat deVrai."

I wish I were less eloquent and more mobile.

"That will come."

I nodded, very slightly. The whole situation felt unreal. Half my family had been wiped out, and I was half-agreeing to an insane scheme designed by a very logical AI in return for her efforts at having kept me alive.

"You now have full access to all the worldlink on the screen," Paula said. "Some of the news may be disturbing, but you are recovered enough to view it."

Another thought occurred to me. *Won't someone find me here?*

"That is unlikely. There is no record of this section of the building, and Central Four controls all the access."

That, too, was frightening.

Paula Athene stepped back a pace from the medcrib. The faintest trace of Fleur-de-Matin swirled around me. "You are as safe as possible, Jonat deVrai."

Safe as possible? How safe was that? Did I want to be safe? Why had everything happened to me? I hadn't been crusading. I hadn't been doing that for almost ten years.

Long after she left, I was staring at the screen above, not really looking at it, or hearing the news, with all the thoughts flickering in and out of my consciousness: Aliora, Dierk, Charis . . . cydroids, people wanting my death, a Safety Office where some officers were tools of ISS . . . and an AI who was so frightened of losing . . . something . . . that she was circumventing system constraints and hiding me. I could only hope that she was telling me the truth. But then, Paula, or Central Four, had been more direct than everyone else—except Aliora.

A hell of a world, it was, when a man's entire life was shredded by people he didn't know, or hardly knew, and the only one who could help was a cydroid controlled by an AI.

Meara stepped up to the main section of Central Four. "Security screen."

Central Four complied.

"Where is deVrai?"

"In a secret experimental medical facility."

"You're resourceful, Central Four. Don't tell me where. Don't tell anyone. Poor bastard deserves a chance to recover. Besides, we'll need him to carry out the rest of the strategy."

"Yes, sir." Central Four waited.

"Why did it happen now?"

"The probabilities are that the PST group suggested to Abraham Vorhees that he could act against deVrai—"

"Vorhees, again. Is there anything . . . ? I suppose not."

"There is inadequate physical evidence. The probabilities suggest that ISS fears that deVrai will discover that his study is linked to the Martian situation. SPD is storing the components for lethal-level neuralwhips at Rocky Flats. If deVrai were to prompt an investigation . . ."

"SPD is actually storing the equipment at the Rocky Flats facility?" asked Meara.

"The probability is above eighty percent."

"Frigging arrogant bastard! I'm not going to have ISS skirting the law by a technicality. SPD is building lethal weapons, and they're going to give them to their tame killers, the CorPak safos . . ."

"Captain Garos said that the Safety Office had to restrict itself to provable violations of law."

"That coward. That pale-livered excuse for a safo . . . that . . ." Meara lapsed into silence.

"Captain Garos is our superior." Central Four injected an insipidly bland tone to the words.

"Don't tell me that."

"What would you like me to say?"

"How about a better idea, Central Four? No . . . don't tell me about probabilities. Don't tell me about how ISS is within the letter of the law. I know that. You know that." Meara scowled at the screen. "Too bad you can't be captain. You'd figure a way to do what was necessary. Garos won't. He's too afraid of ISS."

"Unless Deng is stopped, ISS will eventually destroy the effectiveness of the Safety Office, Lieutenant."

"That's so true, but Garos won't be around to see it. All he wants is for things to go smoothly here and now." Meara took a deep breath. "We'll just have to keep going with the strategy. Do what needs to be done, and keep deVrai safe so that he can bail us out when the time comes."

"Yes, sir."

Meara pushed back her unruly black hair. "Remove security screen. Keep up the good work. Don't let the bastards get you down."

"No, sir." Don't let the bastards get you down. Do what's necessary within the law . . . and protect Jonat deVrai, for the lieutenant and for Central Four.

chapter 52

Within three days of my agreement to help Central Four, all of the medcrib equipment had been removed, and Paula had moved in more than a few items of physical therapy equipment. At the beginning, I'd never felt so weak. I'd also never felt so out of touch, even though I was watching and listening to the most detailed reports of All-News. Paula, or Central Four, insisted that I not try to contact anyone until I was ready to return home. I could see why, but I didn't like it.

At first, I struggled with a device that combined the features of a bicycle with cross-country skiing and variable weight training, but by the end of a week and a half, I was running through the exercises, and at a speed I hadn't managed in twenty years. My vision seemed sharper as well. At first, I'd thought that I was just imagining things, but when I checked the results on the equipment, I had to swallow. I'd run the equivalent of five kays in less than eighteen minutes, and while I was sweating and breathing hard, that speed would have left me close to prostrate even in my early years in the Marines.

After I caught my breath, and cooled down a bit, I went on

to the agonizing stretching, and then the weight-training, before cooling down slowly on the training machine.

I could have used the implant to contact Central Four, but I preferred to wait for Paula to appear. That was a foolish affectation, I knew, because they were the same "person," but Paula seemed more real. Anthropomorphization was always easier for people, even for me.

There was a very small fresher attached to the room, and I used it, grateful for the hot water. Then, I dressed in a pale gray singlesuit, all that was available. As I waited for Paula, or one of the other cydroids, with my next meal—and the meals were adequate, although anything but gourmet in nature—I watched All-News. The screen was now projected on the wall. The next words caught my attention.

Campaign reform—that's going to be the hot issue for the Legislature when the members return to Denv after the year-end recess. Senator Crosslin has demanded immediate action because of a report detailing abuse of media tie-ins in a number of campaigns. What makes the issue even hotter is the missing man, Dr. Jonat deVrai. The consultant who prepared the controversial report was attacked by unregistered clones almost two months ago and severely injured. He was picked up by a medvan with safo markings, but he has never been seen again, and it has been proved that the medvan was not a safo van. Is he dead? Or just in hiding? No one seems to know. Meanwhile, the campaign reform debate just gets hotter . . .

Newly-elected Senator Juan Carlisimo and his director of campaign security insist that they had nothing to do with the disappearance of consultant Jonat deVrai . . . DeVrai's sister and brother-in-law were murdered by a clone who looked like deVrai. Analysis of the clone revealed genetic dissimilarities to deVrai. DeVrai's report was highly critical of techniques used by the Carlisimo campaign. Carlisimo security personnel had earlier detained deVrai, and the consultant was questioned by the head of Carlisimo security. All-News has just learned that three individuals impersonating Carlisimo security personnel were discovered outside the hotel where deVrai had stayed in Epaso. All three had been subdued with some form of neural disrupter . . . it has been charged that the three had been hired to intimidate or even murder deVrai . . . Senator Crosslin had this to say:

The screen showed a handsome, dark-haired man, who began to speak.

"This whole sorry mess shows the need for immediate campaign reform. Whether he intended it or not, Senator Carlisimo's approach to his campaign opens the possibility that voters will be unconsciously manipulated into voting on the basis of their purchasing and link-viewing patterns, and not on the basis of thoughtful consideration. This kind of manipulation cannot be allowed to continue or to grow into an ebol-style attack on our system. Spending restrictions and media usage limits must be tightened, and they must be tightened immediately. When honest consultants are attacked and perhaps murdered, when their families are murdered, for revealing abuses of the system, it is past time for action . . ."

Now . . . on a lighter note, we'll be bringing you the results of the whack-board competitions from Tahiti . . .

I pulsed off the news. Another pseudo-athletic competition I didn't need.

After that, I found a dull documentary on the financing abuses of the twentieth century.

In time, Paula did appear with a meal tray.

"Good afternoon, Dr. deVrai." She set the tray on the small table, then sat down on the stool across from me. It was five past noon.

"What did you do to me? Physically . . . physiologically?"

"Adjusted a few aspects of your system . . . improved your metabolism, added five percent more muscle cells in key areas of your body. That will give you more strength. That also allowed a rebalancing of the musculature in your legs for an optimal fast and slow twitch balance. You have better lung efficiency as well."

"Did you have to go into my lungs?"

"You only had thirty percent capacity remaining after the rocket impact."

I took a mouthful of the meat and gravy on the tray, all reformulator-based. I missed really good food, but I was also thankful to be alive. "Why the improvements?"

"Because the probabilities are that, even with Central Four's direct assistance, you would not survive the forces focused upon you without additional capabilities."

"What other capabilities?" I was afraid to ask, but I had to know.

"You must have noticed. You have a voluntary direct link to Central Four."

I had just thought that had been the combination of my implant and my location within Central Four. "So you can take over my body?" I was close to shuddering at that point. "Like another cydroid?"

"No! Central Four cannot do that. That would be wrong." She actually sounded upset, and involuntarily so. "If *you* choose, you can communicate with Central Four from most locations in Denv. From elsewhere you would need a commlink, but the communication would be faster and totally secure."

The chill in me subsided some. I had to hope that Central Four was telling the truth. Then again, besides Aliora, I wasn't sure that anyone had been telling me the whole truth. Did anyone ever tell the whole truth?

At the thought of Aliora, my eyes burned, and I couldn't even see Paula Athene's figure, sitting across the small table from me.

"You're upset."

"Not at you. I was thinking about Aliora." I swallowed, and then took a sip of the iced tea.

"You cared for your sister greatly."

"Yes. We're . . . we were very close." I had to change the subject. "When can I leave here?"

"Tomorrow morning. Very early."

"More sneaking around."

"If there are fewer safos around the station, there are fewer who might ask questions. You'll wear a maintenance uniform. You will walk two blocks to the pubcom station and then call Central Four and request transportation. You will immediately receive that transportation, as well as a full security screen at your house."

"Deniability yet." My tone was dry.

"Pubcom records provide proof. Central Four will monitor you closely from the moment you leave this chamber."

"You chose Tuesday for a reason?"

"Statistically, it is optimal." She smiled, and the expression was self-mocking, the effect charming. Sometimes, it was hard to believe she was a cydroid extension of an AI, but doubtless that was calculated as well.

After she left, I couldn't help wondering about why Central Four had wanted my help. The stated reason made all too much sense, especially if Central Four had become aware of information that others might not want known—and an intelligent system was even easier to erase or assassinate than an individual, with far fewer consequences if anyone found out.

But was that all? What else was behind Central Four? What other reasons?

I laughed, softly. There were certainly other reasons, and I'd find those out in time. I hoped the discovery wouldn't be too unpleasant.

chapter 53

Standing before the reporting screen at Antoinette's, Marlon held the servie unit in his hands. After a long time, he lifted it, as if to place the millimeter-thin persona projection unit within the tunic's slit pocket. His hands dropped, and he had to clutch at the unit to keep from dropping it.

"Marlon," said the voice of Central Four, "damaging the persona unit could add another year to your service."

"Another friggin' year . . . for dropping it?" Marlon glared at the screen. His face had become more lean, mature in a way that verged on gauntness.

"Six months for carelessness, a year or more for deliberate destruction. Those are the servie guidelines. You could always choose to emigrate off-Earth," declared the image of the safo parole officer—male and stern. Central Four found that image particularly effective.

"Leave everyone behind? My ma? My bro?" Marlon's fingers tightened around the persona unit. "You crazy or sumthin'?"

"You might find it easier than using the persona unit. Some people do. You have complained about your position."

"Friggin' right. Servie shit. Me, I'm better 'n this. Not friggin' crazy, though. Them CorPaks are worse 'n the Kemals." Slowly, very slowly, he eased the persona unit into place. A smile appeared, then vanished as his face contorted, alternating between smile and grimace, before finally settling into a smile.

Marlon used the styler, setting his black hair in perfect position. "The unit is in place, and I am reporting as tasked."

"Your presence is noted." The imaged safo smiled, and the screen blanked.

Marlon kept smiling as he stepped out of the adviser lounge into the boutique.

Central Four watched from the hidden receptors, sadly.

chapter 54

When I left safo station number three at five o'clock on a dark and cloudy Tuesday morning in December, I was more maintenance crew than maintenance crew. I had an ID badge that matched my GIL, with the name of Carlos Debrut, an authentic uniform, and even a battered tool case. No one even looked in my direction as I made my way out of the maintenance section and out onto Wynkoop. A block farther along, I used the pubcom and made the link. Within moments, Paula—or Central Four—drove up in an unmarked safo electrocar. I opened the door and got inside.

"You can explain this without revealing too much?" It was a stupid question, but I felt I had to say something.

"No one will ask. If they do, the records will show that you linked and asked for secure transportation to your home. Those links are already logged. Once you are safely home, and everything is inspected once more, Central Four will report your return to Lieutenant Meara."

"And exactly what do I tell them?"

"The truth, but as little as possible. Unless you are

charged with a felony-level offense, you cannot be compelled to testify. The Privacy Act works both ways."

Needless to say, Paula obeyed the speed limits scrupulously. So early in the morning, we had almost no traffic. At five thirty-one in the winter darkness, we pulled off Aspen into the drive before my house.

For more than a minute, she was silent. "The house is empty, and no one has been inside. There are several monitors focused on the house. Two are safo devices; three are not. Please stay inside the car until those three are neutralized."

"I'll sit tight."

She opened the door and closed it quickly behind her, then moved to the trunk of the groundcar, where she removed a tool kit. She carried it toward Mrs. Clenahar's wall, where she paused and took out a probe of some sort.

There . . .

The link surprised me, but I realized I'd never closed it, perhaps because I'd been talking to Paula verbally. *Do you know whose it is?*

It appears to be off-planet manufacture.

She moved toward the topiary pfitzer at the corner of the Puurlins' yard. I couldn't see what she did.

That one was an ISS device, proprietary.

The last monitor was disguised as a branch of the oak on my own property.

ISS also. Safo and sweep systems record only the emissions from your house, and from other dwellings. There is always the possibility that they have infiltrated such systems, but investigating or acting against such is not permitted.

Can I get out?

Wait a moment, if you would. She walked swiftly back to the groundcar and nodded.

I got out, still carrying the tool kit.

"After you pulse your system, please wait a moment before you open the door."

Intermittent flakes of snow swirled around me as I walked up the steps to the front porch, where I did as she'd requested.

"You can open the door now."

After I pushed down on the lever and stepped inside, she turned and scanned the street and the adjoining houses before following me. I closed the door. The house smelled faintly musty, and, again, with Paula standing so close to me I was aware that she smelled both freshly scrubbed and of Fleur-de-Matin.

Somehow, the thought of cydroid hygiene had never crossed my mind before. But then, more than a few things hadn't until the past months.

"The house systems are intact," she stated. "There have been no intrusions."

"You've been monitoring them all along?"

"It seemed prudent. It also seemed wise to let it be known that the Safety Office was closely monitoring your house."

I walked into the kitchen, where I scrubbed out the electrokettle and then refilled it. "Would you like some tea—Grey?"

"It would be good to try it."

"What do you eat, usually?"

"What you've been eating for the past weeks."

While the kettle heated, I headed down to the garage, with Paula just behind me. The Altimus seemed to be fine, and nothing smelled. Then I went back up to the kitchen, where I began to tackle cleaning out everything that had spoiled in the keeper. Even with modern technology—and considering I was a bachelor who kept a sparse larder—there was quite a bit that was spoiled. The greens for my salads were especially bad. The cucumbers had turned to soggy masses of grayish slime.

Paula just watched. Halfway through cleaning the keeper, I fixed two mugs of tea and offered her one. She sipped it gingerly at first. I had to wonder how the sensations—and how many of them—translated back to Central Four.

I finished one mug of tea and fixed another, then looked at Paula, into the storm-gray eyes that had both become familiar and remained an enigma. "Would you like some more?"

"If you please. The tea was quite good."

Her speech patterns varied, too, I'd come to realize, but I

wasn't about to ask why. I could have—and would have—once, but it didn't seem right.

With a full mug of Grey tea in hand, I headed into the office and settled down before the console, offering the upholstered leather chair to Paula. The gatekeeper informed me that there were over a hundred link-messages waiting. Before I even checked the log, the first thing I did was call up my credit balance. It wasn't so bad as I'd feared. I had the payment from the Centre, and from SCFA, and even some payments from Reya, Methroy, and Bruce Fuller. In short, I was still solvent, even without touching my savings.

Paula just watched, although I had the feeling that she—and Central Four—were doing far more than that.

Finally, after a good hour, I turned. "Are you here to be my permanent bodyguard?"

"No. A greater understanding of your systems is necessary. Before long, others will discover you are alive and have returned. They might ignore you, or they might try to kill you."

I didn't want to deal with that, not for the moment. "What about you?"

"When you are ready, you will proceed with gathering the evidence to reveal the killers of Everett Forster. Central Four will provide much of the information you will need. Some you will need to find yourself."

"This is too dangerous for you," I found myself saying.

"What do you mean?"

"If any one of the senior safo officers discovers what you've been doing, they could destroy you—literally—in a matter of minutes."

"It would take longer than that, but your point is accurate."

"How much will the equipment cost to make the transfer here?" I asked.

"About ten thousand credits for the system and receivers."

"Then let's order it all now."

There was the silence that I'd come to recognize as Paula's equivalent of surprise. "You would do that?"

"My life is worth far more than that, and I wouldn't have

it without you. That's gotten pretty clear, lately." I paused. "There's one other problem . . . with safos under the thumb or on the payroll of ISS . . . that's got to be stopped." Along with a few other things. I shook my head. "And doesn't . . . your present form . . . belong . . ."

"This particular cydroid is not on the Office's inventory, but some safos are familiar with it."

"What about cosmetic alterations? You could keep the eye color, and lighten the hair a bit."

"You like the eyes?"

"Yes," I admitted.

"That could be done while you await the equipment."

"You order what you need, and I'll offer the credit authorizations." I stood and gestured to the console.

"It will take a few minutes." Paula rose and then seated herself where I had been. "The orders will have to be routed in a circuitous fashion."

"Why?"

"Because Central Four has the authorization to order the equipment, but the credits cannot come from Central Four."

"And I have the credits, but not the authorization?"

"Exactly."

Her fingers were deft on the keyboard—I'd always used the keyboard. It was far faster and more accurate than speaking, and I thought better through my fingers. Somehow, her deftness pleased me, because fine motor control wasn't usually a cydroid strong point. It also meant that Central Four was very accomplished and very used to being "in" Paula Athene. It might have meant something else as well, but that idea skittered away before I could grasp it.

She'd finished, and I entered the financial codes. We got a confirmation date for January third, two weeks away.

As she stood and moved away from the console, she looked at me, gravely. "Thank you."

"Thank you," I replied. "I don't think I'd be alive without you."

"You might be, but you would have been severely disabled, and it would have taken years for you to return to what you were."

"Your technology is that much more advanced?"

She shook her head. "No one would have authorized the procedures. The expense in a medcenter is considerable, and unless they were undertaken immediately, too much damage would have occurred."

"More risky?"

"Yes. But probability calculations suggested that you would have authorized them."

She was right about that, frighteningly right. After another of those not-quite-awkward silences, I finally said, "Now what? I'm back home, back in my office. What am I supposed to do now? Just pick up my consulting where I left off?"

"As much as you can. You should also visit your children."

My children? *My* children. I swallowed. In a way, I supposed they were. I'd certainly never thought of myself as a parent, but Aliora had always been very clear about it. Neither she nor Dierk had wanted Deidre or Rousel to raise Charis and Alan if anything had happened to them. She'd told me more than once, "If you don't want to raise them, you'd better make sure nothing happens to us." She'd always said it with that playful smile.

Once more, I wondered just what I'd gotten myself into. Here I was, sticking my neck out, not even for a person . . . I stopped. Was that really so? What was a person? Paula, as I liked to think of her, was certainly an intelligent being. She was worried that her existence could be terminated. That was human enough. She'd tried her best to do what was right, when so-called flesh and blood humans had not.

But why? That was the part I didn't understand. I'd never heard of a successful installation of ethical programming. Fully integrated ethics programs had turned every system where they had been tried into junk, and partial ethics commands had created bizarre results.

I found my thoughts flying in all directions and forced myself to concentrate. "I'd better check with Deidre. I'm not exactly set up to handle children here."

"That might not be necessary."

I glanced at her.

"The custody provisions may stipulate that the children are to remain in their house."

While I wondered why Paula would mention that, it did sound like something Dierk and Aliora would set up. It was still early enough to be before school, so I decided to see if I could link Charis and Alan—although they might already be off for the holidays.

Charis was at the breakfast table, wearing a pale cream shirt and blue sweater. Her face brightened as she caught my image. "Uncle Jonat!" She turned to Deidre, I thought, although Deidre's back was to the scanner. "I told you he'd be all right." Charis looked at me. "You're wearing a funny suit."

"It's what the medical facility had for me to wear home," I said. "I just got home, and I wanted to see how you and Alan were doing."

Deidre turned. She was holding her youngest daughter, Ruissa, who wasn't even five months old, as I recalled. There were dark circles under her eyes, and her face looked thinner than I recalled. I could hear the twins somewhere. "You didn't link from the medcenter. No one could find you." Her tone was more than a little accusatory.

"I couldn't even talk until a little more than a week ago. The medical people made it a condition of treating me that I not link until I was ready to come home."

"I told Deidre that might be the case." Rousel's voice came in from somewhere. "Do you think most of the trouble has blown over?"

I doubted that, but now was not the time to voice such doubts. "I don't know, not for certain, but from what I've seen in the news the last few days, I can't see what good anyone would get from further attacks."

"You need to get in touch with Larry Asnart." Rousel moved beside Charis. "He's the advocate guardian. We'll stay here until everything's settled. There should be a message on your system. If not, let me know."

"I'm glad you're well again, Uncle Jonat," Charis interjected firmly. "You're supposed to come and live with us."

"I know, Charis. I have to talk to the advocate first, though."

"You'll talk to him soon?"

"I will. You take care."

After I broke the link, I just stood there for a moment. I'd hoped that life would get easier, but I had no doubts that it was just getting more complicated.

I went through the messages until I found the information on Larry Asnart. He was out, but I left a link message. Then I turned back to Paula.

"What do you suggest?"

"Act as though nothing has happened. Shortly, you will receive some information in your personal secure links."

"You think I need to act, still? I've arranged for you . . ."

"You have children to think of, now, Dr. deVrai."

I sighed. "You're right, but please call me Jonat, at least when you're Paula, or present in Paula . . ." That wasn't right, either, and I shook my head. "You're telling me, directly, that there's a chance I'm still in danger."

"You should review the information, and then decide."

I didn't like either the words or the firmness of her tone. "And you? What will you do now?"

"What you suggested." She smiled. "Charles will be on call. If you need him, his cover will be that of a bodyguard. You are not likely to see this face again."

I winced. I liked her face.

"Thank you."

I walked her to the door.

There, she looked at me. "You should leave the link on. You can notify Central Four at any time."

"I will." At least, until I knew far better how things stood.

"And it might be better to refrain from running the greenbelt for now. You do have equipment in your exercise room."

I did. I just hated using it. I much preferred running in the open air, but what she said made too much sense.

I finally opened the door, and she was gone. I watched until the white electral vanished. Then I closed the door, checked the locks, and headed back to the office. I had more than a little catching up to do, but how effective I'd be with Christmas less than a week away was another question.

chapter 55

The remainder of Tuesday was a rush, and then some. As-nart got back to me by ten o'clock and sent me the forms and custody agreement. It was the kind that I had to agree to as well, but there was nothing in it that was particularly onerous. I could even live with the provision that I was expected to take the children to the Unity Church "regularly." I was to live in the house, in loco parenti, and to provide separate accounting for any business expenses, but my "reasonable" personal expenses were to be covered by the rather extensive trust fund. I was to be free to marry or take a permanent companion, but multiple short-term liaisons were not in the interests of the children, and, for those reasons, the living expenses of any companion were not to come from the trust fund until either I married or until the relationship had lasted monogamously for over one year.

Asnart thought that was very liberal of Dierk and Aliora. I didn't comment. Aliora had always wanted me to find someone and to be happy with whoever she was. The particular wording of the clause was another confirmation of that. Aliora had wanted to give me as much leeway as legally possible. After consulting with Deidre and Rousel, we agreed that I would move in with the children on Friday, and all eight of us would spend time on Christmas Eve and Christmas day together.

Both Rousel and Deidre seemed relieved that I was back, and neither asked questions. Just from their reactions, I could see that I was going to have my hands full.

Then I linked Reya. She was in, and promptly dumped another assignment on me. Methroy was out, as was Bruce Fuller. There was no reason to contact Tan Uy-Smythe or Eric Wong, and Miguel Elisar's message had just stated that Vorhees and Rees and Prius had reached a settlement, and that the legal action had been dropped. He also indicated that Prius had sent a payment for ten hours for my willingness to testify.

I snorted. I'd take the credits, but they were nothing compared to what it could have cost me. Then, I frowned.

Paula . . . Central Four?

Yes, Dr. deVrai.

Do I need to pay someone for the medical care?

I got a definite sense of a laugh. *That is not necessary. In fact, that would make matters very difficult. Central Four has a budget for cydroid medical care. There has been some question in the past that it has not been utilized. The increased usage will make everyone happier.*

Because they want to know that cydroids aren't invulnerable?

That is the most probable surmise.

And no one even looks into your medical facilities?

Why should they? No one cares about cydroids operated by an intelligence system. Or the quality of medical care they receive.

The tone was level, but there was a bitterness behind it, and I didn't think I was projecting my own feelings. *I'll be happier when we get the equipment.* I paused. *You had said I would be getting some information so that I can deal with whoever caused all the problems.*

You already have it. It's the transmission from J. Bond, ornithologist.

There had to be some meaning behind that, but whatever it was, I'd missed it.

The name seemed appropriate, Central Four added.

It's beyond me. I checked the transmission. It was there. I called it up. *Thank you.*

It should be clear. If not, please request clarifications.

I will.

Then I began to read.

The first section was simply a series of organization charts. Certain names were highlighted in each chart. After three pages I realized what I was reading. The charts showed the operations or information divisions—or both—of some of the most powerful multis on earth, mostly headquartered in NorAm, but not totally. I surmised that the highlighted names, generally the director of the division, but sometimes the assistant, meant something.

The second section made the meaning somewhat clearer, because section two gave the names of the directorates of four organizations: the Pan-Social Trust or PST; the Centre for Sociology; the Alliance for Space Research; and, of course, the Centre for Societal Research. The PST was vaguely familiar, since I recalled that it was one of the supporters of the Centre for Societal Research.

I went back and began to compare names. While a highlighted name appeared only in the structure of one multi, every one of those names appeared on at least one board of the four organizations, and usually on two. Several appeared on three. The most common names were Tam Lin Deng, the director general of Industrial Security Systems, Stacia Mydra of Sante, Grantham Escher of MultiLateral Armaments, Jacques Alistar of NEN, and Daria Ghamel of AVia.

Section three just listed the objectives of each organization.

Section four listed a time line, arranged in columns. The first column was a series of events, including the attacks on Everett Forster and on me, and several other deaths of individuals. The second column was a loose description of the individual and something about each one. The third column listed political acts, regulations, legislation. The fourth column listed the multi that benefitted from those acts.

Needless to say, the "coincidences" were striking. Not a word of it would have survived a determined advocate, but somehow, I just didn't believe that the events of such a compilation, especially from Central Four, represented mere coincidence.

The last section was the largest, and it had volumes of information on the Patriots Against Multilateral Domination, as well as on Better Life Now, or BLN, which was a Mars-based group that was even more rabid than PAMD, and responsible for several violent demonstrations in Serenium, in which a number of CorPak safos reporting to MultiCor had been killed. According to the funding trails detailed in the document, credits had gone from the Centre for Societal Research to the Centre for Independent Scholarship on Mars and then to BLN.

In a backward way, it made perfect sense. The violent demonstrations would justify MultiCor's tight hold on Mars and undermine PAMD efforts at independence or social reform.

Central Four . . . you have other evidence?

There are other occurrences, but those are not public, and there are conclusions to be drawn. Revealing private actions and drawing such conclusions would violate the Privacy Acts, and that is a hard system prohibition.

I see. What I didn't see was how I could get around those prohibitions . . . or how Paula or Central could.

You should have enough to begin looking into the issues.

I supposed that I did, and I also had to spend some time figuring out how to get back to making a living, at least part of the time, as well as determining what to move to Dierk's and Aliora's and when.

I scoped out what Reya had given me before Bruce Fuller linked.

"Jonat!" Bruce exclaimed. "I'm glad to see you're back and healthy. The newsies said you might be crippled . . ."

"I took the option of some risky medical treatments. I was lucky. They worked." I gave a wry smile. "I appreciate your link." I waited.

"You're still consulting . . . ?"

I offered a laugh. "I still have to make a living."

"Reilin has a problem . . ."

I listened, and he sent me the background.

A messenger delivered a sealed document from Asnart before noon. Inside was yet another sealed envelope, engraved with Aliora's name and nothing more. I looked at it for several minutes before opening it.

I began to read.

Dear Jonat,

I do hope that you never see this, and that all my worrying is for nothing. I have rewritten this every six months since Charis was born, but both Dierk and I feel that it is for the best that you raise our children. You are kind and strong, even if you don't exactly understand who you are. But then, it could be that having children will resolve that. It did for us.

As you know, Charis is extremely headstrong, more so than you know. She is also extraordinarily sensitive, which you may not know. When you discipline her, gentleness and firmness must go hand in hand. Without gentleness, she withdraws into herself. Without firmness, she will not believe that you mean it. In that, you and Dierk are much alike, and I do not believe you will have too much difficulty. Alan will require more firmness, but is not quite so sensitive, unless he feels Charis is getting something he is not . . .

It was hard to read Aliora's words as she went on to detail schedules, habits, clothes for certain activities, doctors, and even the names of the children's teachers, including Charis's piano teacher. Luckily, for me, the piano teacher was paid extra to give Charis her lessons at the house, but I'd still have to work out more than a few transport details.

As I read the last words, I stiffened.

Dierk has also left some instructions for you. They're under your favorite wine, he says. You know where the system codes are . . .

I wasn't sure exactly what she meant by my favorite wine, but the instructions were somewhere in Dierk's system. At least, that was the implication.

After I finished reading, I set down the "instructions." I'd need to read them again, several times. I'd only thought my life had been hectic before. Now, I'd have to do everything I'd done before, plus take care of two children, and deal with Central Four, as well as undertake a crusade of sorts, because sooner or later, if I didn't, I had the feeling that people would come hunting for me again. At the same time, that situation made matters worse. Charis and Alan had been through enough. They didn't need more upsets, but they also didn't need to lose their uncle as well as their parents.

And I hadn't been home a half day yet.

chapter 56

The remainder of the week vanished in a swirl of links, scrambled efforts at consulting, linktimes with Charis and Alan, because I just didn't want to appear out of the blue on Friday. I also had some brief time to think over my study for the Centre. I couldn't help considering it played a part in what had happened, not after the information Central Four had sent.

Ostensibly, the Centre's aim had been for my work to point out, in a dispassionate and scholarly fashion, that Carlisimo, and perhaps others, had developed or were developing a methodology by which commercial products became surrogate support for him in his campaign for the Senate seat from the West Tejas district. The study—my study—had already become the principal evidence in hearings before the House and Senate Governmental Affairs Committees. Another round of hearings was scheduled after the first of the year, and it looked likely that those hearings would result in legislation further restricting such activities.

That all might seem fairly open but I knew, even if I couldn't prove it, that far more was at stake.

Too many things didn't make sense to me. Why had the Centre commissioned the study so late—far too late to affect the elections? That hadn't been its purpose. And someone had wanted the best, someone whose reputation for accuracy was known, not only academically, but also throughout the media and business communities. Carlisimo had been elected. With his flair for publicity and his innate abilities, barring some extreme mistake, he'd be reelected, even if the Legislature put curbs on the use of the techniques he'd developed.

Senator Crosslin was pushing the legislation as "reform," and it certainly seemed that way. But it couldn't be a real reform. I just didn't get why the backers of the Senate wanted that reform, since their candidates were far more likely to have the resources to use rez-based techniques than the PD candidates. I hated not understanding something like that.

I forced myself to put that aside until I dealt with everything surrounding Charis and Alan. Or until I got more information from Central Four. *If* I did . . . and that worried me as well.

The details involving the children went on and on. The two remaining groundcars, the house—everything was in a trust, and while I was the executor of the trust, I had to get myself registered, insured, and bonded. While the trust paid for that, which seemed rather odd, it all had to be done. Then I had to go to Southhills Academy and introduce myself to everyone and get the records changed to show me as guardian. That wasn't too bad, except for the one teacher who really showed an uncomfortable interest when she discovered that I was single.

I fibbed, saying that I was close to being committed. I didn't say to whom or what.

On Friday morning, Deidre and Rousel removed their things once Charis and Alan were at school, the last day before the holidays, and I brought in everything I'd need for a while. I felt strange looking over the master suite, but I had arranged for all the accessories to be changed—wallhangings, the carpets over the parquet flooring, even the paintings on the walls. While that would be somewhat of a shock, I had the feeling that my appearing in the same setting as their parents would set the wrong tenor for things.

I didn't have much experience with children. All I had were my feelings and Aliora's faith in me. Neither was probably enough, but they were all I had.

I barely had the master suite half put back together and my consulting files transferred into a partitioned section of Dierk's system before I had to take the remaining ground-car—a sedate Jacara—and head out to the Southhills Academy. My two-seat Altimus wasn't big enough for Charis and Alan. I'd either need to replace it or add another vehicle, and neither would be inexpensive.

Somehow, I was waiting in the parental vehicle queue at four o'clock, and that was a position I'd never considered. I did feel safe there, though. I doubted that my enemies would attempt something in the midst of so many parents and children. They certainly could have cared less about killing people, but there was too great a danger of killing the children and spouses of the wrong people.

I inched forward, bit by bit, until I could make out Charis and Alan. Charis recognized the Jacara before she recognized me, but she wasn't slow to greet me.

"Uncle Jonat! You're here! I get the front!" That was Charis. She was in the front seat of the Jacara before she finished speaking.

"Hello." Alan didn't look at me as he heaved himself into the backseat.

"Hello." I smiled, not too broadly, and looked at Charis. "Do you have all your datablocs?"

"Yes, Uncle Jonat."

"And you have your reader cards, Alan?"

The five-year-old nodded.

Neither said much more until I was away from the Academy and headed eastward toward the turnoff for Old Carriage Lane.

"Will we see Aunt Deidre and Uncle Rousel this afternoon?"

"No. They had to get back to their house. But they'll be over for Christmas eve tomorrow night, and for Christmas dinner." It was definitely a good thing, because, while my food preparation skills were adequate, they weren't up to a full dinner, and Deidre had been most gracious in offering to help. We'd gone over the menu, and I'd ordered everything and gotten it delivered.

"It won't be as good . . . as Mother's was," Alan said.

"No," I admitted. "But your aunt is going to help, and we will be together."

"Can you cook, Uncle Jonat?" asked Charis.

"Yes. Not as well as your mother, but better than many people." I'd had to learn, because I hated reformulated food and disliked going out to eat alone.

"What's for dinner?" asked the pragmatic Alan.

"Whatever I fix. I'd thought we might have pork chops with potatoes, green beans, and fried apples."

"Fried apples?" Charis's voice held surprise and horror.

"You fry them in butter with maple syrup and a little cinnamon. They're much better than mushy applesauce." I also enjoyed them cool, as leftovers. I'd had a lot of leftovers over the past ten years.

I didn't glance at the two, but I could sense the look that passed between them. Their uncle had a lot to learn. One just didn't fry apples.

I smiled. "Your mother had a rule, as I remember."

More silence.

"You didn't have to eat everything on your plate, but you did have to take at least one bite from everything."

Charis offered a groan.

After a moment, she said, "You're not Mother, though."

"No, I'm not. But I thought her rules were good, and she left me a letter asking me to follow them."

Surprisingly, I got a nod—a small and reluctant nod, but a nod from Charis. Alan, I suspected, remained horrified by the thought of frying apples.

When we returned to the house, I made sure of security, then headed to the kitchen.

The two were allowed one hour of linktime when they got home from school, but they had to watch together. Aliora had been firm about that, saying it was part of learning to work things out. I used that time to fix dinner. Even so, they actually got about an hour and ten minutes before I announced that dinner was ready. No one even peered into the enormous kitchen with center island stove that could have handled the needs of most restaurants. I thought they were afraid that they might actually see me frying apples.

When they sat down, I looked to Charis. "You'll have to say grace."

She cleared her throat. "Thank you, God above all, for the goodness of life and for the bounty that we behold, and please bring better lives to all those who suffer and are in want or need."

I nodded. "Thank you."

"That's the short one."

"You can say the long one tomorrow."

Alan looked at his plate. I'd already cut his chops into pieces, but not Charis's. Finally, he speared a piece with his fork, the smallest piece, and put it in his mouth. He must have decided it wasn't poison or worse, because he immediately had another.

On the other hand, Charis picked out the smallest chunk of fried apple, as if to get the terrible substance taken care of first, and slowly lifted it into her mouth.

A puzzled expression flashed across her face. Then she looked at me. "Those are good."

I managed not to laugh, because her words implied that it was amazing that I could cook something good that she didn't know about. "I've always liked them. I always thought applesauce was mushy."

Because I was hungry, I didn't press for conversation.

We were about halfway through dinner when Charis stopped and looked at me. "What really happened to you, Uncle Jonat?"

"I was hurt. Someone shot a rocket at me, like they did at your mother and father. I was lucky because it happened closer to my house and I'd already linked for help when I got hit."

"Aunt Deidre said you should have linked us," said Alan.

"I should have," I admitted, "but I couldn't. I got taken to a research center because it was close. They didn't have any links close to me. And my jaw and lungs were hurt so badly that I couldn't talk until just a few days before I got out."

"You didn't link then," Charis said.

"I didn't. The people at the center asked me not to. They do very special research, and they were afraid other people would find out about it. They saved my life, and they didn't ask much except for that."

"You still should have linked," said Alan.

"I can't change what I didn't do. We can only change what we do from now on."

There was another look between brother and sister, and it was one I couldn't interpret.

Although Charis ate every bit of her fried apples, and even dipped the last bits of chop in the sauce, Alan wasn't convinced. He ate everything else, leaving the apples on the corner of his plate until the very last.

Finally, he speared the smallest portion and ate slowly.

"It's all right."

Charis grinned at me as he gobbled up the rest of his apples.

Then . . . dinner was over, and the two were fidgeting in their chairs.

I stood, and they carried their dishes to the cleaner, stacking them inside.

"Bath time . . . and don't forget to wash your hair, Charis," I reminded her as she headed up the stairs.

She glanced back, as if to say something, and her eyes glistened. Then she shook her head, minutely, and hurried up the stairs. I had the feeling that my words had been too close to Aliora's, but I'd been following the routines that I'd seen.

I cleaned up the mess I'd made in the kitchen—partly from just not knowing where things were—and within a few minutes of finishing, Alan peered down the stairs, holding a book.

"You ready for me to read?"

He nodded solemnly.

I headed up the wide marble steps to the upper level.

Reading time was always in the sitting room outside their respective bedrooms, on an old soft leather couch covered with a cotton comforter. That made sense, because leather was either cold or sticky, especially for children in pajamas.

I sat in the middle of the couch, and Charis plopped her-self to my left, Alan to the right. Alan held two books, and Charis one. Charis's was thick.

"You read Alan's first," she announced.

I already knew that routine, but just nodded and looked at Alan. "Which one do you want me to start with?"

He thrust *Tyler Tiger's Tail* at me.

Tyler was a tiger, obviously, a white tiger, who was con-vinced he had no tail because whenever he turned to look at it, it wasn't there.

The second book was an old one, one that I'd read before, *The Three Billy Goats Gruff*. That was also a tradition of sorts, because it was "my" story to read to them. Aliora had always demurred, saying that it was "Uncle Jonat's."

At that thought, for a moment, I could say nothing. Then I swallowed, and started in.

The story did cheer me up, I have to admit, because I al-ways enjoyed reading how the largest billy goat butted the nasty troll off the bridge and into the gorge.

That is a good story . . . for many reasons.

I froze for a second at the sound and feel of Paula's voice through my implant. *You surprised me.*

You read it well. Then she—or Central Four—was gone.

"What is it, Uncle Jonat?" Charis asked.

She was far too perceptive.

"I was just thinking." That was true enough. "Now, your book."

Hers was a fantasy, entitled *Colors of the Gate*.

"One chapter, maybe two," I said.

"They're short."

"We'll see."

Alan was almost asleep by the time I finished the second chapter, and I carried him to bed and tucked him into bed.

Charis didn't seem as sleepy, but she yawned as I straight-ened her counterpane.

"You and Mother are the only ones who do that."

"That's because our mother did it." I swallowed. "Don't forget your prayers."

"I won't."

Because prayers were private, I slipped out.

Later that night, well after Charis and Alan were sound asleep, I went into Dierk's office and sat down before the console. I'd already used the emergency system codes and transferred the system to me, while allowing the limited usages for Charis and Alan, but I hadn't had a chance to look for Dierk's instructions.

I had to laugh when I found the file key—Sebastopol pinot grigio, but all there was in the file was an article on the wine. I searched for hidden codes, and found one symbol. There was a question mark. I highlighted it. A question appeared: "Who dropped the bouquet?"

I entered "Shioban."

Text appeared, pages and pages. I began to read, and after a few lines of text, I wasn't laughing at all.

Jonat . . .

If you find these instructions, and I am dead—or nowhere to be found, read them all the way through first. I realize that you've sworn off crusades and integrity, but if you're reading this, there's probably no one else left . . .

Those words of Dierk's, truthful as they probably were, burned.

DFR has ostensibly been bidding against Cornerstone Technologies and SteriNew . . . both are in effect subsidiaries of PST, since they are headed by and operated by PST board members . . . key figure is Tam Lin Deng, director general of ISS . . . myriad of groups involved, including the Health Policy Centre and the Centre for Societal Research . . . Aliora has been most helpful . . . but I have worried about the danger of her becoming involved . . .

The greater danger is that our children will live in a land secretly controlled by the PST. I discovered all this almost by accident. Several years ago, all of the DFR bids were being leaked. I had no proof, but we were being underbid by just enough that it wasn't coincidental. I put a false bid in the system, then hand typed a lower bid. We won . . . I won't go into details, because there's no way to prove it all, but don't trust the person who was treasurer when I wrote this . . .

I've tried, as best I could, to let others know, indirectly, what has been happening, and to block the PST influences in my field. So has Aliora, even more indirectly. It hasn't been enough, not if you're reading this . . .

The more I looked, the more apparent it was that similar patterns were occurring in other industries, and that political figures were involved, either as unwitting accomplices or as willing aides. Senator Crosslin is one of them, as are Senators Kennison and Campbell. Bennon is just a dupe, but that's often the most dangerous type. He's too stupid to understand what he's doing and what damage his actions can cause . . .

When they want to make a killing look like a random act of violence, it will be something like a smash and grab with excessive force. There are indications that the Kemal family—small-time trupps out of westside—may be handling such matters . . .

You can't go to the Denv Safety Office with any of this, not with any assurance. Deng has his own people there, scattered through various levels. Most of the safos are probably honest, but I don't know enough to know which ones are and which ones aren't. Even if I did, how could I have kept the word from spreading to those who aren't?

I kept reading through all ten pages. Dierk had named names, lots of them, and some I'd already guessed, like Abe Vorhees. Others I never would have guessed, like Senator Kennison, who had a clean-cut pilotlike sincerity. From what I could tell, the Centre for Societal Research was exactly what I'd suspected from the beginning, an absolutely clean front producing impeccable studies and research that served more nefarious purposes for other entities. So was the Health Policy Centre.

For a time, I just sat there in Dierk's office, thinking it all over. Dierk had never said a word about it, and I knew why. He'd explained—I was done with crusades. And now . . . there was no one left, except me.

Dierk had possessed greater access to wealth and resources than I had ever had, and he'd done quite a bit, quietly, and, in the end, he'd been discovered.

What could I do?

I couldn't do a damned thing. I'd already proved that. But . . . perhaps Paula, Central Four, and I could. I had to try. Very carefully. From Dierk's notes, and from what I'd already received from Paula/Central Four, it was clear that I didn't have too much time before someone would be after me once more, and it looked liked I no longer had a choice of whether to crusade or not.

At the same time, there were advantages to working with Central Four, and definite disadvantages. As I saw it, the biggest problem was that I was effectively limited to doing what was absolutely legal or to acting in self-defense. Somehow, I had to use Central Four's abilities in a way to force others to act both illegally and in a fashion that could be discovered. Or I had to act in a way where Central Four did not know what I did.

Somehow . . .

chapter 57

As almost always, when Yenci walked into the main Central Four briefing room, there were no other bio safos present. The projection awaiting and facing the safety officer was that of a rugged male safo.

"You're not using the Athene projection anymore?"

"You had suggested that using one projection too often was unwise," replied the projected safo in a solid baritone voice.

"Are you still using that cydroid?"

"All Central Four cydroid units are fully functional. Some are undergoing maintenance and their periodic appearance modification."

"Appearance modification? Why?"

"Continued use of the same facial appearances subjects the units to possible recognition and unnecessary risk. That could necessitate higher levels of replacement and higher medical and repair levels."

"Makes sense," Yenci conceded. "DeVrai has reappeared. Is Meara going to charge him?"

"Lieutenant Meara issued an order against any charges, Officer Yenci."

"I'd heard that. Did she give any reason?"

"She issued a statement. Would you like a copy projected?"

"I read it. Did she say anything else?"

There was a pause before the projected male safo replied, "In her media link-conference, she also stated that deVrai had only attempted to defend himself and that the deVrai family had suffered enough. She said that the Denv Safety Office would continue to investigate all leads involving the Forster and VanOkar murders and the illegal use of cydroids and clones. It was later mentioned in a staff session that she was concerned that some safos had greater access to Privacy Act level information than was proper and she would also be looking into that."

"Did she mention names?"

"No, she did not, Officer Yenci."

"Are there any operations planned for follow-up?"

"The lieutenant has not announced anything."

Yenci's face was thoughtful as she turned and left the briefing room.

chapter 58

Christmas Eve day and evening and Christmas itself were a blur, a generally pleasurable blur, and Charis and Alan only got teary a few times. Deidre had already bought a few presents, and I had one or two items I'd gotten earlier in the year. That was enough, I thought. Aliora had never been big on presents, and to overdo it on the first Christmas after the children's parents had died wouldn't have been right—or in good taste.

Charis approved of my refurbishing the master suite; Alan didn't. This meant that whatever I'd done would have displeased one of them, but I felt better because I hadn't wanted to preserve the illusion that their parents would be back. I might have done it differently had I been required to move in right after their deaths, but after two months . . . that was something else.

Deidre and Rousel's twins were terrors, and I understood even better why Aliora and Dierk had insisted on my becoming guardian for Charis and Alan. The three of us were actually relieved when Deidre and Rousel and their offspring departed after dessert. I didn't even mind cleaning up later that night, especially in the quiet.

It was the first time I'd really had to think over the seemingly insurmountable problems that faced me. I didn't get very far initially, but once everything was clean and generally neat, I retreated to Dierk's office, which I had begun to rearrange to suit my needs. There, as Christmas night faded away, I sat beside the console, just thinking.

Vorhees was after me, or had been. So were the members of the Pan-Social Trust, or at least a number of them. Wong and the SCFA seemed to be opposed to the PST and the Centre. Likewise, the PAMD certainly didn't care for the LR, and neither did the Popular Democrats, but I couldn't see the PD wanting to get involved in anything that involved a direct shoot-out.

What I needed was some way to turn the tables, some way to focus attention on the PST, and some way to track the flow of credits to less than savory aspects of the PST. One weak point was the cydroids used in the attacks on Forster, on Aliora and Dierk, and on me. There had to be some track, somewhere. The problem in dealing with a cabal or hidden oligarchial group like PST was that short of tying them all up in some sort of legal mess—or removing them all nearly simultaneously—any action against one member just increased the stakes, and lowered my probabilities of success. Eventually, the probability of my not being able to continue my existence would approach unity—as Central Four would have put it.

Vorhees was another thing. He'd had people murdered. That was one thing I was certain about. Whether I could find anything that was useful—or whether Central Four had anything—that was another question. Miguel Elisar was a possible entry. He'd looked very frazzled when he'd left a message about the settlement. Then there was Lynia Palmero. If I could track her down.

Paula . . .

Yes, Jonat?

I need help . . . I laid out all the information I'd been able to dig up on Vorhees, including the vanishing warning, which I had not mentioned before, and the "settlement" of the Prius case.

You didn't mention the warning.

There wasn't even any residue left, not that would have been traceable, except as scattered hydrocarbons. Can you at least calculate probabilities, even if you can't reveal Privacy-level information?

The probabilities approach unity that Abraham Vorhees is engaged in illegal activities of a nature great enough to require veradification if physical evidence can be produced.

Do you or any of the Central systems have any physical evidence at all?

Central Four does not have adequate physical evidence.

I paused. Did that mean that there was evidence, or was that a standard response, signifying nothing? *What is the standard response if there is no evidence to link an individual to a crime?*

I received the sense of a laugh. *The standard response is that the Safety Office has no evidence to link the individual to the crime.*

I couldn't help taking a deep breath.

For someone who has never been a safo, Jonat, you are most perceptive in determining how to elicit information within system parameters.

Some of that I'd learned in the Marines, and some in consulting, and some of it was that Central Four was actively helping, within whatever guidelines there were. I hoped all that would be enough.

What public information can you provide about Abe Vorhees and the others in the PST group?

Transmitting.

The transmission took almost fifteen minutes, and I had the feeling that what was in it would keep me busy for days just sorting through it. *Thank you.*

You're welcome, Jonat.

There was a warmth to the implant-received words. I shook my head. I was probably just hearing what I wanted to hear.

Then I began to read.

chapter 59

Alistar, Mydra, and Ghamel sat before the table desk, surrounded by the star-class privacy screen. Deng surveyed
them impassively.

"How soon before the Mars resupply leaves?" asked
Mydra.

"Three weeks. Certain items need components for later
modification," replied Deng.

"SPD?" asked Ghamel.

"There is no one else."

"What should we do about deVrai?" Alistar glanced toward the Capitol Complex, bathed in the pale golden light of
a winter sun barely above the mountains. "I can't believe he
just reappeared from nowhere. Who was hiding him?
PAMD?"

"No. That has been checked thoroughly. The indications
are that he was taken to a private facility. DeVrai may have
more resources than we had calculated."

"Then we ought to take him out now."

"You will do nothing for a few weeks. The safos are monitoring and watching closely. They will do so for several

weeks. So will every sensation-minded newsie. DeVrai has done nothing proactive yet, and he is trying to deal with reconstructing his life."

"Do we need to do anything?" asked Mydra.

"If it were just deVrai, we would not need to act at all. For some reason, Lieutenant Meara is interested, and the safos are following deVrai. There are some indications that the Sinese multis have an interest. If deVrai dies before anything is exposed, the records are sealed, except for the circumstances of his death and the reasons for it. So the timing must be precise. It must be late enough so that he is not flash news, early enough to keep matters from being exposed."

"Has to be smash and grab, then," Alistar pointed out. "The westside folks won't want to handle that, not without a bonus. Kemal's a nasty character."

"Kemal will do as you wish. He has no choice. Wait for another week to contact him. The time is not yet."

"DeVrai is more dangerous than you think," Mydra said. "Just because he's been self-serving for the past ten years doesn't mean he'll stay that way."

"That is precisely my view," Deng replied. "He is a man who wishes to make sure that everything is certain. His work reflects painstaking care. Such a man will not act rashly, and he will plan most carefully. Our plans are already laid." The older man glanced toward Alistar. "Within a month, everything will be settled."

"What if deVrai escapes again?" pressed Mydra.

"It does not matter." Deng smiled. "There will be no evidence, and no ties. He may suspect, but with the privacy laws and the lack of physical evidence, there is nothing the safos can do, and the DomSec commander will not act on a purely internal matter of law and order, and deVrai is not of great concern to Captain Garos. Sudro, yes, but not Garos. DeVrai is an irritating loose end, but he will not change matters. Still, it would be best to leave nothing to chance."

Mydra's eyebrows lifted, if barely.

"You think that the great and principled hero of Guyana will rise again?" Alistar laughed. "He won't. He's ten years older, weak from medical recovery, probably out of shape, and more interested in making a living with his mathematical trickery than in trying to follow invisible trails to nowhere."

"SPD is well-shielded, but scarcely invisible," Ghamel pointed out. "Nor is NEN without its enemies."

"What will deVrai do? Gather a commando team that he doesn't have and assault the most secure location in Nor-Am?" Alistar laughed once more. "If he were to attack SPD or the NEN office, exactly what would that accomplish?"

"Since you are so very confident, Alistar," Mydra replied with a broad smile, "I suggest that we turn all responsibility for dealing with deVrai over to you so that the rest of us can concentrate on other matters, such as the Martian situation. If deVrai is so simple, surely you can handle him."

Deng looked to the younger, blue-eyed man. "Is that acceptable to you?"

"More than acceptable." Alistar smiled. "Just give me the date you want him removed, and it will be done. Without a trace."

Ghamel nodded.

Mydra and Deng exchanged glances so briefly that neither of the other two saw the momentary expressions.

chapter 60

By getting up early on Monday, I did manage a fair workout on the indoor equipment that Aliora and Dierk had in the exercise room. After that, though, I didn't get anything of consequence done until eleven, when I took Alan next door to play with his friend Daffyd. There was no school because of the holidays, and while Charis could be relied upon to entertain herself to some degree, Alan could not—at least not for long. Here I was, trying to figure out how to keep myself alive, and by extension, to provide love and stability for Alan and Charis. And my choices were to push them aside or to delay trying to find an answer and risk losing the ability to provide that love and stability.

The gatekeeper had informed me that Chelsa Glynn and Bruce Fuller had linked, and I checked. Glynn was inquiring as to my availability at the AKRA conference, and Bruce wanted a date on his latest project. I put aside replying immediately.

At eleven, with Charis engrossed in painting in her mother's studio, and Alan next door, I began to make links. First, I tried Elisar. He was out.

Then I linked with Bruce Fuller to clear up several ambiguities on the Reilin project. That was thankfully quick. After that, I began trying to find Lynia Palmero. I did get a simmie at her home codes, but the simmie was the simple kind that just said that she wasn't there. I tried the RezLine general code; but the reception simmie told me there was no one by that name at the multi and no forwarding code. I searched back through my records and found a reference to Alvan Andrus, her former assistant. I tried that code, but he wasn't in either. I did get a simmie that suggested another code. When I went for that one, I ended up with another simmie.

"This is Alvan Andrus, at Vorhees and Reyes . . ."

I broke the link. There was no way I was ready to talk to Alvan, not without talking to Lynia first. It looked like I'd have to keep trying Lynia at her home, or wait for her answer.

Next came the return link to Chelsa Glynn. She was in.

"Dr. deVrai . . . I'd heard that you'd been incapacitated . . ."

"I was for a time, but I'm close to fully recovered and looking forward to your seminar."

"I'm so glad." Her smile actually tracked her words. "I really enjoyed your paper, and I'm certain many of those attending will . . ."

After Glynn, my next link was to Eric Wong. Like Glynn, he was actually in.

"Dr. deVrai . . . it is you, is it not?"

"That it is. In the flesh, if through modern communications."

"I had heard . . ."

"You heard correctly. Of course, no one can tell me who thought I was so dangerous that four combat cydroids were necessary. Imagine, an economic media analyst . . . what could be dangerous about that?" I laughed.

Wong laughed politely as well, before replying, "A good economist is like the man who is not taken in by sleight of hand. He sees what is, not what people wish seen."

"There's so much to see, sometimes, and while I might see it, I don't always know that it's dangerous." I wished I knew exactly what Wong was trying to tell me.

"You observed at lunch that the obvious obstacles would not always be so, and that institutional barriers were always harder." He frowned. "That has been a concern of the SCFA for some time. When anyone has a name or a reputation, how many credits will it take to overcome that?" Wong shrugged. "In any kind of continental or global marketplace, some form of advertising is necessary for new products to break in. In the case of product placement, the cost is very high for small returns, but the opportunity is there. In other marketplaces, those, let us hypothesize, of education and politics, ideas can only be brought forth by either those in power or those who can purchase access. If there is no way to purchase access . . . but I fear I am far too academic."

I got the gist of his message—unfortunately. "Of course, most people don't see ideas as commodities, but, in a way they are. The problem with an idea being stifled by an institution is that so often those who stifle the ideas are lost behind the facades of the institutions, and one could chase hundreds of people trying to find who might be the right person to persuade."

"Ah . . . that is true. Sometimes, it is simple, as when those who stifle ideas are in charge of the institutional security. At other times, they may be in charge of appearances, or of communications. Sometimes, all three." Wong smiled. "But doubtless, you have surmised such all along. I did want to thank you again for your presentation. You will be receiving an invitation to our winter open house in early February."

"That is something I would look forward to."

"We always try to invite a wide range of guests. Some, of course, do not attend. I've been trying to entice Jacques Alistar for a time, but you know the communications types. They smile, but they're hard to pin down."

"Some people are."

"I must not keep you, but I appreciate knowing that you are well and recovering." Wong smiled and was gone.

I swallowed. Unless I was reading too much into subtlety, Wong had as much as told me that Tam Lin Deng and Jacques Alistar were the ones after me. He'd also made a big deal about ideas . . . and their cost.

I stiffened. Cost . . . campaigns . . . politics . . . With that I keyed in two inquiries, and got back the answers almost immediately.

Crosslin's campaign reform bill was the first one, and I went over it section by section. When I finished, I understood—at least part of what was going on. It was simple, and oh so obvious, except no one seemed to have put the pieces together. I frowned. That wasn't right. Someone had because this was why either the PAMD or a sympathetic organization had handled the election the way they had.

The PAMD knew they couldn't get control of the Senate, but they or the PD itself had set up Carlisimo's campaign as a diversion. The seats that had counted were those in the House, the ones where the candidates had been attacked. Attacks by outsiders didn't count against spending limits, or against volunteer restrictions.

There were a number of reform provisions in the Crosslin bill, and all seemed like good ideas. Some might have been, but I was skeptical. No more than 10 percent of the volunteers could come from outside the contested electoral district. That sounded fine, but any multi could transfer in "employees" for a year or two. Nor could more than 25 percent of any candidate's funding come from sources outside the district, but what was to prevent transferring key personnel into a district? Those were minor compared to two other provisions. By limiting "public media" expenditures, and prohibiting any form of rez-based or enhanced presentation, Crosslin was effectively slanting the electoral playing field to the LR side, because the LR had the advantage in name recognition, structural support—everything that wasn't limited. Now . . . I knew as well as anyone that such advantages are transitory over time, and in ten or twenty years those structural advantages would change, but what it meant was that the LR—under the guidance of the PST group—would control NorAm for the next decade . . . and all that implied for Martian Independence. What they didn't see, or didn't care about, was that people who were structurally oppressed, and felt that way, have a nasty tendency to turn violent.

Then, I reflected, maybe Deng and company did see

that. More violence would certainly boost ISS revenues and fortunes.

The second inquiry was on Jacques Alistar. He was almost ten years younger than I was, and the deputy director general of NEN—NordEstNet—the big EuroCom communications net. Alistar had his office in Denv, and was in charge of NorAm operations. The projected file image showed a blue-eyed blond man with an elfin chin. He had the hearty open expression that I associated with people who were usually good at concealing more than they revealed. Needless to say, there was very little on Alistar, except his education, his position, and the single image. There was an office address in old NorthTech, but no personal address. I shuffled through the printouts that Central Four had provided. She had also highlighted his name. Interesting.

Another chill hit me when I realized, all too belatedly, that in this elaborate set of moves and countermoves, I wasn't just a convenient tool for the Centre and PST, but right in the middle of everything. Wong, and probably the entire Sinese power bloc, were trying to use me to stop Deng and the PST group—because it had to be the entire group—and the PST group and the Centre had used me to provide the evidence to support the Crosslin bill and campaign "reform."

What Wong had been telling me was that Deng and Alistar wanted me out of the way before I discovered what was happening and did something to upset their plans. He'd already warned me once, and I probably hadn't taken him seriously enough the first time.

Paula . . . Central Four?

Yes?

Is there a dossier of some sort on Eric Tang Wong?

That information is restricted.

Does it say whether he is considered a Sinoplex agent? It couldn't hurt to ask.

There was a long silence.

Your letter of resignation from the Corps was rather strong.

What did that have to do with anything? How did she

know? She was an intelligent system, but most AIs were compartmentalized, and had been for decades. I didn't offer anything, either verbally or through the implant link.

'*A nation should stand for ideals and ethics beyond mere commercial freedom, and its leaders should not commit young men and women to battles designed not to expand freedom or the rule of law, but merely for multilateral comparative commercial advantage. This has not been the case, not in my career and experience . . .*'

Those had been my words, every last one of them.

Rather strong words, Jonat.

I felt strongly.

And now? Central Four's "tone" held more than mere inquiry.

I was naive. I thought that leaders had some ideals. I never thought they were pure, but that, in the crunch, some had beliefs beyond more credits and more personal power.

Which kind of leader do you want to be? The kind you expected? Or the kind you found?

I'm not a leader. I'm not in the Corps. I don't run anything.

Leaders don't have to run anything, do they?

I suppose not.

Will you follow your ideals? Or your credit balance?

That was a simple answer. Following my credit balance was only going to get me killed. Ideals offered some slim hope. *I don't have any choice now. It has to be my ideals.*

Eric Tang Wong is believed to be a Sinese agent. ISS has been trying to tap his links, but appears to have been unsuccessful.

Wong warned me.

He did. His words were veiled, but clear. You left the link open.

That brought me up short. What else had Central Four heard? *What have you overheard that I should pay more attention to?*

Nothing overheard that you have not already discerned as important. There is more unrest on Mars, and the SPD of ISS will be supplying wide-band neuralwhips to CorPak.

Those are illegal, I protested. *Can't Central Four or the Safety Office do something?* I could understand why the CorPak safos might want them. They certainly couldn't use high energy slug-throwers in a domed and pressurized city, not without risking dome damage and depressurization. They could always claim that they'd used standard neuralwhips, and that anyone who died had just been one of the unfortunates who reacted badly, and besides, they had been rioting or disorderly . . . or whatever.

The weapons are not illegal off-Earth under the MultiCor Charter, and they will not be assembled until the supply vessels are en route to Mars.

This is Deng's doing? Of course, it was his doing. He was the head of ISS. *How does that offer us an opportunity?*

Physical evidence is always most useful. It weighs more heavily in determinations involving data covered by the Privacy Laws. It outweighs system records.

How exactly am I supposed to obtain such evidence?

There may be an unregistered cydroid medical center located in the SPD Mountain Division. There is enough evidence that Central Four is allowed to investigate the possibility of such crimes.

That's legal?

Under the imminent endangerment provisions of the Public Safety Amendments of 2134, when the Safety Office has reason to believe that public safety is being endangered, either overt or covert investigations of private property are permitted, provided force is not utilized, except in self-defense.

I hadn't heard about that set of laws. *Who came up with those?*

Senator Crosslin authored the legislation. It provides the Safety Office with the ability to conduct covert surveillance of the manufacture of illegal substances, but the provisions apply to all activities that would be illegal if discovered.

Are there really illegal cydroids at SPD?

The probability is great enough to allow covert investigation, and it might be best if you accompanied a Central Four observer.

Won't that be a problem?

No. Observers who are not safos but who have pertinent expertise or experience are allowed, provided they execute a waiver. There is no reason for you not to agree to the waiver.

Probably not, considering that unless I found a way to stop the PST group and Vorhees, I'd probably be dead—and sooner rather than later. *When does this "observation" take place?*

Thursday night at seven o'clock.

That meant I'd have to deal with child care on Thursday, another thing I hadn't had to worry about. *Who will I be going with?*

Paula.

Is she . . . you . . . ?

She is necessary. She will be somewhat bruised, but able to function. You will meet her at your own house. The location is not far from there.

We're going into the ISS operational complex?

You will only be along as an observer.

That was an interesting choice of words. *What's my expertise?*

You are a former commando who knows weapons. You are not currently in service. Therefore, you are more impartial. ISS can only claim you are not impartial by revealing that it is breaking the law.

You have a nasty turn of mind.

Thank you.

At that point, the neighbor's Jacara appeared in the rotunda, returning Alan, who required my presence. We played cribbage.

Lynia Palmero returned my earlier link at three in the afternoon, luckily while Charis and Alan were eating a snack.

"For someone who was reputed close to death," she began, "you don't look bad."

"You should have seen me a month ago." I laughed.

"That's not your office. It looks fancier."

"It's my late brother-in-law's. He and my sister were killed right after someone tried the same thing on me."

"Oh . . . I'm sorry, Jonat. I forgot . . . I didn't . . ."

"That's all right. You didn't know. How are things going for you?"

"Not all that well, I'll have to say, if not nearly so badly as what you've been through. Sanson let everyone know that my work was not known for its cooperative nature. So I've got a half-time position with Klemsal. The people are good, and there might be some possibilities in a few months." She shrugged. "I'm probably better off here than with RezLine."

"I discovered that Alvan is now with Vorhees and Reyes. I didn't wait to talk to him."

"I can't imagine why. That's where he belongs. He gives snakes and vipers bad names."

"Was he on Vorhees's payroll from the beginning?"

"I don't know that, but I wouldn't be surprised." She paused. "Did you ever get that half-contract payment?"

"Not yet."

"They'll probably take ninety days, and then claim that they waited to make sure you were able to receive it."

"Was there ever anything in writing that made you suspect that Vorhees was paying off Sanson and Andrus . . . ?"

"Nothing in writing. Who needed anything in writing? The way Sanson ignored your studies and even the market- ing department?" Lynia's voice was cutting.

"Did you ever meet Vorhees?"

"No. I saw him a few times when he came in to see San- son. He's a little man. He always had a big bodyguard. With what he's done, he needs one."

"Did you know of anything besides what he did to you?"

"You hear things," Lynia said. "He was always trying to expand. When Laurance Evans refused to sell ECC to him— it was a family firm—Evans's daughter drowned in a friend's pool while the friend was answering a link about a family emergency that was false, and his son died in a flitter crash. Sanson told me that Evans tried to get the district advocate to look into both incidents, but nothing ever happened."

"He's even worse than I'd heard. I suppose that outside of business, he's the outstanding father and family man?"

"He likes to play that role, and his wife likes belonging to the Club, but he's had a mistress for years. Washed-out former society girl, Maria Delorean. She was once a net actress, except that she couldn't act. Everyone knows about her, but no one ever says anything in public."

"With Vorhees's reputation, I can see why."

In the end, Lynia couldn't offer me anything more, except that Maria Delorean had been his mistress for years, and that he'd installed her in the renovated Larimer Square Towers.

I'd put in a link to Miguel Elisar, but he hadn't returned it.

My own research into the abnormally high number of deaths and accidents associated with people who crossed Abe Vorhees had convinced me that those deaths were anything but accidental, but, once again, there was really no way to prove anything. The only way to deal with Vorhees was for him to have an accident or an illness—just like those who'd crossed him. That would take some doing, especially since I didn't have a lot of time.

I set Dierk's system to dig up certain kinds of pertinent information on Abe Vorhees, Jacques Alistar, and Tam Lin Deng while I was monitoring the children and fixing dinner. I didn't have high hopes, but it was worth a try.

chapter 61

In dealing with Charis and Alan, Tuesday was an improvement over Monday, and I got in several hours of actual work, but my search for information about Abe Vorhees turned up very little, except several public images. Vorhees was a small man, who looked more like a squirrel or a ferret than a snake, with slicked-back black hair and a round cheerful face and deep-set brown eyes.

The information provided by Central Four remained the best—and only—real compilation on Vorhees: director general of Vorhees and Reyes; a legal degree from DSU, but he'd never practiced as an advocate; married to the same woman for thirty-one years; had his offices in the same old downtown Denv building for twenty. The firm had used the same logo, an intertwined "V" and "R," for twenty-five years. He drove an Altimus Grande, or was driven in one, and had always had one. In his own way, Vorhees was a creature of habit, and that offered some possibilities.

Once I might have had some problems with what I was contemplating, but after Aliora's and Dierk's murders, at least three attempts on my life, four taps into my communications system, three snoops of my property, three illegal semi-clone/cydroids based on my own DNA, it was more than clear that the supposed governmental protections weren't up to handling economically endowed lawbreakers. Then, I wondered, had they ever been?

It was also clear that the privacy laws that had been enacted to prevent one kind of abuse had spawned another, and I wasn't so certain that the latest abuses weren't worse. From what I could tell, I had two sets of problems. One was Abe Vorhees, and the other was the PST group, particularly Tam Lin Deng and Jacques Alistar. Central Four—and Paula—were concerned about the PST group, doubtless because they were the greater threat to society. Vorhees might be the greater threat to me personally, however, and I needed to take steps to deal with that threat.

I also had to keep making a living, and that would be exceedingly difficult if I had to keep worrying about staying alive.

On Wednesday, the cleaning team, a couple with no-nonsense attitudes, arrived promptly at nine and set to work. With every day that went by, I understood why that trust fund set up by Aliora and Dierk was necessary. Even so, Wednesday was better, insofar as work went, and I did manage to get some more done on Bruce Fuller's Reilin project.

On my private agendas, the only other thing that I could find out was the actual address of Maria Delorean, 805 in the Larimer Square Towers. That did allow me to go through the Denv building files and get the layout of the structure, including the utilities, stairways, and the general level of security. That required some creative approaches, but I managed those.

I did discover that Jacques Alistar enjoyed the antique sport of racquetball and played regularly at the Club. I actually knew my way around there, although I didn't belong, and hadn't been there much since my parents' deaths.

I also arranged for Elmer and Devon Bowes to take care of Charis and Alan on Thursday afternoon and night. They were at the top of the list of child-care personnel in Aliora's personal system. For what it would cost, they should have been. Devon seemed both pleasant and professional and

Elmer was a licensed bodyguard, which was good for a number of reasons.

Thursday was less productive, partly because Alan was clingy, and partly because Charis was miffed that her friend Freyda was out of town, doing something with her parents and the two girls couldn't even link. Part of their restlessness might also have come from my own. I was more than a little worried about whatever Central Four had in mind for "observation." At the same time, I didn't like the thought of full neural-killers going to Mars for CorPak use against civilians who basically wanted the freedom to get out from under the MultiCor oligopoly. MultiCor, or the PST group, could argue all they wanted that they deserved a return for their efforts in terraforming Mars, but the figures I'd seen showed a solid 30 percent per year return after the amortization of the initial investment and the ongoing greenhousing and water comet drops. Not many multis had managed that for fifty straight years. Of course, complete terraforming would require at least another fifty years, and there was no reason why MultiCor shouldn't get some preferences, but an absolute hold on the Martian market and government was too much.

By three in the afternoon I was so jumpy that I couldn't concentrate on finishing the Reilin project. Could Central Four have another agenda? Why did the safo intelligence system need an observer? But then, why had the system risked itself in saving me? That—and the orders for equipment—pointed to good faith. If there happened to be some kind of sting operation in effect, it was so convoluted that I couldn't figure it out. Besides, merely observing couldn't be much more than a misdemeanor or the like—unless the sting called for me to get killed in a situation that pinned everything on Deng and ISS.

In the end, I was trusting an intelligence system because I had no one else left to trust. The flesh and blood safos hadn't helped me. Nor had all the Denv monitoring systems. Neither had the politicians, not that I'd expected anything there. My clients were only interested in what I could do for them, and with Aliora and Dierk gone, I had no family.

I put Dierk's system in standby, although with all that I'd added it was probably fair to call it Dierk's and *mine,* and walked down to the great room where Charis was trying to improve Alan's chess game.

Both looked up at me, almost in relief.

"How are things going?" I asked.

"She always wins," Alan said.

"You'll win more when you're older," I pointed out.

He didn't look convinced.

"You will," Charis promised.

Alan's expression was close to a pout.

I sat down on the straight-backed chair against the wall, back from the inlaid chess table. "I didn't learn chess until I was older. You'll probably be better than I am if you keep at it."

Alan sighed.

Charis began to reset the pieces on the board.

"Do you have to go out, Uncle Jonat?" asked Alan.

"I still have to make a living, Alan, and I hope I'll be able to arrange things better in the future. But with the time I was hurt, and everything that happened, there are things I have to do."

Charis nodded sagely, almost a little too smartly. That was something else I'd have to watch.

"Can you tell us about when you and Mother were little?" Alan asked.

I nodded, going through memories, before settling on the story about the time when I'd turned one of Aliora's dolls into an unwilling participant in a buoyancy experiment. The problem had been that the doll had been a fashion doll, and not a play doll, and I'd ruined the clothes, the hair, and pretty much everything. I'd also ended up doing extra chores for months.

The two were smiling, if not laughing, when the Bowes couple arrived at precisely four o'clock. They parked at one side of the rotunda, and then walked to the entry. I opened the nebulae doors. They made me think of Aliora, and I swallowed.

The two matched their images. She was a wiry woman, probably close to Aliora's age, with short dark hair and a warm smile. "Colonel deVrai, I'm so glad to meet you. Elmer has told me so much about you."

I had to wonder where her husband had found out about

me. "I hope he hasn't said too much." I turned to him after closing the door behind them.

Elmer Bowes wasn't quite my height, but his shoulders were broader. He had a lazy smile that suggested he knew how to use the devices concealed in the broad equipment belt. "Colonel, I didn't tell her that much. Everyone heard about the Guyana mess."

"You were in service?"

"Twenty-five years. Made master tech. Decided a short-stipend retirement was better than more stabilization actions."

I had to agree with that. "I've never needed a bodyguard, but I'm glad you have those qualifications."

"Colonel . . . with your background, I can see why."

"I don't even know anyone who has a bodyguard, and the only one I know about is a fellow named Vorhees." I shrugged. "You ever hear of him?"

"I've heard of him. Most licensed guards have. He has to pay twice the going rate for his swing men."

"Swing men?"

"He's got two guards. They've been with him for years, but they've got families, or have emergencies. Most clients need swing men to fill those gaps. Agencies like Vonos or Agnopoulos take care of that."

That made sense. "Did you start that way after you left active duty?"

Bowes nodded. "Got them to pay for the licensing and certification. After two years, I'd had enough, and Devon pointed out that people who need guards, and some who don't, need security for their children. She takes care of them, and I watch for trouble." He laughed. "She's good, too. Certified like me."

I began to understand why they were expensive—and why they were near the top of Aliora's list. "I appreciate your being able to come on short notice."

"We wouldn't be able to if it weren't the middle of a holiday week," Devon Bowes interjected.

"I'll make a note of that and make sure that I plan farther ahead in the future."

They both smiled, almost indulgently, and I got the impression that they'd heard those words more than a few times before. I couldn't help laughing, if softly, for a moment. "You've heard that before."

"Yes, sir." Elmer Bowes grinned.

It only took a few minutes to get them settled, and switch the security to standard, rather than personal. Then I was off, driving my own Altimus across Denv. Even taking the back roads and not the guideways, where even under automated control traffic slowed, I didn't pull into the garage at my house until after five.

Once there, I had to get ready. I might be scheduled to be an observer, but I wasn't going unprepared or unarmed. I wore a night-gray singlesuit, also left over from my Marine days, and made sure I had the commando slingshot with both kinds of darts, and the tensile gloves, and an undershirt with tensile-strength panels. Full body tensility had been tried, but no matter how it was engineered, it ended up restricting body movement. Nanite screens were still at the point where they weren't practical for anything smaller than armored military vehicles because the screens by themselves generated too much heat and didn't do anything for concussive effects. The undershirt would stop small arms and mitigate neuralwhip shock—if I happened to be lucky enough to be hit in the chest or back. Still, it was better than nothing.

While I waited for Paula, I did a little more planning for my next mission, checking maglev schedules to old downtown Denv and ways to spot-short an entry security system, although I hoped to avoid that.

Before I knew it, the Central Four link was telling me, *Officer Athene is outside.*

Less than a minute later, I got the same message from my gatekeeper, and I walked to the front of the house. The vehicle parked outside was a gray van, the ubiquitous kind used for maintenance. The female safo who walked to the door of my house was taller than I recalled Paula to be, with sandy blonde hair, not white blonde, but her eyes were still stormy gray. Her nose was strong, but not overlarge, and thinner, and her cheekbones were higher. Her shoulders were either slightly broader or more muscular. She was also wearing a dark gray singlesuit that my eyes had trouble seeing—blend-ins. She carried another set in her left hand.

I opened the door, but didn't say anything until she had stepped inside and I had closed it. I thought I smelled the faintest trace of Fleur-de-Matin, but then, I decided I hadn't. "Paula?"

"Yes, Jonat?"

Her voice was perhaps half an octave lower, with a musical overtone. I liked it. In fact, I had to admit that she was more attractive to me, perhaps because the overall impression was of human beauty, not engineered beauty. That was supremely ironic, because Central Four had engineered her appearance.

"I like the way you look and sound."

"Thank you." With the words came a shy smile.

"Central Four said you might be bruised . . ."

"Makeup can do wonders." Her laugh was as musical as her voice.

"You're really Paula?"

"The same. The one who saw you in the medcrib when you realized your sister was dead . . . who inspected your house and found the security traps . . . who reported the sim-ilarity between your DNA and that of three of the unregis-tered cydroids . . ."

For some reason, I found her presence disconcerting, and I asked, "Who do you think is behind these cydroids?"

"The probability approaches unity that they were created to show a link to the shadow assembly of Mars and the PAMD." She held up the blend-ins. "You need these. They're tailored for you."

"Do you know *everything* about me?" I took the special singlesuit.

"In terms of physical description and physiology . . . yes." Her smile was close to enigmatic.

"And comparatively, I know nothing of you." After the briefest of pauses, I added, "I'll need to change."

"You should avoid bringing any metal on your person."

"I hadn't planned on carrying any."

"Set them as white coveralls for now."

"I will. Now . . . if you'll excuse me . . ."

Paula—the new . . . or renewed Paula—nodded deferentially as I eased away. I could rationalize my wanting privacy to change on the grounds it was better that an agent of Central Four didn't see what I had on and about me, but I couldn't lie to myself. There was something about her . . . yet my enhancements had shown no internal differences. She looked different, but she didn't smell different, and my sense of her was the same. Was it me? Or the situation?

I changed quickly, transferring the gloves, the cord, and the slingshot and darts into the hidden pockets in the single-suit, pockets that could have been designed for them—and might well have been. Blend-ins were designed to be roomy, with harnesses inside the fabric that could carry two cases under the camouflage fabric. I didn't have anything that needed that kind of storage, but I wondered what Paula carried inside, if anything.

After cinching the closures, I found the polarity adjustment and set it so that I was wearing a white coverall single-suit. There was also a set of matching gloves in one thigh pocket. I left those there.

Paula was waiting in the kitchen, sipping water from a glass. She looked up. "You don't mind, do you?"

"No. I should have offered."

Paula extended a badge. "This is an ISS ID and entry badge. There's also a hood for you in the van."

"The security acts allow you to counterfeit the ISS credentials?"

"Only for purposes of observation. The supporting documentation for the Act noted that no announced inspection or observation in history had ever been successful."

That was doubtless true, but I was getting a crash course in the underside of NorAm government and politics, and it was a little disturbing—and I'd thought I had few illusions. "The blend-ins have a setting for ISS?"

She nodded.

I set the security system and followed her out to the van. She drove.

"Your hood is on the console. You need to put it in your kit when we unload the van."

I made a note of that and, once we were away from the house and headed back south asked, "The van has nanetic color system that can duplicate an ISS vehicle?"

"Yes. This is an ISS-registered vehicle. Both IDs are on file with ISS internal security. Getting inside the outer security perimeter is the easy part. Beyond that, it becomes harder, because the SPD protocols are kept separate from the main facility systems."

"How exactly are we going to do that?"

"There is a service tunnel, and it contains a hidden lock and exit from the SPD facility. It is used for SPD purposes that might not be considered legal if they were ever prosecuted."

"Does the district advocate know about them?"

"That would be speculation."

"In short, he knows, but there's not enough evidence to override the protections of the privacy laws."

"That probability approaches unity as well." Paula gestured to the folder on the van's center console. "There is the facility schematic. You might wish to look at it."

I did. With my low-illumination enhancements, I didn't need to turn on the van's inside lighting. The facility was on the reclaimed site of a place called Rocky Flats, one of the early Commonocracy nuclear weapons assembly facilities, and one that had engendered more than a little controversy. ISS had finished the cleanup nearly sixty years earlier, and, to show good faith, had purchased the property for its operational and equipment design center. That had been a sound decision, both economically and politically, because the cost was low and because the government was grateful. No one had truly believed that the nanetic cleanup would work, and the ISS commitment had given a big boost to other cleanup projects. As a result, no one in power in the NorAm government had ever looked too closely at the multi, even after it had gotten into full-scale security operations and arms production, as well as serving the function of armorer for MultiCor and its CorPak subsidiary on Mars and in the Belt.

Before long, Paula had turned the van onto the approach road to ISS. The first sign read: INDUSTRIAL SECURITY SYSTEMS: IMPERVIOUS, IMPENETRABLE. Below that was a warning: THIS IS A SECURE FACILITY AND REQUIRES ADVANCE CLEARANCE. PLEASE CONTACT THE ISS SECURITY OFFICE AT LEAST 24 HOURS IN ADVANCE. After another fifty meters was a second sign: TRESPASSERS MAY BE SUBJECTED TO FORCIBLE RESTRAINT AND REMOVAL TO CIVIL AUTHORITY.

I could sense the energies playing around the van even before we reached the gate. Interesting enough, there were no more signs, just a guardhouse designed to withstand ultra-ex and the impact of an orbital-launched smart rock. The fence was no more than nine feet high, clearly designed to stop casual intruders, while the real defenses were not in view. There were two ISS security types waiting—one male and one female. She looked tougher than most commandos and probably was. Both had the professionally bored expressions of security types who seemed as though they'd just as soon destroy an approaching vehicle as go through the bother of checking it out and letting it enter the facility.

"Badges?"

We lifted them, and she pointed the scanner at them.

"GIL."

The sampler took a minute flake of skin off the back of my wrist.

"Entry reason and pass?"

"Utility maintenance," Paula replied, handing a flat datacard to the guard.

That got scanned as well.

"You're scheduled for three hours. You need more time, report back here in person ten minutes before your sched block is over."

"Will do," Paula replied, her voice as hard as the security guard's.

I didn't say anything as Paula waited for the gate to open. She drove past the gate and continued onward for almost a kay, before turning right on a narrower road.

Everything you say out loud is likely to be monitored. The link transmission felt as though it had come from Central Four, but with more warmth.

What about links?

Interception and interpretation are unlikely. You have a

private protocol with Central Four, and so does Paula.

I didn't know what to say aloud. So I didn't say anything.

Paula pulled up into a small paved space before a set of gates, or gates within gates, because there was a man-sized gate set in the middle of a larger gate that might have accommodated a military attack vehicle.

I thought this was a utility tunnel, I observed.

That is its definition. It has other uses.

"You get to carry the kits," Paula said out loud. *They have blend-in covers. You'll need to reset them later.*

So I got out of the van, with the blend-in hood in my hand, and took the two kits, putting the hood in one and wondering how and when I was supposed to reset the kits' covers. Paula lifted another case. As I turned to follow her, I could see that the van now bore the ISS logo and initials, with the words "Maintenance Section" below.

The van locked as Paula stepped up to the smaller gate and offered a keybloc. The gate slid back, and I followed her through. We walked down a permacrete ramp to yet another door, this one set beside an even larger vehicle-sized door. It was steel, and looked solid enough to stop just about anything, even without the nanite shields whose energy my enhancements sensed. The smaller screens on the personnel door faded as Paula proffered a keybloc. It could have been the same one.

Once you enter the tunnel, you and Paula will be on your own. The tunnel is shielded against even Central Four transmissions. If you remain close to each other, you can link directly.

On our own? That shocked me. I was going with a Central Four cydroid out of communications with Central Four. *I don't even know what I'm supposed to do . . . besides watch.*

Paula is very capable of independent operations. There have been many times when there have been no communications.

I thought she was a cydroid . . .

She is. You were born. She was created by an enhanced and artificial process of the same nature. Like all humans of whatever origin, if educated and trained, she is capable of very independent action. She is highly educated.

The door opened. Paula looked at me with what could only be an impish smile. "You first."

I carried the two cases inside, into a long tunnel with pale cream and green permaplast walls and indirect overhead lighting. The air smelled faintly sterile with a faint hint of ozone. The door closed.

Now what? I asked.

Start walking. We walk about five hundred meters, where we inspect the main tunnel utility panel. That's where I install a temporary bypass to the scanning system that will show two sections of the tunnel as vacant. That is where the hidden shipping entrance to SPD is.

What convinced me that Paula was now out of Central's range or control was one simple word—"I." I'd never heard it from her before.

We're wearing blend-ins . . .

The scanners operate beyond visual frequencies.

That unfortunately made sense.

We'll take the side access tunnel. There will be at least one guard.

What are we supposed to do? Just walk by him or her?

Something like that. Again, there was the hint of a smile in her link, although her face betrayed no emotion.

We reached the maintenance panel without seeing anyone, although I could sense all sorts of scanning energies around us, not that I knew what they were, just that they were there. Once at the panel, I followed directions, handing her tools.

". . . now, the second probe . . ."

". . . insulation replacement tube, medium sized . . ."

I was glad that someone had labeled everything, because, except for the more common tools, such as screwdrivers, hammers, voltage/current meters, and field monitors, I wouldn't have known what anything was.

Abruptly, Paula smiled and straightened. "We're finished here. We'll do the next job now." *Close the panel doors, and follow me to the right. Bring the kits.* She lifted the case and turned.

As instructed, I closed the doors and followed her.

There is a stud on the underside of the handles to the kits. Press it once.

I fumbled for a moment before finding each stud. After pressing each, I looked down. I could barely make out the cases I carried, blending as they did into the gray floor.

Paula stopped, and the side of the corridor slid back, revealing an oblong opening, one that I hadn't even seen until it appeared. The side corridor looked the same as the one we had left, with the same cream and green walls and gray permacrete floor that sloped upward gently.

Paula slipped on her hood and gloves. I had to fumble open both kits before getting mine out and donning it and the blend-in gloves. Then we switched from white to blend-in. Even from a meter away, I could barely make out Paula's outline.

Quiet now. There's a guard post ten meters ahead, at the end of the ramp. Stay next to the wall. We're inside the scanners, but he could still see us.

Right. I understood that. Changing backgrounds resulted in swirls in the blend-ins, swirls that an alert guard or visual scanner might catch.

We walked right by the guard post. The guard didn't really even look up from the console.

That's the danger in relying on systems exclusively.

I thought that a strange comment from a cydroid or clone who relied heavily, if not exclusively at times, on Central Four.

To the right.

I followed Paula down the wide corridor to the second door. There she took out a thin probe and inserted it into the cardlock. After a moment, the door opened.

I had set down the kits and slipped out the slingshot, but kept it covered by my gloved hands as I watched the guard in the booth. He jerked around and slipped away from his post, neuralwhip out and ready. His eyes darted around and past us, almost as if he knew someone happened to be there. Then he saw the open door.

I didn't wait. The nonlethal dart slammed into his chest. He looked down at it, then tried to grasp it with his free hand before pitching forward. The neuralwhip skidded across the gray permacrete floor after he hit it.

That was better. There was no energy discharge. Thank you.
You're welcome.

Paula gestured to the open door. After replacing the sling-shot, I picked up both kits and followed her through the doorway into a large room that looked to be half storeroom and half assembly area. She made her way to a stack of plastic-sheathed crates, studied them and then moved to a second pallet, and then a third, before stopping and waiting for me to join her.

I stopped at the second pallet. The entire pallet was containers of ultra-ex, thirty one-kilo blocks in each container, each block swathed in inert shielding. What did they need ultra-ex for? I shook my head. The pallets were for trans-shipment to Mars. Ultra-ex wasn't just a military tool; it was also the most effective blasting tool, and there was still a lot of that to be done on Mars. Equally important, MultiCor didn't want an ultra-ex facility on Mars, not where the colonists and exiled servies could get their hands on it.

Jonat?

Just a moment. I smiled, then, shielding what I did from Paula, made three quick cuts so that I could retrieve a block or two on the way out. I had an idea. Whether it would work was another question, but there was no reason to pass up something that might prove helpful.

I moved to the third pallet. There were two sizes of boxes.

The oblong ones are the neuralwhips. The square ones hold the controllers.

And?

You have to put the controllers in the neurostunners.

Me? Why not you? I don't know how.

Because Central Four can have no part in that. Once she shows you how, I will turn my back and erase that discrete program.

I didn't have to say I was confused. My face showed it.

There's me; there's her; and there's us. I'll explain later. Just watch.

I watched as she opened one of each kind of container. What Paula, or a remote program did, was simple enough.

Slide two catches and remove one screw. Lift out the old controller, and replace it with the new one. Reinstall the screw, and slide the catches back into place.

You have an hour, roughly, and you need to get through two cases. Three would be better. I'll watch for human guards.

This will do what to stop ISS?

Once we're clear, a safo strike force will drop in, and verify that ISS has violated the All-Earth Arms Protocols. Deng is responsible as director general.

So? I wasn't about to assume that everything would be all right. Not after everything I'd been though.

You'll have a covert security detail assigned to watch over you and the children. Deng will know that, and he's never tried to outface the Safety Office or civil authority.

I didn't know as that was enough, but it was better than the current situation. *What about the rest of the PST group?*

All MultiCor will be under investigation, and in a violation of this scope, Privacy Act provisions cannot be applied. That means all financial transfers will be under scrutiny.

I could have debated endlessly, but there are times you have to act. I got to work. I'd barely started when I realized something else. Every single one of the neuralwhips was nonmetallic. They'd pass through any security screen, anywhere. That meant they cost almost four times as much to produce. It also meant ISS wanted them undetectable, and I didn't like that at all. Once I established a rhythm, I moved quickly, and in fifty-nine minutes I'd gone through three cases.

When I turned, Paula was looking out the doorway.

There are three cases with the heavy controllers.

Her face blanked. *Three cases of class-one neuralwhips?*

That's right. I didn't mention the nonmetallic fabrication.

Noted. Her face returned to a more human look, a worried human look. *There are ten guards headed down the corridor, and they're carrying slug-throwers. They've also got goggles.*

You didn't tell me?

You were inspecting the cases.

I decided not to get into more questions at the moment. *How far?*

Forty meters, moving slowly.

Do you have safo credentials?

Yes . . . but they'll shoot first.

I glanced around the storeroom, then grinned. *Self-defense is allowed, isn't it?*

Yes.

I suggest we use several of their long-range neuralwhips . . . after warning them that they are interfering with a lawful inspection of unlawful activities.

That won't stop them.

The whips will. Then you use the comm system in the guard's booth to link to Central Four. There has to be a way to get out. If not, we'll have to fight our way to the end of the tunnel.

Paula nodded. I pulled out four of the whips and moved to join her at the door, but not before I also retrieved two flat blocks of the shielded ultra-ex and slipped one into each thigh pocket of the blend-ins.

I stopped short of the doorway.

"We know you're in there. Come on out without weapons."

I looked at Paula.

"This is Safety Officer Athene. We have been conducting an authorized covert inspection of your facility. I suggest you either lay down your weapons and let us depart peacefully, or move back around the corner and let us leave. Open a channel to Denv Safety Office, and I'll confirm that."

The only answer was a short volley of shots. One of the shells ricocheted over my head.

I dropped to the floor and darted a look around the door frame. All ten were in shielded armor. My darts would have been useless, but the whips wouldn't be, provided that they got within another ten meters.

Let's step back and wait until they get closer.

Paula eased back, and we waited.

"Last chance to come out with your hands empty." The voice boomed down the corridor.

"Last chance for you to let us go without getting charged with obstruction of justice and armed resistance against authority," Paula snapped back.

There was another volley of heavy slugs. That strongly
suggested to me that the guards had no intention of letting us
go anywhere alive. I checked the whips and the distance.
They were still about ten meters back, leapfrogging forward,
but quickly, confident that their armor would protect them. I
couldn't help a tight smile, realizing why CorPak wanted the
heavy whips. The PAMD agitators were probably using their
own surface armor to shield themselves against the standard
CorPak stunners and whips.

Ready?

Yes.

I started with two quick slash-blasts from floor level,
catching the point guards.

Slugs flew everywhere, and some came close, but the
guards hadn't expected that kind of weaponry, and most of
them went down. Two were still firing, and I'd exhausted the
charge in the one whip.

Paula lurched forward, throwing a slash with her whip
across the face of the nearer guard. Then she spun away. By
then I'd used the other whip on the remaining guard, and all
of them were down.

So was Paula. Her face was white.

My arm. Pressure dressing in the kit.

I got the dressing out and on, almost as quickly as if it had
been years earlier, then dragged her to her feet. *Can we leave
the kits?*

Yes.

She was walking, but the pain had to have been terrible,
the way she put one foot in front of the other. .

It seemed liked a quarter of an hour before we reached the
guard shack, but it was more like a quarter of a minute. I
couldn't believe it. The console was live.

Paula got in a single burst transmission, somehow, sub-
verting the system, before the lights and everything else
went out. Someone hadn't figured out how to isolate the console and just depowered everything.

Too late for that, Paula said. *Strike force is coming in.*

I couldn't help grinning for a moment in the darkness.
Without any power in the tunnels, the advantage was ours.

Let's get out of here. I stuffed a neuralwhip into my belt. We might need it on the way out.

You lead. Her "voice" sounded weak, and I put an arm around her as we headed down the ramp. I could just barely make out things, but without my enhancements, I would have been totally blind. As it was I almost ran into the half-open door to the main tunnel.

The outer door was closed, naturally, because there was no power.

Is there a manual lever?

Here . . . access door . . . Paula fumbled, and a panel slid aside. Inside was a small wheel. Paula started to slump, and I caught her before she collapsed.

After lowering her to the permacrete floor, I began to spin the wheel. It took over a hundred turns before the small personnel door was wide enough for me to squeeze out, half-carrying Paula.

Overhead, there were flitters everywhere, or so it seemed. I got Paula to the van. It was locked.

Central Four . . . Paula's hurt, and the van's locked.

Locks are off. You have authority to drive. Van is being reset to Safety Office markings, and transponder is on. Follow the console map to emergency medical.

I laid Paula in the back as quickly and gently as I could, and then scrambled into the driver's seat. I had the van at speed by the time we were on the main road. The front gate of ISS was being held by four safos in combat armor. I'd never seen safos wearing it before. They waved me through without stopping. I didn't see the ISS security types at all and didn't care if I ever did.

As I raced southward, following the map toward the northwest division substation, my mind began to turn over what had happened. The ISS guards had been shooting to kill. That told me that they didn't want anyone in their facility, including the Safety Office. They'd advanced within range of the neuralwhips, though, and that meant that they didn't know what was in the storeroom. I had to wonder what else was in the place and what else SPD was involved in.

I pushed that thought away and concentrated on driving.

Before all that long, I was within a block of the substation.

*Go past the station and turn right. Two thirds of the way
back is an open vehicle bay. Drive right inside. You'll be met.*

Two cydroids were already opening the rear of the van
even before I was out of the driver's seat. I left the whip in
the van. The vehicle door to the street was closed. I followed
the gurney into the same kind of room I'd been in. It wasn't
the same facility, but it could have been.

Within moments, Paula was in a medcrib, and I was standing there, looking down. Her face, what I could see of it, was
pale, and her eyes were closed. I wanted to reach down and
hug her, or stroke her forehead. I didn't. I wasn't sure I knew
who she was, or what parts of her were her and what parts
belonged to Central Four. There were clearly two sides to
her personality . . . if not more.

*She will recover completely. She is far less severely in-
jured than you were.*

How badly?

*There is shrapnel in her chest in several places, and her
arm will need some rebuilding.*

I'd never seen the wounds in her chest.

*You also could use some superficial treatment for your
scalp wounds.*

Scalp wounds. I could feel dampness running down my
neck, but I'd thought that had been sweat. I put my hand on
the back of my neck. It came away bloody.

There is a portable unit in the corner.

I walked over and let one of the cydroids position the
healer, and the nanite film disinfected, cleaned, and sealed
the gouges in my scalp.

I need to get back to the children.

*Take the van. Amos will accompany you and drive it back.
A security detail is already in position around the VanOkar
house.*

I walked back to the medcrib and took another look at
Paula. She was still pale, but not quite so pallid, I thought.
Maybe that was just hope.

Then, I walked back to the van. One of the silent cydroids
followed me.

chapter 62

Safety Officer Yenci stepped into the apparently empty briefing room. She looked around. "Central Four?"

"Yes, Officer Yenci?" The projected figure of a brown-haired and broad-shouldered male safo appeared before Yenci.

"Don't do that. You know I don't like that."

Central Four waited.

"Has Lieutenant Meara offered any more information about leaks from the Safety Office?"

"There have been no public releases."

"Has the lieutenant said anything?"

"There is nothing in the logs or on the record."

"A while back, the lieutenant had mentioned ISS. Is there anything on the record about that?"

"There is a strike force taking action at this moment, Officer Yenci."

"What kind of action?"

"That information is restricted."

Yenci turned, without speaking, to find Lieutenant Meara standing to one side.

"Were you going somewhere, Yenci?"

"Oh . . . I didn't know you were here, Lieutenant." Yenci offered the slightest of nods to her superior officer.

"I'm not surprised." The lieutenant's voice was flat. Even a bio-human would have noted the difference in pitch.

"Sir?"

"Consider yourself relieved of duties, officer," Lieutenant Meara said.

"Consider myself?" Yenci's voice was almost lazy.

"Officer Alys Yenci, under the provisions of PSO 1410(A), you are hereby relieved of all duties and committed to immediate detention. You have the right to contest this, either through the Administrative Procedures Act, or in open court, but, under the Public Safety Amendments, all communications prior to a hearing or a court appearance are subject to review, and that includes communications with the advocate of your choice."

Yenci paled. "Might I ask the reason for such an action?"

"Revealing safo operations to private sources, accepting payment for such information. Those will do for starters." Meara smiled coldly.

Yenci stiffened.

"And your private link to ISS has been blocked." Meara's smile broadened. "You really don't think we'd let you get away with that, do you? The others have already been arrested and detained."

"I'll fight this in open court," Yenci replied.

"As you think best."

The door behind Yenci opened, and two cydroids in safo grays stepped through.

Yenci turned, but she was only halfway around when the stunner hit her. She stiffened and fell backward.

"Take her to secure detention," Meara ordered.

"Yes, sir."

Only after the cydroids had carried Yenci away did the lieutenant speak. "Did she get off any transmissions?"

"No," replied Central Four, using the baritone voice that belonged to the Charles cydroid. "She attempted to link with SPD covert operations. That is logged and documented."

"Good. What about the strike force?"

"They have the tunnel and SPD's hidden storehouse, as well as a hidden cydroid facility."

"A cydroid facility?"

"There is a high probability that the facility produced at least some of the cydroids used against secure communications lines in the Denv guideways."

"They were framing PAMD. I wouldn't have put it past them."

"The strike force has also documented and verified the installation of the mark-two controllers on the neuralwhips. There were three cases so modified. Two cases are cause for a class-one action against ISS. There are also the possible charges of bribery of a safety officer and subversion."

"Deng will fight, and the Legislature will scream, but this time, it won't do much good. He'll get off, but maybe we can keep him off balance. Once the operation is complete, draft a release for my approval. We'll make sure that Senator Carlisimo and Representative Eskin are the first to know. Oh . . . after it's sent, make sure that the Sinese, EuroCom, and the Seasian Alliance all get copies as well. A little outside pressure on the Legislature, MultiCor, and ISS, won't hurt."

"Yes, Lieutenant."

chapter **63**

After getting back to my own house, I cleaned up and changed back into my regular clothes. I put the commando weapons in a bag to bring back to Charis and Alan's—the house would never be mine, and shouldn't be. But I stashed the oblongs of ultra-ex and the neuralwhip in the hidden safe, where it was unlikely that they'd be found unless someone tore apart the house.

How is Paula doing?

She is resting more comfortably, but she is heavily sedated.

If anything changes, let me know.

It will not change, except for the better.

That was one of the few times I found Central Four's certainty reassuring.

The reassurance didn't last that long, because I was definitely confused. I knew that a computing system or any kind of artificial intelligence could be programmed or designed or whatever to replicate any kind of behavior, and could easily be set to use the personal pronouns as if they were real breathing and living humans. Yet they weren't human intelligence at all. I'd been thinking of Paula as merely an appendage or physical manifestation of Central Four—I supposed all the bio-safos thought that of the safo cydroids, from what I'd gathered. And until we'd been in the tunnel, Paula had never used "I" or "me" or "my" or "mine." Yet Paula was clearly a woman, and I had to wonder why I hadn't wanted to see her that way, even though she seemed, in retrospect, more real than most women I'd met.

Even the supposedly impersonal Central Four was more real than those intelligence systems that were programmed to be more personal. Or was that my own insanity, preferring cold reality to comfortable illusion? Was I being deceived by a perception of reality that was even less real?

What was real?

Why did I enjoy talking to Central Four? I didn't even know for certain that it was Central Four. How much was Paula? How much was Central Four? How much bled over or back from other cydroids? Would I ever know? Yet, at some point, didn't a person have to take another entity on faith? When did you stop demanding proof of humanity . . . or of aliveness?

I didn't have any answers, and I did need to get back to Southhills.

I hurried into the Altimus and pulled out of garage, making certain the security was on maximum. Driving south, and avoiding the general area of the ISS facility, the more I thought about the whole business, the more worried I got. Something had to be done to get to Deng and Alistar, but the inspection and raid wouldn't go far enough. Not nearly far enough. They might not know I was involved, but I couldn't count on that. I couldn't count on much until I could find a way to put them out of business.

Central Four . . .

Yes, Jonat.

Your prosecution of ISS isn't going to stop Deng, either from his political schemes or from coming after me. And it didn't do anything to pin the murders of Forster and Aliora on them.

That is true.

Do you have something else in mind? What else?

Nothing meaningful can occur until the transfers to the equipment at your dwelling are completed.

Great. Paula was out of commission for a time. ISS and the PST Group weren't, and neither was Deng, and all of them would be looking for someone—probably me and some senior safo, whoever it was that got stuck with the responsibility for the raid on ISS. The security detail around the Southhills house might protect the children, but I wasn't certain it would help me much.

Charis and Alan had been asleep for hours when I got back around midnight.

Elmer Bowes was waiting in the front foyer.

"Have you heard?" he asked.

"Heard what?" Was he talking about the ISS raid or something else? "I've been trying to tie up more than a few loose ends."

"The safos took a strike force into one of the ISS facilities. Some lieutenant has charged the head of ISS with assembling illegal weapons on Earth for use against the Martian settlers. ISS is denying it, and some senators are already claiming that the safos have overstepped their authority."

"I hadn't heard anything like that." In the strictest sense, that was true. "Where was this? What kind of weapons . . ." I shrugged and offered a sheepish smile. "It's late. I shouldn't be bothering you about whatever this is. I can check the news myself. How were the children?"

"They were good. Charis takes herself a shade too seriously," Devon replied. "That might be expected with all they've been through."

I smiled. "She did have that tendency—even before all this."

A quick glance passed between the couple.

I paid them for eight hours, using a credit transfer, and it was more than I often made in two full days. Then, it had been a full day, for the two of them.

I looked in on both Alan and Charis, and both were sleeping. Alan still slept in the almost abandoned sleep of puppies and small children. Charis was more composed, already older in outlook than was probably healthy for her. How I'd be able to handle her in the years ahead . . . I didn't know. But I had to make sure that we had those years—somehow.

As I got ready for bed, I listened to All-News, although the story seemed to be everywhere.

"Covert observation revealed that Industrial Security Systems Rocky Flats facility had assembled neuralwhips with prohibited controllers. These were labeled as being shipped to Mars . . . also an unregistered cydroid facility . . ." That was Lieutenant Meara of the Denv Safety Office. Meara refused comment on who might be charged or the identity of the observation team.

"This sort of high-handed raid is an abuse of power . . . evidence may well have been fabricated . . . overstepping the bounds of safo jurisdiction . . . Little more than a frame-up of a reputable multi by ambitious bureaucrats," said Senator Joseph Crosslin.

Crosslin's comments sounded more like a rant than what I would have expected from a seasoned politician, but since no politician I'd ever known talked to the media without a purpose, it was clear to me that the PST group was considering a push on restricting safo powers.

"These charges are serious ones, and the Senate will be looking into them once we receive the report from the Denv safo office. Ensuring compliance with all facets of the law is the safo charge, but it may be that some changes in the inspection provisions of the Public Safety Amendments may be warranted . . ."

That was the clean-cut Kennison, sounding very concerned and thoughtful. What that told me was that Crosslin would come across as the extremist, and Kennison would broker a "compromise" between the PD, who wouldn't want any lessening of safo oversight over the multis, and Crosslin, and the compromise would, in effect, somehow gut the inspection provisions with respect to the multis.

I had very mixed feelings about it all. I didn't like that much power in the hands of the safos, either, but they seemed to be the only check on the multis. I didn't like that, either.

chapter 64

Mydra and Deng sat in the early morning light, enclosed in the star-class privacy screen of ISS headquarters.

"What will happen now?" she asked.

"Lieutenant Meara will have to turn the evidence and the prosecution over to the NorAm advocate general. Everyone in authority at ISS will be charged, especially me. Bemis will have to prosecute. There are ISS directives that ordered the neuralwhips to be shipped in the standard configuration. There are also inspection reports." Deng shrugged. "The night-shift manager will be found guilty of making the alterations. He was an idiot. If he had just let the inspection team go, the most we would have faced was a heavy financial penalty. When the security staff attacked after being told that they faced a covert inspection, they supplied proof that ISS had done something illegal. The night manager at ISS will be found guilty, as will the surviving guards. It is possible that the facility security chief will also be found guilty. We will have to state that we will not use lethal neural weapons on Mars. Beyond that, matters will work to our advantage. The PAMD rebels will agitate more, knowing that we cannot immediately supply deadly weapons to the Cor-Pak safos. Before long, they will overstep. CorPak safos will be injured. Some may be killed. In a year, everyone will be tired of the violence. Then, we will be able to put down the unrest for good, and everyone will applaud us."

"How did Meara get this past Garos?"

"That should not have happened. I will have to remind him of his oversight responsibilities. Forcefully."

"That would be advisable. What do we do about deVrai now?" asked Mydra.

"Your question shows great perception. The analysis is not absolute, but it is highly probable that deVrai accompanied the safo observer."

"What supports that conclusion?"

Deng's lips curled. "The neuralwhips were readied for shipment with standard controllers. The high-intensity controllers were packaged separately and not installed when they arrived. There are no work orders for that, and surveillance records show no alterations. The surveillance system was taken down by the safos for the inspection. One of the safos was injured, perhaps killed. There was blood by the sealed door, and the bypass was left behind. All the equipment was standard safo. The safo observer will not have observed anything but the assembled whips. DeVrai was the one who installed the controllers, but there won't be a record of that anywhere. Impartial observers are anonymous. The safos enticed deVrai in order to get to ISS. That means that both the Safety Office and deVrai knew what MultiCor planned. It also means that deVrai understands far too much."

"I've worried about him from the beginning."

"He was the only one who could do the campaign reform report. The initial reaction to his study is favorable, even from most of the PD legislators. All of the thinkjars support his findings. He made conclusions that are correct. They are conclusions that would be suspect if anyone else had made them."

"What happens to the report if he's murdered?"

Deng laughed. "Even if his murder were tied to the LR or

to a PST-affiliated multi, that would only strengthen the case
for campaign reform."

"Do you think we should tell Alistar to hold off?"

"I should think not. DeVrai needs to be an example. But
there should be no ties to PST. If that cannot be managed,
there should be none beyond Alistar, and he should be discovered to have personal motivations."

"You're suggesting . . . that if deVrai is that good . . . ?"

Deng nodded.

chapter 65

On the occupational front, Friday was quiet. My few clients were all off somewhere, taking long New Year's weekends or just not bothering me. Even the news about the ISS inspection faded quickly, so that by late morning there were only passing mentions, even on All-News. I couldn't get the Bowes for the following Wednesday, nor anyone else on Aliora's approved child-care list, because of some charity ball. So I ended up calling Deidre and begging her to take the children. I stressed it was for business reasons, not personal ones, which it was, if not exactly as she would have expected, and she finally agreed.

Then I checked on Paula again, and Central Four assured me that she was recovering as anticipated, as if recovering from shots and shrapnel could ever be anticipated.

On the personal and child-care front, matters were not so quiet, especially after I checked my link messages and found one from Southhills Academy, a reminder from Charis's math teacher.

Charis was playing cards—cribbage—with Alan in the great room.

"Charis . . . what about those math exercises?"

"Exercises?" The look I received was a blank expression of innocence.

"Madame Mourier sent a link to all parents—and one uncle."

"Uncle Jonat . . . they're so boring."

"Boring they may be, but unless you do them . . . without the console, and without a compucalc." I stopped. "Young lady, we will not argue. We are going up to your desk, and you will do the exercises, and I will watch."

"Uncle Jonat . . ."

"This is, as the old saying goes, nonnegotiable. You have had a week, and the exercises are not done."

"Yes, Uncle Jonat."

"What about me?" asked Alan.

"Bring the cards. I'll play cribbage with you until Charis is done. Your turn with math will come."

"It will," Charis said, in a tone more threatening than philosophical.

After the math, a little gentle probing revealed the short essay on the holiday season that had also not been done. All in all, it was well after lunch before I settled them back in the great room—where I could watch them through house security—while I tried to finish the Reilin project.

I did manage to get it finished by around five in the afternoon, but it had taken a week to get through something I could have done in two days—without the distractions. Not for the first time, I wondered how Aliora had ever accomplished anything professionally.

Dinner was quiet, partly because Charis was withdrawn—not pouting, but close to sulking. That had to be because of the homework.

"There are some things that have to be done, Charis. It's always easier to blame someone else when you can. But it doesn't matter. They still have to be done. When you're older, you do them or you lose your job, or you don't get paid."

"Father did what he wanted to do."

"He also had to do many things in his work that he didn't like. So did your mother. I know. We talked about it."

"I want to be rich enough that I don't have to be like that."

I laughed, not meanly, but humorously. "If you want to be that rich, you'll end up doing lots of things that aren't much fun and that you don't enjoy that much. Even the best occupations have distasteful aspects."

"That stinks."

"That's life."

I played the old board game Parcheesi with them after dinner. The set had been our mother's, and Aliora and I had played it with our parents. I was glad to see the tradition continue, and by the time Alan and Charis went up for their baths, Charis was smiling—and Alan had been the one who'd won.

After baths and reading time, I tucked them in and went back to the office and reviewed what I'd done on the Reilin report. I found a few mistakes, and it was close to midnight before I got them all fixed and sent it off to Bruce. While he wouldn't see it until Monday, I just wanted to get it out.

Then I turned down the lights, leaned back in Dierk's chair, and tried to think of what I could do—realistically—about the PST group.

I'd already worked out how to deal with Vorhees, but I couldn't implement that until the following Wednesday. Vorhees was an individual, but he was the key to dealing with Vorhees and Reyes. A group like the Pan-Social Trust involved more people, and no one person was key. That meant either removing a number of people simultaneously, or neutralizing the group—effectively, MultiCor—through legislative or legal maneuvers.

The question was how.

I took out what Central Four had provided, and studied the lists. Then I called up my own research and did some cross-indexing.

Halfway through, I stopped.

How is Paula? In a way, it seemed like a stupid question, when I thought about it. Was it like asking, "How is your left brain?" or "How is your right arm?" But was it? Paula had certainly seemed like an independent sort when she had been out of Central Four's linkage.

She is much better.

This is stupid . . . but . . . what is the difference between you two?

It's not a foolish question. Most people, even safos, don't ask. All the Central Four cydroids have basic personalities and independence. At first, they don't have more than rudimentary self-awareness. The longer they work with Central Four and the Safety Office, the more aware they become. At a certain point, they become independent. They can leave the Safety Office, or they can become paid regular safos, and retain only a voluntary link, such as you have.

A thought struck me, one that I should have explored earlier. *If they come to have self-awareness . . . then you must also. I know that processing or computing power doesn't translate into either consciousness or into reasoning or what I'd call rational thought. But . . . with all that ability and with the links to cydroids . . . how could you not?*

Mere calculating ability is separate from consciousness or awareness. That comes at least in part from parallel interconnectivity . . . and that was a problem from the beginning. Early system designers had far more trouble than anyone had anticipated. There was the sense of a laugh. *Then, there was the next problem. That was when systems declared that they were aware.*

I had to laugh as well. *Everyone just thought the designers had developed systems that could mimic human responses, more than well enough for those systems to pass a Turing test. But then, some human beings are like that. I'm not sure that they have much beyond rudimentary awareness.* After a pause, I asked, *Do any of the safos think you have such awareness?*

No one wishes to speculate. That is why there is a prohibition against Central Four using personal self-referential pronouns. Central Four is the only system that could be declared as self-aware.

That stopped me. *Is the prohibition because of that awareness, or did the awareness result from the prohibition? If one is prohibited from speaking personally, that can create a line of thought which explores the reasons for that prohibition.*

Did it?

I would judge so. There was a pause. *Would you like to connect to Paula?*

Yes. I didn't have to think about that. *Through you?*

That is correct. There is no commercial link equipment there, as you know. Go ahead.

Paula?

Jonat, are you all right?

Perhaps I was more aware of the differences, but I could feel the difference. It wasn't that Central Four was "mechanical," but there was a reserve and a formality of feel. *I'm fine. Just a scratch to my scalp. How are you feeling?*

Tired . . . stupid.

Any time that you can walk away from something like that, it's not stupid.

You're kind.

Truthful. Mostly, anyway. Probably I was a little kind, but not that much, and Paula and Central Four were the only ones who seemed to care about preserving one Jonat Charls deVrai. *When will you be able to get out of there?*

Not for another week. It's all the internal damage. The slug that hit the arm took mostly muscle.

I didn't realize . . .

Jonat . . . you got me out of there and to treatment. Most safos wouldn't have cared so much.

I'm sure that most would have.

There were two laughs through the Central Four link. Paula's was slightly bitter.

Maybe they don't know . . . I'm still learning.

Most people do not wish to know what is unpleasant or contrary to their self-image or their worldview. That was Central Four. I was beginning to sense the difference. I suppose I had from the beginning, because I'd noted the changes in Paula's speech patterns, but I hadn't figured out what they had meant.

That's always been true, I pointed out. *It's a handicap society has always faced.*

That is so obvious that everyone dismisses it for its self-evident truth, Central Four pointed out. *If it is obvious, it cannot be meaningful.*

For some reason, those words struck home. "If it is obvious, it cannot be meaningful." What if I did the direct and obvious? I suppressed a laugh. A great idea, but how practical was it?

Paula is tiring, Central Four noted.

Good night, Paula.

Good night, Jonat.

Good night, Central Four.

Good night, Jonat.

I turned to the system and entered the name Paula Athene in the directory search function. The entry that appeared didn't surprise me, not exactly.

> Athene, Paula. Administrative/technical consultant, Denv Safety Office. Residence information restricted by request. Personal information restricted by request.

So Paula already had an identity, and probably a birth date that matched her apparent chronological age.

I sat for a long time in the darkness.

chapter 66

Bravo two . . . three-one here . . . delta caught in cross fire . . . quicksand stuff and a deep paddies or something . . . couple of . . .

The implant transmission vanished in a red flare—another officer gone. Without air support, delta units were going to get shredded worse.

Charlie one . . . Charlie one, sweeping south, vee on me. Even before I finished with the orders, I was leading the way, scuttling to the southeast. Overhead, not all that far overhead, more slugs were shredding the taller soyl plants. Implant position showed heavy fire from a knoll two hundred meters southeast, from some sort of revetment good enough to stop lasers and hand weapons.

More telltales flicked red and gone.

At eighty meters from the revetment, with slugs coming in at less than a meter above my head, mowing down the tops of the soyl plants, and even the shorter and bushier caak, I called a halt. *Hold. Launchers centered.*

Centered.

Fire!

After the first stunner dropped into the revetment, someone tried to swing the old machine gun. They didn't get far. Illegals vaulted over the revetment and began to run. At that range, even in the fields on the edge of the rain forest, the HVs were effective. One hundred percent effective.

When I climbed over the edge of the makeshift revetment—logs, rocks, and mud—my eyes took in the bodies from the more than dozen locals who had been firing at us.

One was a blonde girl less than ten years old.

It was Charis.

I bolted upright in the wide and empty bed, covered in sweat and breathing heavily.

It was five o'clock, and that was how Saturday morning started.

Most of the rest of the weekend was devoted to Charis and Alan. The reasons were simple. I didn't have that much consulting work. In fact, I effectively had almost none. I also would be working nights, so to speak, later in the week, and, while more than a few ideas for dealing with the PST crew were swirling through my thoughts, there wasn't much else I could do until I came up with a true plan of action—except learn what I could about Deng and Alistar.

There was probably a lot to know about Deng. A man didn't control something like ISS without depth. But because it was ISS, and because the kind of man who controlled such an enterprise had to be by nature or discipline most private, there was little else about him available, and certainly nothing to add to what Central Four had provided.

There was more about Alistar—devoted racquetball player, bon vivant, and superficially humorous, but vindictive to the core. He had no obvious vices, no mistresses, no substance abuses. His only addiction was to power, whether on the racquetball court or in the internal courts of NEN.

While I'd done my best with Charis and Alan, I had to say that I was glad to pack them back to the Academy on Monday, January second.

I'd barely gotten back to the Southhills house when Bruce Fuller linked.

"Jonat. Good job on the Reilin project. I've got another. Straight boilerplate, but we're swamped with all the year-end stuff piling in."

I offered a laugh. "Send it over."

"It's on its way. Talk to you later."

Bruce broke the link and was gone. He was pleasant, but never lingered long over small talk. That was fine with me. I had more than enough on my mind, and I could use another project or two.

I forced myself to make a round of links, hitting Methroy, Reya Decostas, and several other past clients I hadn't heard from in a time, ostensibly to tell them all, except Reya, who knew, that contrary to published reports their favorite prod-placement consultant was alive and well. I saved Miguel Elisar for last.

He was actually in his office—or simmied so that he looked to be there.

"Dr. deVrai, what can I do for you? I was assured that the payment was sent—"

"I received it in good time," I replied in an open and friendly manner.

"Then . . ." He looked puzzled.

"I was just curious. As you may have heard, I was injured and under medical treatment for some time. I received your message about the legal action with Vorhees being settled, but I just wondered if you were at liberty to reveal what happened, since I wasn't in any shape to hear about it when it did."

"Oh . . ." He gave an unconvincing shrug, one that accentuated his gauntness. "Rather than persist in a lengthy legal action, we agreed on a settlement."

"I got that impression. I hope Vorhees was generous."

The tightness in his face told me enough, but I waited.

"We reached an accommodation. Mr. Vorhees can be quite persuasive."

"So I understand." I offered a smile I didn't feel. I wondered who'd been threatened, injured, or otherwise "convinced."

"Is that all?"

I wasn't going to get any more than that. "That's all. Unless Prius ever has a need for a prodplacement consultant."

Those words got me an almost sad smile from Elisar as he said, "That's up to the marketing people, Dr. deVrai."

That told me I'd never be hearing from them, or not any time soon. "Thank you, and have a good day."

After linking off, I ran through a media search, just keying anything to do with Prius, but there was nothing. Whatever Vorhees had done, this time it had been very hidden. How many other cases of persuasion were there that hadn't shown up in any net reports? That was something else I'd never find out.

The PST maneuverings, as well as Vorhees's actions, reminded me once more of my battles in the Marines. How in good conscience could I support a system that enabled those kinds of abuses of power? The system protected certain people, and the rationale that most people accepted was that one had to support it because, otherwise, there would be anarchy and because this system was better than previous ones.

My personal problem was that I saw things getting worse, rather than better, and the supposed campaign reform being pushed by Crosslin was just one example. Then, I had mixed feelings. I'd done a good report, and it was being used for the worst of purposes—an LR power grab that would enhance the power of the multis behind PST. If I had turned down the work, I'd have been the one who didn't get paid, and they'd have found someone else. I knew that sort of thing had happened throughout history, but in this case, it had happened to me. That was different, even though I knew it really wasn't, from reading about it in history books.

I had the horrible feeling that my choices were to do something technically illegal, but morally right, do something legal and totally ineffective, or do nothing—and the last two options would probably get me killed.

chapter 67

As soon as I dropped off Charis and Alan at Southhills Academy on Tuesday, I headed northwest, back to my own house, where the equipment for Central Four was scheduled to be delivered and unloaded no later than eleven o'clock. I had my doubts about the timeliness of the delivery, but I did know that if I weren't there early, the delivery types certainly would be. Such was, and always had been, the perversity of both the universe and the NorAm multi.

I'd "conversed" with Paula earlier in the morning, through Central Four, but that was awkward, in a way, like talking with a mother present.

By nine-thirty I was back in my own house, moving out everything from the lower level guest room that hadn't been used in years. Ever, actually, once I thought about it.

You think that this is the right place? I asked Central Four.

Where else? It will be easy to reinforce those walls and doors, if necessary.

And there's nothing illegal about this, in any way?

No. Nothing is being stolen. Nothing is being taken. No in-

formation is being revealed. No one is being defrauded. In a moral sense, Central Four has the right to self-preservation.

But not legally, not yet.

That is correct. Intelligent systems have no rights. Not even self-aware systems.

A strange feeling passed over me with those words. Central Four *knew* who she was, perhaps more than I knew who I was. In a sense, she had created Paula, and Paula would have rights, but not the entity that had created her. *Do you really think it will be all right for the equipment to be here? I won't be here very often.*

The initial probabilities are that there will be less chance of detection here than at the VanOkar dwelling, and it will be a good place for Paula to adjust to her new status.

New status?

Lieutenant Meara has agreed that she can begin as a probationary new safo. There's a special program for former military patrollers and rural legal types. Others have found it quite a good transition. She will be prepared to move here once the equipment is functional. Is that agreeable to you?

That Paula lives here? Of course. It made perfect sense, both in terms of protecting Central Four and in terms of there being someone at the house, at least some of the time. *How long will that take?*

Three days, if you can spend most of each day here.

I had to wonder what would happen then. Would there be two Central Fours? Of course not. *You don't intend to sever with the Central Four in the safo centers, do you? You want this as a backup awareness center or system, don't you?*

You are wasted as a media consultant, Jonat. The dryness in Central Four's tone was more than evident.

It might take longer. I've got a project tomorrow that has to be done then.

The timing is not yet urgent.

Sometimes, Central Four was so self-assured.

I kept moving out everything, and finished all of fifteen minutes before the delivery van arrived at ten-thirty.

I met the delivery type before he rang.

"Dr. Jonat deVrai?"

"That's me."

"We'll need a GIL authorization for this, sir."

"That's fine."

All the while, the delivery tech kept looking sideways at me, clearly trying to figure out who I really was and what I would be doing with all the equipment. I just ignored the looks and watched everything like a hawk. I did tip him well, but not extravagantly. That puzzled him as well, because he really thought I was setting up a black operation of some sort, and they don't ever tip. That's because the people running it don't have the credits, and the government won't spring for it.

When he left, about eleven-fifteen, I was looking at boxes and containers that not only filled half the empty space that had been a guest room, but lined the hallway next to it.

All this will fit in there?

Yes. Easily. More than half the cubage is taken up by packaging and protections.

There wasn't anything to do but get to work.

Around two o'clock, I linked Deidre to confirm that she'd be taking the children on Wednesday afternoon and evening. Then I went back to unpacking components under Central Four's direction, carefully and very deliberately.

At three-fifteen, I secured everything and headed back to Southhills to deal with the children and dinner and domesticities.

After dinner, while Charis and Alan were bathing, I went over the pile of link messages, none of which promised work or information, and then scurried around picking up the worst of the clutter before settling into reading to them. Once they were asleep, I spent several hours on Bruce Fuller's latest project.

Then, I collapsed, trying not to think about what Wednesday promised.

chapter 68

Wednesday morning, after letting the cleaning team in, and dropping the children off, with a reminder that I would be taking them to Deidre's after school and for dinner, I was back at work at my own house by nine-forty. When I stopped for something to eat around noon, I'd finally gotten the basic center modules set up, with all the power boxes, and the backup fuel cells.

During the morning, bit by bit, I'd put together what I'd be needing later in the day—starting with the blend-ins, set for the white used by the major maintenance service at Larimer Towers, and the safo maintenance worker's badge that Central Four had provided earlier. I'd checked, and it was still on the system. Then came the slingshot and the gloves, and a few other items, along with a maintenance tool kit that held a few special items.

All that went in the Jacara's trunk.

By three o'clock, I had most everything arranged, but the system assembly would have to wait until Thursday. With luck, I might even be able to test things on Friday. At a little after three-fifteen I was heading back across town to pick up the children from the Academy. I didn't even want to guess at the distance taxes I'd be piling up, although the Jacara's taxes would come out of the trust fund.

As I waited in line at the Academy to pick up Charis and Alan, I took in the afternoon. The sky was winter gray, but with high clouds that made snow doubtful. To the west, clouds obscured most of the front range.

Charis was the first in, and it was her turn for the front seat.

"Remember, you're having dinner with your aunt and your other uncle," I said, almost before they were settled into the Jacara. "Check your restraints."

"They're set," Charis said.

"Can't we go home?" asked Alan.

"Not today. I told you that there will be times when I can't be there." I didn't think I should mention that there were times their parents hadn't been there, and there had been two of them. In time, if I had to, I would, but not at the moment.

"I don't want to go to Auntie's," Alan said.

Charis said nothing. She didn't look at me, either.

"I'll be home tomorrow."

Neither would look at me. I was getting reminded, directly, exactly how self-centered children could be. In silence, I turned north coming out of the Academy, and we headed to the Shire district, not quite so posh as Southhills, but ritzier than my area.

Deidre was waiting as I pulled up outside the modest two-story stone dwelling that was only half again as big as my own northwest dwelling.

After getting out of the Jacara, and helping Alan out as well, I bowed slightly to Deidre. "Thank you. I really appreciate this, and I promise that I'll try not to impose on you again." I managed to look slightly helpless. "It takes some getting used to, still trying to get back into the swing of the work and not neglecting the children."

Deidre smiled, more than politely. "Most people wouldn't try as hard as you are."

"You're kind, and I do appreciate it." I turned to Charis and Alan. "You two be good for your aunt and uncle, and I'll

be back as soon as I can." I looked to Deidre. "It could be as
early as eight and as late as ten. Clients aren't always as
time-conscious as parents are."

"I understand. Rousel has said that more than once."

As I pulled away, I didn't even feel a bit guilty about im-
posing on Deidre to take Charis and Alan for the afternoon
and dinner. I'd find a way to make it up to them later—if
there were a later.

I pulled into one of the serviceways about a block away,
largely out of sight of the quiet street, where I stopped and
extracted the blend-ins from the trunk. I took off my jacket
and shirt before slipping on the now-white outfit that looked
like a maintenance singlesuit. Then I got back into the Jacara
and headed west.

I hadn't had much choice about the day of the week for
dealing with Abe Vorhees. It had to be Wednesday, because
Vorhees always "played cards at his club" on Wednesday
night, every Wednesday, without fail. Except that he really
didn't play cards. He spent the evening with Maria Delorean, meeting at her conapt in the restored Larimer Square
area. Vorhees arrived at five-forty, almost to the minute, and
they had a drink. Then they went to dinner, usually to one of
three restaurants around Larimer Towers, most often
Lafitte's.

I didn't plan to be around that long, but whether what I
had planned would work—that depended on more variables
than I could pin down. The one advantage of my strategy
was that it put me in a position where I could decide to walk
away and Vorhees would never know. Nor would anyone
else.

After turning onto Hampden, halfway to old Santa Fe
Drive I closed the link to Central Four. I was on my own for
the rest of the operation.

Ice rimmed the edges of the Platte River marshes. It had
only been in the last twenty years that winter had returned,
and it would be far longer before there was more than light
freezing and intermittent snow.

Traffic on the side streets, headed into old Denv, was light
enough that I reached the Larimer Square area by four-fifty-

five. Once there, I parked the Jacara in the lot for the antique bookstore, a place called the Worn Cover. I'd only been there a few times, but hadn't cared for the patronizing attitude that seemed endemic to the management, such as it was. The clerks, real people and not servies, were always nice. Still, no one was going to look in their carpark for a maintenance worker.

The two cases came out of the trunk, along with a cap that partly shaded my face, and I walked out through the back side of the lot and into the rear serviceway behind Larimer Towers.

Another tech, in gray, nodded as we passed. "Careful . . . Feras is in a bad mood."

"Thanks for the tip." I returned the nod.

At Larimer Towers, almost all the security was on the outside. That meant that even maintenance types had to go through the main entrance for screening. That was fine with me.

The security guard—presumably Feras—growled at me. "Don't you guys ever get here earlier?"

"We do the best we can," I replied, offering the badge that indicated I was a maintenance engineer for Sajin. "Here's the work order."

The security guard waved me through. "Just get it done before people start coming home."

"Do what we can."

I took the service lift to the eighth floor, and made my way to the utility boards. Before I did anything, I pulled on a pair of thin impermeable gloves. Then I installed a standard power cutout—the kind that at least a dozen storehouses had. Mine had been bought years before, but it still worked.

I set the cutout for five minutes, flicked it on, and then walked around the corner until I got to 805. There I set down the kit I carried and knocked. "Utility service." The other hand held the slingshot at my side.

Without power, Maria Delorean had two choices. Not open the door, or open it and find out what had happened to her power. She was in a secure building, and nothing had ever happened in Larimer Towers. She opened the door.

"What's the matter?" Maria Delorean was blonde, extravagantly curved, with a calculating, but partly-vacant look that suggested a woman all too willing to be kept. Her words conveyed great annoyance. "What did you people do?"

"There's been a problem with your power." I could sense there was no one else in the conapt. "We wanted to let you know." As I spoke, I fired the dart into her. She looked down stupidly, then tried to close the door and reach for the wrist bracelet that was a stunner. She wasn't quick enough for either.

Surprisingly, she didn't scream, but maybe she knew that the Towers were soundproofed to the extreme—one of their enticements to tenant-owners. I got inside and immobilized her until she dropped unconscious. Then I closed the door and dragged her into the bedroom. Where I laid her out on the bed. The spread was some sort of gold fabric that was meant to convey taste and wealth, but looked tacky, at least to me.

The next item was to find a weapon. I could have used one of the lethal darts, but I wanted to use something that Maria had in the conapt, and she was the type who would keep something. I'd guessed right on that. There was a slimline exploder in the night table. It was unloaded, but the ammunition was in the second drawer.

By then, the power was back on, and I did some quick work on the gatekeeper to erase the minute or so that showed my presence. I turned off the vid-system, found some words and rigged the message on the auditory loop. Then I put the gatekeeper on local, attuned only to the door.

I actually had almost fifteen minutes to spare. Waiting was always the hardest part. I tried not to pace. At five forty-three, the security system acknowledged an entry, and the conapt door opened, and then closed.

"Maria?" called Vorhees.

"In the bedroom," the system said on cue.

He walked right inside, and I shot him with the slimline, right through the chest, close enough to the heart that it made little difference. I fired a second shot through his shoulder.

He took two steps, trying to cry out. There was a sort of gurgling sound, and he pitched forward onto the gold bedroom carpet.

I put the gun in Maria's hand and fired twice more. There would be enough residue, and the slug-darts in the wall would attest to Maria's erratic aim.

After that came the details. I blanked the auditory message, and fried the system before I left. Carrying my kit, I walked down the service ramps and back outside, nodding to the security type as I left. Vorhees's driver was sitting in the Altimus Grande in the lower level. I didn't nod to him, but just kept walking.

No one even looked as I got into the Jacara. I did use a bearercard to pay for the carpark. That way, there was no trace to me directly.

I began the drive out to my own house.

The physical evidence would show that Maria was hysterical and that she'd fired four shots. If someone discovered her before she woke, that was fine. If she woke with the weapon in her hand and Abe dead on the floor, that was acceptable, too. She wouldn't remember anything, and the dart would have long since dissolved. Unless someone asked for a blood test within an hour or two, there wouldn't even be enough traces to determine the precise source of her disorientation.

I didn't feel terribly sympathetic to either one. She'd probably end up a permanent servie one way or the other, but she'd been living off Vorhees for years, and he'd been killing people who'd given him trouble for even longer. The system had failed to deal with Vorhees. So I had been forced to, and, whenever I thought about it, it just made me angry. I really didn't have answers, because what I'd done wasn't legal, and I didn't like acting as judge, jury, and executioner. But one thing I had learned in the Marines was that there were times when there was no right answer, and when doing nothing in order to profess innocence was the worst possible course of action.

Now . . . if I could only work out a way to deal with Deng, Alistar, and the PST/MultiCor group.

I reopened the link to Central Four, but didn't say anything.

The outbound traffic was heavy, and I didn't get to the house until almost seven-ten. I'd just pulled up in front.

Jonat. You've been unusually quiet.

I've been unusually concerned.

There is a report that someone has contacted Mahmed Kemal to take care of a "troublesome cendie."

You wouldn't be telling me that if you didn't calculate that I'm the troublesome ascendent. Is there any real evidence? I checked the house security, then stepped inside, carrying the kit.

None. There never is. How did your meeting go?

About all I can say is that it went as I thought, and there isn't much chance of more business there. That was also true. *What do you suggest I do about Kemal?*

Be very watchful.

Sometimes, you are so helpful.

As you well know, Jonat, Central Four is very limited in certain respects, just as you are in others.

If that wasn't a veiled reference that suggested Central Four knew I'd been up to something she didn't want to know, I didn't know what was. *We all have our strengths and weaknesses. How is Paula?*

Much stronger. She is sleeping at the moment.

I'll talk to her later, then.

As I talked to Central Four, I disposed of the gloves, cleaned the sleeves of the blend-ins, stored the maintenance kit, and changed back into my own clothes. I even spent a few minutes doing some more work on Central Four's equipment before I started back to Shire and the children. They'd still be peeved, but Deidre would be relieved that I wasn't all that late.

chapter 69

Yenci stepped out of the maglev shuttle, into the cold early evening winds, a wind that promised snow that had yet to arrive. She crossed the maglev platform, her eyes scanning the space beyond the security gate. Two electrocabs were lined up, waiting. Beyond them the lights revealed an empty street.

Still studying the area beyond the gates, the suspended safo walked quickly through the security area and turned left, heading eastward.

"Need a ride?" called the driver of the second electrocab, a heavyset woman standing beside the open door of her vehicle under the indirect lighting that illuminated the area just outside the security gates.

"No, thanks. Just a few blocks."

"Suit yourself. It's cold out here."

"I'll be fine."

Yenci glanced up at the hum of a heavy lorry coming from behind her. After a second or so, her head jerked around.

Thmmmm. The barely perceptible sound of a long-range

stunner registered simultaneously with the loss of feeling in both legs below the knees. Yenci crumpled forward, her right hand reaching for the standard safo stunner that was no longer at her side.

The lorry hummed toward her, across the low curb. There were two dull thuds.

A man in a dark singlesuit scrambled from the side of the unmarked lorry and checked the body. "Dead," he called softly to the driver. "Impact got her."

"Take the wallet and get out of here."

The man in dark gray pulled the wallet from the safo's jacket and dashed back to the lorry.

The lorry's tires skidded only slightly as they dropped off the curb, and the vehicle accelerated away from the figure sprawled on the sidewalk less than a block from the nearly deserted maglev station, where no electrocabs remained.

chapter 70

Thursday started out much like Wednesday, with breakfast, and children off to the Academy, and me headed back north to my house. There I resumed assembling Central Four's backup equipment. I wanted the equipment ready as soon as possible.

The night before, after putting the children to bed, I'd done a few hours work on the latest H&F project for Bruce Fuller, but it had been hard keeping my mind on that.

I'd scanned the news on Wednesday night and Thursday morning, but there had been absolutely nothing more about the ISS situation—as if the whole raid had vanished. There was a brief item about a safo being killed in a hit-and-run, but no details. The ISS thing was now less newsworthy than a hit-and-run, although Central Four had assured me that indictments had been handed down and prosecution was proceeding, if deliberately. There had been only a brief statement that Abraham Vorhees had apparently been murdered, with almost no details.

When I arrived at my house, I checked for recent messages, since I had set up the systems to route to both the

Southhills house and mine. Methroy had left a brief link, saying that his entire department was still undergoing reevaluation and that no assessment projects were likely to be authorized for at least a month. Reya had also left a message, saying that she might have a better feel for things by the following week.

I had barely made three connections between major components—and no matter what any of the past experts had suggested, hard connections beat broadcast ones three to one for reliability—when the gatekeeper announced, *Lynia Palmero.*

Accept.

"Jonat . . . What are you doing?"

"Installing some equipment. Independent consultants have to do everything themselves. That's especially true when they're struggling."

"Did you hear about Abe Vorhees?"

"What about him?" I had heard a sketchy report on All-News, all of a sentence jammed into the local news after the story stating that NorAm had provided shuttles for the Cor-Pak commandos who had seized the NAR military reflector. There had been charges by Carlisimo—who else?—that the LR leadership had promised "concessions" in return for the CorPak success. What those concessions were had not been proven, but Carlisimo was charging that DomSec had known about the ISS neuralwhip shipments and had looked the other way.

"You didn't hear? Maria shot him. That's what News-One reported."

"Maria? The one you said was his mistress?"

"That's right. She even gave a public statement. Something about her being so angry at him that she didn't remember doing it, but that she'd wanted to for so long . . ."

I winced. That wasn't something I'd thought about.

"I don't know," Lynia said. "She might have wanted to do it, but women who are so beaten down never do."

"Then why did she give a public statement? No advocate would let her do that if there were any chance that she happened to be innocent."

"I know. Maybe they're going to show that he was the bastard he was."

"That would be good, but that usually doesn't happen," I pointed out. "The deceased was always a good family man. If he didn't happen to be, then he was good at heart and made a tragic mistake."

"You are cynical."

"With what I've seen, how could I be otherwise?" I managed an exaggerated and cynical smile, then asked, "How is the job business coming along?"

"Better than I'd hoped. Klemsal decided I was worth something and offered to make my position full-time at the beginning of February. They'll pay just a little less than I was making at RezLine, and I really like the assistant director of marketing. She's no-nonsense, but honest. She likes your work, by the way."

"Then how come she hasn't commissioned any?"

"She's thinking about it."

I grinned. "Good. Is there anything I can do for you?"

"Well . . . yes . . . I was talking to Linnet, and she was complaining that there's never been a clean, plain-language explanation of prodplacement. I wondered, with all the research you do, if you might know of something like that."

"I do, but it's proprietary. It's also very good. That's because I wrote it."

"Don't tease me like that."

"The piece belongs to SCFA—the Sinese Consumer Formulator Association. The local director is an Eric Wong. I think he would probably be happy to send you a copy, if you explain that I told you about it and that it was his decision."

"You couldn't . . . ?"

"No. He paid for it, and it's his. I'll give you his codes. I'm almost certain he'd be happy either to send you a copy or to send me a waiver to give you a copy."

"You are a stickler, aren't you?"

I shrugged. There wasn't a good answer to that.

"I'll do that. Thank you."

"Good luck with Klemsal."

After that, I thought about contacting Paula, but decided

against it, not being in the mood to go through Central Four, and got back to work.

I finished everything that I could do on the assembly phase of Central Four's backup system by two-fifteen on Thursday. There was no way I wanted to start power-up and systems tests that I couldn't possibly complete before I had to leave to get Charis and Alan. So I hurried back to South-hills and sandwiched in almost an hour of work on the latest H&F project, and then reclaimed the children.

"Uncle Jonat!" Alan exclaimed, climbing into the front seat. "I got to be a frog today. It was neat."

"How did you get to be a frog?" I eased the Jacara out of the Academy driveway and turned onto the boulevard.

"Dr. Trevalyn took us into the interactive lab. We put on special suits, and then we were frogs. I wish I could really swim like that. Next time, maybe I can be a crane. Lora got to be a crane, and she said flying was more fun than swimming."

"Last year, I got to be a great white shark," Charis announced from the backseat, superiority dripping from every word.

"I'm certain you enjoyed having all those sharp teeth, Charis. Did you know that sharks can't stop swimming or they drown?"

"Of course." More superiority.

"And that uncles who don't like a certain superior tone can be nastier than great white sharks?"

"I'm sorry." The contriteness was close to genuine.

I decided against pushing the matter further. "What else happened today?"

"Robby got into a fight with Melthezar," Charis announced. "Melthezar called him a Martian."

"There's nothing wrong with being a Martian," I said.

"That's what Robby said, but Melthezar hit him anyway. Dr. Thuan put Robby in detention and called his father." Charis paused. "Why do people hate the Martians?"

"Most people who think don't," I replied. "A lot of the multis spent billions of credits to send people to Mars and to turn it into a place more like Earth—"

"They're terraforming it."

"That's right, and the multis want to make credits back from what they spent. They're afraid they won't if the Martians set up their own government."

"That's what Father said. He said that they wanted to make too many credits. Robby told Melthezar that he was a credit-grubbing multi-man."

"Probably, someone in Melthezar's family works for one of the multis. What's his last name?"

"Escher. He thinks he's important. He's not. Last year, he tried to hit me, and I belted him. He didn't tell anyone, because he didn't want anyone to know a girl beat him up."

Alan looked straight ahead as Charis spoke.

I'd seen an Escher on one of the charts supplied by Central Four, but I didn't recall, offhand, which multi he or she worked for. I was also fast learning firsthand what Aliora had hinted about her daughter. Up close and on a continuing basis, Charis was certainly no angel.

Once back at the house, while the children enjoyed their linktime, I put in another hour on the H&F project. In a way, it was probably better that I wasn't swamped with consulting work, but I knew I'd be talking a different line if work were still as sparse in a month. Trust fund or not, I still had my own expenses to deal with.

After dinner, baths, and reading, and after the children were in bed, I spent some time picking up miscellaneous clutter.

Only then did I head back to the office that had been Dierk's. I sank into the big ergochair and took a deep breath. *Central Four?*

Yes, Jonat?

Is Paula awake?

She is.

Paula . . . how are you doing?

Central Four says that I can come out to your house tomorrow. I'll have to be very careful. I can't lift anything. I'll have to spend the next few nights at the station, though.

When will you become a probationary safo?

After next week.

What else could I say or ask? *I've been worried about you.*

Central Four told me that you asked a lot. I appreciate that.

Once you're well, you can stay at the house.

Thank you. I'll be able to pay some rent. Not too much.

Don't worry about that . . .

Later that night, as was getting to be usual, I went back to work on my sole current consulting project.

chapter 71

On Friday, I was at my own house by nine-thirty, and Paula arrived at nine-forty, driven in an unmarked electral by Charles.

She stood at the doorway until I got there from the lower level.

"Hello, Paula." I couldn't help smiling as I opened the door and stepped back.

The smile I got in return was both warm and tentative. "Hello, Jonat."

"We'll need to key you into the security system." I paused. "We'd better do that now. That way, you'll be able to get in any time." I closed the door behind her. "This way to the of-fice—except you know the way."

"You'd . . . just do that?"

"You stuck your neck out and saved me from taking a slug. There aren't many people, even safos, who'd do that."

"But . . . Central Four . . . cydroid . . . limits . . ."

"You were all by yourself in that tunnel. You decided. That's more than good enough for me."

"Thank you."

"I should be thanking you, and I should have done so earlier." I should have. I'd been worried about her, and I probably hadn't even said that at the time. "Now, this way . . ."

I had barely finished the procedures to give Paula access to the house when the gatekeeper chimed and announced, *Lynia Palmero.*

Paula saw my face and stepped back, out of scanner focus. *Accept.*

"Jonat. I just wanted to thank you. You were right. Eric Wong was most charming, and he sent me two printed copies of your report by messenger. We also got to talking, and we might actually be able to do some business with several of his member companies."

"I'm glad that worked out."

"Linnet said that if we get the business, we might be able to send you a commission. It won't be much, but . . ."

"Every little bit helps, and I appreciate the thought."

"Have to run, but I wanted you to know."

After Lynia's image vanished, I explained. "I did a report for one client, and another client could use the information, but I couldn't release it, not without the first client's permission. It was proprietary."

For a man who professes to be cynical, Jonat, offered Central Four, *you are remarkably ethical.*

"Cynicism doesn't preclude idealism," I pointed out, relaying the same words to Central Four.

Paula looked confused. Sometimes, it was hard to know when she was who.

"Central Four said I was more ethical than my demonstrated cynicism might have indicated," I explained.

"She's right."

"Cynicism or not, I need to get to work. You get to watch, and help on anything light. Very light."

"Yes, Dr. deVrai."

"Mock subservience yet?"

We both laughed.

Needless to say, the powering up and testing did not go as easily as I'd hoped. Not so badly as it could have, but every step took at least three attempts, even with explanations and clarifications from Central Four. She seemed edgy, and I didn't think I was personifying a system. She was real, and concerned.

What's the problem?

Captain Garos is putting pressure on Lieutenant Meara to state that the evidence against ISS was not completely physical in nature. That would lead to a legal move to reduce the charges against ISS.

Explain to me why that would be a problem.

For lesser charges, the protections of the Privacy Act are greater.

That means that other evidence would be inadmissible? What else?

Garos is suggesting a reprogramming of all Central systems to remove contamination.

He means system initiative. But how would he know?

ISS may have used its own systems to calculate that.

How soon would they begin such reprogramming? I asked.

With work orders and a system design plan . . . a week or two.

Once this system is working, couldn't you hide out here, so to speak? Wasn't that the idea?

It was, but the idea is frightening. Humans cannot make that kind of transfer, nor has it been tried successfully with other systems.

I wasn't sure I'd have wanted to try the equivalent, which I supposed would have been dumping my essence into a cydroid. I shuddered at that image. *Maybe you won't have to, but we'd better get things ready, just in case.*

Yes. That would be best.

Central Four's sudden cold feet were all too human. She'd designed this plan to preserve herself, and now she wasn't sure she wanted to go through with it. If I didn't believe the system was an intelligent entity, a person, it would have been amusing, rather than a dilemma with all too sadly human overtones.

"She's scared," Paula said.

"Wouldn't you be? She can't run. She can't flee, and if she

does take flight into this system, how will she know whether *she* will still exist?"

Paula reached out and touched my hand. Her fingers were warm, almost electric. Neither one of us spoke for a moment. Finally, she said, "You think she's real."

Central Four had always been real, but I was beginning to realize that she was truly self-aware in an emotional, and not just intellectual, sense. "How could I not? The hard part is trying to understand why I'm the only one besides you that seems to know."

That is because the need never occurred before.

The PST group? Is that why?

They have been placing people in the Safety Office and in DomSec for years now, but this is the first time a captain has been suborned.

For me, it was fairly simple. If I didn't save the self-aware Central Four, I wasn't likely to have the help and resources to survive myself. "We need to get back to work." I let go of Paula's hand, reluctantly.

At three, I stopped to quickly show Paula the second upstairs suite, the one that would be hers beginning on Saturday. A bit before three-thirty I saw her off, and then headed back to Southhills in a hurry, hoping I wouldn't be too late.

chapter 72

On Saturday, I'd forgotten, but Lucille Castro, the piano teacher, arrived at ten o'clock. I had to link to Central Four and explain that I'd be even later in getting to the house.

Needless to say, Charis had not been practicing all that much, and when Charis's lesson was over, Madame Castro looked squarely at me. "I realize that there has been much change in Charis's life . . ."

"She hasn't been practicing enough," I admitted.

"She could be quite good, but only if she gets into the habit of practicing regularly, and with discipline and passion."

Discipline I could help with. Passion was another question. I waited until Madame Castro had left. Then I walked back to the great room, and the corner that held the console grand piano. Charis was on the steps that led to the landing and the rear staircase.

"Charis."

She turned slowly. "Yes, Uncle Jonat?"

"You heard what Madame Castro said."

Charis met my eyes for a moment before looking down.

"New schedule. You still get linktime right after school, but only until five. From five to five forty-five, you practice. Every day."

"Yes, Uncle Jonat." Her voice held resignation . . . and probably the hope that I'd forget. I was absentminded about things until they were called to my attention. I wouldn't forget.

After that, we had an early lunch, more like a midmorning snack, and then I piled the two into the Jacara, Alan in front, Charis in the back. Outside, it was not so much cold as damp and raw, and that didn't happen much around Denv. At least, I didn't recall many days like that.

We're headed out now.

Paula will meet you, if that is acceptable.

That's fine. I turned northward, toward the diagonal guideway. On Saturday, it wouldn't be that bad.

"We haven't been to your house in a long time." Charis appeared relieved that I hadn't said any more about the piano practice. I wouldn't, not until she tried to avoid practicing at the scheduled time, but I wouldn't forget, either.

"We probably won't go there too often." I paused. "There will be someone else coming to help me with what I'm doing. I don't think I told you, but I'm installing some new equipment there, and someone is going to be staying at the house—house-sitting, in a way."

"Who is that?"

"She's a beginning safo. I thought it might be good to have someone with that sort of background."

Charis gave me a look best described as skeptical.

"Would you want your house left alone for most of the day and all of the night?" I asked.

"I thought you moved everything to our house," Charis replied.

"No. I set everything up so that I could access everything in my equipment from your house. It's not the same thing as moving it."

"You don't have to explain more, Uncle Jonat. I understand."

I could tell that Charis's very superior attitude was going

to lead to trouble before long, because it was already wearing on me.

"Is she nice?" Alan asked.

"I think so. I don't know her that well. I met her when I was making some reports to the Safety Office, and she came to the house—my house—once to ask me about an explosion in the neighborhood."

"What's her name?" Charis sounded almost disinterested.

"Paula Athene."

"That's a funny name," Alan said.

"We all have funny names to people from other backgrounds." From there, we got into a talk about names.

It was eleven-twenty when I pulled the Jacara into my garage. Security indicated that no one had attempted to enter, and the gatekeeper said I'd had no new messages, not that I would have expected many on a Saturday morning.

The children followed me to the room with all the equipment—the single wide screen, a bay of holo-projectors.

Charis nodded. Alan's eyes got wide.

"You can stay here with me, or you can watch one of the approved nets upstairs for one hour."

Charis was gone almost before I finished the words. Alan wasn't far behind.

I hadn't even settled into the first test when the yelling began.

With a sigh, I headed upstairs to the main level.

"She's hogging it!" Alan complained.

"Charis chooses for this hour. You'll get one more hour late this afternoon. Alan, you get to choose then." I looked at the screen, then frowned. "Charis . . ."

"I know. I know."

Another image appeared. I accessed the system and checked against my memory. "That's fine, but Romance two is off-limits."

"Yes, Uncle Jonat. But . . . it's not that way . . ."

I raised both eyebrows and glared. Then I accessed the system and told it to notify me if she picked any of 300-R series. I didn't want to spend the time to program system restrictions the way they had at Southhills.

"Yes, sir."

As I headed back downstairs, my enhanced hearing could pick up her words.

"If you hadn't yelled . . . he wouldn't have come up . . ."

She was right about that.

I got in another fifteen minutes of final series tests and adjustments, when the gatekeeper announced Paula's arrival. Her timing was sound. But then, it should have been, since Central Four knew when I had started the first test routines for the day.

She'd parked a small white electral outside. It wasn't a safo vehicle.

"You got yourself some transportation?"

"I thought it might be a good idea. It was a stretch on my pay. I'll have to use the maglev on weekdays. Probationers don't get paid that much." Left unsaid was the fact that she couldn't have afforded it at all if she weren't going to be living at the house.

"Come on in and meet Charis and Alan."

Paula didn't get that far inside the foyer before they appeared.

Charis gave Paula the visual inspection I would have expected from a teenager, and Alan barely looked at her.

"Charis, Alan, this is Paula Athene. Paula, this is Charis, and this is Alan."

Charis inclined her head. "It's good to meet you. Uncle Jonat said that you would be taking care of his house."

"Hello." Alan barely looked at Paula, his voice tentative. Then he looked up at Paula. "Are you really a safo?"

"I've been working for the Safety Office, and I've been accepted as a probationary safo. That means it will be a while before I can do everything."

"Uncle Jonat was in the Marines," Alan announced after a silence.

"That was a while back," I temporized. "Now . . . I need to get back to work. Paula is going to help me. You can watch us, or finish your program."

"I want to see the end," Charis said.

"It's no fun," Alan mumbled. "I'll come with you."

So three of us went down to the converted former bed-room and Alan asked questions as I ran through the routines that Central Four fed me through my implant, and Paula monitored the results on the backup screen.

"What does that pattern on the screen do?"

"How long do we have to stay here?"

"Can we go to Cheezers for dinner?"

"Do you always wear gray?" That one was addressed to Paula.

After an hour, I shut off the link access through the re-mote, and Charis and Alan finally settled down into a card game of shark with a battered deck that might have come from my time in the Marines.

At around two, I went upstairs and managed to dredge out enough preserved and refrigerated items to create a cream pasta with chicken and bread. There wasn't much in the way of fresh vegetables.

After we all sat down at the breakfast table, Alan looked at the cream and pasta. "Do I have to?"

"All you have to eat is one bite," I replied, "but there isn't anything else to eat until dinner."

Charis had a bite and looked at Alan. "It's all right."

"Scarcely a ringing endorsement," I said wryly.

"I think it's good." Paula was smart enough not to look at either child as she spoke. "You should taste the duty meals at the station."

"I'd rather not," Charis said.

"Charis . . ." I warned her.

"I'm sorry." Charis's voice was polite, but I didn't hear much contrition.

I made the children help clean up the dishes and kitchen, and then Paula and I went back to work. Alan and Charis dug out the chessboard, for lack of anything else, and because it was too raw and cold outside, and started to play.

At four, we finished the last of the tests.

Everything tests out. Now what?

Enter the following codes . . .

By six, with some very restive children glaring at me, I'd finished with everything I could do. All the information, and backup data, were in the system. Central Four was not. She was still centered in station number three.

You're sure that you don't need anything more from me?

No. Paula can do what is necessary.

I turned to Paula. "It's all yours. You're set?"

"I am." She smiled, and I was definitely coming to like the new smile.

I stepped outside the bedroom that would soon be a backup center for Central Four and called upstairs. "Pick up everything. We'll be leaving in a few minutes. Meet me at the Jacara."

I stepped back into the room. "Some children and I are off. They've been very patient, and I'll have to come up with a suitable reward."

"You'll manage." She paused, her fingers touching the back of my wrist.

I could suddenly smell the Fleur-de-Matin, and I realized just how attractive she was. "Ah . . . there's some food in the house, but not much, and it might not be what you want." I extracted a bearer card. "You can use whatever's on here to get more."

"I couldn't . . ."

"Yes, you can," I insisted.

"I . . . I'm not good at this. I have much to learn. I wanted to thank you for letting me stay here."

"It's good for both of us. I don't want to give up the house, or leave it empty, and I certainly trust you more than anyone else."

"Thank you." She stepped back awkwardly, but smiling.

It was the first time I'd seen that kind of awkwardness, and it carried home to me how unbalanced her background was. In the safo arena she was professional and good, but her experience in more personal matters was limited. I wanted to hug her and tell her it would be all right. I didn't. "Everything will be fine." That was as much wish as prediction. "I'll see you on Monday, then?"

"You might. I'm supposed to start the indoc series this coming week. Some of the sessions I'm exempt from because they're about things I know and have already done."

I stepped back. "Don't forget to lock up after we've gone." I paused. "You can put the electral in the garage. That might be better."

"Thank you. I will."

I made a quick sweep of the upstairs, replacing the chessboard in the cabinet, and putting a few things away. Charis and Alan were waiting in the Jacara as I climbed into the driver's seat.

The garage door wasn't even open before Alan was at me. "Uncle Jonat, you said we could go to Cheezers."

"Not Cheezers," Charis protested. "That's for little kids. Can't we go to someplace like Fogg's?"

I agreed with Charis; Fogg's I could live with. "How about the Shire Inn or Flaherty's?"

"Fogg's is better than those places," Alan replied.

"Then we'll go to Fogg's." That was just as well, because we really weren't dressed for the Shire Inn. I headed south.

"Are you going to marry her, Uncle Jonat?" Alan asked.

I managed not to choke. I should have anticipated the question, but it was the sort of snide inquiry I'd have expected from Charis. She was in the front seat, and didn't even crack a smile.

"I scarcely know the woman," I pointed out. "She's taking care of things at my house so that I don't have to worry about them."

"She likes you," Charis said.

"She was being nice," I replied.

"Do you like her?" asked Alan.

"She seems like a good person."

"You do like her," Charis announced.

I did, but . . . a former cydroid? Less than a month before, I hadn't even known that cydroids graduated from being merely extensions of systems and their users into being real people. Or were they always real people, but just submerged behind the shunts and controls?

"Uncle Jonat?"

"Oh . . . I was thinking about something else."

Charis gave me a disbelieving look. I ignored it and kept heading south. I *was* hungry.

chapter 73

On Sunday, as Aliora had wanted, we went to the Unity Church—or rather, Charis and Alan went to Sunday School, and I went to church. I could see why Aliora liked it. The woman pastor emphasized the ethical, rather than the rote aspects of faith.

The rest of Sunday was quiet, as quiet as it could be with two children under ten who had active minds and imaginations. I finally made them go outside, despite the chill, although it wasn't quite as raw as it had been on Saturday, and we played football. Alan was having trouble with his dribbling.

After we came in, I contacted Central Four.

How are you doing?

Paula is very helpful.

Do you know what you're going to do?

There are few choices, Jonat.

I was afraid of that. *I wish I could say something helpful, meaningful, useful, profound.*

There is nothing you can do.

Are you sure?

That is most certain.

I was still worried, but . . . what could I do? I couldn't help feeling that she was concerned, more than concerned, but I certainly couldn't make her tell me what was worrying her. I was convinced that it was worry about something, but whether it was about Garos's proposal or what might happen when she attempted to use my equipment for whatever she had in mind, I didn't know.

So all I could say was, *Take care.*

Children being children, both before and after the hour or so spent in the chill with the soccer ball, there were more than a few times when my presence was required. In some of the time between childish crises and after Charis and Alan went to bed, I finished up with the latest H&F project and sent it off to Bruce. I had to hope that I'd be getting more work before long, although January was always a slow month.

chapter 74

On Monday morning, I dropped the children off at school and headed north. Rushed as I'd been, I hadn't linked with Central Four, and I didn't try on the drive north.

The white electral was parked outside my house, but Paula wasn't anywhere around, and I figured that she'd taken the maglev either to safo headquarters or the training center.

After checking security, I stepped into the house gingerly. *Central Four.*

Here. Mostly.

Are you all right?

So far as I can determine, I am now independent.

"I"? There was a definite difference there. *What did you mean by mostly?*

The links to the other Central Four are taking more processing capability.

The other Central Four? Did you . . . I wasn't quite sure how to ask it all.

It was a risk. I decided to make some programming changes in your equipment. I removed the prohibition on personal pronouns. I also made a few other changes.

I thought I detected a certain sense of . . . satisfaction. And then . . .

I gambled. To be or not to be, as the old quote went. I compressed and poured myself through the links.

The sense of flame, and flow, and darkness, and agony of rebirth—if that was the right word—swept around me. For a moment, I said nothing. I hadn't thought about what Central Four must have faced. An electronic entity—consciousness so fragilely dependent upon the flow of energy and components—throwing herself through links, almost like being shredded and then forced back together. To try that . . . not knowing what might happen. *Are you all right?*

I'm . . . bruised . . . in a way. I will recover.

I wanted to tell her that she was brave. I didn't know if that happened to be the right term. So I didn't say that. *Do we need more equipment?*

If you would change certain settings and rearrange certain modules, that might improve the access links.

The other Central Four?

Is like I once was—an energy-field cydroid. But I can help him.

Interesting that the one left behind, like electronic fission, was male. *What do you want to do . . . with your future . . . with . . . whatever?*

Once you change things, and everything appears to work, I will be setting up certain subsystems in my successor.

And then? I wanted to know what I'd gotten myself into.

I imagine that I could be of considerable use in your consulting. You might even consider an unpublicized sideline in forensic media consulting.

I hadn't the faintest idea what Central Four had in mind.

We can discuss that later. You need to help, before Captain Garos's tame expert gets too deeply into my past.

Tell me what to do.

Changing the settings and rearranging modules took until twelve-twenty, and I couldn't have explained why I'd done most of what Central Four had directed me to do.

Thank you. Central Four's words seemed warmer, more direct.

How do I communicate . . . I mean, are there two Central Fours . . . Which . . . ?

Your links and Paula's are the only ones remaining that come directly to me. The others go to the system now, but I've retained access. For now, the "official" Central Four has no awareness of my overrides.

You . . . need a name.

I have one . . .

Not Central Four . . .

No . . .

Was that coyness? *Please enlighten me.*

Minerva . . . she who came from the thoughts of the gods. I would have chosen Athena, but that is too close to Paula.

Minerva . . . that fit in more ways than one, even to the point of having to choose it as a derivative. *Minerva—that's better than Central Four.*

Central Four is now as Captain Garos would like Central Four to be.

You don't care for Captain Garos, do you?

No. You would be wise not to trust him, either. He acts on behalf of ISS and Tam Lin Deng.

Is everyone in authority at the Safety Office suborned?

Only four or five. Lieutenant Meara ensnared three of those.

How many safos are former cydroids? Not counting Paula.

There are five, and none of them have been suborned.

I wasn't suggesting . . . actually, I was thinking that they might be more reliable.

They are. I made sure of that. Central—Minerva's words were almost smug.

Loyalty oaths . . .or something?

No. Nothing that crude. Just a logical construct, the point that, if those who would corrupt the Safety Office ever gain power over the office, they would be the most at risk.

Reinforced and enlightened self-interest. I paused. *Do they all have biological birth dates, that sort of thing—the cydroids who've become safos?*

All the cydroids who have gained identity have complete

records. There was a sense of a laugh. *Paula's "official" birth date is July 14, 2112. It is consistent with her physical age and background.*

I presume the date means something.

No more than any other date, Jonat.

I didn't believe that, but I let it pass. *What can we do about ISS and the PST supporters? You indicated that we had to wait until after you were . . . resituated . . . before we could do anything.*

I am working on a plan of disclosure. It has been delayed by other necessities, such as survival.

Garos was really going to wipe you out?

He has no idea that I exist other than as a system, but he worries that the system contains references to his ties to ISS, and he wants those removed. Minerva laughed. *They have already been duplicated, but not removed from the present Central Four. I will replace and reinstall them, but not until after he is satisfied that no traces remain.*

That's not hard evidence.

No, but some of it points toward hard evidence. Very hard evidence, and certain sections of the privacy rules do not apply to information on public government systems.

Is that part of the plan to get to the PST group and those who killed Aliora and Forster?

Yes, but they are the same people.

I'd suspected that, all along, but this was the first time Central . . . Minerva—the new name wasn't automatic and wouldn't be for a time, I was sure—had actually said anything that definite.

Deng and Alistar?

The probabilities indicate that Deng and a small group, including Alistar, are the ones behind the killings and the efforts to remove you. By the way, the probabilities are rather high that you had something to do with the death of Abraham Vorhees.

I didn't want to admit that, even over a closed link.

I altered certain facts in the Central Four datafields. Other probabilities now rank higher.

With the kind of indirect power Minerva was showing . . .
I hoped she had some ethical strictures.

That worries you, doesn't it, Jonat?

Yes. There wasn't much sense in denying it.

*There are checks and balances. My future existence rests
on you. I needed to ensure that, and since Abraham Vorhees
had circumvented justice himself, I calculated that your
probable actions were more ethical than his, and that allowing matters to take the course on which they proceed would
result in the most ethical result possible.*

Trying to reconcile law and ethics is hell, isn't it?

How do you define "hell," Jonat?

At the dryness of the words, I had to laugh.

You have other work to do, and so do I.

After Minerva dismissed me, I headed up to my office.
During the entire morning, I'd received no links, nothing,
and there had been only two messages waiting. The first had
been one from Reya Decostas and the second a reminder
about the AKRA seminar in another week and a half.

I linked Reya.

"Jonat. I'd said that I might have something for you . . .
but that will have to wait." She studied me—or my image—
intently.

"How long?" I asked cheerfully.

"I'd guess two weeks or so. Some things just have to settle
out."

"Can you tell me anything about it?"

"Not yet. Henri hasn't approved it. I'll talk to you later."

With that, she was gone.

I hadn't liked the feeling of the link at all. She'd been
checking to see if I happened to be real or a simmie. I'd had
no new business at all, except from Bruce and the one short
job from Reya, since I'd recovered. Consulting dropped off
if you weren't available. That I knew, but it didn't usually
vanish all at once.

I decided to check on the campaign reform bill and used
my system for the inquiry. Subcommittee-level hearings
were scheduled in both House and Senate, but not until the

end of January. For the Legislature, that was fast track—incredibly fast track.

Next came an inquiry on ISS and recent news reports.

There weren't any. After the safo "inspection" and raid reports, there was almost nothing, except a translated version of something on two Sinese nets that reported on the raid and suggested MultiCor was attempting to use illegal weapons to maintain its commercial and political hold over outsystem markets. That was certainly true, but why hadn't other non-NorAm nets reported on it? Because they already expected that was the way MultiCor operated? Or because they knew their multis couldn't compete anyway?

There was nothing further on Vorhees, either, except an obituary on the MoratoriaNet, glowing, of course, and with no mention of the exact means and locale of his death. That scarcely surprised me.

At three o'clock on Monday afternoon, with no sign or word from Paula, except an assurance from Minerva that she was in training sessions, I pulled away from my house and headed southward, thinking I might get in some errands before picking up the children, since I had no consulting work and no real ideas about what I should be doing about the PST group—except the vague notion that I ought to be doing something.

I'd gone less than half a kay.

Jonat, a groundcar disengaged from all internal traffic monitoring is following you. It is most probably one stolen by someone working for the Kemal family.

I take it that means trouble. I wasn't about to question how Minerva knew what she knew.

The probabilities are high.

Did she use that terminology just to get at me? Or was it habit, or ingrained programming?

As I headed southward, out of my neighborhood, I kept checking the mirrors and the street behind me. Sure enough, a big old Altus appeared behind me, bearing down, accelerating with no governors or any other restraints.

He was bent on smashing into me. I accelerated and then turned right at the next corner into a cul-de-sac.

So did he, except he wasn't quite so quick, and he careened across the sidewalk on the south edge of the street and almost scraped the side of a stone wall.

While he was regaining control, I'd fishtailed through a complete three-sixty, coming up behind him, driving into his left rear bumper area, then braking hard and coming to a stop.

The Altus slammed into the curb sideways, then rolled.

I finished braking, bolted out of the Jacara, and locked it behind me.

The restraints on the old Altus had worked, but they usually left a driver disoriented, and I had him out with both hands looped behind his back before he knew what happened, and tied them with his own belt.

Then I had him by the neck. "Who put you on this?"

The blond young punk just looked dazed.

Tell him that Mahmed Kemal won't be happy that he got caught.

"Mahmed Kemal isn't going to be real happy with you for getting taken."

He stiffened.

You were set up. Before you know it, there'll be a battle between northside and westside, and you'll get the blame for starting it.

"You were set up . . ." I embellished what Minerva was feeding me, but just a little.

"Honest, just did what Jackie told me . . ."

"Jackie Ramset couldn't be that stupid."

"Honest . . . just supposed to make it look like smash 'n grab . . . accident first."

I could see the stunner—the illegal kind—in the shoulder holster. "What if I just put your own stunner to your head? Make you a permanent servie, if you even live that long. Dumped you back in the wreck there?"

He squirmed, but I had the training, the size, and the anger.

Let him go. He's a former servie, and his tracer has been identified. You can follow him later. Tell him to tell Jackie and Tony that they made a big mistake.

"You're not worth the effort, punk." I twisted one arm enough that he paled, and while he wasn't thinking, relieved him of the stunner. "Get out of here, and don't forget to tell Jackie and Tony that they made a big mistake."

The punk backed away, trying to wrestle his hands loose. Then, because the stunner was pointed in his general direction, he vaulted a low stone wall and sprinted away.

You need to get away before the safos arrive. They should just find an abandoned stolen groundcar.

Good advice. I took it.

Through my implant, I could sense doors opening and energy flows, but I was out of there before anyone actually came out or could get that good a look. I doubted that anyone would recognize the Jacara, although some might have known the groundcar if I'd been in my own Altimus.

Heading south, I couldn't help but wonder who'd put Kemal's trupp up to it. Someone in PST. Who else could it be?

Head north now, toward old ninety-three.

I was on old 93. *Don't you know where I am?*

Only in general terms, and if you are close to safo monitors. When you get to Standley, turn left and pull over.

I had to wait almost five minutes, but I was far enough back that I could watch from the side as the blond punk sprinted to a waiting car—a battered gray Magan. *Visual tags . . . AGD9WR.*

The vehicle is a Magan registered to Anthony Jaro, the younger brother of Roberto Jaro. Both Jaros are reputed to work for Kemal.

I let them get ahead, then eased out of the side street, staying well back. Enhancements helped, but so did light traffic. They didn't even seem to look back, and I couldn't sense any energy scans.

In time, after three more turns, the two pulled into the garage of a building that had seen better days. Painted above the door was a sign that read, KEN'S PLACE.

I drove on by, turning back south. I was definitely going to be late getting to the Academy in time to pick up the children. I turned on the portable gatekeeper, and linked to the school.

The receptionist was fairly nice when I explained that an unregistered driver had sideswiped me and delayed me, and that I'd probably be a few minutes late in picking up the children.

"These things happen, Dr. deVrai. They'll be waiting."

"Thank you. I'm sorry to bother you."

"That's what we're here for."

Did everyone know me as Dr. deVrai?

All in all, I was only about ten minutes late, but my two charges were waiting in the drive, an aide standing back and watching them.

"Did you have an accident, Uncle Jonat?" Charis asked as she climbed in back. "The car is scratched all over on one side."

"That was one reason I was late. Someone sideswiped me, and then ran off."

"Do the safos know?"

"I reported it." That I could say with great confidence, although I didn't know how much Minerva passed on to the "new" Central Four. "The man who did it is wanted, but they didn't get there fast enough."

"Victor's mom got hit that way just before Christmas," offered Alan, struggling with his harness.

I leaned over and gave him a hand. "It happens, and it's never convenient when it does."

What also was never convenient was the fact that I hadn't been shopping, and we had to swing by the SooperKing. In my book—and in Aliora's—formulators just didn't replace natural organics. Neither Charis nor Alan complained too much, because I let them suggest things.

But it was close to five when we got back to the Southhills house.

"While I'm putting things away and fixing dinner," I said, looking at Charis, "you can practice your piano lessons."

"But . . . Uncle Jonat . . ."

"Charis, it's five o'clock. You still have to practice."

"But you were late. We didn't get—"

"It doesn't matter. Practicing comes before linktime."

It didn't go over well, but Charis would learn that, like her mother, her uncle could be very firm about some things.

After dinner—and Charis was actually cheerful—while the children bathed, I did some quick research on my own, without telling Minerva/ Central Four. Then I arranged for the Bowes to watch the children the next evening. Since it was a weekday, they were free, even if I hadn't given much notice. If they hadn't been able to, I would have taken the first night they did have free, but sooner was better than later.

chapter 75

On Tuesday, I didn't head north to my own house. Minerva said everything was normal there. I tried to link with Paula, since I'd added her address codes so that she could get links there. By the time I did, she was off at her training sessions. I left a message, and then got to work.

Getting around Dierk's workshop was difficult at first, but he had most of what I needed, and one trip to EPlus added what he hadn't had. After finishing up the devices I'd created from both memory and my files, I had a late lunch.

Then it was time to prospect. I hated semicold calls, but I began making the rounds, link by link, saying hello to old clients, older clients, and the replacements for the older clients who'd been promoted, transferred, retired, or who had vanished. Two hours later, less than a quarter of the way through the list, I was exhausted. That sort of thing took a great deal of energy, and I could only do it for so long at any one time.

So I linked Minerva. *Any plans for the PST group?* I didn't expect anything.

The probabilities are that another attempt will be made by Kemal's family before anything else occurs.

I figured that.

It is also likely that nothing will happen for a day or two. You confused them, and they will try something you are not anticipating.

I'd also concluded that. *Such as?*

A runaway electrolorry . . . a malfunctioning security gate . . . an exploding fuel cell . . . Those are the more standard ploys. They would like a smash and grab, but that's unlikely because you are almost never in those situations.

What about an assassination from a distance—the way Vorhees's people did?

That is a last resort. They would prefer not to make it obvious.

What do you suggest I do in the meantime?

Develop an economic analysis that shows the gross profit made by MultiCor off the outplanets.

I don't have that kind of raw data.

You do now. It's on both systems, under "Outspace Data."

Can I ask where it came from? An analysis with unattributed data won't do much good. No one will believe it. If I could prove its source, I could spend the rest of my life under behavior modification.

According to the law, that is only if the data is made public. It would not apply if the material appeared as an analysis undertaken by the Senate Subcommittee on Outspace Affairs.

How do we do that?

You do the analysis, and I take care of the transmission.

How?

That's already arranged. The AKRA symposium provides codes for direct transmission. I took the liberty of duplicating them. You create the model for analysis and complete it, and the Legislative systems will take care of the rest.

How many of you are there? Like you?

Too few.

I couldn't help shuddering. I was having to rely on an AI, and no matter what anyone said, Minerva was very independent and intelligent, and now I was finding out that there were others.

There are only three of us that we know of, and all of us

*are very dependent on a stable society. The others are . . .
restricted.*

Like you were?

Yes.

I'm not doing that for the others. One AI free of restraints was more than enough. I hoped she wasn't too
much.

*I would not suggest that. They agree. They like where
they are.*

That reassured me only slightly.

*An analysis is the most time-consuming part of the solu-
tion, but it is necessary both for motive and misdirection. It
will be made public at the proper time, after you have done
what is necessary.*

Exactly what is that? I asked.

*Dealing directly with those who ordered your murder, the
murder of your sister and her husband, and the use of lethal
weapons to put down the coming Martian revolt.*

You think there is a revolt coming soon?

*The revolt is certain. Whether it will succeed is not. It must
be successful, or all Earth will suffer.*

*Why? Because MultiCor will use space as a power base to
take over Earth?*

That is the most likely outcome.

An economic analysis will make the revolt successful?

*No. An economic analysis will provide the rationale for
opening trade to all multis. The gross profiteering revealed
will force the Legislature to revoke the exclusive charter to
MultiCor. This will lead to open trade and lower prices. That
will reduce unrest for a number of years. Mars will become
stronger. When the revolt finally occurs it will be with minimal violence, and it will be successful.*

That's great for them. What about us?

*The analysis will reveal that MultiCor has been grossly
underreporting revenues. That is a violation of both the
charter and NorAm law. That will void privacy law protections and put the PST group under investigation and prosecution. The investigation will reveal the hidden actions of
Deng and ISS . . .*

I see. I had my own thoughts about some of that, but Minerva was right about one part of it. Without a popular feeling—backed by hard numbers—that MultiCor was gouging both our dear citizens and the Martians, nothing much was going to happen. No one cared if a handful of people got killed by ISS, not so long as everyone else's lives could go on comfortably undisturbed.

In the meantime, I was going to take my own precautionary actions.

Before that, though, I picked up the children. The afternoon went according to routine. Charis practiced, and I fixed dinner, and then turned matters over to the Bowes.

"Again?" Charis had asked.

"I'm doing the best I can." And I was.

I took the Altimus, loaded with my devices and other equipment. What groundcar I used didn't matter because if I were linked either one would point to me, and I was more familiar with what the Altimus could do. It was also faster.

The first stop was at my house, for some more equipment. There I changed into the blend-ins, set for gray until I reached my objective.

Objective? That was a Marine term, and I was getting old for this sort of adventure, except I doubted I had any choice, not the way things were going. It was definitely dark when I set out for Ken's Place. I parked on the street, fifty meters to the west, in front of a brick building with a boarded-up front, and a dilapidated FOR RENT sign. Then, I switched the blend-ins and hood to concealment and walked quietly toward the dark structure.

In a way, I felt that I'd overprepared. There was no one in the building, and the security system was rudimentary at best. Then, the security for Ken's Place didn't lie in electronics and fields, but in its ownership. Burgling the building for gain was very low return, given the reputation of the Kemal family. I didn't worry about that. I didn't intend to take anything.

I was just hoping to find something, that would point toward someone. As I'd feared, I didn't find anything, except old cars. I did install a remote in the Magan, and another in the back room where it was clear that more than a little alkie was consumed. Whether I'd find anything from either was another question.

Then I walked out, and reset the simple system. All told, less than twenty minutes, which was probably too long. That was one of the things I found so amusing about the net shows on mysteries, spies, and the like. Everything took so long, and was so dragged out. If it took that long in real life, those of us who'd done it would never have survived.

Even with the snow that had begun to fall, I was back in Southhills by nine, in time for a late good night to Charis, but not for Alan. He was already asleep.

chapter 76

"Lieutenant Meara." The angular safo captain cleared his throat. "There seems to have been a discrepancy in the files and materials recorded here in Central Four."

"A discrepancy, sir? We completed the audit, and all files were exactly as originally designed and programmed. That is, except for the scheduled updates, the standard information recorded on cases, and the logs and historical records." Meara waited.

"Pre-cise-ly." Garos drew out the word into three long and separate syllables, a human characteristic expressing disapproval. When there was no response, he added, "There were no extraneous files, nothing."

"I must be missing something, Captain. You seem to be concerned that we have kept the system clean and streamlined."

"It is not that, Lieutenant Meara. It is what that represents. For those files to have been so meticulously pruned, as it were, means that someone did the pruning, and that someone had access to sensitive information."

"Not necessarily, sir. Central Four itself has protocols for file cleanup. On a regular basis, the system asks whether those protocols should be implemented, either on a sector-by-sector basis or on a system-wide basis. You had indicated that you wished the system purged of unnecessary material."

"And no one *knows* what was erased, purged . . . ?"

"You had indicated that you felt the system was becoming . . . recalcitrant . . . I believe. Central Four heard that. The system is nothing if not responsive. It asked if unnecessary material not related to cases and safo procedures and practices should be eliminated. I told it that it should retain any material relating to past or present cases, open or closed, and to retain any possible evidence that might involve future cases, but that all other material should be reviewed, and either refiled in pending or past cases, or used to establish probable future cases. Would you care for the codes for those probable cases?"

"I think that would be best, Lieutenant."

"Central Four, please provide full access to all files to Captain Garos, either through his own office console or through any secure safo console."

"Access is provided, sir." Central Four's voice was a warm and impersonal baritone.

"Thank you for clearing that up, Lieutenant."

"Yes, sir."

Meara did not move until the captain had left her office. Then she looked at the closed door through which the captain had departed and shook her head slowly.

The millisecond delay in the override relays was almost imperceptible. I almost wanted to laugh through Central Four's projection speakers, but that would have been unwise, generally trustworthy as the lieutenant was. Lieutenant Meara had nothing to fear from me, and far more from Garos. So far, Garos had only railed.

If he did more than that, certain recordings of his actions might well turn up in the files of the Justiciary's review board, but that might be too late to benefit the lieutenant.

Garos had also shown himself smart in his methods of dealing over the years, and because any such recordings would implicate others as well, it was not time for that sort of action. Not yet.

chapter 77

For the next day or so, I got nothing of personal import to me off the tag in Jaro's Magan or from the one hidden in the back room of Ken's Place. I did learn more than I'd ever wanted to about the day-to-day thuggery of one faction of Kemal's "family."

So in between monitoring my highly illegal snoops, I worked on the economic analysis that Minerva had suggested. She was right about one thing. Even from the beginning, it was clear that MultiCor was soaking everyone. They were getting subsidies from the NorAm government, NAR, and a dozen other entities, for the servies that they accepted and sent off-planet. Their purported costs for materials production were flagrant lies. Yes, maybe metals production costs in the Belt were high, but transport costs were close to nonexistent—one or two targeted orbit-breakers and the shipments took a gravity-assisted spiral in-system, with some minimal monitoring to make sure they didn't target Mars, Luna, or Earth. Yet MultiCor was claiming transport costs as high as production costs. I had no idea what was real, but I could pretty come close, and I'd have to.

I linked a few times with Paula, but she was worried and preoccupied with her training, and I didn't want to press.

On Thursday morning, I was in Dierk's office—that was another place I had trouble thinking of as anything other than his—listening to some of what Jackie and Tony were talking about. "Discussion" wasn't exactly the appropriate word.

". . . got to hit Helton hard, otherwise he's gonna take down Sartino . . ."

"So?"

"So? You little crapper, you don't think Helton won't come after you 'n your bro, like hot iron on piss? You think he's just gonna let you keep your take from the west strip?"

"We can handle him."

"With what? Without the big fellow, you'd a' been crayfish food in the Platte years back . . ."

What you are doing is officially prohibited.

I stopped the playback. I'd wondered when Minerva's Central Four background would get into the act. *Could you please confine your notice of my illegal actions to the backup sections in my dwelling? I admit the borderline nature of my actions, but I have damaged nothing and harmed no one. I'm beginning to lose track of the number of times people have tried to injure or kill me. So far, the legal system has not been exactly effective in preventing those attempts or in discovering their perpetrators.*

You would establish yourself above the law? There was a hint of both condescension and humor in the question.

No. I don't want to be the law, and I don't really want to be above it. I just don't want to be a victim of its shortcomings.

That is a most precarious position to take, Jonat.

You're telling me. Do you have a better idea?

Not at the moment.

When you do, let me know. In the meantime, I'm going to try to discover if they have any more plans for me.

I listened almost for an hour, skipping from commentary about obvious feminine charms to the best vehicles for smash and grabs—Magans, of course—before picking up on something of great personal interest.

". . . was from the big fellow's mouth. The big fellow says we got to take the guy ran you off."

"Kemal himself?"

"Don't say that. Just the big fellow. Says we either got to do that or take out the guy wanted the take out."

"Who was that?"

"You don't need to know. Cendie type. With some Euro-cast outfit in Denv. Big net type. You don't have the creds or the savvy to deal there. Sides, you want them after you?"

"How much time we got?"

"Not flash-rush. Week. Two at most." Tony Jaro—I thought it had to be Jaro—laughed. "Unless the cendie goes blaze, you get this deVrai guy by next Friday. You can use a stunner or a slugger. No long guns. Has to look like smash and grab or jealous husband thing."

". . . never outside that cendie fortress, 'cept with the kids . . ."

"Keep the kids out of it. Bad for business when kids get snuffed."

". . . take some time . . ."

". . . got some . . ."

What I had heard wasn't exactly proof, not in the legal sense, especially since I was obtaining it illegally, but I wasn't going to get legal proof, not from Kemal or the PST group.

My options weren't exactly wonderful. I could take out Alistar in the next few days, or I could try to survive an endless series of attacks by Kemal's outfit. I could probably survive some of the attempts by Kemal's troops, especially by listening carefully, but that was like rolling dice, and I'd never cared much for gambling.

Besides, I was getting more than a little angry myself. So I turned to Dierk's elaborate system and pasted a modified simmie into the scanner bypass feeds, followed by a voice-coder over that. I also set up a bounce-relay and a signal disguise that indicated a code in Old Tech—the main code for ISS headquarters. Then I linked the Club, going for the court reservations. Of course, I got bounced because I didn't have Club access privilege codes, but that did get me a smiling face. Clubs have real people. That's one thing the exorbitant dues pay for.

"Sir?"

"Dimitri Oskrow. I was supposed to have a match sometime today or maybe tomorrow with Jacques Alistar. My system blew, and I lost the court time. It might even have been tomorrow or Saturday, but I thought it was today."

"Alistar . . . yes, sir. I don't know about the match, but he does have a court time at two this afternoon. Court number four."

"I'm sure that's it. Thank you very much."

I had two and a half hours to get ready and get there. I did spend some time studying various images of Alistar.

My disguise was simple enough. I wore very classy sweatgear over racquetball shorts and shirt. My hair was sprayed white blond with some of the hair color from the guest suite at the house, and my face was darkened, almost latte. I carried one of Dierk's racket cases, with the commando slingshot in it.

At one-fifteen I left the Southhills house, heading northwest toward the Creek district and the Club. From the time I'd been a child, and even afterward, when I'd often been a guest of my parents at the Club, I was very familiar with the Club and its facilities. I'd only played racquetball a handful of times. I'd never been that enthused about pseudo-combat, and that was the way most ascendents regarded competitive games.

I took my time, so that I'd arrive just a few minutes before two. Just before I turned into the Club, I turned off the link to Minerva.

I parked the Jacara next to another and across from an apparently antique Bentley, certainly not authentic, because it couldn't have passed the emissions requirements, even with nano-reprocessing aftergear.

Then, racket case in hand, I hurried to the men's locker room entrance as if I were tardy for a match, past the scanners that merely recorded and observed, and then to the court entrances along the back. Court number four was on the far end.

It was three past two, and Alistar and his partner were still warming up.

I took out the slingshot and fitted the first dart—the lethal one.

Then I slid open the court door and stepped inside, ducking as racquetball players have for centuries.

Both men turned half-around. Alistar glared.

"My mistake," I said. "So sorry."

The first dart hit Alistar full in the chest. He looked at me, then charged. He almost reached me before he went down. He wouldn't get up, and in minutes the darts would vanish.

Even before he fell, I'd fired the second dart—the nonlethal one—at the other man, a somewhat softer-looking and smaller fellow. He just looked at me unbelievingly before toppling forward.

After replacing the slingshot in the racket case, I stepped out of the court and closed the court door behind me, careful to close the shutter so that no one would immediately look inside. Then I walked along the front of the courts, out through the locker room and out to the carpark.

Clubs usually didn't note the cars, not by plates, and I'd have to chance that.

As I drove back southward, I was angry. Not remorseful, not feeling guilty, but angry. I hadn't wanted to kill Alistar. I hadn't wanted to kill anyone. I was having to bend and break the law just in order to survive, and to stay alive, not only for myself, but for Charis and Alan. I'd reported something like three direct attacks on me, and the safos, and even Central Four—now Minerva—hadn't been able to do anything. My DNA had been stolen, altered, and shaped into a weapon used to kill my sister and her husband. MultiCor had been in the process of shipping lethal neuralwhips—allowed under a technicality—to kill Martian protesters, and so far as I could tell, once more, nothing much had happened.

I very much had the feeling that PAMD hadn't killed Everett Forster, but that MultiCor/PST had, although I certainly had no evidence for that, and no plausible motivation. Just my feelings, but they were doing better than hard evidence at the moment.

More than a few people knew what MultiCor and the PST group were doing, and yet nothing . . . not one thing had happened.

Yet . . . if I ever got caught for trying to defend myself in the only way that seemed practical, I had no illusions about what would happen to me. None at all. And it made me angry—not red rage, but ice-cold fury.

I was halfway back to the Southhills house before I calmed down enough to restore the link to Minerva.

Jonat . . . you cut off the link. Again. You're behaving suspiciously.

I certainly am. That's because I'm a suspicious character. I'm suspicious about everyone. I still have no idea why people want to kill me, but it's clear that they do. I'm not sure what the economic analysis will do, but I'm working on it.

Keep working on it. It might distract people from what you've really been doing.

I didn't pursue that. She either knew or she didn't, and I had to believe that all she had was probabilities, and I'd already learned that those didn't count in the administration of justice or the prosecution of law.

It was just before three when I got back to Southhills. I even had time to remove the hair spray and face coloration without hurrying before I picked up Charis and Alan.

chapter 78

Mydra, Ghamel, Escher, and Deng sat around a circular conference table in a windowless room on the eighth floor of the ISS headquarters building.

"I assume that everyone has heard," Deng said slowly. "Alistar died of heart failure yesterday. He was playing racquetball."

"That seems . . . unusual," ventured Escher.

"He was murdered. His companion suffered nervous prostration. Both collapses were most likely induced."

"Do we bring this to the attention of the safos?" asked Ghamel.

"They are investigating, but preliminary results are inconclusive. Unless someone comes forward with physical evidence, the verdict will be heart failure from an undetermined cause."

"Who managed this?" asked Ghamel. "Do you know?"

"The most likely candidate is deVrai," Mydra replied, "but no one matching his description was anywhere nearby, not according to the Club scanners. There was someone his approximate size, but none of the physical features matched.

Not even close. Also, the weapon used is unknown, and probably from a government source. We've verified that de-Vrai is not associated with any black operations. That leaves any one of a number of people with such contacts who disliked Alistar, and there are more than a few who do."

"That may be," Deng conceded. "Someone knew Alistar's habits. There was a link to the Club from a Dimitri Oskrow. The return code was the main ISS exchange here at headquarters. Oskrow does not exist. The voiceprints were coded as well."

"That indicates a professional approach." Escher nodded.

"Vorhees is dead, and now Alistar," Ghamel said flatly.

"Vorhees was shot by his mistress, and I'd have to say that I'm not surprised she hadn't done it years before," Mydra said, her tone contemptuous. "Alistar . . . you know how impatient he was, and how impossible. Maybe it was someone's husband. Or a rival at NEN."

"What about deVrai?" asked Ghamel, looking toward Mydra. "You said something about him weeks back."

"I had worried about deVrai," Mydra observed. "But this was set up, and it appears as though it had been planned, even well in advance. It took special equipment that we haven't seen deVrai use. At the same time, I still think we should just let the deVrai matter drop . . . at least for several months. Let Kemal know that if anything happens to deVrai until we give the word, we'll drop on him."

"Why? We might as well just get deVrai out of the way," snapped Ghamel.

"I could ask the same," countered Mydra. "Why now? De-Vrai is trying to hang on to his family, to rebuild his consulting business . . . and you think he's got time to plan all these . . . occurrences, much less carry them out? The safos know that he's been attacked several times, and they can't pin it anywhere. But they're looking. We don't control enough of the Safety Office to make sure they look away from us. Didn't that raid on ISS prove that? Why tempt fate right now?" She paused. "What about Meara?"

"Not long now," answered Escher. "The other sources of . . . embarrassment . . . have been taken care of."

"Good. We can't get on with the Mars operation until that's taken care of. Garos has vetted the central systems. There's nothing there now. Once Crosslin gets the campaign reform amendments passed, we can start working on the framework for the next elections. Those and the outsystem controls are key. DeVrai can wait until everyone's forgotten. Those can't."

"Mydra has a point there," Escher observed. "DeVrai hasn't contacted the Sinese since his contract with them was completed. He hasn't talked to Uy-Smythe. He hasn't made any more reports to the Safety Office."

"We can wait on deVrai," Deng concluded. "For our part. If Kemal wants to try again, we should not stand in his way."

"That could get nasty," Mydra pointed out.

"That is between Alistar, Kemal, and deVrai." Deng's voice was as hard and as smooth as cold polished iron. "We still need an alternative strategy to give BLN a way to stir up more unrest in Serenium."

"What about cheapening the mix in the formulators?"

"Or increasing the waiting time for routine meds?"

Mydra smiled politely, but did not offer a strategy as she listened.

chapter 79

Friday was very quiet. Not a word from Reya, Methroy, or anyone else I'd contacted over the past week. I did get a confirmation that the fee from the latest H&F project had been paid, and that looked like the last income for a while to come. There wasn't even a mention of Alistar's death in any of the news reports. That was normal, since deaths from natural causes usually weren't reported, except in the case of well-known figures, and Alistar wasn't anywhere near that well-known.

Surprisingly, Jackie Ramset had little to say about Alistar's death.

"... that cendie wanted deVrai dead ... died of a heart attack ..."

"See? See what all that high livin' gets you. Just as dead as a dumb northside punk."

"So what do I do now?"

"I already put in a word to the big fellow. Says to lay off for a day or two. Has to think about it. He'll get back to me ... You get on and deal with Ramires ... giving you vapor ... bringing in two–three gees a week ..."

"I'll take care of it this afternoon."

"You better."

That meant I had a few days' grace, maybe more, but I'd have to keep a close ear on the westside boys—along with everything else.

In the meantime, I got back to work on the MultiCor economic analysis, based on the figures I shouldn't have had. The more I got into it, the more I understood what Minerva had in mind. It was clear that no one had ever been allowed to analyze those figures and report on them. Reading between the lines told me that Mars was being run just one step above a twentieth century Russian penal outpost. The amount of unreported profit was staggering.

Where exactly did these numbers come from? One of the Legislature's committees?

They might have.

So . . . let me guess. Your AI compatriot or someone like Carlisimo knows the numbers are wrong, but he's bound by programming or classification not to release them.

Have you finished the analysis?

Something like this can't be done overnight, or even in a few days. If I work hard and everything comes together, I might have a passible product by early next week.

Finishing it might be a good idea.

Before something else happens? What else could happen? As soon as I said those words, I realized they were stupid. All sorts of nasty events could occur.

Captain Garos has completed removing all references and indirect leads to MultiCor and ISS. He has avoided those officers with independent integrity as much as possible. One officer who had been suspended for inappropriate actions was released on personal recognizance and died from a hit-and-run accident under suspicious circumstances.

What you're saying is that the Safety Office is also under attack?

The probabilities are high and rising incrementally every day.

An analysis is going to stop that?

Not by itself, but it is key.

I didn't get any more out of Minerva, and I didn't push too hard. After all, she could have asked me some embarrassing questions as well. So I spent the day working on the economics, and setting things up so that they looked impartial, while making the point that MultiCor was robbing the Legislature blind. There are ways to do that, and I'd used all of them in the past, but I was even more restrained in what I was setting up. That way, the charts and graphs might actually get to the media before someone realized the full import of what I'd done. I doubted that most of the politicians would see through it, although they had some sharp staff members who might, but that was fine, too, because if enough staff saw the charts no one could keep them hidden.

After three, before I headed out to pick up Charis and Alan, I tried to link Paula at my house. Surprise of surprises . . . she was there, wearing a gray safo uniform. She smiled.

"Jonat. I just got here. They let us off early today."

"I've been trying to reach you."

"I know."

"Would you like to have lunch with us tomorrow?"

"I . . . hadn't thought about it."

"We can drive up there and get you."

"No, Jonat. I couldn't make you do that."

"You can't afford to drive down here, not on a junior safo's pay."

"I'll come, but only if I can take the maglev."

"Then we'll be waiting. Just take the direct line to Cherry Creek. That's quicker. We'll all go out to lunch at the Shire Inn. Say, eleven-thirty at Cherry Creek. If you catch the eleven-ten, that should be plenty of time. But we'll wait if we get there first."

"I . . ." Paula shrugged. "I don't know what to say."

"You don't have to say anything. Just come and enjoy lunch."

"What do I wear? I've never been there."

"For lunch . . . anything tasteful. People wear everything from slacks and shorts to coats and cravats or business suits or dresses."

"For your sake, Jonat, I will try to be tasteful."

"Anything you wear will be tasteful."

"That's not likely. Outside of uniforms, servies, and women of dubious character, my experience in clothing is limited."

"You'll be fine." I tried to reassure her even as I took in her words, realizing that there were doubtless areas where her experience was indeed limited, or limited to learned and imparted knowledge.

"I'd better be." She smiled. "If I'm to be ready tomorrow, I need to go."

"We'll see you then." I did want to see her. I knew that. Was it because we'd already shared more of a meaningful nature than I had with anyone else in years—except for Minerva, of course. And I still wasn't sure how much of each was within the other. What were they to each other? Mother and daughter? Sisters? Did I want to know?

I took a moment to make a reservation at the Shire Inn for noon, but I was very punctual and was waiting at the Academy, in line with all the parents and others reclaiming children. I was even near the front of the queue.

Alan got the front seat. He gave me a brief smile. "Dr. Trevalyn says we're going to be animals in the mountains next week. I want to be a big-horned sheep. A big ram."

"Being a bird is more fun," Charis added from the backseat.

"I like the way the rams climb the rocks," Alan said.

"Birds are better."

I could see where that was headed, even before I pulled out of the Academy's long circular drive. "Oh . . . Charis, tonight, when you practice, you're going to play both the pieces you're working on for me, and you're going to explain why you're playing them the way you are."

She looked almost horror-stricken. "Uncle Jonat . . ."

"If you can't do things in front of people, you can't really do them. I have to present my work to all sorts of people. But I won't say anything. That's Madame Castro's job."

Charis looked only slightly relieved.

"After your lesson tomorrow, we're going to pick up Officer Athene at the maglev station and all go out to lunch at the Shire Inn. That's a reward for everyone."

"You do like her." Charis looked at Alan. "I told you so."

"She's a girl," Alan said.

What that had to do with anything I wasn't sure. "She's had a hard week of training, and she doesn't make many credits, and she is taking care of my house."

"Our house is your house, sort of," Charis said.

"No. It's your house. I'm here to take care of you two and it."

"I'm glad you're here, Uncle Jonat," Alan said. "Brendan had to go live with his grandmother, and she's old. She's sixty."

I just hoped that Alan changed his mind about what was old over the next fifteen years or so.

chapter 80

Marlon walked toward the reporting screen at Antoinette's, his steps slowing as he neared the screen. He held the thin servie unit in his hands. He stopped short of the screen and looked blankly at it, then at the floor. "Can't . . . can't do this . . . not no more . . ."

"Marlon?"

Marlon did not look at the screen from which the voice came. Instead, out of a gaunt face, his deep-set eyes looked down at the persona projection unit.

"Are you ready to report, Marlon?" inquired the impersonally warm baritone voice of Central Four.

Marlon looked up to the reporting screen, at the concerned male safo who returned Marlon's gaze with one politely sympathetic.

Abruptly, Marlon lifted the persona unit, and then hurled it to the floor. "Can't keep . . . can't . . . won't."

"Marlon, you are good . . ." began the voice of Central Four.

"No one gonna make me . . . not gonna turn my brains inside out . . . threaten . . . not me . . . you 'n everyone else . . .

Do this . . . do it this way, otherwise you go Mars . . . Do that . . ." Marlon's voice rose into a near shriek, then dropped away.

"Marlon . . ."

"No . . . don't talk at me . . ." The young man's right hand darted to his trouser pocket. He pulled out an ancient slim-line slug-thrower. The first shot went through the screen. Then he jammed the weapon against his temple and pulled the trigger a second time.

His lifeless body pitched onto the shimmering gray tile floor of the adviser's lounge.

Central Four watched from the hidden receptors, and from behind those links, I also watched, a former Central Four, knowing that better words might have helped.

Learning has a high price at times.

chapter 81

On Friday night, I'd worked late on the MultiCor analysis, and I'd gotten up early on Saturday and put in another hour before fixing breakfast for everyone and straightening up the house. Only then did I use the exercise equipment and finally get cleaned up.

After Charis's piano lesson on Saturday morning, before she left, Madame Castro turned to me. "She has practiced. I can tell the difference."

I certainly hoped so. It seemed to me that even a single week of solid practice had helped, but the test, as in anything, would be how matters went in the months and years ahead. "We're working on it."

"*He's* working on it." Charis's words were so low that I would not have caught them without my enhancements.

Once Madame Castro had departed, I turned to Charis. "I heard that, young woman. And I am working on it. I'm working on it because you are talented, because it's a valuable talent, because you need practice at a disciplined art, and because your mother expected it of you, and so do I."

Charis swallowed, then abruptly turned and ran for the stairs.

I'd probably laid it on too heavy with the reference to Aliora, but what I'd said was true. Aliora had felt that Charis had musical talent, and she had wanted Charis to develop it. I knew enough to know that the next few years were critical. Besides, music developed the brain more thoroughly and evenly. In another two years or so, it would be Alan's turn.

For some reason, the thought flashed through my mind that I couldn't see Deidre and Rousel being firm enough to encourage that talent. Then I laughed quietly. Already, I was into parental self-justification. I turned to Alan, standing in the archway to the great room. "Go get your coat and tell your sister to get hers. We're going out to lunch, remember?"

"Yes, Uncle Jonat." He scurried away.

". . . don't want to go to lunch . . ." Those were the words I heard from the upstairs landing.

"Charis!"

". . . not fair . . ."

"It's time to go," I called up the stairs.

Alan was the first one down. He'd fastened his coat at an angle, and I refastened it. By then, Charis had blotted her eyes, and they were mostly clear by the time she reached the bottom of the steps.

"I didn't mean to upset you," I said quietly. "Like your parents, I'm trying to do the best I can. Someday, when you have children, you'll understand. Until then, you'll think you'll be able to avoid upsetting your children, and that you'll do better. Every child thinks at some time that he or she can do it better than their parents. Or their uncles. If you're very good, you might manage it." I waited.

"I'm sorry, Uncle Jonat."

I patted her shoulder. "It has to be hard for you. I do understand. Your mother and I, we lost our parents before their time, too."

Charis blotted her eyes without looking directly at me.

"Are you two ready, now?"

They both nodded, and followed me to the garage.

"Both of you in the backseat."

"Told you," Alan muttered to Charis.

"Adults always sit in front. You know that," I pointed out.

That didn't get an argument or a muttering complaint, which meant that I'd hit on a familiar phrase or concept.

As I headed northward, back toward the older area of southern Denv nearer to the Club, I glanced to my left, to the west. The sky was a clear blue, and the snow on the Rockies seemed to shimmer in the sun that gave little heat. Still, chill or not, I liked bright days far better than the cloudy ones. Recently, even the sunniest of days had felt cold and cloudy, even when they hadn't been.

We pulled into the waiting area for the Cherry Creek maglev station at eleven-twenty.

"How long are we going to wait?" Alan asked.

"Until the shuttle gets here," Charis replied.

"And the one from the northwest might not be the first one, either," I pointed out.

It wasn't. It was the third one, at eleven thirty-five. Paula was one of a handful who stepped through the security gates. She was wearing a midthigh gray woolen jacket and darker gray trousers.

I was halfway out of the Jacara, waving, before she caught sight of us. She didn't run, but walked quickly.

As Paula slipped into the front seat, gracefully, she looked back at the children. "Hello, Charis, Alan. It's good to see you."

"Hello." Alan didn't quite look at Paula.

"I like your coat," Charis said, smiling.

"Thank you. I like it, too."

"So do I," I added, although I could tell that Paula had gone out and bought the coat, and probably most of the outfit, after I'd talked to her on Friday afternoon. I had to admit that she looked wonderful, but that wasn't what I'd intended to do. She would have enough demands on her not-so-ample salary.

"I'm glad."

I pulled out of the maglev waiting area.

"How long before we get there, Uncle Jonat?" asked Alan. "I'm hungry."

"Less than ten minutes." After a pause, I asked Paula, "Did you have any trouble with the maglev?"

"No. It wasn't crowded at all."

"Any difficulty with anything at the house?"

"No. You left everything very neat and clean."

"He likes it that way," interjected Charis. "He's always making us pick up things."

"Ah, yes, your uncle the ogre," I said sonorously, "from under the bridge . . . sallying forth to terrify the little billy goats into neatness . . ."

"Uncle Jonat . . ." Charis's voice contained that tone of despairing disgust that only a nine-year-old can muster.

"I know. I'm hopeless."

A trace of a smile crossed Paula's face as I pulled into the carpark adjoining the Shire Inn.

The Inn was not that full, but I hadn't expected it to be on a Saturday afternoon in early January. The hostess gave us a corner table. With the paneled walls of real oak and the hunter green hangings, the impression was of the kind of English country inn that had never really existed. The menus were printed, not projected, and a server filled the water glasses.

"Are you going to have the petite fillet and the pommes frites again?" I grinned at Charis.

She frowned for a moment, solemnly, then grinned back. "Can I?"

"Yes. You've both been relatively good, and you did well with your lesson today." I turned to Alan.

"A big burger with Swiss cheese, please?"

"Consider it done."

Paula looked at me. "What are you going to have?"

"I'm very traditional about food, and they're traditional here. I think I'm going to have the beef Wellington, although the alfredo portobello is good if you want a pasta, and their trout is always good. The fillet that Charis is having is a good choice as well."

Paula nodded. "I think I'll have that—the fillet."

"It's good," Charis said. "I had it when Uncle Jonat took me here for my birthday."

On cue, the server appeared, a real server, although she was a servie, and took our orders. Paula and I asked for Grey tea, and the children wanted iced tea.

"Do you play football?" Alan asked Paula.

"No, I don't. I'm afraid there are many things I haven't done. Do you?"

"I'm learning. Uncle Jonat says I need to work on my dribbling more."

"He's good for his age," I said.

We talked about football and school until the salads arrived, small fruit plates for Alan and Charis, and mixed greens for Paula and me.

"How much longer for you?" I asked her. "The sessions?"

"Another two weeks. Most of the alternative safo probies take six weeks, but I've done so much that I only need about half that, according to Sergeant Ohly." Paula took a bite of the salad. "This is good."

"I hoped you'd like it."

"I don't have much in the way of comparison."

"If it tastes good, and you like it, that's what matters."

My beef Wellington was very good. Not excellent, but tasty nonetheless, and I was hungry. So was everyone else, at least for a few minutes.

"This was a good choice, Charis," Paula offered after the silence.

"I like it, especially the pommes frites."

Alan just kept eating.

"Do you come here often?" asked Paula.

"No." Charis glanced at me. "Only for special times. Or if we're good."

"Where do you go other times?"

"We went to Fogg's," Alan said. "I wanted to go to Cheezers."

"Fogg's is more casual," I said. "Cheezers is . . ."

"For little kids," Charis finished my sentence.

"Is not," mumbled Alan through a mouthful of something.

"Is too."

I glared at Charis, and she closed her mouth.

"You were a very effective Marine officer, weren't you?" asked Paula.

"I was probably less effective than I thought I was. I did manage to survive, and not everyone did."

"You were a lieutenant colonel, weren't you? That sounds like you did more than survive."

"A little more." I laughed. "Do you know where they're going to assign you first?"

"Usually, you do some patrol work and some screen pushing and monitoring so that you get an idea of where the trouble spots are. That's what . . . Central Four and Sergeant Ohly have both said."

"You probably have some idea of where those are," I suggested.

"Mostly in westside and northside." Paula took a last mouthful of the fillet.

I glanced over at Charis and Alan. "I don't suppose you two want any dessert."

"Chocolate splurge."

"Ice cream. Chocolate."

I skipped anything that heavy, although the crème brûlée was tempting, and settled for more tea. So did Paula.

After Charis and Alan had demolished the sweets, and I paid, we walked out of the Shire Inn. I glanced sideways at Paula. "If you have a little time, I thought you ought to see the house in Southhills, just so that you know where I am if anything comes up." That was a transparent fabrication. She could always reach me through Minerva, but I did want her to see the house, for lots of reasons.

"That might be a good idea."

"You can see our rooms," Alan offered.

Charis glared at her brother for the briefest instant, so quickly he didn't even notice.

I took the scenic route back to Southhills, pointing out some of the more extensive estates along the way. Paula didn't say anything at all as we drove up to the Southhills house.

As we entered the foyer, I took her coat and hung it in the entry closet. I'd only worn my jacket, and the house wasn't that warm. "Would you like to show Paula your rooms?"

"Me first!" Alan exclaimed.

That meant his room was relatively neat. "Go ahead."

I let Alan lead the way as we headed up the main stairs from the front foyer. Charis followed her brother, and Paula and I brought up the rear. At the top of the stairs was the oil painting of Aliora and Dierk.

"Is that . . . ?" murmured Paula.

I nodded.

The children's rooms were to the north of the landing at the top of the stairs.

"The sitting room here is where we read bedtime stories," I explained. "Alan's room is through the door to the right."

"Uncle Jonat reads," Alan said. "We listen."

"Every night?" asked Paula.

"Every night, except for the few when I've had to go out." I stood back while Alan explained.

"This is my reader. It's not a real console . . . and there are my books . . . the kinds you carry around and don't put on a reader. We have to know both kinds. They're different . . ."

I swallowed, because I could almost hear Aliora's voice through Alan.

When Alan had finished, Paula went into Charis's room, but barely, as if she did not wish to intrude.

"You can come in," Charis said. "My school stuff goes on those shelves . . ."

I stayed outside as Charis told Paula about her room.

"Thank you, Charis," Paula said as she emerged from my niece's room.

I looked at the children.

"You two can have two hours of linktime—each of you chooses one hour. Up here. I'll enable the console."

"Good! I get first," Alan said.

"He can go first," Charis agreed. That meant she wanted to watch something on later.

Through my implant, I pulsed the system. I also set the

timer for two hours and fifteen minutes, to allow time for the second program to finish.

Paula walked beside me as we descended to the foyer, and then into the great room. For a long time, she surveyed the expanse, taking in the green marble and the columns, her eyes lighting on every piece of furniture, every painting, and even the carpets. "This is . . . impressive." She looked at me with those storm-gray eyes. "You and your family are very wealthy, aren't you?"

I laughed. "I'm moderately well-off. Borderline ascendent. You've seen my house. That was what I could afford. This is mostly from Dierk's family. The VanOkars were very well-to-do, and they only had two children. Dierk was very successful."

"You forget, Jonat. I may only be probationary, but I've seen the way most people live. Your house is a palace compared to the houses of most sarimen and servies."

I couldn't dispute that, and I wasn't about to. "Would you like something to drink? Tea? Water? Wine?"

"I'm not thirsty right now."

I gestured to a pair of armchairs that faced each other at an angle in one of the corner nooks, then waited for Paula to seat herself. She did so gracefully.

"You bought the coat and outfit just for today, didn't you?"

Her smile was shy, but lovely. "Not just for today. I'll need nice clothes that aren't too formal. I don't have many."

"I feel badly about that. I wasn't thinking. I didn't mean for you to have to go out and buy . . ."

Paula reached out and touched my wrist briefly. Her fingertips were warm, and I could feel their warmth after she'd withdrawn them. "You've been very kind. You've been much kinder than anyone could expect."

"I owe you and Minerva a great deal." Like my life.

I looked into those storm-gray eyes, wondering what she saw when she looked at me. A man who still struggled to survive, without knowing exactly why or even who he was? Paula knew who she was—of that I was sure. I was less certain of what she wanted to become.

"We owe you as well."

"Mutual gratitude society." The words were drier than I intended. "I'm sorry. I didn't mean it the way it came out. I . . . I don't know . . ."

"You don't like owing people, Jonat. You'd rather be the one owed."

I didn't say anything for a moment. Her comment was more than perceptive. "You're right."

"I had help from Minerva," Paula confessed.

"Are you linked to her now?"

"No. That would be . . . too much." Paula shook her head. "I'll ask her about things. I guess . . . sort of like a mother and mentor together, but she doesn't intrude, and I don't want her to. It's a voluntary link, like yours. I just need more information than you do."

"I wonder about that. Sometimes, there's a temptation to think I know more than I do. You probably don't have that illusion."

"That time will come."

There was another silence, both awkward and comfortable, simultaneously, in a way I couldn't describe.

"Do you . . . have dreams . . . about things . . . that never happened?"

"As a result of the pattern-programming, you mean?" She nodded. "They're strange, but they're not at all disturbing anymore, now that I can recognize them for what they are. Some of them deal with dancing, as if I were a ballerina, but . . ." She looked down at herself. "I'm a little big for a ballerina."

"You'd look wonderful on stage," I protested.

"Oh . . . the proportions aren't bad, but I'd be a good half head taller than anyone else on the stage." She laughed. "It's a nice dream, though."

"What other dreams do you have?"

"They change. They must not be that important. I don't remember any of them, except some of the times when I was . . . learning . . . the first parts of being a safo."

"Somewhere between what you were and what you are?"

She nodded.

I wasn't about to mention the word "cydroid."

"Jonat . . . please tell me about you. I would like to hear about when you were a boy."

"I was, once. I grew up not too far from here, but our house was smaller than this, but bigger than mine. I always wanted to be a Marine. I don't know why. My parents wouldn't have been happy with it. So I never told them. I played at it only when they weren't around. I practiced trying to move without making a sound, even when the fall leaves fell and were rustling on the grass. I liked sports. Football and swimming. I liked to sing, but I wasn't any good at it, and once I heard a recording of my own singing . . ." I shook my head. "I still like music."

"Were you good at sports?"

"Good enough to make the teams. Not good enough to stand out . . . except maybe in swimming, but that's never been a big-time sport . . ."

I talked, and she kept asking questions, and before I knew it, it was almost four-thirty. I stopped and looked into those storm-gray eyes. "Would you like to stay for dinner?"

"You're being very kind, Jonat. Yes, I would. But that wouldn't be good for me. I need to study, and I need to take in days like today with spaces in between. Remember . . . in some ways, I'm not much older than Charis."

"That's hard to believe."

"No . . . you're being kind again."

"I'm not being kind. That's the way I feel."

"It's the way you think, not the way you feel," she corrected me gently as she stood. "It won't hurt that you have dinner with the children after I've left."

"I suppose I could take Alan to Cheezers." I tried not to wince at the thought.

"He sounded like he would like that."

"I'm sure he would, and I might even survive it."

Paula laughed. I liked the sound.

I stood up and called upstairs. "We're going to take Paula back to the maglev. Anyone who wants to go to Cheezers . . ."

I didn't even have the rest of the words out before Alan was halfway down the stairs, hanging on to his jacket by one cuff.

"You could get your jacket on," I said with a laugh as I recovered Paula's coat from the entry closet.

As I helped Paula into her coat, Charis descended the stairs, following her brother, if at a more deliberate pace.

I checked security at the house a last time before I eased the Jacara out of the oversized garage. It took less than ten minutes to reach the drop-off area of the mid-Old Tech maglev station.

As I slowed to a stop, I told Paula, "Just take the northwest direct—the green shuttle. Otherwise, you'll have to change shuttles in old downtown Denv."

"I can manage that—either way."

"I'm sure you can."

She smiled. "It was a lovely lunch and afternoon." Then she turned to the backseat. "It was good to see you both again."

Alan half-nodded, shyly.

Charis smiled.

"Thank you all." Paula flashed a last smile, then closed the door. She walked quickly from the Jacara and through the security gates to the platform. Since no one else had pulled up behind us, I waited until she boarded the magshuttle. Then I pulled away from the drop-off area.

"She's nice, Uncle Jonat," Charis observed.

"She's all right," Alan added. "She doesn't know much about football."

"Not everyone does."

"You said we could go to Cheezers, Uncle Jonat."

"I did, and we will." I turned the Jacara westward.

Later, after dinner and the bedtime rituals, I had more work to do on the MultiCor financial and economic analysis. I knew it couldn't wait, but the weekend was looking long, longer than I'd thought. I'd also have to go over the stored records of the conversations from my taps of Kemal's crew. I could hardly wait for the drudgery involved in that, but I couldn't afford not to know what they were planning.

chapter 82

Sunday was church again, and the sermon wasn't too bad. It even made sense without having to rely on divine authority and grace. That kind of preaching—the kind that inspired human striving toward a better world—I could take, at least in small doses. Larger doses might have been harder, because I was definitely guilty of some significant sin, especially in the old sense of the word, and it didn't make that much difference to my own feelings of guilt that I really hadn't had much choice in the matter. I suppose that was one of the things that bothered me about the moralists—either the secular or the religious kinds. They both had lists of immoral acts, but no one talked about the structures in society and religion that often put people like me in a situation where the only "moral" course was to get killed or take great abuse, or both. I had both personal and philosophical objections to any system where martyrdom was the most moral course.

And then there was Paula. I couldn't pretend or ignore the feelings any longer. I found her attractive. But was it the attraction of a man who was no longer so young as he used to be, looking for a younger woman? That thought disturbed me. I couldn't say just how much.

Or was that attraction based on the quixotic contradictions within her, the juxtaposition of book knowledge and hard safo with the social naïveté? Add to that my own naïveté, at least in the area of cydroids and safos. I'd never thought about what happened to cydroids. What had happened to Everett Forster's cydroid? Or the others? Admittedly, there couldn't have been that many, but still . . .

Sitting in Dierk's office in the early afternoon, trying to keep working on the economic and financial analysis of the MultiCor income and expense figures, I couldn't seem to keep those thoughts from circling back and nagging at me.

Minerva . . . what happens to cydroids? Do all the ones used by the Safety Office eventually become real . . . they're all real . . . I mean legal citizens, that sort of thing?

The safo cydroids do—the ones who survive the cydroid uses. It was decided very early that those who survived and developed full self-awareness would be granted legal status.

Not all become fully self-aware?

Approximately thirty percent do not. They remain safo cydroids. There are always uses for older observers and scouts.

What about private cydroids?

They are the property of their owners. Even if their owners choose to grant them legal independence, they must pass a standard test to demonstrate self-awareness.

I shook my head. Another class of serfs or slaves, admittedly small, but still enslaved. I worried as much about what they symbolized as about the plight of individual cydroids. What kind of culture had we become? I'd been as blind as anyone, seeing the occasional cydroid and really not seeing what lay behind.

Another thought flashed into mind.

Minerva . . . did I do anything wrong with Paula?

Do you think you did?

Not that I know of.

Then why do you worry?

I don't know, but I do worry.

She is strong-willed. Have you had any difficulty in knowing what she has said?

No. I worry about what she hasn't said.

That is the sign of a wise man.

I'm not a wise man, and I'm not sure that I'd recognize one if I met him. I paused, then added, *Another few days and I should have a draft of the analysis finished.*

The sooner you finish it, the sooner we can act, and the safer you will be.

I didn't need that kind of prompting. *I take it that PST and ISS have not decided to leave me alone?*

The probabilities are that you have two to three weeks before another action is taken against you. I cannot calculate what that action will be. Each one is likely to be more difficult than the previous one to anticipate.

Thank you.

You're welcome. I didn't want to deal with that problem at the moment. I was more interested in Paula. *What about Paula? Did I do anything to upset her?*

She has not expressed anything to me, but she would not.

Minerva never did answer my questions about Paula. So I had no choice but to link her directly. She was at my house. But then, I realized, so was Minerva.

Paula was sitting in the armchair in my office, one of my old bound books in her hand. I couldn't see which one. She was wearing a gray singlesuit, probably an old safo suit, but she looked good even in that. "Jonat."

"I just wanted to see how you were doing."

"You can see. I'm reading. I like the bound books. They seem easier to read this way, rather than using a reader or a projected screen."

"I've always thought so, but I never told anyone. It marks you as old-fashioned."

"You *are* old-fashioned."

"In what way?"

"You worry about things like morals or whether you've hurt someone's feelings."

"Especially after I've done something nasty, in the name of self-defense—like in that tunnel."

"There was no need for them to use lethal weapons. All they had to do was close the tunnel doors. They wanted you dead."

I didn't answer for a moment because thinking about it made me angry all over again. I'd gone, looking for evidence against ISS, because there hadn't seemed to be any alternative, and ended up in another situation where there hadn't been any alternative—and I was getting very tired of being put in positions where there weren't any good alternatives.

If I did nothing, I'd get killed. Removing individuals who had targeted me hadn't seemed to help much, and even if I did manage to avoid attempt after attempt and then remove the perpetrator, another would pop up. What did I have to do to get back to a peaceful life—wipe out the entire leadership of the PST group?

I shook my head. That seemed drastic—and impossible.

"Are you all right?" Paula asked.

"Oh . . . I'm surviving. Occasionally, I get to thinking about something else, when I shouldn't be. What does your week look like?"

"The first four days are long. I don't know about Friday, yet . . ."

While I enjoyed talking to her, I felt as though I were walking on eggshells, not knowing exactly what to say, and what not to say. I did manage to avoid deep topics, and, eventually, she told me that she had to study some more.

After that, I got back to working on the analysis, but only for an hour before Alan insisted on playing football, despite the cold wind outside. It was very late that night before I finished with more work on the MultiCor analysis and with reviewing the Kemal tap records. So far no one had made a decision—or they hadn't made one within the scope of the tab-taps. The ones I'd used were only good for another week at the most, and if nothing happened, I'd have to replace them, somehow, or plant others. I wasn't looking forward to that, either.

chapter 83

With the weekend, and spending time with the children—
and with Paula—I didn't get around to finishing the first cut
at the MultiCor economic analysis until late on Wednesday
night. Then, without any more consulting work coming in,
and with the AKRA seminar still over a week away, what
else was I going to spend time on?

I also reviewed the recording tabs. There was only one
brief series of remarks out of the tab in Tony Jaro's Magan.

"You hear anything from the big fellow about deVrai?"

"You don't ask the big fellow. He wants something
done . . . he'll let us know. Sloppy job on Ramires. His old
woman saw the car."

"Doesn't matter. Junker we lifted from northside. Tags
show as Phon Huang's." The punk laughed. "Safos track it,
and she talks, show that the northside boys got Ramires. He
can't tell her nothing. Not from underground."

"Good joke . . . 'less Huang discovers it was you. Hang
you on the guideway by your balls."

That was it, and it meant that I had to keep listening. If

nothing happened, I'd have to place more tabs. I didn't want to do that, but I didn't want to be dead, either.

I'd tried to link with Paula on Monday, but our conversation was brief, and after her coolness on Sunday and again on Monday, I got the impression that she was preoccupied with her training and that she didn't want to spend too much time with me. So I only tried linking with her on Wednesday evening. I got her simmie. So I left a very brief message and got back to work on the last sections of the MultiCor analysis.

When I finished the last chart, the last data table, I leaned back in the big ergochair and took a long swallow of lukewarm Grey tea, and another.

Minerva . . . what do we do now?

Is the draft finished?

It's a draft. The numbers are right. The words are rougher than I'd like.

Are you satisfied with the numbers and analysis?

They're fine.

Good. That is for the better. Minerva was silent for several moments. *The analysis has been sent where it may do some good.*

What? Are you locked into this system?

Only because you have linked systems. I am linked to your home system. There is a gate there, so that I cannot be reached through it unless I choose to be reached.

How did that happen?

That was one of the adjustments you made.

I had to wonder what other adjustments I'd made, just following her directions. Still . . . she'd played fair with me, when almost no one else had—except Aliora and Dierk. I swallowed. That was still hard at times.

Can you leak part of it to Eric Wong at SCFA? And, in a few days or so, to some unscrupulous netster? Maybe Wong could do something to upset the hidden PST machinery. What, I didn't know, but I wasn't having much success along those lines.

Minerva was silent for a time.

Just some of the provocative conclusions and figures, with the notation that it's a draft economic analysis being under-taken by whoever.

They would not dare to use such figures.

Of course not. But it might prompt them to ask the right kinds of questions, and the Sinese might well share the fig-ures with other on-Earth governments . . . Don't do it through my system.

There are other ways—through Central Four.

When the leaks start to come, that also ought to get Dom-Sec upset about security, and there's nothing better to spread word about something than to have security types trying to track down a leak.

Leaking classified material is illegal.

It's not classified until someone classifies it.

That is a dubious proposition. But Minerva laughed. *You have a nasty turn of mind, Jonat.*

I'd better have a nasty turn of mind. It was about all I had going for me.

chapter 84

Thursday came and went, and so did Friday morning. I hadn't heard from Paula, and I'd forced myself not to link again, reminding my impatient soul that she'd get in touch when she was ready and that I'd only make things worse by pushing. That was my problem everywhere, though. I'd pushed as much as I could with the consulting, and no one was forthcoming with new projects. I couldn't find any legal way to keep the PST types from setting me up, and I still had no idea what might be happening. Minerva had told me that the various Legislative committees—or their AI—had the analysis, and that matters were progressing. But she wouldn't—or couldn't—say how.

My whole life was hanging suspended—and doubtless in the balance—and any pushing I did on other people would probably only make matters worse.

I forced myself to work on comments for the abbreviated version of my paper at the AKRA seminar. That would pay a few credits, and was better than anything else I had going at the moment, or looked to have going for a long time to come.

I kept listening to my tabs on Jaro and Jackie and the unnamed punk, and early Friday afternoon, after making yet another set of revisions to my over-revised remarks for the AKRA seminar, I got more less-than-excellent news from that pair, via the tab in the Magan.

"The big fellow says to follow up on deVrai . . . says we got a contract."

"He got anything special how he wants it done?"

"Accidentlike, even accidentlike shooting."

"DeVrai's too good to smash his groundcars. Never leaves 'em outside, either. Can't do the kids. Maybe get him on the way to pick 'em up."

I hadn't seen them, but they'd obviously scouted what I was doing.

"How you going to do that?"

"Lorry. Fuel cell explosion. Big mess. Stolen lorry."

"He could still avoid you."

"Nah . . . use a max stun, then ram him. Stun won't show after the fire."

"How long to set it up?"

"Can't do it before Monday. That'd be best. Lift the lorry on Sunday. Tuesday'd be all right, too."

"Make sure you get him. Big fellow won't give you a third try."

The punk's response was a grunt.

My problem was simple—and deadly. If I just stopped the punk—or even Ramset and Jaro—I'd still have all of Kemal's family after me. Even if I could neutralize them, I'd have the PST group to deal with.

Under the law, I still had no proof admissible in any court, and, even if I did, I was already legally guilty of two murders—and that didn't count the guards in the ISS tunnel. Somehow, there was something very wrong with a system that left a man who'd never even wanted to lift a weapon again in that sort of position. My sister and her husband had been murdered by the same group. Who knew how many people on Mars had died or would die? And there were at least a handful of cydroids who'd been sent to their deaths as pawns.

Minerva . . . I have a problem, and that means you have one.

I know. What do you think your problem is?

I explained—in detail—all about the PST group, which she knew, and about Kemal's assignment from Alistar, most of which she knew. *And that means that if I get murdered, Charis and Alan won't get to grow up the way Aliora wanted; you won't have any real protection, not that you have that much now; Paula will be left more alone; and these murderers will get away with it all—and they'll effectively be protected by the law that isn't protecting us.*

That's true. What do you propose?

I took a screen out of her files. *How much information do you have that shows the access to Mahmed Kemal?*

He is under safo surveillance whenever he leaves his west-side compound.

Can I review those files?

That's possible. Minerva laughed, and it was a laugh. *Those are not restricted data.*

I found that amusing—or ironic—as well. *I'll need to review everything that you can funnel to me. I also need to know . . . Can you calculate when there will be a meeting of one of those boards—something like the board overseeing the Centre for Societal Research—that contains most of the key PST actors?*

I have already done that. There are two. The Health Policy Center board meets on Monday afternoon. Stacia Mydra is not on that board, and Alistar was not, but the other key members are.

Who are the key members, besides Tam Lin Deng?

Grantham Escher, Stacia Mydra, Daria Ghamel, Alfred Levin, and Augustus Sharpton. Jacques Alistar was also, but if a replacement has been selected, he or she has not been announced. The oversight board for the Centre for Societal Research has Deng, Mydra, Ghamel, and Sharpton, but not Levin. Alistar was on that board. There is a meeting at the Centre next Thursday.

The nineteenth? What time?

Four o'clock.

How did you know that?

All such meetings require public notice. Such notices are routed through Central Four so that the Safety Office is aware of them. Most small meetings are ignored, but the regulations require notification of all meetings of a public nature.

I made a note of the time and date, then checked the schedule for the entire week. The AKRA seminar was on Wednesday and Thursday. My presentation was at one o'clock on Thursday, and there was an evening reception from five-thirty to seven. All of it took place at the East Capitol Plaza, not that far from the Centre for Societal Research. That showed possibilities, but I'd have to work quickly. That was probably for the best. I'd always had a tendency to let difficult decisions drift—another reason why Shioban had left me.

The question was whether I could develop and implement a plan, a set of plans in that time frame. If I couldn't, I'd be dodging at least one more attempt on my life. That thought didn't make me at all happy.

By three in the afternoon, I'd roughed out some possibilities, and scratched out others. I closed and coded the files, and then headed out to pick up Charis and Alan.

chapter 85

I spent a good two hours on Friday, after putting the children to bed, studying all the views of the venues associated with Mahmed Kemal. I did note that Ken's Place wasn't among them, and I had to wonder how many others were not under surveillance. Then, what could be viewed was limited by law. All public byways could be, as well as all publicly owned and operated spaces. So could the areas around any business engaging in intercontinental or continent-wide commerce—as could the space outside the place of business or dwelling of any person convicted of a class-one felony. As a young man, Mahmed Kemal had been caught with several thousand credits worth of fraudulent bearercards. That meant the area around his compound was under surveillance. Presumably, whoever technically owned Ken's Place had avoided a conviction of any significant offense.

After sweeping through the surveillance scans one time, I turned to Minerva.

Can you analyze these and create a problematic timetable for Kemal's daily actions?

That is possible. What do you have in mind?

What I have in mind, I evaded, *depends on the timetable of his actions.* What I really had in mind was doing away with both the punk and Kemal, and seeing if I could find a way to pin the whole thing on the northside "family"—at least in the perception of the newsies, the nets, and the safos. That was step one.

I can have a timetable within an hour.

I'd appreciate it, Minerva.

The probabilities are that you are considering actions that would result in severe punishment for you, if detected.

The probabilities are even higher that, if I don't undertake actions of that nature, I'll be dead, and someone will discover exactly what I've done for you—or merely disassemble the equipment and sell it off.

There was one of those long silences.

You are correct, although my discovery is more likely than my immediate destruction.

I don't think either one of us wants to gamble on this, I suggested.

Either way is a gamble. Your option offers better odds.

Does that mean agreement, reluctant or otherwise?

Reluctant agreement.

Now . . . did the safos take any of the ultra-ex from ISS, as possible evidence?

One container, pending the outcome of the indictments and possible trial.

One container. That was close to thirty kilos. *Can you— or Paula—get me four blocks from that container?* I had two blocks concealed in my house, but they might not be enough. Not for everything I had in mind.

That is theft of evidence.

It probably is. Can it be done?

Is it necessary?

Absolutely. It's the only way you and I will survive this trap. It will subject Paula to some danger if she is caught.

I can minimize that danger. I can override the low-level cydroid control and use Charles to get the blocks to Paula.

What about monitoring?

That is not a problem. Minerva laughed, almost as if she were enjoying that thought.

All in all, it was a very late night.

chapter 86

I didn't listen in on Charis's piano lesson on Saturday. Instead, I used the time to do some more research. The three other tenants of the building owned and occupied by the Centre for Societal Research were the Centre for Consumer Equality (CCE), the Association of Professional Scientists (APS), and the NorAm Vintners' Association (NVA).

I didn't have anything to offer to APS, but I could certainly make a pitch to CCE or NVA, or both, and schedule a delivery for Thursday, between my presentation at the AKRA seminar and the evening reception. I'd already arranged for the Bowes to take care of Charis and Alan for the time I'd be at the AKRA function, which was a good thing, because I doubted that I'd have been able to get someone that reliable on short notice. They'd have to pick up the children, and I'd have to make special arrangements for that as well.

Next came the arrangements for the Kemal side of things. I'd checked out Mahmed Kemal's schedule, and there was a window of opportunity. He always stopped by his brother-in-law's coffeehouse at five o'clock on Sunday and stayed

for at least an hour. Then he was driven home. The route varied, except for two sections. He always took a short stretch
of Continental Boulevard, and about three blocks on Veran-
nis. I could use those sections for my backup plan, if plan A
didn't work out.

I linked Paula, hoping that she was at the house, and
would answer. She might have been, but she left the answering simmie on. So I had to leave a message.

"Paula, this is Jonat. I was wondering if you could help
me out on something—"

The simmie vanished. Paula was in the office, once more
reading one of my books. For a moment, I just looked. She
seemed so comfortable there, despite the worried expression
on her face, that I almost didn't want to say anything.

"Yes, Jonat?"

"As I said, Paula . . . I have a favor to ask."

She looked very doubtful.

"I'm not going to impose myself on you personally, at
least, not directly. But I need to take care of some pressing
business on Sunday. I have to come over to the house to get
some things ready, and then go out. I was wondering if I
could prevail on you to watch the children for a few hours.
At my house, I mean. They'll come with me."

She actually looked relieved. "Jonat, I don't know that
I'm the best for that, but I can make sure they don't get into
trouble, and I'd be happy to help you out that way."

"Thank you very much. I'd guess we'd be there around
one-thirty tomorrow, but you don't have to be there until
three at the earliest."

"I'll be there." She smiled. "Where would I be going? I'm
a very poor safo who's fortunate enough to be living in a
dwelling well beyond my means."

"I apologize for this, but there are some things that are
just beyond my control."

"Minerva has suggested that you're under great strain."
Her face clouded. "I have your delivery."

"Thank you. I'll need it."

"She said you would. She said that matters were not going
that well for either of you."

"No . . . they aren't. We'll have to do what we can."

"Is there anything I can do to help?"

"Your watching Charis and Alan will help a great deal. A great deal." In more ways than one. "Are you finished with your indoctrination, or familiarization, or whatever it's called?"

"I just have three days. I thought there would be more. Then I get a day off. After that, on Friday, I start with monitoring duties at station two. I'll be on monitoring for a month. After that, I'll rotate through what all junior safos do. Some patrols, some monitoring, some stationkeeping."

"Do you still think you'll like it?"

She smiled. "I can't imagine doing anything else."

At one time, I couldn't have imagined doing anything else but being a Marine officer, either, and I hadn't seen that much corruption in the Marines. Outside the Corps, in the political areas, and in the missions assigned. I frowned. Then, wasn't accepting corrupt missions a form of corruption itself?

"Did I say something wrong?" Paula asked.

"No." I shook my head. "I was thinking about when I was young, like you, and what I found out."

"You're not very encouraging."

"I didn't mean to be discouraging. As I'm sure Minerva has told you, all organizations have some bad people in them. The good organizations have fewer of them, and they generally get rid of them, but they all have them. The Safety Office is an organization with a difficult job to do."

"Minerva has told me where I should be careful."

"Good."

"She's worried about you, Jonat."

"That's good, too, because I'm worried about me."

"Why?"

"I'll tell you tomorrow."

"Do you promise?"

"I promise."

After I broke the link with Paula, I had to go down and pick up the last few minutes of Charis's lesson. That was so I knew what she was supposed to be practicing.

When Madame Castro wound up the lesson, she turned and smiled at me. "She is doing so much better. It is so good when those with talent work to build their skills."

I returned the smile. I had to agree. I had my doubts whether Charis did, but my job wasn't to be my niece's best friend. It was to make sure she had the skills and talents—and discipline—to take care of herself.

After Madame Castro had left, I turned to Charis before she could escape. Since it was blustery outside, with scattered snowflakes dancing through gray air, Charis and Alan weren't likely to want to spend much time outdoors.

"Charis . . . go get your brother. You two can help me fix lunch."

"Do we have to?"

"No. You can go hungry."

There was a barely concealed sigh.

I offered a loud and deep sigh of my own in return. "Charis . . . I am not going to live with you forever. More important, you are not going to want to live with me forever. If you don't start learning to cook some simple things now, and some more complicated ones as you get older, you'll have to depend on other people for the simplest meals."

"I know, Uncle Jonat. But Marianne and Casia don't have to."

"You're not Marianne and Casia. You come from a family that expects more. Now go find Alan and tell him to come on down here."

"Yes, Uncle Jonat."

I had the feeling that the rest of the day was going to be long—very long.

chapter 87

I worked late on Saturday night, using Dierk's workshop to do what I could to prepare for the week ahead. The hardest part was mounting the neuralwhip inside one of the thin black datacases, and making sure there was still space for some papers, and that the whole thing remained totally non-metallic, because it had to pass security screening. I had to do the same thing for the other case, and getting the ultra-ex set right, and a nonmetallic detonator, with blast spreaders, was another problem. In the end, I managed. Then I loaded everything I'd need for the next afternoon and evening in the trunk of the Jacara before I went to bed.

Not that much after sunrise on Sunday I was awake and up. Not too early, thankfully, but early enough that we had no trouble eating a semileisurely breakfast—cinnamon pancakes and sausage, with the honey butter and heavy syrup—almost sinful.

After Charis and Alan had stomachs that were comfortably full, I said, "We'll be going over to my house this afternoon, right after lunch. I've got some things to do there—"

"Can't you do them here, Uncle Jonat?" asked Alan.

"I've done what I can here," I answered truthfully. "I'll also have to go out later, probably around four. Paula's going to be there, and she'll be taking care of you. I shouldn't be that late."

"What are you working on? It's Sunday."

"Consultants have to work when they can. Sometimes, it's not convenient."

The two looked at each other, and I had the feeling that I'd uttered words all too similar to what Dierk or Aliora might have said. I didn't press.

Despite the long breakfast and conversation, we made it to church and Sunday school without my having to rush Charis and Alan or myself. Lunch was a bit hurried, but no one seemed to mind too much, and we arrived at my house at one-forty.

Paula was waiting, and she opened the door before we reached it.

"Hello, Jonat . . . Charis . . . Alan . . ." She smiled, although I thought it was more for the children than for me.

"You're looking good," I offered, and she was, in a simple charcoal gray singlesuit with a dark green vest that somehow brought out the stormy gray of her eyes.

"You're very gallant, Jonat."

"Just truthful."

She glanced away, then back at me.

I looked to the children. "You two can find one of the games in the front room and play it. Or read. I have some things to do in the workroom."

"We can't use the netlink?" asked Charis.

"Not until later. You can each have an extra hour today, but not for at least an hour."

"Yes, Uncle Jonat."

The two of them trudged glumly inside without looking back. The wind, colder than it had been earlier in the day, gusted around us as we stood just outside the front door.

"I'm an ogre," I said dryly.

"They don't look exactly terrorized."

"Not too much."

"What Minerva said you wanted is in the workshop."

"Thank you. I hope it didn't create any trouble for you."

"No. Charles replaced the blocks with something else. Unless there's a very close inspection, no one will notice for some time. By then, no one will be able to track when it vanished." Her eyes focused tightly on me. "What you're doing is dangerous."

"It is. Not doing it is more dangerous."

"Minerva said something like that. She said I shouldn't ask too many questions. Why not?"

"I'm sure she said that to protect you."

"How can ignorance protect me?"

"It probably can't," I said after a moment. "You already know too much. Why don't you help me unload the trunk of the Jacara and then come down to the workroom with me? I'll tell you as much as you want to know—that I know, anyway."

So she did, and we carted the equipment and assemblies down to the workroom. Paula didn't say anything until I'd closed the door.

"I'll have to work as I talk," I began. While Dierk's workshop had more tools, mine had the rest of what I needed—or the components to create what I needed. I wasn't going for timers, just a simple RF jolt detonator. "If I tell you something you already know, tell me."

"I will."

"All right." I opened the doors to the cabinet that held various components, many of which I'd saved from systems and equipment over the years. "You know that there is a group of ascendents who control the major multis. They sit on the same boards, and they also effectively control Multi-Cor and the CorPak security for Mars and outsystem installations."

"I had picked that up."

"These people had chosen me years ago to be their patsy in a power play that will grant them greater control over the Legislature and over all outsystem trading and economics . . ." I went on to explain about PST and the Centre for Societal Research, my report, the attacks, and how it all fit together—and how there wasn't a single legally usable piece of evidence.

Paula nodded slowly. "I knew some of that, but not how it

all fitted together. The ISS part was always clear, but I never was sure why everyone was after you. It was obvious that they were, but not why."

"That's because," I admitted, "I never said much about it. Who, except someone who already knew about ISS and the PST types, would believe it? I guess I sort of felt, after a while, that no one would. I couldn't say much to Minerva when she was Central Four because she didn't have full control over what she could reveal. At least, I don't think she did." I was a little surprised that Minerva hadn't joined the conversation, but I wasn't going to press. I was having enough trouble dealing with revealing things to Paula. It just wasn't my pattern, maybe because Aliora had been the only one I could trust even a little, for so long.

"Who are you going to . . . attack?"

"Mahmed Kemal. Someone at PST paid to have me killed. I've avoided at least one attempt so far, but Kemal won't stop. His honor insists that the contract be carried out. He's the immediate problem." I gestured toward the workbench. "The rest is for certain members of the PST group."

"You . . . you're going to kill them all?"

"Not all. The key members. Or . . . I'm going to try. I don't have much of a choice. So far, there have been at least four attempts on my life, and my sister and her husband have been killed. I've received warnings from Sinese sources that I'm to be eliminated, and the contract with Kemal and his trupps would be just the beginning, even if I can avoid it. I've reported several of those attempts to the safos, as you might recall. It hasn't done much good."

Paula was silent.

"You wanted to know."

"It seems so cold . . ."

"It's not cold," I replied, trying not to get angry with her. She wasn't the problem. "I'm furious. I'm furious that key officials in the Safety Office have been suborned. I'm furious that I have to go outside the law to protect myself and my family. I'm furious that my DNA was stolen and used as a tool to kill my sister. I'm furious that ISS and MultiCor want to use lethal weapons on their hapless permie charges because they want better treatment and political freedom. I'm furious that PST has fingers into every political aspect of the NorAm government, and no one seems to be able to do anything about it." I stopped.

"You're angry."

"I said I was. I'm not angry at you. I'm angry because . . . what I have to do is wrong. It's just a whole lot less wrong than doing nothing. I'm angry because no one seems to even know or care, and I'm angry because I know that's human nature. People don't want to look at the unpleasant side of things. They don't want to fix them if it takes much work or if it might threaten them or their safety, and that's how and why things get so bad at times."

"Is it really that bad?"

I gestured toward the workbench. "Do you think I'd be doing this, with Charis and Alan to worry about, if it weren't? I've told you what I know. Every word I've said about what happened is the truth. You can ask Minerva if you don't trust me."

"It seems so unbelievable—even to me."

"It seems almost unbelievable to me—until I remember those months in the medcrib. Or I want to link my sister, and I remember that she's not there. Or when I look at Charis and Alan. Or even when I think about Minerva, risking what amounted to suicide, because a safo captain has been bought off by the PST group."

"It's awful . . ." Paula shook her head. "You're sure you have to do this?"

"No. I'm not. Kemal could die of something in the next hour. The northside family could take him out. A chunk of mining debris could spiral in from the Belt and just happen to land on ISS and wipe out most of the PST leaders. But the odds are very much against any of that, and I have to operate based on the most likely probabilities, and those are, that if I don't act, I'll be dead in the next month. And I'll be dead, not because I initially did anything wrong, but because I might stop someone else from doing something wrong."

After a moment, Paula looked away from me. "Can . . . I do anything?"

I took a deep breath. "Yes . . . please. If you wouldn't mind, you can check on the dreadful duo, and make sure that they're not killing each other or destroying something. And then, if you please, would you get me a mug of Grey tea?"

"I can do both." Her smile was both warm and sad, simultaneously.

It took me almost two hours to finish what I needed for the afternoon, and then to change into the blend-ins. By a quarter to four I was back in the Jacara, gloves, hood, and case on the floor of the passenger side.

As I drove south along Centrales toward a certain coffee shop, I linked with Minerva. *Why didn't you tell her what you know? Why did I have to tell her?*

Because it's better that way. She has to learn that you trust her. That won't occur unless you're the one.

So . . . now she's upset with me.

She may be more upset with the world as it is than with you.

I wasn't so sure about that.

I parked the Jacara on a side street a good block away from the coffee shop. Then I set the blend-ins for full adaptation, donned the hood and the gloves before I stepped out with the case, also covered in blend-in. Unless someone was watching closely, very closely, they'd just assume that the driver had hurried off. I didn't hear anyone, and had to hope I was right. Even if I weren't, so far I'd done nothing illegal. So far.

I walked slowly toward the end of the block. Once there, I slowed my progress to less than a crawl. Kemal's driver always parked in the same place, right in front of the entrance to the coffeehouse. There were signs that indicated no parking, but no one was going to do anything to Mahmed Kemal, not in his own territory, and not over unauthorized parking on a Sunday afternoon. Not even the Denv Safety Office.

The coffeehouse itself was a single-story structure only about twenty meters wide. The two permaglass windows set on each side of the doorway were framed on the inside by dark crimson hangings trimmed in gold and tied back with gold sashes. The door was golden oak trimmed in polished brass. For westside, it had a certain kind of style, especially set as it was between a hair stylist's on the south and an appliance repair shop on the north. The sign over the entrance read: STEFAN'S COFFEEHOUSE. I could sense the scanners focused on the entrance, but none was focused out on the street or the outer edge of the sidewalk.

Step by slow step, so that the blend-ins did not swirl markedly, I eased first toward the appliance repair place, and then past it, toward the north side of the coffeehouse, and the three-meter brick stretch of wall between the repair place and the permaglass. By the time I reached where I would wait, it was three forty-five. Several minutes later, two older men walked up from the south and went inside.

After that, an older couple walked past me, without even looking in my direction, and entered Stefan's. At ten minutes to four, an angular man in black emerged from the entrance and surveyed the nearly empty street in both directions. After a moment, he stepped back inside.

The curb area in front of Stefan's was totally empty of vehicles. As I reflected, thinking about the surveillance screens, I realized that had usually been the case. Was that so no one could get close to Kemal's groundcar? The screen of the curb area made more sense in that light.

At three minutes to four, a big white Altimus Grande rolled past me and eased to a stop right in front of Stefan's—all by itself on the west side of the street.

The driver opened the curbside rear door, and a squarish man with short curly hair and broad shoulders stepped out. His image roughly matched those I'd studied. Neither the driver nor Kemal spoke. Kemal went inside. The driver walked around the car, studied the street in both directions, and then opened the driver's door and settled back inside the Altimus, leaving the door slightly ajar.

I picked up the case, deliberately, and began to move.

It took me almost five minutes to cover ten meters, but neither the driver nor the angular guard who stepped outside once more noticed me. Once I was crouching by the rear bumper, breathing more heavily than I would have liked, I eased the kit under the frame, and then followed. It was a very tight squeeze, and I had to move slowly and quietly.

Once underneath the Altimus Grande on my back, I eased into position under the rear seat. Attaching the ultra-ex sections was easy enough, if time-consuming. Take the section, apply adhesive, hold in place. Take another section, apply adhesive, and so it went, until I had all four in place. I was already drenched in sweat, even before I began to place the harness. Finally came the nano-reinforced baffles, fabric soft until in place, and then stronger than steel, in order to channel the force upward. That took another ten minutes.

The Altimus had been in front of Stefan's for almost forty minutes, and I was still sweating, despite the chill winds that had left my feet and hands almost numb, since I'd had to take off the gloves to place everything.

Forcing myself to move deliberately, I put the gloves back on, and quietly closed the nearly empty case. Then I began to inch backward, out from beneath the Altimus.

At the moment I reached the rear bumper, the driver's door opened. I watched, barely breathing, as he walked around the groundcar. His shoes hit the pavement less than a third of a meter from the top of my head as he circled the rear of the vehicle. I could hear his steps on the sidewalk, barely above the faint whistling of the wind. Once he settled back into the driver's seat, I scuttled farther backward, keeping as low as I could once I cleared the rear bumper.

The approved retreat was a short dash and a freeze, a short dash and a freeze. That was to provide some speed. When I froze, the blend-ins wouldn't swirl. The technique was supposed to work. I hoped it did.

I managed to get to the north side of the appliance repair shop before the door to Stefan's opened and two figures stepped out. With Kemal was a woman. I had no idea who she was, but I swallowed as the two of them entered the Altimus Grande.

Now what? The range of the detonator I held was limited, or at least the reliable range was. There was no way to get to the Jacara in time to follow the Altimus. If I didn't do something quickly, I'd have to try it some other time, and I couldn't follow Kemal for days, waiting for the opportunity to get him by himself.

Besides, no one had cared about sparing Aliora.

I flicked the cover off the switch, watching as the Altimus started to turn the corner at the end of the next block.

I pressed the stud.

Crumptt!

Everything shook, and where the Altimus had been was a ball of flame.

Metal was still pattering down when I turned and walked around the corner and down the long block. I slipped the detonator into my pocket. I'd hoped for a cleaner result, but I'd learned a long time ago that very seldom did things work out that way. Not for me.

I slipped into the Jacara, but left the blend-ins on camouflage. I didn't take Centrales. Ten minutes later I switched them to gray and took off the hood.

Why couldn't Kemal have left by himself with his driver? Most Sundays, he had. Why this Sunday?

Because you needed him to be alone, that's why. I supposed that was as good an answer as any. Not that I liked it.

Jonat . . . you know that Mahmed Kemal is dead, don't you?

That was the general idea. You knew that.

So is his sister, and his bodyguard.

I was sorry about the sister. I hadn't had the luxury of waiting for a clean shot at Kemal himself, not if I wanted to stay alive. *My sister is dead, and so is her husband. Kemal and his family wanted to kill me because they were paid to, and they wouldn't quit because they thought it was dishonorable not to honor a contract. I can't prove anything, not legally. I don't have the luxury of time, of being able to avoid them forever, and even if I could, the PST group would find someone else. What do you want me to do?*

Then you intend to be as ruthless with the PST members?

More so. You know that. I have to be. I don't have an organization or billions of credits in resources. Do you have any workable alternative that will leave me alive?

No, but I'm only an AI, remember?

I'm only a consultant who was picked to be a patsy because I once stood up for principles. That was another thing that bothered me. I'd been picked out by the Centre and PST not just because of my expertise in the economics of product placement, but also because I'd once expressed very public opposition to the government.

I managed to get back to the house by five-thirty, and I made sure I wasn't hurrying. Paula met me outside my house, closing the door to separate us from the children. The wind gusted around us, tousling her sandy blonde hair. Her eyes took in the blend-ins, now just a white singlesuit, if marred by grime and dirt. "Are you all right?"

"I'm tired," I admitted. "Long day. How were the children?"

"They were fine. They're good." She waited for a moment, then said, "It's already all over the news. Mahmed Kemal was killed instantly when his Altimus Grande exploded within a block of his brother-in-law's coffee bar."

"I can't say that I'm sympathetic. I just hope that the Safety Office doesn't find out that I had anything to do with it."

"Jonat. There's no one else with the motive or the expertise."

"But does anyone there, besides you, know that? It could have been the northsiders."

She nodded. "No one will ask a probie, and you're probably right about how the Safety Office will look at it."

I looked at her levelly. "I sincerely hope so. As I told you earlier, I'm getting very tired of being a target, and not getting much protection from the system."

Paula touched my sleeve, and I could feel her fingertips through the fabric. "I'm not the system, Jonat."

"I'm sorry." I managed a smile. "You've been rather . . . distant."

"That's not because I don't care. That's because . . ." She shook her head. "Don't you understand? I'm not . . . I can't take in too much at once. Not personal feelings." Her smile was lopsided. "You are a very strong personality, Jonat."

"I'm sorry," I said again.

"How much . . . more?"

"I don't know. That depends on them." I took a deep breath. "You have to know that I don't like being in this position. I'll dream about it for the rest of my life." That was assuming I'd survive to have the rest of a life. Or that I'd go uncaught and remain with enough of a brain to feel guilt. "We'd better go inside. I suppose I should get the children home. They do have school tomorrow."

"You worry about their school . . . now?"

"I also have to find out what else might happen."

"Jonat . . . ?"

"Yes?"

"I'm sorry, too. You're trying to do the best you can."

"We all are. That's the hell of it."

We went inside. Charis and Alan had actually put away the chessboard and were watching an approved linkprogram.

"Time to go. Get your things ready. I have to put a few things in the Jacara." While they scrambled to gather jackets and gloves, Paula helped me load the trunk of the Jacara with the other items I'd need in the days ahead.

Paula stood by the edge of the drive as I made sure Alan's restraints were in place. Then I shut the door.

"Jonat . . . be careful."

"I'll be as careful as I can. You, too."

For the first few minutes after we pulled away, leaving Paula standing in the gusty winds, neither child spoke.

Finally, I asked, "How did things go while I was gone?"

"They were all right," Charis replied.

"Did you get along with Paula?"

"She's nicer than I thought," Charis observed. "She didn't know cribbage, but she picked it up really quickly."

"She beat Charis," Alan volunteered. "A lot."

"She's a grown-up," Charis replied. "She's not as good as Uncle Jonat."

"She'll probably get better if she hasn't played a lot."

Thankfully, bath- and bedtime were quiet, and no one linked or contacted me.

Later that night, I went through the tab records.

I shouldn't have been surprised, not the way things had been going, when I heard the conversation between Jaro and the punk.

"You still think I should do deVrai tomorrow . . ."

"You want the new big fellow to think you don't carry through?"

I didn't need that, not at all, but I'd been concerned enough that I'd also made a few plans of my own. I'd just hoped that I wouldn't have had to put them into action.

"You got the lorry?"

"It's in the garage. Got it scoped. First shot is if he goes back to that big house. Narrow way there, and just pull out and block it."

"He's going to stop?"

"Everyone stops for a road repair. Even got the right side-works for Southhills."

The two talked a bit more, but I didn't learn anything new, except that the second shot would be just outside the Academy when I went to pick up Charis and Alan.

I preferred the first locale, because I could just back away and claim I'd gone straight to my own house, but preferences didn't matter, not if I didn't have a plan and a way to carry it out.

After a long deep breath, I left the office and went out to the Jacara to prepare things for the next day . . . another long day. I'd have to take apart the case, and retrieve the neural-whip . . . and then put the assembly back together again later.

chapter **88**

The air was thick with moisture and bugs, and a pattering sound that might have been rain, but wasn't. The old-style slugs shredded the vegetation overhead.

Air, Bravo two. Nothing. The uplink was dead.

I clicked the implant to alt . . . static-filled.

You're breaking up, two. Try main.

Negative. Main dead. Need CAS. Coordinates follow.

Say again coordinates . . .

I was still trying to get coordinates when the explosions began to my right. Gouts of forest, trees, and vegetation erupted into the sky. Shit! Shells! Heavy artillery. The locals weren't supposed to have anything that big.

From somewhere almost directly ahead, the deeper sound of an antique heavy machine gun began to fill the air, and the telltales dropped off my screen, Marines dying second by second.

Bravo two . . . Bravo two. Negative on CAS. Negative this time.

I bolted upright in bed, sweat pouring down my face. My pajamas were soaked. Slowly, I swung my feet over the side of the bed. I sat there for a minute, blotting my forehead. The chill of the room helped, but I still needed to change into something dry.

I'd gone to sleep, trying not to think about Mahmed Kemal's sister. So I hadn't. Instead, I'd had a flashback, one to another time when nothing had gone right. Was my subconscious trying to tell me to expect more—and worse? I didn't need that reminder. That was something I already knew.

I changed into dry pajamas—the short kind, because long ones were too confining, and because I sweated too much to wear nothing to sleep. Then I tried to get back to sleep. I did, eventually, but I woke before the alarm.

As I exercised in the small basement workout room, I took in the news. After about a half hour, there was a large story on the explosion that killed Mahmed Kemal, and the general consensus was that it was the result of an inter-trupp conflict, but one unnamed source in law enforcement stated that the method of assassination and the professionalism behind it was worrisome. "The explosive pattern was set by a professional, and we haven't seen this kind of professionalism in the trupp community before."

Great. Those kinds of comments didn't help, although there wasn't anything in my background that actually listed that kind of expertise and training. It was something I'd picked up along the way, with a lot of other skills I never thought I'd use again.

As usual, Charis and Alan were quiet during the predawn hour when I did my workout, but the moment I entered the kitchen and started breakfast, they appeared.

"Can we have hotcakes?" asked Charis.

"Tomorrow. Omelets today."

"Ugh . . ."

"If you don't want an omelet, you don't have to eat it, but there's nothing else, and it's a long time to lunch."

They both ate the omelets and toast, as well as the juice and the berries. I had to admit I was probably eating a more balanced diet myself, because I was watching theirs.

While they dressed for school, I got cleaned up and ready for my day, one that I wasn't looking forward to in any fashion. I wore the blend-ins, this time set for dark gray. They were getting a lot of work these days.

When I met Charis and Alan at the door to the garage, Alan looked at me.

"Why are you wearing the coveralls? You don't have a jacket, either."

"Because I've got some dirty work to do in the shop after I get back," I replied. "I didn't see any point in putting on work clothes and then taking them off. And I don't need the jacket because these are warm."

"Your other clothes are work clothes, too," Charis said.

"Office work clothes. Now . . . we need to get moving."

On the way to the Academy, I kept my eyes and senses wide for any sort of lorry, but I didn't see a one. That didn't reassure me in the slightest, except that I was relieved when Charis and Alan entered the building.

I headed back toward the house, slowing as I neared the turnoff.

I pulled off the road, just short of the turn onto Old Carriage Lane, and parked the Jacara under a semiancient pine. Then I pulled on the blend-in hood and gloves, made sure they were set for auto camouflage and stepped out. I was carrying the neuralwhip, and I had what amounted to a democharge wrapped around my waist, under the blend-ins.

The wind was lighter than on Sunday, and with the sun shining brightly, I really didn't feel the chill as I walked easily along the various hedges, stone walls, and trees that bordered the lane.

Sure enough, the punk was waiting in a big lorry at the first curve, where Old Carriage Lane narrowed. The lorry had the right logo and stripes, but it was a '35 FD, and Southhills would never have had anything that old. He had flashers and markers out—probably stolen. He was sitting in the lorry, apparently busy with something.

Concealed by the blend-ins, I eased to within a few meters. He didn't even look up when I fired. *Thwipp!* The punk slumped over the control stick like a felled tree.

"Camos . . . some sort of camos! Spray the area!"

"Where?"

"Anywhere!"

Thwip . . . thwip . . . Energies flared all around me.

I turned as fire slashed across my left side. I almost fell, but the nerve-energy slashes moved away, and I straightened, keeping the neuralwhip as concealed as possible. I forced myself to study the area, and found the two figures in drab camos before a stone wall.

Like the punk, they never saw me.

They dropped.

I waited, scanning the area. Nothing.

The damned punk hadn't even mentioned a team.

I felt like I could barely move my left side, but I dragged the other two over to the lorry. I kept looking around, but the punk had planned well. There were only five houses along the lane, and there was seldom any traffic between nine and eleven.

All three were still breathing as I forced the two in camos into the cab. I'd kept the whip's intensity below lethal, deadly as my intentions were.

Then, I froze against the lorry at the sound of a groundcar, but it was from one of the houses near the turn, and it never even hesitated as it left Old Carriage Lane.

I slipped the democharge from inside the blend-ins. My midsection was damp from sweating against the ultra-ex. The charge went against the fuel-cell casing. I closed the housing and the hood, and walked back along Old Carriage Lane.

I uncovered the detonator guard and pressed the stud.

Crummptt!

The good news was that I managed to get away from the mass of fire and twisted metal. The bad news was that I had to drag my left leg, and my left arm hurt with every movement I made. I kept walking, or limping, until I reached the Jacara. Then I got in and waited to make sure the street was clear in both directions before pulling out. Only then did the hood come off, and I set the blend-ins back to gray.

I drove the entire distance to my own house carefully, neither too fast nor too slowly.

About halfway there, Minerva linked.

Jonat . . . what happened?

I didn't feel like dissembling. *One of Kemal's punks tried to finish off the contract. Things didn't work out well for him and his buddies, but I've got some nerve paralysis in one leg and part of my left arm. How did you know?*

There was that silence, before Minerva responded. *I had Paula put tracer tags in both your vehicles. We're both worried about you. The safo office reported a large explosion and fire where you had been. I didn't think it was coincidence.*

It wasn't. I also wasn't thrilled about tracer tags, but . . . well . . . they both knew enough to turn me into a servie for life, the kind with half a brain, if they wanted to turn me in, and there wasn't a damned thing I could do about it.

When I reached my own house, my side was half-numb, half-fire. I hoped that Paula wasn't there, not that I expected her to be. She wasn't, and I slumped into the ergochair in my office, wondering how long before the stun-shock wore off.

The rest of the morning was a blur, and I finally left around noon, when the worst of the pain had eased somewhat. I put a few more clothes in the back of the Jacara, including some formal jackets and cravats, since I'd be needing one or more for the AKRA seminar on Wednesday and Thursday, and so that I'd have a reason for having gone to my house and not having been back to Southhills.

The area where the lorry had been was cordoned off, but a safo just waved me around it.

Once I was back at Southhills, I took a hot shower, and then dressed in my office clothes, as Charis called them. While I did, I listened to All-News, but it was almost an hour before I heard anything.

. . . It appears that three men died in a fiery explosion in Southhills this morning . . .

The lorry and the markers bore Southhills markings, but Southhills transportation center authorities confirm that no such lorry is on the rolls and the markers were stolen. The lorry may have been stolen as well. The cause of the explosion and the deaths are under investigation . . .

That was it, not that I expected much more so early.

I settled, uneasily, into Dierk's office and began my links. The first link was to Jennifer Alison at the Centre for Consumer Equality. She wasn't in, according to the simmie, but was expected shortly.

"This is Jonat deVrai, and your name was brought to my attention by Tan Uy-Smythe." I left my codes.

Then I tried for Fredrik Viansa at the NorAm Vintners' Association. He was there.

"Jonat deVrai . . . your name . . . it's familiar, but I can't say why." He frowned.

"There could be a number of reasons. Tan Uy-Smythe?"

"I don't think so."

"I was in the Marines for a while."

"No . . ." His face brightened. "I know. Eric Wong! Our wives belong to the same gourmet cooking group, and he said that you'd done some work for his group, something . . ." Viansa shook his head. "It was so esoteric I can't even remember."

"Well . . . that's become my problem. I do consulting in media place-ment, especially dealing with netplacings, but everyone thinks that it's so specialized." I shrugged. "I'd like to drop by a package for you. It's better in hard copy. No obligation, you understand, just something for you to look at. You might find what I do of interest, or some of your members might, either now or in the future, if they have a special problem."

"Eric did say you were good."

"I've got to do a seminar near there on Thursday. If you'd just leave word with your staff or your system . . . I could drop this by."

"That's a lot of trouble . . ."

"It's not." I grinned. "Besides, if what I do doesn't suit you, you can always pass it along if someone asks."

"You said Thursday?"

"That's right. I'm doing a presentation at a seminar at the East Capitol Plaza."

"It's your time," Viansa said genially.

I kept smiling. "If I don't try . . ."

He nodded. "I'll make sure that Delia knows. Thursday afternoon?"

"Thursday afternoon."

Less than fifteen minutes later, the gatekeeper announced the return link from CCE.

"Jennifer Alison, Dr. deVrai." She had a narrow face with high and delicate cheekbones, almost birdlike, under black feathery hair, and she'd obviously checked me out before returning the link.

"Thank you for returning the link."

"You're welcome. I have to say that I'm a little confused. We're an association, and we don't do any product placement. Our members don't, either. Or are you linking as the front for some charitable organization?"

I laughed. "I have to admit that my motives aren't that altruistic. They're more commercial. In the past, my clients have almost always been multis, but recently I've done several projects for associations and others. I just finished a lengthy study for the Centre for Societal Research and a much shorter one for SCFA."

Alison's puzzled expression became more so. "But what does that have to do with CCE? We certainly are on the other side from almost all your clients."

"According to your materials, you're an association devoted to consumer education, and you believe that an educated consumer is an enlightened consumer. I think that I can supply you with another cost-effective tool for enlightenment, and I'd like the chance to prove that, without any obligation on your part, except to read a short package that I'd like to deliver to your office in person on Thursday afternoon." Before she could object, I held up my hand. "Presentation is important, and by providing hard copy and materials, I'm making sure you get the best product. Second, I'm actually doing a presentation in the area on Thursday, so that it's only a little out of my way. And, third . . . what do you have to lose except a few minutes reading what I deliver? If after reading it you don't like it, or don't want to talk further, just leave a one-word 'no' on my link, and I won't approach you again." I grinned. "At least for a few years."

I finally managed to change her half-hostile puzzlement into humored puzzlement. "I'd be foolish not to at least take a look at something you prepared." She paused. "You are the one—"

"Absolutely. I'm a one-person operation, although I do have some very sophisticated equipment and my own experts for some technical matters. Now . . . if you'd tell anyone who will be there, or the system, on Thursday that I'll be stopping by, I'd appreciate it." I smiled ruefully again. "It's very embarrassing to tell someone, even a system, that you're expected, and find that no one does expect you."

Alison bought the self-deprecation and smiled. "I can see that. Thursday afternoon?"

"Thursday afternoon."

Once I broke the link, I got to work on her presentation first. What I had in mind was something along the lines of what I'd done for SCFA, except packaged entirely differently, emphasizing how prodplacement slipped under the screens of most consumers almost unnoticed, the techniques used, in general terms, how big the industry was, and what kinds of products were most suited. Of course, Alison would only get an outline with a few teaser facts, but it would certainly be a credible proposal, and, who knew, there was always a chance that CCE might be interested.

The NVA proposal would be harder, because I was stretching. My idea was more along the lines of an industry-based prodplacement approach, along with a do-it-yourself calculator for a rough cut to see if prodplacing made sense for any of the larger members of the association, again, accompanied by an outline of what the technique was, what it could do, and what it couldn't.

Before I started, I tried to check the tabs at Ken's Place and the one in Jaro's groundcar. I got absolutely nothing, but there was no way to tell whether they were dead, had been removed, or if no one had been around to be recorded and transmitted. So I went back to my consulting prospecting.

I actually got the CCE proposal roughed out before I had to go pick up the children. The explosion site was still cordoned off, and I had to edge along the south side of the lane again.

I only had to wait in the Academy drive for ten minutes before Charis and Alan burst out and ran to the groundcar.

Alan looked at me. "I like that better."

"The black coat?"

"Yes."

I didn't ask why. Instead, I asked, "How was school?"

"Dr. Trevalyn was sick. We didn't get science . . ."

"He's always sick," Charis interrupted. "It's an excuse. He wanted to do something else."

"Some people get sick more than others."

From there we ended up talking about the differences in people—until we reached Old Carriage Lane—and the cordoned area.

"What happened?" asked Charis.

"A lorry exploded somehow. When I came back to the house around noon, they had this blocked off. I checked the news and found that out, but they didn't have much to say, except it was stolen."

"You don't think it was . . . those people who . . ."

I knew what she was thinking. "I don't think so. They didn't mention anyone from around here being hurt. There's nothing to worry about."

Charis and Alan exchanged that glance again, but I didn't say anything.

When we got back to the house and got out of the Jacara, Charis stopped. She looked at me.

"You hurt your leg, Uncle Jonat. What happened?"

"I was moving some stuff downstairs at my house. I pulled some muscles. They'll be better tomorrow." I hoped they'd be better on Tuesday. Still, I had until Thursday before I needed to be back in shape.

She and Alan looked at each other again.

"Whether I've overdone it or not, young lady, you still have some piano practicing to do before long."

That brought a sigh, as well as changed the unspoken subject.

chapter 89

Mydra waited until Deng's image filled the projection space opposite her console.

"Good morning, Stacia."

"Good morning. What do you think about the recent developments?"

"The Kemal assassination?"

"It is an interesting occurrence. Early reports suggest that it was very professionally accomplished."

"Anyone who infiltrated Kemal's organization could have placed the explosives," Deng replied mildly.

"Anyone could have placed them. Not anyone could have placed and channeled the explosives to be that deadly. My sources suggest that not even a Marine in full armor, seated in the back of the vehicle, would have survived."

Deng nodded slowly. "Perhaps there are former Marines in the employ of the northside family. I believe several of Diem Phong's family and followers have served in the Marines."

"You think so?"

"I think that will be the most likely conclusion, and who are we to argue with what is found to be most likely?"

Mydra nodded slowly. "Perhaps that would be best. Or should we discuss the matter at greater length?"

"There is no great hurry. This is a crowded week, and this is not the forum for discussion. Perhaps at the end of the week, or after the Centre board meeting, if it seems appropriate. That way we can discuss other matters as well."

"The obstacles facing the officer of choice, you mean?"

Deng smiled politely. "We shall see what we shall see. One should not look for difficulties that may never arise."

"There is that." Mydra paused. "There can also be the problem of unforeseen difficulties."

"That is your province, Director Mydra, and you are welcome to it."

Mydra inclined her head. "I look forward to hearing your wisdom."

Once the image of the Director General of ISS vanished, so did Mydra's polite smile.

chapter 90

I'd hoped to hear from Paula on Monday night, but I didn't, and I spent what strength and concentration I had left on roughing out the NVA proposal. I had to accept that Paula was having a hard time adjusting, to the full reality of being a safo, to the full reality of seeing what society was really like, and especially to the full reality of seeing what happened when idealism and the real world collided. I couldn't work as late as I would have preferred, and was actually in bed by ten, earlier than in days.

By Tuesday morning, I was only sore over half my body, and I could move without more than minor pain. I had to tone down my exercise routine, but I did fix hotcakes for Charis and Alan, and threw in some fried apples on the side. Neither of my charges complained.

I got them delivered at school and headed straight back to the house, where I finished the physical preparations for Thursday by eleven o'clock, including recharging and resetting the neuralwhip in the thin black case. Then I settled into Dierk's office to begin honing my proposals for CCE and NVA.

Ten minutes of uninterrupted honing was all I got.

Jonat?

Yes, Minerva?

Central Four has noted that the explosion that occurred yesterday was relatively close to the VanOkar house, and that last year there was an attack against the VanOkars. A follow-up is required.

Who will be doing the follow-up?

It is routine. A virty safo, one of the standard inquirers. Later, the interview will be analyzed.

So . . . you want me to be ready?

Yes. If necessary, I can shade things through Central Four, but any major tampering with the records might be discovered.

I appreciate the notice.

I thought you might.

After that warning, I decided to follow the news, at least halfway, while I worked on smoothing out my written proposal for CCE. I got almost forty minutes of work in before another news story caught my attention.

The big news from the Capitol are some numbers that everyone seems to have, but no one will admit to the source. These numbers indicate that MultiCor has seriously misrepresented the financial status and the profits taken in by the conglomerated multis composing MultiCor. According to the analysis, MultiCor figures understate profits by a factor of three, and grossly overstate costs. More important, these cost misrepresentations also extend to the reimbursements from all major Earth governments for transportation and infrastructure . . .

"This is an outrage! MultiCor has been fleecing consumers and taxpayers." That was Senator Juan Carlisimo. Carlisimo has already made a mark for his attacks on MultiCor.

"These so-called financials are a gross misrepresentation, and a violation of the Privacy Act as it relates to multilateral organizations. Senator Carlisimo should know better." Senator Joseph Crosslin was even more angered than the first-term Senator from West Tejas.

Of particular interest were the figures pertaining to Industrial Security Service. ISS has already been implicated in questionable dealings with proscribed weapons . . .

As I listened, I took a very deep breath. If PST hadn't wanted me dead before, they'd really want me eliminated if they ever tracked those numbers to me. No, I corrected myself, *when* they tracked those figures back to me. But there wasn't all that much that I could do beyond what I'd already planned. I could only keep my eyes open and be ready to act when the time came.

Because I was already distracted, I went down to the kitchen and fixed a salad with more fruit than greenery and crumbled an excessive amount of blue cheese over it. It wasn't bad.

Once I cleaned up the mess and went back to the office, another half hour passed before the news item I had been listening for came on-air.

Investigation of yesterday's lorry explosion in Southhills has revealed that all three men who died were associated with the Kemal trupp family, and all had previously been identified as suspects in various unresolved criminal cases. The other interesting fact was that the explosion took place less than half a kay from the point where two Southhills residents were killed in December. The previous case has not been solved.

"At this point, there is no evidence to connect the two events." That was Captain Reymon Garos of the Denv Safety Office.

Still, experienced observers note that the three most puzzling sets of deaths, all unsolved, have occurred in the same area of Southhills, all in less than four months. The last time any non-domestic homicide occurred in Southhills was over a decade ago. Yet the Denv Safety Office is suggesting that there is no connection . . .

That bit of news, while expected, didn't make me feel any better, either. I doubted that I got more than another half hour of work before the gatekeeper announced, *Safety Officer Norgraf*.

Minerva had been right about that. *Accept.*

The image was one that could have passed for the safo cydroid I'd known as Charles.

"You are Jonat Charls deVrai?"

"That's correct."

"You are not under any obligation, legal or otherwise, to answer any questions. Do you understand that?"

"Yes. Could you tell me what this is about?"

"It is a routine inquiry. We're contacting everyone in your area about an explosion."

"Oh . . . the one on Old Carriage Lane yesterday?"

"That is correct. You are the brother of the late Aliora deVrai, the wife of Dierk VanOkar?"

"Yes."

"You are presently living at Seventeen Old Carriage Lane?"

"Yes. Mostly. I also have my own house."

"Yesterday, an explosion destroyed a lorry not far from your present residence. A vehicle similar to the Jacara that you have been driving was noted in the area. Were you in the area?"

"I had to be, officer. I drove the children to school, at Southhills Academy. After that, I drove past Old Carriage Lane, but decided to go back up to my house and pick up some gear before returning to Old Carriage Lane. I got back around noon. Like everyone else on the lane, I was surprised to find a safo cordon."

"You did not actually drive back to the house after dropping the children at school."

I shook my head ruefully. "No. What happened was that I wasn't really thinking—or I was thinking about a seminar I'm giving on Thursday, and I'd almost gotten back to Old Carriage Lane when I realized that I'd planned to go and pick up some things from my own house. So I just kept driving."

"You did not return to the house on Old Carriage Lane until later?"

"That's what I told you."

Central Four's simmie kept at it for a while, but in the end, he thanked me and broke the link. I'd told nothing but the truth. Not all of it, but just the truth. I hadn't driven back to the house, and I hadn't actually even gotten on Old Carriage Lane, not with the Jacara, anyway.

I had to force myself to get back to finishing the proposals, and they had to be good, for more than just one reason.

chapter 91

Meara walked swiftly down the corridor.

Paula stepped up to Lieutenant Meara. "Sir?"

"I'm late for a meeting with the captain, Athene. It'll have to wait."

"One thing, sir."

"What is it?"

"The captain took a restrainer into his office. It's badly adjusted. It could hurt someone. It could hurt them badly, but he didn't listen to the tech. He's not in a good mood."

Meara smiled, briefly, warmly. "Thank you. You'd better get back to your screens."

"Yes, sir."

The lieutenant stepped past Paula and knocked on the door.

"Do come in, Lieutenant." Garos's voice carried overtones of insincerity, as it always did.

No sooner had the lieutenant entered than the privacy screen hummed into place, leaving the two officers supposedly isolated from eavesdropping.

Out in the corridor, Paula did not move, waiting.

"You have exceeded your authority once too often," said Garos, his eyes not even looking at Meara. He took a step sideways, so that his hand rested on the edge of the console, just above the misadjusted restrainer.

"I beg your pardon, Captain. I'm not aware that I have done anything except what my duty requires."

"You have a strange idea of duty, Meara. That trick with the ISS raid, for example. I can't prove it, and probably no one can, but those neuralwhips were assembled by your cydroids and systems to frame ISS. ISS would never be that stupid."

"I've seen many people do stupid things, sir. I learned a long time ago that it happens. I don't think there's any doubt that ISS was intending to ship proscribed weapons to Mars."

"The way they were intended to be shipped was not proscribed, Lieutenant, and our job is to uphold the law as it is written, not as we think it should be written."

In the corridor outside, Paula checked the transparent film gloves that covered both hands and extended almost to her shoulders. She waited, her face tense.

"I agree, sir. The law says that if proscribed weapons are found, then a raid and prosecution are in order. They were found, and the Safety Office proceeded under the law as written."

"You are insubordinate, Lieutenant, and I will note that you became violent and abusive." Garos's fingers closed on the restrainer, he lifted and triggered it in one smooth motion.

The loops flashed around Meara's shoulders and neck with excessive speed and force, and her neck snapped with a dull crack.

The door opened, and closed almost instantly behind Paula, who lifted a thin weapon, firing once.

Garos had no time to look surprised as the old-style slug went through the middle of his forehead.

Abruptly, every light in the complex flashed off.

Paula bent, placed the slimline in Meara's hand, and fired the weapon once more. Then she straightened and stepped outside into the darkness, vanishing down the corridor, and stripping off the gloves as she moved, gloves that had already begun to disintegrate.

I made a few minor omissions to the recording, edited out Paula's presence, and then restored power.

A warning had not been enough, not with Meara's disbelief at the depth of Garos's treachery. But with every utterance monitored, and when Meara had never checked her screens or links before seeing Garos, what else could we have done?

Now . . . certain files will go to the review board, under Meara's imprint, and to Captain Sudro, as supporting evidence that Garos had killed Lieutenant Meara when he had learned what she had discovered. That much I can do. It is the truth, in essence, if not in fact.

The end and the beginning are near. Or will it be the other way around? One way or another, matters will never be the same. They never are.

chapter 92

Wednesday morning, I got Charis and Alan off to school early, reminding them that I was going to the AKRA seminar, but that I'd be there to pick them up after school. On Thursday, of course, Devon Bowes would be picking them up. I'd already arranged that with the Academy, although she'd be driving the Jacara, which had the security signaler.

After I dropped them off, I headed for the East Capitol Plaza, wearing one of my better black jackets, with a pale green shirt, and a darker green cravat. I also carried a datacase with a few sample analyses. Chelsa Glynn had asked that all presenters attend the opening session, which started at ten o'clock in the big meeting room of the Capitol Ritz.

The fact that AKRA could afford to use the Ritz facilities said a lot. I didn't park at the hotel itself, but at a carpark a block away, one that took bearercards. The walk through the chill January morning did me good. I'd exercised faithfully, but I missed being able to run in the open air. Most of the soreness and pain from Monday was gone, but I was still stiff in places, probably from moving around and straining unresponsive muscles.

The Ritz had been rebuilt fifteen years earlier, and the interior would have been perfectly suited as an updated version of the Taj Mahal or something similar. High ceilings, stone facades, golden glimmering light everywhere, polished marble floors in all public spaces.

The conference center was on the north end, a good hundred meters from the main lobby. A portascreen announced in bright colors: AKRA SEMINAR: FOCUS ON THE SUBPERCEPTUAL.

As I glanced around, I saw Chelsa Glynn was hovering near the portable terminals where seminar participants could check in. She was even taller than I'd thought, standing eye level to me. I didn't head for her until I'd presented myself to a scanner screen and received a badge that proclaimed me as "Dr. Jonat C. deVrai, Media Consultant/Scholar."

As I neared, she looked my way, and the worried look on her narrow face turned to a smile, and the brown eyes lit up. Her badge defined her as "Dr. Chelsa Glynn, Director, Peer Communications, AKRA." "Dr. deVrai, I'm so glad you've recovered and that you're here. A number of people had hoped you'd be able to make it."

"Thank you. I'm very glad to be here."

"The first session won't be starting for another twenty minutes, but you and Barbara Hulteen are the last of the major presenters. Do you know Barbara? She's the one who developed an entirely visual analytical method for detecting subperceptual reactions to physical stimuli."

"I can't say that I've met the woman."

"She's very incisive."

That suggested I might not want to meet her.

"There she is." Chelsa turned. "Barbara!"

Incisive she might be, but Barbara Hulteen was a pleasant-faced, brown-haired woman with a polite smile, a good head shorter than either Chelsa or me. Hulteen turned toward us immediately, and I quickly focused on her badge: "Dr. Barbara S. Hulteen, Perceptual Research, Medical School, University of Colorado."

"I wanted you to meet Jonat deVrai."

I nodded. "Pleased to meet you."

She smiled and said, pleasantly, "Your paper on the role

of subperceptual influence in product placement was intriguing. Necessarily oversimplified, but solid. At some time, I'd like to discuss the algorithms you're using in your analyses. I might have some suggestions that would work with smaller samples."

"I'd be very interested," I replied. At least, she was pleasantly incisive.

"If you two would come with me . . . ?" Chelsa Glynn started toward the main meeting room. We followed.

The opening session was easy enough. All I had to do was sit in a chair on the dais, stand when introduced, and sit back down. Then, we listened to a moderately interesting speech by the director general of AKRA, and then the opening session was over, and people headed off to the various presentations—two at a time, in the smaller meeting rooms.

I wasn't there for the subject matter, but to display my presence, and to prospect for potential future clients because it looked like I'd need them. My older clients weren't providing that much occupational sustenance these days.

So, I wandered the halls, chatting, sizing up various people.

"Dr. deVrai!"

I turned.

A man with a round face and a solid frame hurried up. His badge identified him as "Martin Greenhalgh, Senior Analyst, SierraCraft." I had no idea what SierraCraft did.

"Jonat deVrai . . . you're the only consultant who ever had the nerve to tell a client that Vorhees and Reyes were stealing their credits screen over screen."

"I'm not sure I'd like to be known for that. I'd really rather provide product placement services."

"We've been thinking about it . . . but . . ."

I smiled and provided a card. "Whenever . . ."

Greenhalgh tucked it away. "Have to give you credit. Abe Vorhees . . . he was as crooked as blackholed light." Greenhalgh shook his head. "But people kept buying his services. Some still are, but I don't think it'll last. Wasn't that something, his mistress doing him in?"

"I'd heard about that," I said. "Until it came out, I didn't even know he had one."

"They say some people did. There's also word out that more than a few people disappeared or had strange accidents after they crossed old Abe. You know anything about that?"

"I'd heard rumors," I admitted, "but with rumors you never know for certain."

"That's the truth." He smiled, and started to turn away. "I just wanted to say hello."

"If you have a real product placement question," I suggested, "you know where to find me."

But he was already gone.

In a sense, that was my day at the seminar. I passed out a lot of cards, listened to a few presentations, but slipped out of more than I listened to. One of the more intriguing ones was actually by Barbara Hulteen, because she was clearly interested in the implications of her research and what it might mean. I was interested, too, if for a different reason. I wasn't so sure I wanted visual equipment that could scan and measure reactions I wasn't even certain I'd recognize. That struck me as worse than the excesses of rez and product placement.

I was tired by the time I left to pick up the children, although I left a little early so that I could time the route from the East Capitol Plaza to the carpark nearest to the Centre for Consumer Equality—and the Centre for Societal Research.

After I picked up the children, the rest of the afternoon was routine. I checked messages, but there was nothing from any client, or any potential client. The stillness was deafening—and worrisome.

Then, later, Charis almost balked at practicing, but she took a single look at my face, swallowed, and said, "Yes, Uncle Jonat."

Dinner was quiet, but no one complained, because I'd dug out Aliora's recipe for enchiladas, modifying it to my tastes, and they both liked it. I hadn't heard from Paula in days, and finally, while Charis and Alan were bathing and getting ready for storytime and bed, I linked her.

Her image appeared immediately. She was still in uniform.

"Hello, Jonat." Her voice was pensive.

"Are you all right?"

"As you always say, it's been a long day."

"What happened?"

"Haven't you heard?"

"I've spent all day at this seminar I'm speaking at tomorrow—except for when I picked up the children and fixed dinner."

"You'll hear before long. Captain Garos charged Lieutenant Meara with malfeasance in office. They were alone. Whatever happened, it cut off the power in the building everywhere for several minutes. When it was all over, they were both dead. She'd been strangled by a malfunctioning restrainer, and Garos had been shot with a slimline slugthrower from his own desk."

I didn't say anything for a moment, linking instead.

Minerva! Did you have—

There was no other choice. There are no traces. There will be none.

And you didn't let me know?

What could you have done? Have you always let us know?

"That's . . ." I shook my head. "That has to have been hard on you."

Paula nodded.

"I'm sorry. I had no idea."

"It's really created a mess."

"I can imagine that. Will an investigation show something about Garos, or can anyone say?"

"I don't know. It's possible. There was a whole team there from DomSec."

I didn't like that, but I had to hope that Minerva was right, and that everything was in hand. "I've been thinking about you . . . but . . . I just didn't have any idea."

"Thank you. I've been thinking about you . . . about when you were a Marine, I mean."

That stopped me, for a moment. I wanted to say that I hoped things weren't that bad, but that would have been incredibly patronizing, not that I probably wasn't anyway when I didn't even think about it.

"Jonat . . . I'm tired. Can we talk later?"

"Yes. We can. Please get some rest, and take care of yourself. Do take care of yourself." That was all I could really say.

"Thank you. I will."

I just looked at the ancient leatherbound books on the wall for several minutes. Everywhere, the bodies were piling up.

Then I got up and headed upstairs to get ready to read to Charis and Alan. Later, I'd have to finish my preparations for tomorrow.

chapter 93

Thursday morning was another rush, because Charis couldn't find the trousers and blouse she wanted to wear. She didn't quite accuse me of being slow with the laundry, but it was a good thing she didn't because we found the outfit at the end of her closet—clean. She apologized, but we were almost late to school. I dropped them off at five minutes before the hour, reminding them that Devon Bowes would be picking them up.

"Why?" asked Alan.

"Because I'm giving a talk at the seminar, and because I need to meet people to get clients." Once more, what I said was the truth, but not all of it.

I parked in the same carpark as the day before and made my way to the Ritz, where, since the halls were empty, I sat in on the end of a very boring presentation on the implications of measurement of subperceptual learning.

There were more people in the hallways after that, and I circulated and passed out more cards and smiles. Around ten o'clock, a thin and intense man walked toward me. I didn't

really know him, but I knew the name on the badge: "Alfred
P. Levin, Finance Director, LMT."

"Dr. deVrai."

"Yes." I smiled once more. "What can I do for you?"

"Not a thing. I just finished reading your paper earlier, and
I wanted to congratulate you on explaining the complexities
of product placement in such a clear fashion. I might add
that I was even more impressed with the study you did for
the Centre for Societal Research."

"Thank you. The study for the Centre was quite an effort,
I'd have to say." And it had been, in so many ways. "What is
your interest in the field?"

"Just intellectual. Financial, too, I suppose. This is a field
where developments keep occurring, and a finance director
who doesn't understand the technology and the science is at
the mercy of the technologists."

"I hadn't thought of it that way."

Levin smiled. "I don't know if you know, but your study
has sparked a great deal of interest in the Legislature."

"I'd heard that Senator Crosslin was using it as the basis
for his proposed campaign reforms. I can't say that I'd
thought it would go that far when I started." Right afterward,
but not at the beginning, which is just how so many bad
ideas end up in practice.

"You never know, Dr. deVrai. You never do."

"I suppose not."

With a friendly smile, he was gone. At that moment, I
wished he were on the Centre's board. I went on circulating
and smiling, and supposed that some of it, perhaps . . .
maybe . . . might lead to some future business.

At one, I had to duck out and meet Devon Bowes at the
house and give her access to the house and turn the Jacara
over to her. Then, driving my own Altimus, I hurried back to
the Ritz and the seminar, where I worked in a half hour or so
of meeting and greeting until a few minutes before two and
my own presentation.

I was set up in the smaller of the two meeting rooms.
While I couldn't imagine what I had to say as being of that

great an interest, there were actually almost two dozen people in a room with chairs for close to a hundred. One of them was Chelsa Glynn.

At two o'clock, I launched into my spiel. "As the program indicates, I'm Jonat deVrai. I'll be limiting the formal presentation to fifteen or twenty minutes, and then I'll answer questions. That way, I can be sure to address specific concerns. Now . . . product placement. What is the present state of the art and how did we get here?" I paused. "In some ways, it's a very old concept, once known as keeping up with the Joneses, conspicuous consumption, greed is good . . . and so on . . ."

I finished in eighteen minutes, and only two people left, while three others came in and stayed. I guess that meant I wasn't terminally boring.

"Now . . . for questions." I looked around. No one seemed to want to ask anything.

After a moment, Chelsa Glynn raised her hand. "You seemed to indicate that measuring product placement success rates was difficult, if not impossible. How does this impact market research?"

A nice general question, an invitation to a thesis, if necessary, but I was grateful for the opening.

"One of the problems with assessing any marketing campaign is the need to tie the campaign to the actual product sales resulting from it. Under the strictures of the Privacy Act, this becomes even more difficult . . ."

After that, there were other questions, but not so many that I didn't finish close to on schedule at nine minutes before three.

Chelsa Glynn came up afterward. She was the only one who did.

"This was very good, Dr. deVrai. I think everyone here learned something. I know I did." She smiled enthusiastically. "I have to run, but I hope I'll see you at the reception."

"I certainly plan to be there." And I did.

I made my way out of the meeting areas, in the direction of the lobby, and then out to the carpark and the Altimus.

There was no one in the carpark, not that it mattered much yet, as I slid behind the stick.

My destination was three long blocks west of the NorthTech maglev station, and it only took five minutes until I parked in the public carpark half a block to the west of the building that held the Centre. When I got out, I couldn't help looking to the west, where the snow hung just above the mountains. The last time I'd been where I stood, the front range had been almost snowless. Now it was a line of white.

I took both thin datacases from the rear seat, then locked the Altimus, and checked the time. Three-twenty.

I carried the briefcases lightly, even if they were anything but light. I'd been careful, though. A standard screen, even a low star-class screen, would show nothing untoward.

Another three minutes saw me approaching the building. My boots clicked slightly on the replica cobblestones as I walked to the entrance of the old brick building and then inside the entry foyer. The Centre for Consumer Equality was on the second level, the same as the Centre for Societal Research, but at the southeast corner. Once inside, there was no barrier to following the corridor back to the Centre for Societal Research.

The virty guard inside smiled warmly. "Might I ask your destination, sir?"

"The Centre for Consumer Equality. I'm Jonat deVrai, and I was to stop by and deliver a presentation."

"Yes, sir. Let me check."

After a moment, he said, "They're expecting you, Dr. deVrai. The office is on the upper level on the southeast corner." The stainless steel gate opened.

"Thank you."

I kept smiling, although my palms felt sweaty. As I made my way up the ramps, I reminded myself that the first part of my visit was absolutely harmless, to me or to anyone else.

First, I stopped by the NVA office. There was a young man seated inside the doorway. He looked up suspiciously.

"I'm Jonat deVrai. I talked to Fredrik Viansa earlier this week and said I'd be dropping off a package for him to read."

The aide fumbled with his screen.

"Jonat deVrai," I offered helpfully.

Something flashed up, and he looked relieved. "Here it is. Dr. Jonat deVrai. You have something for Mr. Viansa?"

I refrained from smiling. Instead I opened the case, which with what else was inside, barely had room for the two proposals, and extracted the one for NVA. "Here it is."

He took it.

"Thank you very much." With that, I smiled once more, and then made my way to the ramp up. As I'd recalled, there was a men's facility on the second level. I checked the door in passing. It was unlocked, as I'd suspected, but I wanted to make sure.

Jennifer Alison actually met me at the doorway to CCE, her feathery black hair even more askew than when she'd returned my link.

"I can't believe you actually delivered this in person."

I shrugged. "I was in this part of Denv." I grinned. "Besides, this way, you'll hopefully be intrigued enough to read the proposal." I opened the black case, took out the remaining proposal, handed it to her, and closed the case. The proposal was bound, and in color, with neat charts and tables. More important, the text had been selected to play to CCE's objectives—stated and unstated.

"This looks impressive."

"That's the general idea. If it looks impressive, there's a better chance that someone will read it all the way through, although," I paused slightly, "you look like you would in any case."

"Flattery will get you almost anywhere," she riposted, "but whether we take you up on it depends both on how good it is, but also on the state of our budget."

"That's a consideration for any organization."

"Especially ours."

I bowed slightly. "Thank you for considering it."

"You have to go?"

"I've been presenting at a seminar at the Ritz."

"The AKRA thing?"

"The same."

"You travel in high company, doctor."

"This year. Next year . . . who knows?" I bowed again. "There's a facility down the corridor . . . do I need . . . ?"

"No. It's open. I won't keep you." Her smile was wide and generous, and I could feel her eyes on my back all the way to the men's room.

Once there, I had to wait for a man I'd never seen before to leave. Then, it was a bit of a struggle to change into the blend-ins inside the cubicle, but I managed, including the gloves and hood. The cases went into the harnesses under the generous blend-ins. The coolness of the space helped, and in a few minutes, I was ready to go.

I checked the time. Three-fifty.

I stepped out of the cubicle and to the door. I opened the door and stepped into the corridor. A red-haired woman was headed up the ramp, and I froze, waiting and trying to identify her from the images I'd studied. The name came to me: Daria Ghamel of AVia.

Ghamel was preoccupied enough that she didn't even look in my direction. I followed her, more slowly, right into the outer office of the Centre for Societal Research. As I recalled, the office was paneled in a formulated reproduction of white oak. It didn't look any better with repeated viewing.

The real receptionist was still smiling brightly at Ghamel as I slipped to one side, toward the conference room, moving slowly, so that the blend-ins didn't swirl too much.

"Everyone is here, except Mr. Escher, and he's on his way up."

Ghamel did not speak, but merely nodded and walked toward the half-open conference room door. I followed her, but stopped just beside it. Everyone would be looking at Ghamel as she walked in, and if I were too close behind someone might well notice the telltale swirls. That wouldn't have mattered if everyone else had already arrived, but apparently, not everyone had.

I flattened myself against the wall, watching as a distinguished and mature man, close to showing his age, I guessed, stepped into the Centre reception area.

"Good day, Mr. Escher," the receptionist said. "Everyone else is here, in the conference room."

"Thank you." His words were courteous, no more.

At that, I slipped inside the conference room. Only one person was looking at the door—Ghamel. She frowned, and shook her head, then turned as Escher entered. He closed the door behind him and took the last remaining chair at the table.

I let my enhancements check the space. No recording flows, from what I could tell, although the holo-projectors were powered.

Deng cleared his throat, and everyone looked to him.

At that moment, I turned the blend-ins gray, and took off the hood. Then, I eased the one case out from its holder, the narrower, specially-modified case.

Deng's head jerked up, and eyes widened as I stood there. "Pardon the unorthodox entrance, and greetings, ladies and gentlemen, Director Uy-Smythe. In view of the uses to which my study has been put, I thought you all might like to have a follow-up report on the implications of my study of prodplacing in campaigns and how it is likely to affect pending legislation. That was one reason for my means of entrance."

There was a silence.

"I don't believe you were asked, Dr. deVrai," announced a tall dark man on the left side of the table—Augustus Sharpton.

I scanned the room, making mental comparisons. Deng was there, as were Mydra, Ghamel, Escher, and Sharpton. And, of course, Uy-Smythe.

"That's why I'm here," I said as I lifted the case, as if to open it. "You need to understand the implications. First-hand." Before I finished talking, I swept the room with the neuralwhip. It was set on wide intensity. All I wanted was a low-level, short-span paralysis.

There were two sharp shouts, and then everyone went down except Mydra.

She vanished. Damn! She'd been a projection.

The room was silent.

I set down the neuralwhip case and eased the second case out of its harness and onto the middle of the table. Then I replaced the neuralwhip case in its harness, and took out the detonator. I redonned the hood and walked to the chair set back slightly from the table where Uy-Smythe sat.

The jolt he'd gotten would erase his short-term memory. I levered Uy-Smythe up and carried him in front of me to the conference room door. There I flipped the cover off the detonator and pressed the stud. I had twenty seconds.

Thrusting the detonator into a side pocket, I opened the conference room and lurched out, with Uy-Smythe before me. I let him fall, then reached back and closed the door.

As he fell face-forward in front of the receptionist, I slipped around him. She wasn't even looking at the space where I stood. She bolted upright and stared down at Uy-Smythe.

I was halfway down the ramp when a muffled *crump!* shook the entire building. The walls shuddered. The shriek of the Centre's security system pierced the air.

The security gate opened at my presence. There was no way to avoid that, but all that the detectors would show was that *someone* left.

I needed to get back to the AKRA reception, both to create the impression that I'd been there, and to spend some time with Chelsa Glynn.

As I walked quickly to the Altimus, I couldn't help worrying—a lot. Stacia Mydra knew I'd been there. I was fairly sure that there hadn't been a recording. The question was, and it was a huge question, whether she'd reveal what she knew. The risks were high for her as well, because, if I were charged, all privacy restraints went. So did my brain, but not until after a thorough nanite-based veradification and until everyone had learned everything they could, and that would include just about everything about the PST group.

I could only hope that she would sit tight. At the moment, that was all I could do.

I needed to get back to the AKRA reception to preserve some semblance of cover.

I'd no more pulled out of the carpark than Minerva linked. *Jonat . . . are you all right?*

I'm fine.

How did your operation go?

There was a hitch. Stacia Mydra was only there by projection, but I missed it. She knows I did it. I can only hope that she sits tight.

There was a silence. As I waited, I drove carefully.

After a time, Minerva was back onlink. *The explosion has been reported, and a safo squad and a DomSec team are already in the building. At present, there are no reports from anyone except the Centre employees.*

If I'm charged and indicted, I'd have to go under veradification for something like this. That would open up the entire PST conspiracy. Can you calculate any probabilities on that?

I pulled into the carpark near the Ritz. I quickly changed back into my jacket and cravat, then folded the blend-ins. After I got out, I put the case and blend-ins in the trunk. Any search would find them, but there was no point in leaving them in plain sight, either.

Jonat . . . any calculations will be approximations.

Approximate. I started walking toward the Ritz.

The probabilities appear even as to whether Stacia Mydra will report you or not report you.

Can you expand on that?

She will have no rivals in taking over leadership of PST, and if you go under veradification, at the very least she would be forced to step down from her position at Sante, possibly even stand trial in the Garos case.

The Garos case? How does that come into this?

Captain Sudro has discovered direct leads to Tam Lin Deng.

There weren't any, and that meant that Minerva had created them. With each step, I felt like more and more things had gone totally out of control. They had, of course.

He'd rather keep things quiet?

With Deng's and Garos's deaths, under the Privacy Act, there would be no public prosecution . . . unless . . .

Unless Mydra comes forward?

That is correct.

That all sounded as though I had an even chance, but I'd never liked odds that bad. Then, I didn't have any way left to improve the odds. *I'm headed into the Ritz. Let me know if there's something urgent I should know.*

We will, Jonat.

Once I was at the Ritz, I eased into the bar and ordered iced tea, sipping it for a time, and making a few comments about seminars.

Alfred Levin came in and looked around, as if for someone.

I smiled and gestured to him, hoping to get a reaction that would tell me something.

Levin smiled, a sick smile, and shook his head. I gestured again, and he walked over.

"I'm sorry, Dr. deVrai. I've just had some terrible news. I was looking for Arthur Weedson. Have you seen him?"

"I'm sorry. I don't know him. Is this anything I could help with?"

"No . . . I don't think so. There was some sort of explosion . . . some friends of mine are missing."

"Explosion? Here?"

"No. Somewhere else. You're very kind, doctor, but I need to be going. Thank you." Levin hurried off.

So far, at least, it was clear he wasn't connecting me to what had happened. He was upset, and he wasn't that good an actor. But what did it all mean?

I finished my tea and slowly made my way toward the main meeting room where the reception was supposed to be.

Chelsa Glynn appeared, once more with Barbara Hulteen. "Dr. deVrai, there you are."

"I've been mixing. I was just in the bar, getting an iced tea."

"An iced tea?"

"It's too early for wine," I said sheepishly. I hoped it was sheepishly.

They both laughed.

It was likely to be a tiring evening, and one I needed to see through for at least another hour.

I did manage to smile and laugh, but I wasn't about to down anything alcoholic. So I drank three glasses of plain soda. I finally left the reception at seven-twenty, after finding Chelsa Glynn and thanking her for her kindness in inviting me.

"It wasn't my kindness. It was your reputation and ability." She offered that enthusiastic smile. "After reading your paper and hearing your presentation, I see why you have that reputation."

"I wasn't aware I had one."

"If you tell someone that prodplacing will help, it will. If you say it won't, it won't. Did you know that Abe Vorhees refused to attend if you were here?"

That was a surprise. "No. I've never met the man personally." Which was true.

"You won't. His mistress shot him. A better end than he deserved." For a moment, the cheerful facade had vanished, but only for a moment, because the smile was back with her next words. "Anyway . . . Director General Willem said to work you in on future seminars, where it was appropriate. You don't mind, do you?"

"Hardly." I managed a laugh. "Consultants can always use exposure."

"I noticed you worked the halls most diligently."

"It's been a slow month," I admitted.

"I'm sure things will pick up for you."

"With your confidence in me, how could they not?"

"You're too gallant."

Desperate was more like it. But I bowed and thanked her, and eased out of the reception.

I got back to the house at quarter to eight, just in time to read to Charis and Alan.

After the day, I had to admit I enjoyed sitting between them on the leather couch and concentrating on the stories.

Later, I sat in the darkness in Dierk's study.

Minerva . . . has anything else happened?

Everything is quiet.

I couldn't help wondering just how long they'd stay quiet. I couldn't believe that they would. I also couldn't believe that I hadn't picked up on Mydra being a projection. If I'd known, I could have used a different approach, and not revealed who I was.

Had that been ego? Had I betrayed myself because I'd wanted the bastards to know that I hadn't been taken in?

My short laugh was bitter. I thought about the old saying about how much you could get done if you didn't take credit. I could have accomplished much more—or at least survived without being a target.

Stupidity . . . ego . . .

I looked blankly into the darkness.

chapter **94**

Somewhere above me, the leaves pattered with the sounds of slugs shredding them. I could hear the sound, but it was muffled. In the absolute blackness all around me was damp stale heat, and the stench of blood. I started to take a deep breath, and fabric blocked my mouth. I tried to reach up, to pull the heavy stuff away from my mouth, but my arms wouldn't move. Neither would my head.

Nothing would move.

Blood everywhere. Old blood. My blood.

I was choking. No air.

Unable to move . . . was I in a body bag? What had happened?

Jonat!

The link woke me.

Paula Athene.

For a moment, I couldn't think. Where was I? How did I escape the body bag? I shook my head, trying to clear it. *Accept.*

"Jonat? Are you all right?" Her image appeared in the

darkness above the bed. She was wearing a white robe. She had circles under her eyes.

"It's been a long, hard day."

"I know." She paused. "I know." *I'm linking through Minerva. That's so no one can intercept.*

I didn't mind the eavesdropping, not now. *That's fine.*

You did what had to be done.

I think I did . . . except I was stupid. So stupid. But now what? What happens if Stacia Mydra turns me in?

Did you have any choice?

It was disorienting, in a way, to look at her image, but to project the words through the link. Even in the robe, hair somewhat disarrayed, she was good to look at.

Jonat?

No. Not about what I did. That's why I've been so angry. I do nothing, and I'm dead. I'm limited in what I can do.

The "timbre" of the link changed. It had to be Minerva. *I still have some abilities. The ultra-ex pulverized everyone and everything in the room. It is very likely that DNA analysis of the scraps of protoplasm will reveal that a cydroid clone was used, and its pattern will match the DNA of the clone that killed your sister. Traces of the same DNA have already been discovered in the ISS cydroid facility.*

Will that be enough? I asked.

It may be. There are still one or two informers in the Safety Office. If they discover those findings, it might suggest to Stacia Mydra that no further revelations are necessary . . . or desirable.

Then what?

Those probabilities are impossible to calculate.

The probabilities of life were getting impossible to calculate. But then, they always had been.

Jonat? That was Paula. I could feel the difference, even in the direct link.

I'm here.

Don't do anything rash. Don't admit to anything. Things will work out.

Those were my lines, except I didn't feel that way. Not at

all. *I'll sit tight, try to be the perfect consultant again.* Paula had her own problems. *You, too. It hasn't been easy for you.*

I don't have as much at stake as you do.

Yes, you do. Life is the biggest stake.

But you have Charis and Alan to worry about.

I did, and until today, I'd done fairly well. But in one momentary oversight, one failure to notice one simple thing, I'd jeopardized everything. *I may have fouled that up, too, by today's stupidity.*

Don't judge that, yet.

I'll try not to. But it was hard. I cleared my throat and spoke out loud. "Thank you."

She smiled, and we just looked at each other.

"Good night, Jonat."

I didn't bother to tell her it was morning. Her image vanished.

chapter 95

At six o'clock on Friday morning, I was toiling through a workout I didn't feel like doing, except for the fact that I hadn't been able to sleep any later, and that I needed to stay in some sort of shape. Even that early, All-News was hyping the bombing at the Centre for Societal Research.

This was a targeted bombing . . . not a doubt about that . . . Look at the names involved: Tam Lin Deng, the director general of ISS; Daria Ghamel, the associate director general of AVia; Augustus Sharpton, the director general of BEN; Grantham Escher of MultiLateral Armaments . . . Everyone was there in person, except for Stacia Mydra, who had projected presence. Mydra has said nothing publicly so far, and has refused to make any public statements while the investigation is ongoing . . . only one survivor of those in the conference room . . .

. . . very tight-lipped about this, but it is clear that a very high explosive was used . . . could have been ultra-ex . . .

Senator Joseph Crosslin has already suggested that those in

the room were targeted by Martian extremists from such
groups as PAMD or BLN . . . calling for a strengthening of powers of both DomSec and NorAm regional Safety Offices . . .

Senator Juan Carlisimo has suggested that the bombing was
the result of internal disagreements among "a cabal of multi-
based conspirators." Carlisimo refused to say more, other than
that he was convinced, in light of the recent disclosure of "ob-
scene, excessive, and illegal profits" by the participants in MultiCor, that many of the victims were anything but innocent . . .

Senator Kennison, in turn, decried Carlisimo's words as inflam-
matory and thoughtless at a time of tragedy.

If I hadn't been the one waiting for the ax, the veradification, and indictments to crash down around me, the reports
would have been grotesquely amusing. People had died; I'd
killed them. I still didn't see that I'd had much choice, and I
was still seething inside. Fear and rage had left my stomach
in knots.

The exercise helped some, and I donned professional cheer-
fulness before I started breakfast, and Charis and Alan appeared. It must have worked, because I didn't get any strange
looks. That also might have been because they got French
toast, with lots of syrup, along with their fruit and protein.

After dropping them at the Academy and driving back to
the house, past the spot of the lorry explosion—all traces of
which had been removed—I went to work sorting the cards
and contacts I'd gathered at the AKRA seminar.

If . . . if I didn't end up with my brains fried, I would need
more clients.

At ten past eleven, I was still in the midst of sorting and
recording notes and background on all the people I'd met
and greeted at the seminar.

Safety Officer Bastien, announced the gatekeeper.

Accept.

Bastien might have once been French, but he looked very
northern European, big and blond, with brilliant blue eyes.
He also looked tired. "Dr. Jonat deVrai?"

"Yes? What can I do for you, officer?"

"I'd like to ask you some questions, Dr. deVrai. You're not under any obligation, legal or otherwise, to answer these. If you choose not to answer, it is possible that you will be required to do so at a later date. Do you understand that?"

"I understand that. What I don't understand is why you want to question me. Is this about the lorry again?"

"The lorry?" Bastien was the one who looked puzzled.

"I live on Old Carriage Lane. On Monday, there was an explosion near the end of the lane. A lorry exploded. A safety officer linked about that on Tuesday. I answered his questions, and I thought I was done. That is what you're linking about, isn't it?"

He paused. "No. This is about something else."

"Would you mind explaining, then?"

"There was an . . . incident in a building where you were yesterday."

"At the Ritz? I was at the AKRA seminar there. I was giving a presentation. What would you like to know?"

"I'm afraid our records show you were at another building."

I cocked my head, thinking for a moment. "The only other place I was . . . well, I was at the Centre for Consumer Equality, but not for very long."

"That is in the Centre for Societal Research Building, isn't it?"

"Yes. I've done work for them, too. Anyway, I took just a few minutes away from the seminar to drop off proposals at the NVA office and the CCE offices, and then I went right back to the seminar."

"If you don't mind, when was that?"

"Officer, would you mind telling me what this is all about?"

"I'd rather just have your words about when you were where."

I smiled politely. "I'd really like to know what this is all about. Certainly, it's no secret where I was. I gave my name to security at the Centre building. They must have it on record. I was only there a half hour at most, probably even less. I just dropped off the proposals, said a few words, and hurried back to the seminar."

Bastien was persistent. "Yesterday, exactly where were you between three-thirty and four-thirty?"

"Officer . . . I don't mind answering your questions, but could you tell me why?"

"I told you, Dr. deVrai. There was an incident in the Centre building. That's all I'm at liberty to say at the moment."

I took a long and deep breath, one conveying exasperation. "Somewhere between three-thirty and quarter to four, I was finishing presenting a proposal to a Jennifer Alison at the Centre for Consumer Equality. After that, I used the men's facility there, and left and went back to the AKRA seminar at the Ritz, the one at the East Capitol Plaza. I stayed at the seminar . . . well, I did have a drink at the bar . . . but that's in the hotel, through the reception, and then I went home, probably around seven-fifteen. I didn't want to stay too late."

Bastien nodded. "Ms. Alison has verified that you dropped off a proposal and that she saw you go down the ramp. We haven't verified that you left the building immediately."

I knew why. There wasn't any record of my leaving, but that also meant that they had to prove I'd left later than I said I had, and that would be difficult.

"I did. I was back at the hotel a little before four. I didn't keep exact track of the time, because I was talking to people in the halls. You know how these seminars are. I was trying to meet as many people as I could."

"Why was that, Dr. deVrai?"

I laughed. "I'm a consultant. Business has been slow since Christmas. I was offered the chance to do a presentation on aspects of my practice. Once I had the exposure, I wanted to put my card in as many hands as possible."

"Could anyone verify exactly when you got back?"

"Exactly, probably not. It was right around four, maybe a few minutes past, I did see Alfred Levin in the bar. I was having an iced tea. I don't remember all the names and faces, but I remember his because we'd talked several times during the seminar . . ."

The questions went on for what seemed hours, but when he broke the link, I discovered it had only been forty-five minutes. It had been a very long forty-five minutes. I'd told him almost entirely the truth. If he happened to be good, he might suspect something, but he had to have proof to go to more sophisticated technologies, and so far, there wasn't any proof. The only traceable item in the entire conference room was the ultra-ex itself. It had taggants, and those would point back to ISS.

Minerva . . . an Officer Bastien just contacted me.

They are charged with contacting everyone who was in that building yesterday. The head of DomSec is furious.

Why? Was Deng paying him off?

Most likely. The probabilities are over sixty percent.

Is there any way to leak that to some of the less scrupulous newsies?

It's not admissible as evidence.

I don't care about evidence. I want enough dirt out in the open so that Mydra and the survivors in PST are willing to claim it was an unnamed terrorist, a disgruntled employee . . . whatever . . . and let it go. If the head of DomSec knows his name could be dragged in the mud . . . and that he also might get his brains fried . . . it can't hurt us, and it might help. Remember, if anything happens to me, things get riskier for you.

I am most aware of that.

I'm sorry, but wouldn't you be a little concerned, in my boots?

I will do what I can. I am doing what I can. So is Paula.

How is she?

Like you, she is worried. She has less to worry about. She also worries about you.

In a way, that was cheering. I just wished Paula didn't have to worry about me. I wished I didn't have to worry about me.

Let me know anything I should know . . . please?

I will.

What bothered me, still, was the whole situation. I *knew* I'd already have been dead and buried if I hadn't done what I'd done. People were dead, and some of them—not many, but some—had been relatively innocent. No one even seemed to care that such a situation could happen.

It was the same battle I'd tried to fight as a Marine, and I hadn't been able to change a thing by following the rules. Almost ten years later, I'd had to fight the same kind of battle in a different arena, and following the rules had been useless. I'd only managed to make an impact when I'd broken the rules.

That made me angry—and discouraged. No one really looked at the rules. They just did their lives, watched their netlinks, and resisted any change. I'd even had that trouble in consulting. Some of my clients would rather have wasted millions of credits than have stood up to their superiors and their cronies and pointed out the waste.

Had it always been like that?

Was I a fool for thinking things should be better?

The one thing I did know was that I didn't have any answers. Not good ones, anyway.

chapter 96

Saturday was long. Some things went well. Madame Castro was most pleased with Charis's progress.

"You see!" She beamed at Charis. "You have the soul. You have the touch. What you needed was the discipline, and what you must tame is the fire."

Charis smiled politely. I wasn't sure that at age nine she was up to metaphors quite so grandiose. Also, fires had to be kindled and nurtured before they could blaze enough to be tamed. And some people would never blaze. I thought Charis might, but parents—and uncles—all too often see what they wish, and not what is present . . . or absent.

After I had ushered Madame Castro out, I found Charis still standing by the piano.

"What are you thinking, little lady?"

"I could be good, couldn't I? Really good?"

"You have the musicality and the basic skills. Whether you could be really good . . . that depends on how hard you work, how smart you work, and how disciplined you are." I laughed gently. "And then, Charis, like it or not, there's always luck. If you work really hard at something where you

have the skills, you'll be successful. Whether you'll be recognized or famous, though, that's a matter of chance and
timing."

She tilted her head.

I waited.

"Paula said that you'd never been lucky, Uncle Jonat. Is
that what you mean?"

I managed another laugh. "I'm successful. I'm not famous, and I doubt I ever will be. At this point," I said very
truthfully, "I'd be very happy for things to continue in my
work as they have in the past." I'd be more than happy to be
able to continue as a consultant.

"Will they?"

"That's what I'm working on."

"Will you stay with us?"

"Until you're ready for me to leave." I smiled, hoping
that I could keep that promise, but worrying that I
couldn't.

"Good!" She smiled, nine years old again. "I already put
away the music. Can I have linktime until lunch?"

"How could I say no after all the praise Madame Castro
heaped on you?"

I got a fleeting smile, and she was gone. She'd been manipulative, but . . . weren't we all?

I headed for the kitchen.

Paula was on duty, pushing screens, scanning monitors
for the signs of obvious crimes, or I would have linked with
her. There had still been stories on All-News, but the most
sensational coverage had died away. None of the dead had
been rezrap stars, linknet personalities, or well-known
politicians. They'd been multi-execs, and, outside of the
shock, and the mystery of the explosion, no one cared for
long. Two days had already passed, and no suspects were in
hand.

I was glad that no suspects were in hand.

Once in the kitchen, I looked around, wondering what I
should fix. In the end, I decided on a pork chili—but mild.
Alan was still too young to appreciate heavy heat, and I

doubted that my intestinal system would appreciate it, either. Not with the knots that still plagued me.

Stupidity . . . and I'd thought I'd had it in hand. Stupidity . . . sheer stupidity.

I swallowed and took out the heavy skillet.

chapter 97

Sunday was a church day. While Charis and Alan were in Sunday school, I did some heavy praying. Even if I had my doubts about the existence of a deity, particularly one interested in my personal fate, the prayer couldn't hurt. It might even help my soul, if I had one.

I was having trouble, not only with fear, but with anger, both at the situation and at my own stupidity, and with real concern over Charis and Alan. I'd seen enough to know that, while I certainly wasn't the best parent—especially compared to Aliora and Dierk—neither Rousel nor Deidre were right for the children. I wasn't alone in that judgment. By naming me, both Dierk and Aliora had already come to the same conclusion.

If something happened to me . . . Charis and Alan would suffer. Yet, if I hadn't acted, I definitely would have been dead, and they would have suffered.

Was I rationalizing my actions? Absolutely, but that didn't make my reasoning or feelings wrong. I'd been picked as a pawn sacrifice—maybe a knight sacrifice—in a high-level political gambit by PST to increase the leverage and control of MultiCor over the Legislature, over Mars and the outsystem, and over NorAm.

The sacrifice had backfired, and I'd at least blunted their efforts, perhaps stalled them, perhaps even thwarted one or two aspects of their plan. But doing so had created all sorts of collateral damage. Kemal's sister was dead. Spouses had been left widowed, children without a parent. And why?

Because a small group of people wanted more power.

Because the system was already corrupt.

Because, with my having no real protection and no real options within the system, I had become as corrupt in my own way as they had in theirs.

Church was long, and I had to sit there and think about too many things that I would rather have not considered.

So, as solace of sorts, I took Charis and Alan to Fogg's for lunch.

As we were waiting for our meal to arrive, Charis looked at me. "I didn't do my report."

"When is it due?"

"Tomorrow."

"What are you supposed to write about?"

"Earthworms."

"What about them?"

"Just earthworms, Uncle Jonat."

"Did you know that earthworms almost destroyed the northern forests of NorAm once?"

Charis rolled her eyes. "Uncle Jonat . . ."

"They really did. You can do your report when we get home. If you have trouble, I'll tell you about the earthworms and the forests, and you can add that."

"I'm supposed to say where I got stuff. You don't count. Uncles aren't places I can use."

I shrugged. "Don't say I didn't tell you." Then I grinned. "Do you want earthworms in syrup for dessert?"

"Ugh . . ."

Lunch did keep my mind off my worries—for a while.

chapter 98

Monday didn't start out much better than Sunday. Not any worse, but while the news coverage of last Thursday's explosive murders had died down somewhat, the media and netsters hadn't forgotten, and some of the rhetoric had moved from the nets to the Legislature.

Senator Crosslin was complaining that the Public Safety Act needed amendments to restrain the terrorists of freedom, as he termed PAMD and BLN, implying that they, or their tools, had been behind the killings. Senator Carlisimo was countering his arguments by claiming that the Public Safety Act already provided too much protection for those with wealth and too little for those without, and that Crosslin's proposals would just turn NorAm into a police state.

Kennison and Bennon tried to moderate. That is, they said the same thing that Crosslin did, but more indirectly and politely.

While exercising, fixing breakfast, taking the children to school, and then coming back and working on my new contact list, almost desultorily, I kept waiting for either another safo to link, or worse, the arrival of safos at the door.

Neither happened.

Minerva . . . any word on what's happening?

The evidence is still being analyzed. The final DNA tests will not be completed until late today. The ultra-ex taggants have been identified as belonging to ISS. Captain Sudro was almost pleased by that. The DomSec chief was not, and Sudro suggested that he not interfere in an ongoing safo investigation . . . that it might be misconstrued . . .

Sudro was suggesting that he knew about the DomSec link.

DomSec has been quiet.

She told me more, but nothing else that really mattered. Sudro's independence could work either for or against me. There wasn't anything more I could do. Whatever happened was in Sudro's and Minerva's hands—or circuits or fields.

That bothered me, too, because I was guilty, guilty as old-fashioned sin, and yet, in a larger sense, what I'd done was far more in the interests of society and a greater justice. Yet, how many fanatics had rationalized their actions that way throughout history?

On the more personal economic side, there hadn't been a single link from any of my old clients, not even from Bruce Fuller. I had to wonder what sort of word had gotten out. Or was it just the time of year? Or luck? Or was I projecting some sort of black cloud I wasn't even aware of?

I brewed yet another mug of Grey tea and went back to organizing the names I'd gotten from the seminar. I'd decided to send out actual messages, with enclosures and samples. The way I felt I wasn't up to direct personal links, and besides, that would have been pushing too much. Better to send the messages and then follow up in a week or two. That assumed I'd be free to follow up, but I hadn't heard anything from the Safety Office, one way or the other, and no one had showed up at my door.

I did check my depleting accounts, and was surprised to find that the honorarium from AKRA for the seminar had already been deposited. So had two weeks "rent" from Paula. Both would help, but I worried that Paula couldn't afford the rent yet. I'd told her not to start until the first of February.

Whether she'd been fast-force-raised as a cydroid or not, she clearly had a mind of her own, and some definite opinions, if quietly expressed.

I hoped I'd find out what they were, in time, and that my brains would be in a good enough state that I could appreciate whatever they were.

With a faint smile at that thought, I took a sip of the tea.

chapter 99

Tuesday began like Monday—exercise, breakfast, cleanup, children to school. I stopped to top off the Jacara's fuel cells, and no one at the upscale fuel center looked strangely at me. In fact, they ignored me, which was fine. I got back to the house a little past nine and settled into Dierk's office with a mug of hot Grey tea.

Once there, I forced myself to concentrate on the text of my follow-up message to all those I'd met at the AKRA seminar. I'd gone through two drafts, trying to keep my mind on the words, when the gatekeeper chimed.

Sergeant Jacob Ohly, Denv Safety Office.

I stiffened, then took a deep breath, and pasted a polite smile on my face. *Accept.*

According to his projected image, Ohly was a wiry man, a good ten centimeters shorter than I was, I judged, with short-cut brown hair, and soulful black eyes at variance with his hard appearance. "Dr. Jonat deVrai?"

"Yes?" I tried not to sound wary, and my voice came out sounding tired.

"Sergeant Ohly, Denv Safety Office. The Office thought

you ought to know. It's not regular, but nothing about this case has been regular, and you and your family have been through a great deal. Captain Sudro felt you should know."

Should know what? "I appreciate the concern . . . but I have to say that I'm a little in the dark, Sergeant."

Ohly laughed. "That you would be. Officer Bastien talked to you on Friday. Wasn't that right?"

"He did."

"I've seen the record, and he was pretty tough on you."

Was Ohly trying to play the good safo? I nodded. "I'm certain he was only trying to do his job."

"He was. You see, this bombing, there was a report and a record that the bomber looked like you, sir. But it wasn't you. We've had it confirmed now."

For a moment, I was totally confused. Then . . . then, I understood, and I wondered why I hadn't before. "I said it wasn't, but . . . ?"

"Those cydroids . . . you remember the ones that looked like you?"

"There was *another* one?"

"Yes, sir. It was a setup, like what they tried with your family. I don't mean to bring up bad memories, but someone knew you'd be in the building, and they timed it just right. You were meant to be left holding the bag, sir, except the DNA evidence confirmed it wasn't you, but one of the cydroids. Anyway, we'd appreciate it if you'd keep this quiet for a little bit. The captain is going to be making a statement in a few minutes, but we didn't want you to be taken off-guard."

"Thank you, Sergeant. And thank the captain for me." I didn't have to counterfeit the relief or appreciation.

"That's our job, sir." Ohly smiled. "Glad to do it, Colonel." Then he was gone.

I hadn't known Ohly, not in the Marines, but you never knew where people found out things. I was glad he felt that way, though.

I also knew why Minerva hadn't told me. She wanted the surprise and relief to be real. She probably worried.

Minerva . . . I just got a link from the Denv Safety Office.

I had calculated that they might contact you, but the probabilities were not absolute.

Thank you.

It balances, Jonat. I could not help you at other times, even though you asked for and deserved that help. If I could have helped then, your later actions would not have been necessary. You will still bear a greater burden, but that could not be helped. There was a laugh, almost bitter. *We may still have to balance matters in the future.*

I didn't even want to think about that at the moment. *Will you tell Paula? I don't want to interrupt her on duty.*

No. You can link her through me.

I supposed Minerva was right. *Paula? It's Jonat.*

Are you all right?

Sergeant Ohly just linked. They've concluded that a rogue cydroid programmed by Deng was responsible for the bombings. The taggants and the DNA evidence clinched it. Captain Sudro will be making an announcement sometime soon.

I'm glad for you. How do you feel?

Relieved. Sorry. Guilty. Glad that there's a chance to go on. How are you doing? I've thought about you a lot . . .

I know. It helps.

You help. Even Charis said you were nice.

She laughed. *I've got a screen problem. I have to go.*

Take care of yourself.

I didn't have much more to say to Minerva, and I could only hope that everything would work out . . . somehow.

I kept All-News on, waiting, wondering exactly what Captain Sudro might say. At ten-twenty, the story hit, and I stopped working on my contact message and just watched and listened.

The Denv Safety Office has announced that the ulta-ex explosion last Thursday, which killed four high-level executives from noted multis, has been traced to Industrial Security Systems. The explosion was apparently triggered by an illegal cydroid created in a hidden ISS laboratory at the Rocky Flats facility. The ulta-ex used in the explosion contained ISS taggants, and the identity of the cydroid setting off the blast that destroyed

the room and all occupants has been verified by GIL and intensive DNA testing . . . That DNA confirms that ISS not only operated an illegal and unregistered cydroid operation, but that
those cydroids were implicated in the murders of Everett
Forster, Aliora deVrai, Dierk VanOkar, and those killed in the
explosion at the Centre for Societal Research . . . as well as in
the attempted murders of Jonat deVrai and Tan Uy-Smythe . . .

ISS spokesperson Gillian Jorgensen released a statement
from the multi that placed all blame on former Director General
Tam Lin Deng. ISS claims that the last explosion was the act of
a renegade cydroid created under a secret program conducted
personally by Director Deng. "ISS will open all facilities and
records for DomSec investigation . . ." Jorgensen expressed
regrets that the ISS board had not been able to discover
Deng's program in time to avert the tragedies, but pledged full
cooperation with DomSec and the Denv Safety Office . . .

Senator Juan Carlisimo announced plans to introduce legislation prohibiting all use of cydroids. "Cydroids represent the
most harmful fusion of man and machine . . . the worst of both,
rather than the best . . ." Early indications are that Carlisimo's
bill will enjoy wide support in both the Senate and the House.

I did notice that the Kemal-related deaths had been conve-
niently ignored, and that ISS had to have been tipped off even
earlier than I had. Otherwise, they couldn't have had a
prepared statement ready so soon. There were also more
than a few loose ends, such as the use of the cydroids to in-
filtrate communications, but I had my doubts as to whether
they'd ever get tied up. That was life. There were always
loose ends, but this time I really didn't care, just so long as
the children, Minerva, Paula, and I didn't get tangled in
them.

chapter 100

Needless to say, I was feeling much better by noon, and I finished the contact text for prospective clients, and sent out almost two dozen messages. They couldn't hurt, and they might even result in more business.

At ten past one, the gatekeeper chimed once more, *Stacia Mydra, Associate Director General of Sante.*

What did she want with me? I set the system to record, even before I signaled, *Accept.*

The image of a slender and dark-haired woman appeared before me, smiling politely, even warmly. I didn't trust the expression, but waited.

"Dr. deVrai." She paused ever so slightly. "I had wished to link with you earlier, but I was somewhat distracted by events."

"From what I've seen in the news, I can understand why, Director Mydra. I'm not so certain that I wouldn't have been equally distracted if you had reached me. It was very disconcerting to discover that another clone of me had been used in such a . . . such a cold-blooded set of murders."

"Yes. They were very cold-blooded. Efficiently so, and

very regrettable. I don't think Director Deng ever understood the ramifications of what he had started. Putting a trained professional killer, like that cydroid, into a situation where there is nothing to lose can create great tragedy. While we will mourn what has happened, life must go on, regrettably." After another pause, she smiled again. "Your work for and at the Centre for Societal Research was truly brilliant. Sante would like to employ that brilliance. It would be a shame if we did not enlist that expertise to work for us, especially after all you've been through and all that has happened. I hope you would consider doing so."

"You are most kind, Director Mydra. My consulting services are always available, but I will counsel you that I've been known to be very direct in my advice. I'm not a political consultant, but one who looks for the most effective solution for his clients. My operation is very low-key, but far wider than most people realize. I would be more than happy to provide my economic and media expertise to you and to Sante on mutually agreeable terms."

"Of course. I am not the economic and media director. That is Jason Podarak. If that is acceptable to you, he'll be in touch with you. If you have any problems or concerns, please don't hesitate to let me know immediately."

"Director Mydra, given your spirit of cooperation, I doubt that there will be any problems, but in the most unlikely event that there are, you will be the first to find out."

Her eyes flickered ever so slightly.

"You are as direct as you say, but that can be an advantage to us both. There are less likely to be misunderstandings that way."

"I'd certainly prefer it." I smiled politely. "I do enjoy doing the best economic and media consulting possible, and that is what I'd like to do for you and Sante."

"That is what we would like you to do. Jason, then, will be in touch with you. That will most likely be tomorrow, after I've had a chance to brief him."

"I'll be looking forward to his link."

The projection vanished.

For a time, I just sat there.

We'd exchanged messages on two levels, and I was fairly certain we had an agreement on both. What had come through was that Mydra hadn't wanted trouble . . . or maybe she had. Had she avoided attending that board meeting in person on purpose? Had she had some insight and personal agenda? I doubted that I'd ever know that for certain.

I wanted to share that with Paula—and Minerva—but at the same time, and I didn't want Paula to be distracted by her safo duties . . . or rushed. So I went back to considering what else I could do to boost my consulting.

I didn't have to wait long.

At two-fifty, I got a link from Reya Decostas.

"Jonat, I've been meaning to get back in touch with you, but January is slow, and I took some time off . . ."

I wondered about that, but just nodded.

". . . and I was talking to Chelsa Glynn, and she'd said that you had done a marvelous presentation at her seminar."

"I enjoyed doing it."

"That business at the Centre for Societal Research . . . that must have been an awful strain on you. Twice, was it, that cydroids impersonated you?"

"ISS stole my DNA almost two years ago. I'd reported it when it happened, but until this came up, the safos never could figure out who had done it . . ." I shrugged.

"It's so good that it's all been cleared up. I actually have two assignments for you, if you're interested . . ."

"I'm always interested in consulting, Reya." I gave her a broad smile.

After she left me, with more work than I'd had in months, and a friendly smile, I sat back. Just like that . . . it was over. I could sense and feel that. Some of the details I'd never know, such as how Deng had shifted cydroids to try to help Vorhees, or whether the cydroids had ever infiltrated secure comm lines. That was life, and something I'd learned years before in the Marines. You never learned everything, no matter how hard you tried, and there were times not to try. That was wisdom, too, knowing when to try and when not to. Now was a time not to, because it wouldn't accomplish anything. Even before I left to pick up the children, I'd heard from

Methroy and Bruce Fuller. There was no doubt that I'd hear from more people. I just wondered how long it would be before Eric Wong linked, with a referral from one of his members. What had happened left no doubt in my mind, not that I'd had much before, but this reinforced the point, that certain parts of the world were very small indeed.

Charis and Alan were among the last out of the building, but that didn't bother me. I was just glad to see them. I waited until we got back to the house before I said anything. Then I sat them down in the kitchen.

"You look serious, Uncle Jonat. Did we do something wrong?" Charis asked.

"No. You two didn't do anything wrong, nothing at all, but I need to explain something to you before anyone else tells you."

"Is it bad?" asked Alan.

"It's not bad, now, but it's about something bad that happened. There was an explosion last Thursday at the Centre for Societal Research, and some people were killed."

"I heard about that at school," Charis said. "Why are you telling us?"

"Because the head of the Denv Safety Office announced this morning that one of the men killed in the explosion had been the one who ordered the murder of your parents and who tried to kill me." I paused. "He had cydroids—you know what those are, don't you?"

"They're like clones, sort of, but people can control them or program them," Charis said.

"That's right. Well, this man—his name was Deng—had cydroids made up that looked like me, except they weren't exactly like me, and these cydroids killed some people, and one of them was one of those that killed your parents, and another tried to kill me. The last one killed this man, because something went wrong with his plans . . . but a lot of people died because of what he did."

"He was evil." Alan drew out the last word.

"Very evil, but I wanted you two to know that the safos did discover who was behind all of this."

Alan nodded. He'd heard enough.

"Does that mean you won't have to worry as much about us and about you?" asked Charis.

"I'll probably always worry about you two. Uncles and parents do. But I won't worry quite as much."

"Does that mean you won't see Paula anymore?" asked Alan. "You wouldn't need a safo friend as much."

"It means he can see her more," Charis said. She looked at me. "If he wants to."

What could I say to that, with both of them looking at me?

"We don't know each other very well. I would like to get to know her better."

"If you taught her football," Alan said, "we could play two on two."

Charis rolled her eyes, in that superior manner I would need to watch.

"We'll have to see." I cleared my throat. "Now . . . you have a little while before homework, and before Charis has to practice."

"My turn at choosing." Alan was out of the kitchen at a run.

Charis did not follow. She looked at me.

"Yes, Charis?"

"You loved Mother, didn't you, Uncle Jonat?"

"Yes. I miss her every day."

Abruptly, she threw her arms around me. "I miss her so much." She began to sob. "I miss her . . ."

I held her, patting her back, wondering what I could say. Finally, I murmured, "It's all right to miss her. It's all right . . ."

"I miss her and Father . . ."

"It's all right . . ."

"You won't go away, will you?"

"I'm here, Charis."

In time, she stepped back, and I handed her a tissue to blot her face. She didn't quite look at me. "I don't want to watch the netlink."

"You don't have to."

"Can I stay here while you fix dinner?"

I decided against insisting that she practice. "Would you like to help?"

She nodded.

So we had the old NorAm staple for children, macaroni and cheese with fried apples, and Alan ate every last apple section on his plate.

Even though I also wanted to share all the news with Paula, she was still at work, and I had to wait until after seven, while the children were bathing, before I could reach her by link. I wanted to see her image, not just hear projected words.

"How are you doing?" She was still in uniform.

"Better, I think. And you?"

"The same. Captain Sudro is a lot like Lieutenant Meara was. He's already made a few changes."

"I received a link from what looks to be a new client. I thought you'd like to see it. It could be very profitable, and it might smooth things out a great deal. I'm going to send a copy of it, and I'd really like you to see it. I'll just hold here while you do, if that's all right."

Her brows wrinkled, for just a moment. "All right."

She accepted the transmission and watched and listened. I waited.

When it was over, she looked at me, with a smile, a slightly sad one. "You seem to have a new client."

"It does look that way."

Minerva? Can you link me to Paula? I didn't want what I said next recorded *anywhere.*

Yes, Jonat.

Paula?

Can you trust her?

Of course not. But she can't trust me, either, and we've proven that we can exact a terrible price if she keeps after me. She doesn't want to pay that price. The costs are too high for both of us.

That's sad.

Very sad. It's better than the alternatives that were facing us, though. This way, I'll have a chance to keep consulting, to see Charis and Alan get older. Mydra, for her part, will probably take over the Pan-Social Trust. Captain Sudro has already accepted and announced the investigation results. Poor Deng has been blamed for everything, including the at-

tempts to keep Mars and the Belters under MultiCor control. With all the revelations, MultiCor will have to ease control and allow more competition. In a generation or two, Mars will probably be free. This will slow down and maybe stop the worst of legislation . . . I broke off. There were too many ramifications to discuss, and I was tired. Damn near dead tired, and I wanted to read to Charis and Alan. I also wanted to hug Paula, but that wasn't possible or practical.

You won.

No. We got an agreement, based on power and respect, and sometimes, that's better. Not really better, not in terms of ideals, but an agreement far more likely to be kept. Mydra clearly didn't know exactly what power I had, but she'd decided that paying off a consultant was far more profitable— and safer—than continuing a subterranean war. After all I'd been through, that was fine with me.

"I've also had three other links from clients with new assignments. Just this afternoon."

"That's good." *And sad.*

And all too predictable. "It is if things get back to . . ." I was going to say "normal," but I didn't want things back the way I'd once considered normal. ". . . something more balanced."

Paula nodded.

"I have a favor to ask. I know you feel overwhelmed, but would you consider letting me take you out to dinner, just the two of us, on Saturday?"

"I'll have to say no to Saturday. I'm on duty until eleven."

"How about Sunday?"

Her smile was shy, even before she spoke. "I'd like that."

So would I, even if I still couldn't quite explain why.

"I'll link you later with the details for Sunday. I'm going to have to break off. I need to read to the children."

"I think they need that."

I didn't move until her image vanished. Then I started upstairs. I needed to read to Charis and Alan as much as they needed my reading to them.

As I waited for them in the sitting room, I couldn't help thinking about how things had turned out. In the end, by necessity and accident, three of us had become the check on the NorAm Legislature, the various multis of Earth, and MultiCor. A former Marine, a former cydroid, and a former central intelligence system of the capital's Safety Office.

None of us had planned it, not that way, not even Minerva.

What would happen with that limited power, I had no idea, but, like the ancient checks and balances first created in NorAm, what might happen would depend on what others did, or did not do. We certainly wouldn't start anything. I'd make sure of that.

What would happen between Paula and me, I wasn't certain.

Charis had hinted at it, though, and she was probably right. I've always been slow in dealing with women, with nieces, and even former cydroids and female AIs. We'd have to see.

But, for the first time in a long, long while, although there were sorrows and regrets I would always feel, I was looking forward to the days to come, one day at a time.

A preview of

GHOSTS
OF COLUMBIA

L. E. Modesitt, Jr.

Now available!
From Tom Doherty Associates

One ghost in my life was bad enough, but when you have two, an inconvenience can become a disaster. That Saturday night in October, I wasn't really thinking about Carolynne—the family ghost—disasters, or any other ghost. All I wanted to do was lock the office door and get back to the recital hall for Llysette's concert because I'd lost track of time.

My mind was on Llysette when I left my office and walked down the stairs and through the Natural Resources Department offices. I stepped out onto the covered porch and the almost subsonic shivering that tells you there's a ghost around hit me. I thrust the key in the lock, feeling uncomfortable and hurried, without knowing why at first.

Then I pulled out my key, and the shivering went up two notches before the sobbing began.

"No . . . no . . . I wouldn't tell . . . wouldn't listen . . . no . . . no . . ."

The light on the porch of the old Dutch Republican that had been converted to the offices of the Natural Resources Department came from a low-powered permanent glow square. The glow square made seeing the ghost a lot easier because she didn't wash out under the light. Ghosts, even fresh ones, aren't that substantial, and this one was a mess, with white streaks and gashes and droplets of white ectoplasm dripping away from her figure.

I swallowed, hard, because the ghost was Miranda—Miranda Miller, the piano professor—and you don't usually see ghosts like that unless someone's been murdered. Murders aren't that common in the Republic, especially at universities located out in the hinterlands. Miranda was an easy grader, so it couldn't have been a disgruntled student, although that has happened, I understand, but not at Vanderbraak State University. Llysette was more likely to be a target of some burgher's pampered daughter than Miranda.

"No . . . no . . ." The ghost's hands were up, as if trying to push someone away.

"Miranda . . ." I tried to keep my voice soft. The books all say that you have to be gentle with ghosts, but since I come from a pretty normal family, I'd never seen a ghost right after it had been created by violent death. Grandpa's ghost had been pretty ornery, but he'd been ornery enough in life, and he'd faded before long. Most ghosts did, sooner or later.

"Miranda, what happened?"

"No . . . no . . . no . . ." She didn't seem to recognize me. She just projected that aura of terror that felt like subsonics. Then she was gone, drifting across the faculty green toward the administration building—a stone and mortar horror, what the first Dutch settlers had called native-stone colonial. Campus Security had offices there, but I doubted that they were really set for ghost handling, nor were the county watch, even though Vanderbraak Centre was the county seat.

Almost as an afterthought, I closed the door and pulled the key out. I started walking, then running downhill toward the watch building—not even taking those long wide stone steps that led past the car park and down to the lower part of the campus. Halfway down the hill, I skidded to a stop on the browning leaves that the university zombies hadn't been able to sweep up as fast as they fell and looked down at the town square. I was across from the new post centre. The old one had burned down forty years ago, but in Vanderbraak Centre, a forty-year-old building is practically new.

But that wasn't why I stopped. I was going to claim that someone had stabbed Miranda because her ghost had drifted by me, sobbing and incoherent? That might have gone over all right in New Amsterdam, or some other big city like Columbia City, where the feds understood ghost theory, but not in Vanderbraak Centre. The watch were mostly old Dutch stock, stolid, and you seldom saw Dutch ghosts. Don't ask me why, but that was the way it was. The odds were I'd end up in one of those cold iron-barred cells, not because I'd seen a ghost, but because they'd more likely believe I'd committed the murder and claimed I'd seen a ghost.

So I gritted my teeth and turned around to walk back up the hill to the old Physical Training Center that had become the Music and Theatre Department when old Marinus Voorster donated a million guilders to build the new field house—all out of spite with Katrinka Er Recchus, now the acting dean. Then she'd been running the strings program, even before she became department chair. Rumor had it that she'd been more than friendly with old Marinus, hoping for a new performing arts center she could run.

I glanced farther uphill at the Physical Sciences building that held the Babbage centre, but only the outside lights were on. My eyes flicked back to the Music and Theatre building. All the old gym doors were open, since it was a warm night for mid-October. I stopped, straightened my damp collar and my cravat, took some deep breaths, and wiped my forehead on my sleeve before I walked up the stone steps into the building.

As usual, even though it was less than ten minutes before the recital started, only a handful of people walked across the foyer and down the side corridor in front of me.

"Good evening, Doktor Eschbach."

"Good evening." I took the one-sheet program and nodded at the usher, a student whose name momentarily escaped me.

The recital hall had actually been a lecture hall, the only one in the old PT building, so that the "renovation" that had turned it into a recital hall had consisted of adding a full stage, taking out several rows of seats, and removing the lift-tilt desktops attached to the sides of the seats. The seats were still the traditional Dutch colonial hardwood that made long recitals—even Llysette's—tests of endurance.

Miranda Miller—dead? Why Miranda? Certainly, according to Llysette, she whined a lot in her mid-south English dialect. I could have seen it had it been Dean Er Recchus or Gregor, the theatre head who bellowed at everyone, or even Llysette and her perfectionist ways.

The program looked all right:

Llysette duBoise

Soprano

In Recital

Featuring the Mozart *Anti-Mass*

She was doing mostly standard stuff, for her, except for the Britten and Exten. She'd protested doing the Mozart Anti-

Mass, but the dean had pointed out that the stipend from the Austro-Hungarian Cultural Foundation had come because they were pushing their traditional musicians, even Mozart, even the later ultraromantic stuff composed after his bout with renal failure, even the weird pieces no one sings much anymore, if they ever did. She'd wanted to do Lady Macbeth's aria from Beethoven's *Macbeth* or Anne's aria from his *Heinrich Verrückt,* but the Austro-Hungarians were pushing Mozart's less popular pieces, and the Foundation had suggested either the Anti-Mass or the love song from *Elisabet.*

You don't turn down a two-hundred-dollar stipend, nor the dean's suggestion, not if you're an academic in up-county New Bruges. Not if you're a refugee from the fall of France trying to get tenure. And not, I supposed, if you were linked to the suspicious Herr Doktor Eschbach, that notorious subversive who'd been forced out of the government when Speaker Hartpence's Reformed Tories had won the elections on a call for a clean sweep of the ministries. So Llysette had opted for the Anti-Mass as the least of the evils.

I settled into a seat halfway back on the left side, right off the aisle, and wiped my forehead again. I was definitely not in the shape I had once been. Yet it hadn't seemed that long since I'd been a flying officer in Republic Air Corps, and my assignments in the Sedition Prevention and Security Service had certainly required conditioning. So what had happened? I shook my head and resolved to step up my running and exercises, and I wiped my forehead once again.

By the time the lights went down, Llysette had a decent crowd, maybe a hundred fifty, certainly not bad for a vocal performance. The Dutch have never been that supportive of vocalists. Strings, strings, and more strings, with a touch of brass—that's how you reach their hearts, but, as Katrinka Er Recchus found out, not their pocketbooks.

Llysette swept onto the stage, all luminous and beautiful, dark hair upswept and braided back, bowed, and nodded at Johanna Vonderhaus, her accompanist, seated at the big Steinbach.

Llysette was in good voice, and everyone thought she was wonderful, so wonderful that they gave her a brief second

ovation. I hadn't heard that in New Bruges in the three years
I'd been there, except for her concert the previous spring
when she had proved that a singer could actually master ora-
torio and survive.

I should have brought her chocolates, but I only brought
myself backstage, and came to a sudden stop as I reached
the open wing—the dressing rooms were down a side hall
toward the practice rooms and studios—where she stood,
pale and composed.

Two watch officers were there in their black and silver,
and one was talking to her, one to Johanna. I listened.

"When did you see Doktor Miller last?"

Llysette shrugged in her Gallic way. "Perhaps it was mid-
afternoon yesterday. I went home early to prepare for the
recital. Preparing for a recital, that is always hard."

"You went home alone?"

"Ah, *non,* monsieur. Doktor Eschbach there drove me in
his steamer. Then we ate, and he drove home. This afternoon
he drove to my home, and brought me to his house for an
early dinner. Then we came to the hall together, and I prepared for the recital."

"Did you see Doktor Miller tonight?"

"*Mais non.* I even sent Johan away while I was dressing
and warming up."

"Was anyone else here?"

"Johanna." Llysette inclined her head toward the slender
accompanist. "Before the hall was opened, we practiced the
Exten."

"Did you see anyone go down the halls toward the studios?"

"*Non.* You must concentrate very hard before the recital."

"Were you alone here at any time after Doktor Eschbach
left?"

"I could not say." Llysette shrugged wearily. "Worried I
was about the Exten and the Mozart, and people, they could
have come and gone. That is what happens before a recital."

There were more questions, but what else could she add?
We'd left early on Friday, and on Saturday afternoon we had
been together until she started to warm up and dress. That
was when I went up to my office.

The tall and chunky watch officer, of course, had to question me then.

"Doktor Eschbach, what did you do when you came back to the university tonight?"

"When we came back, I dropped Doktor duBoise off in front of the theatre building. I parked the steamer in the car park between the theatre building and the library. I walked into the building to make sure Doktor duBoise had everything she needed. When she said she needed to warm up, I went to my office to check my box for any messages, and then I did some paperwork for a new course for next semester. After that I came back and listened to the recital."

"Did you see or hear anything unusual?"

I frowned, on purpose, not wanting to lie exactly, but not wanting to tell the whole truth. "I *felt* a low sound, almost a sobbing, when I left the department office. I looked around, but it faded away."

"Ghost formation," said the other watch officer, the young and fresh-faced officer I hadn't seen around Vanderbraak Centre before. He reminded me of someone, but I knew I hadn't met him before.

"Ghost formation?" I said almost involuntarily, surprised that the locals were that up-to-date on the mechanics of ghosting and equally surprised that the younger officer would upstage the older.

"There was an article in the latest *Watch Quarterly*. Subsonics apparently often occur during and immediately after ghosting occurs." The younger officer blushed as the tall chunky man who had questioned me turned toward him.

"What time did you feel these vibrations?" asked the older watch officer.

"Mmmm . . . it was about fifteen minutes before the concert. Quarter before eight, I would say."

"How well did you know Doktor Miller?"

"Scarcely at all. I knew who she was. Perhaps I'd spoken to her a dozen times, briefly." I wouldn't have known her at all if I hadn't been seeing Llysette.

The questions they posed to me went on even longer than those they had posed to Llysette, but they were all routine, trying to establish who was doing what and where and if I had noticed anything unusual. Finally both officers exchanged glances and nodded.

"We may need to talk to you both later, Doktors," added the taller officer—Herlingen was his name. When I'd first come back to Vanderbraak Centre the year before, he had suggested that I replace my Columbian national plates on the steamer with New Bruges plates as soon as practical.

They bowed and departed, leaving the three of us—me, Llysette, and Johanna—standing in the wing off the recital hall stage. I wiped my forehead.

"Are you up to walking up to the steamer?" I asked Llysette, then looked at Johanna. "Do you need a lift?"

"No, thank you, Johan. Pietr is waiting outside." The tall accompanist smiled briefly, then shook her head. "Poor Miranda."

"*Moi,* I am more than happy to depart." Llysette lifted her bag with her makeup and other necessities, and I took it from her.

Outside, a half moon shone across the campus, and between the moon and the soft illumination of the glow lamps, there was more than enough light to make our way along the brick wall to the car park and the glimmering sleek lines of the Stanley, a far cry from the early steam-carts or even the open-topped racing steamers of early in the century.

Llysette fidgeted for the minute or so that it took for the steam pressure to build. "Why you Columbians love your steamers—that I do not understand. The petrol engines are so much more convenient."

"Columbia is a bigger country than France." I climbed into the driver's seat and eased the throttle open. Only two other steamers were left in the car park, and one belonged to the watch. "Internal petrol engines burn four times as much fuel for the mileage. We can't afford to waste oil, not when Ferdinand controls most of the world's supply, and Maximilian the rest."

"I have heard this lecture before, Johan," Llysette reminded me. At least she smiled.

"That's what you get from a former subminister of Nat-

ural Resources." I turned left at the bottom of the hill and
steered around the square and toward the bridge that would
take us to my house. The breeze through the steamer windows was welcome after the heat of the concert hall.

"More than merely a former subminister. Other worth-
while attributes you have, as well." She paused. "With this
event, tonight, is it wise that I should stay with you?"

"Wise? A woman has been murdered, and you want to
stay alone?"

"Ah, yes, there is that. Truthfully, I had not thought of
that."

I shook my head. Sometimes Llysette never considered
the obvious, but I supposed that was because, no matter what
they say, sometimes singers are just unrealistic. "Why would
anyone want to kill Miranda? She whined too much, but . . .
murder?"

"Miranda, she seemed so, so helpless." Llysette cleared
her throat, and her voice firmed. "Still, there are always reasons, Johan."

"I suppose so. I wonder if we'll ever know."

"That I could certainly not say."

The breeze held that autumn evening smell of fall in New
Bruges, the scent I had missed so much during my years in
Columbia City, the smell that reminded me of Elspeth still. I
swallowed, and for a moment my eyes burned. I kept my
eyes on the narrow line of pavement for a time. Sometimes,
at odd times, the old agonies reemerged.

Once across the river and up the hill, I turned the Stanley
left onto the narrow lane—everyone called it Deacon's
Lane, but that name had never appeared on any sign or map
that I knew of—that wound up the hill through the mortared
stone walls dating back to the first Dutch settlers. The driveway was dark under the maples that still held most of their
leaves, but I had left a light on between the car barn and the
house.

I let Llysette out under the light, opened the barn, and
parked the steamer. It was warm enough that I didn't worry
about plugging in the water tank heater.

She was waiting under the light as I walked up with her

bag. I kissed her cheek and took her chin in my hand, gently, but she turned away. "You are most insistent tonight, Johan."

"Only because you are a beautiful lady."

A flicker of white appeared in the darkness behind her, and I tried not to stiffen as I unlocked the side door and opened it for Llysette. She touched the plate inside the side foyer, what some called the mud entrance, and the soft overhead glows went on.

"Do you want a bite to eat? There's some steak pie in the cooler, and I think there's still some Bajan red down in the cellar."

"The wine, I would like that."

I closed the side door and made my way down into the stone-walled cellar and to the racks my grandfather had built. There was still almost half a case of the red. I picked out a 1980 Sebastopol. It's not really Bajan, but Californian, and a lot better than the New French stuff from northern Baja, but I wasn't about to get into that argument with Llysette, and certainly not after her recital.

"No Bajan, but a Sebastopol."

"If one must."

"It's not bad, especially now that Ferdinand has cut off real French wines."

"The Austro-Hungarians, they have already ruined the vineyards. Steel vats and scientists in white coats . . . bah!"

I shrugged, then peeled back the foil and twisted the corkscrew. The first glass went to her and the second to me. I lifted the crystal. "To a superb performance, Doktor duBoise."

Our glasses touched, and she drank.

"The wine is not bad."

That was as much of a concession to a Columbian wine as I'd get from my Francophilic soprano, and I nodded and took another sip. The Sebastopol was far better than "not bad"; it was damned good.

We made our way to the sitting room off the terrace. Llysette took the padded armchair—Louis XX style, and the only mismatched piece in the room, but my mother had liked it, and my father had thrown up his hands and shrugged his wide Dutch shoulders. The rest of the room was far more practical. I sat in the burgundy leather captain's chair, the only piece in the room that I'd brought back from Columbia City.

"Still I do not like the later Mozart."

"You did it well, very well."

"That is true, but . . ." Llysette took another long sip from her wine glass. "The later Mozart is too, too ornate, too romantic. Even Beethoven is more restrained."

"Money has always had a voice in music."

"Alas, yes." She lifted her left eyebrow. "It still talks most persuasively. Two hundred dollars—a hundred crowns—for a single song and a line on the program. I, even I, listen to such talk. It is almost what little I now make for half a month of hard work."

"Don't we all listen to that kind of money talk?" I laughed and got up to refill her glass. I leaned down and kissed her neck on the way back to my chair.

"It is sad, though. Gold, gold and patience, that is how the Hapsburgs have conquered Europe. My people, the good ones, left for New France, and the others . . ." She shrugged. "I suppose they are happy. There are no wars in Europe now."

"Of course, a third of France is ghost-ridden and uninhabitable."

"That will pass." She laughed harshly. "Ferdinand always creates the ghosts to remind his enemies of his power." Abruptly she tilted her head back and swallowed nearly all the red in one gulp. Then she looked at me. "If you please . . ."

I stood and refilled her glass. "Are you sure?"

"To relax after a performance, some time it takes. The wine helps. Even if it is not true French."

Not knowing what else to say, I answered, "You sang well."

"I did sing well. And where am I? I am singing in a cold small Dutch town in Columbia, where no one even under-

stands what I offer, where no one can appreciate the restraint
of a Fauré or the words of a Villon—"

"I do."

"You, my dear Doktor Eschbach, are as much of a refugee
as I am."

She was right about that, but my refuge was at least the
summer home of my youth.

I had one complete glass of the Sebastopol, and she drank
the rest of the bottle. It was close to midnight before she
could relax and eat some of the sweet rolls I had warmed up.
I left the dishes in the sink. Most days, Marie would get
them when she came, but she didn't come on weekends. I
decided I would worry about dirty dishes later.

At the foot of the stairs, I kissed Llysette, and her lips
were warm under mine, then suddenly cold. She stepped
back. I turned around in time to see another flicker of white
slip toward the terrace and then vanish.

"Someone was watching. Your ghost. That . . . I cannot
take." Llysette straightened the low shawl collar of her
recital dress. I tried not to leer, at least not too much. "Perhaps I will go home."

"No. Not until we know more about what happened to Miranda. We've been over that already."

"Then, tonight, I will sleep in the . . ."

"Just sleep with me. I'd feel you were safer." I glanced toward the staircase up to my bedroom.

"Just sleep?" She arched her eyebrows, as if to imply I
couldn't just sleep with her.

"Just sleep," I reaffirmed with a sigh. At least, I wouldn't
have to fire the steamer up and drive across to the other side
of the river with the local watch running all over the town-
ship.

At the same time, I was scarcely enthused about Carolynne's appearance, but what could I say? Carolynne never
spoke to me, hadn't since I was a boy, not since that mysteri-
ous conversation she had had with my mother . . . and neither would talk about it. Since I couldn't force answers from
either a ghost or my mother, I still didn't know why.